ROBOT OVERLORDS

To Claire, Emily and George for their
daily dose of inspiration.

PROLOGUE

THE DAY WE LOST THE WAR

They came for them in buses. Street by street. Queuing in the glare of the headlights as the sun went down. Packing everyone in. Standing-room only. Sean squeezed in next to his mum. No one spoke as their bus pulled up alongside dozens of others in the car park outside the hospital.

The crowd surged forward. The huge wave of humanity nearly knocked Sean off his feet and onto the Tarmac. He'd only experienced anything like this once before, when Dad took him to a football match at Wembley, but that had been like swimming in a tide of happy people. They were excited to see the game, fans were chanting and singing, and you didn't mind the pushing and shoving.

But here everyone was fearful, quiet, worried about what lay ahead. This felt like drowning.

Nearby, a woman cried out and fell into a puddle. Sean caught a glimpse of blood. A gashed knee, grazed knuckles. A man helped her to her feet and Sean saw they were both crying.

'Stay close, Sean.' His mum gripped his shoulder. 'Don't get split up.'

That was the first time Sean saw one of them.

It was a Sentry. The different types of robot were named by those who survived the war, and eventually even the VC and

Mediators adopted some of the names: Sentries, Drones, Snipers, Skyships, Lampheads, Cubes, or just Clankers. The Sentries were the most common, posted on almost every street corner. This one towered over the hospital entrance, standing two storeys tall, the high-powered beam in the middle of its faceless metallic skull sweeping across the crowd. Rows of silhouetted heads turned away from it, wincing at the intense light.

Sean felt sick just looking at it. Until now, he'd only seen blurred footage on the news. Shapes flashing by as fighter jets and tanks burst into flames, before the TV cut to presidents and prime ministers making speeches from bunkers, then not saying anything at all. But this one was real. From here, Sean could see small chips and cracks in the blue steel of its outsized arms. The wear and tear of invasion. Its weapon-arm crackled with energy, glowing red in the dark. Thick, clumping legs were attached to a segmented, ribbed torso topped with huge, brutish shoulders, in-between which nestled its tiny head with its circular lamp. Everyone was watching it. Would it turn on them? Had they been brought here to die?

There was a murmur at the front of the crowd, at something Sean couldn't quite see, and now there was a faint drizzle in the air, the fine raindrops and searchlights creating a dazzling mist.

'What's going on?' he asked.

'It's okay.' His mum squeezed his arm as she craned her neck to get a better view. 'Just some people coming out through the main door. I think … I think that's Robin.' She sounded puzzled. 'What's he doing here?'

Sean inched forward for a better look. There were about a dozen people – the mayor, councillors, police officers – all milling about under umbrellas near the hospital's main entrance. They were swapping sheets of paper, preparing to make a statement as someone wired up a microphone to a PA system. And on the fringe of the VIPs was Robin Smythe. Sean's geography teacher, head of Year Ten and terminal dickhead. Sean wasn't surprised to see him mingling with the nervous-looking town leaders. If anyone knew how to kiss the buttcheeks of power, it was Mr Smythe.

The mayor put the microphone too close to her lips. '—this on?' Her distorted voice echoed off the hospital walls and around the car park.

Some people at the front started shouting questions.

'Please!' said the mayor. 'I have a short statement, and then … just please listen.'

The crowd simmered down, still restless.

'As of midnight last night, in order to prevent any further loss of life, every government on the planet surrendered unconditionally to the Robot Empire.'

A wail swept through the crowd as people started crying. The rain began to fall more heavily.

'We are now all subject to their laws.' She was sobbing as she spoke and more voices rose up around her. Angry voices.

Sean felt a tremor beneath his feet and glanced around. More sweeping searchlights; more Sentries moving in, surrounding the car park. No escape.

'Please, listen!' the mayor cried, but the shouting grew louder. More organised. Threatening.

Someone threw a rock. It clanged off the first Sentry's armour.

Without a second's hesitation, the Sentry raised its gun-arm. The casing at the end split open with a whirr and a clank, revealing a glowing red mechanism that spun rapidly as it powered up. The flash of light momentarily blinded Sean and he felt the heat bloom brush across his cheeks. Four times. Five. There were more angry shouts, then, 'No! Please, I didn't mean to—' And another voice was silenced by the searing heat from the Sentry's gun. There was a new smell in the air: a strange metallic tang from the weapon's energy discharge. Around Sean, people exchanged silent glances: most were terrified, some looked angry. A few, their fists and jaws clenched, looked ready to surge forward and attack, but they were also hesitant, unsure. Unwilling to die quite yet. Sean felt completely helpless, and it took him a moment to realise that everyone else around him did, too.

Smythe grabbed the microphone from the mayor. Say what you want about a weasel like Smythe, he had a voice that carried authority.

'*Quiet!*' he bellowed, and he got it. 'It's very simple: we can cooperate or die. The war is lost. If you want to live, if you want your loved ones, your children, to live, then you must do as you are told.' He was getting through to them. The silent, frightened crowd wanted someone to tell them what to do next. 'You have been brought here today for registration. It's a simple procedure, so let's show the robots that we can work with them, that we're better than a rabble. Our lives have changed and no amount of shouting, screaming or fighting is going to change that. The greatest armies in the world couldn't change that.' He let that sink in. 'We're going to read out some street names, and we'd like the people who live in those streets to come to the front. The quicker we get this done, the quicker you can get home.'

It actually worked. Any thoughts of uprising vanished as quickly as those who had died. The promise of home stopped a riot – or worse, a massacre. Only afterwards, when it was too late, did anyone realise the robots planned to make everyone's home a prison for the next seven years.

AN IMPORTANT MESSAGE FROM MEDIATOR 452:

'My name is Mediator 452.

'I have been purpose-built to liaise between the Robot Empire and the humans in this zone.

'Approximately 9.78 million years ago, we were brought to the brink of extinction by our organic creators. We are Data Miners. Our mission is to study all sentient thought in the universe; to scrutinise this data to ensure that no life form can threaten us again.

'Do not be alarmed. We wish you no harm, but disobeying our laws will not be tolerated. With your full cooperation, we will complete our study of humankind in seven years, eight months, six days, eleven hours and nine minutes, approximately. We will then leave your planet and never return.

'Our laws are simple:

1: STAY INSIDE.
2: OBEY ROBOT COMMANDS AND MEMBERS OF THE HUMAN VOLUNTEER CORPS (VC). THEY CAN BE IDENTIFIED BY THEIR ARMBANDS AND GREEN IMPLANTS.

Everything we have told you is the truth.
Robots never lie.'

IMPLANTS AND ROBOT OCCUPATION

Sean remembered getting his implant vividly. He and his mum were some of the first to be called. She held him as long as she could, tears streaming down her cheeks as they dragged him away behind a green hospital curtain. There he saw his second robot, headless, multi-armed like a chrome spider, devices whirring. Two doctors in white coats stained with red handprints strapped him to a bed as the machine went to work.

'Hold still,' one said, voice muffled by his face mask.

Sean, pinned down by the straps, could only look up. The hospital must have taken a few hits during the invasion. Whole panels had fallen away from the ceiling, revealing air-conditioning ducts and pipes swaddled in ragged insulation. A neon light dangled precariously from the damaged ceiling at the end of a couple of wires, glaring in Sean's eyes. He squinted, turning away.

'Keep bloody still,' the other man said in a tight voice. Sean recognised that tone. His dad used it whenever he got angry and then instantly regretted it. This was a good man doing a bad thing. Sean could see it in the doctor's baggy, bloodshot eyes as he grabbed Sean's jaw, setting him straight.

It took less than a minute. An injection to numb the pain, a drill-like device stabbing into his neck, a punch followed by a tight squeezing sensation, and then it was in.

Without a word, the doctors unstrapped him and bundled him out into a hallway tinted a murky green by the flickering emergency lights. Sean didn't know where to go, what to do. His mind tried to make sense of what had just happened. He looked up and down the hall. It was full of stooped, sorry figures, their implants glowing blue as they cried, 'What have they done to us?' and, 'What is this thing?' Howls of pain came from behind the rows of closed hospital curtains as more people were implanted.

Some clawed at them, tried to pull them out. One man had found a toolbox and was attempting to unscrew the implant of an RAF pilot in a tattered flight suit. Sean wondered if he was from the same base as his dad. He was about to ask when a doctor barged past and ran towards them, hands waving. 'No! Don't! It'll—'

The explosion turned the pilot's head into a red mist of brain and pulverised bone. His friend with the screwdriver lost his face completely. It was a mess of red-raw flesh, muscle and white, exposed skull. He tried to scream, but his lungs were burned and all he could manage was a gurgling, rasping noise before he fell dead to the ground.

Sean watched, frozen to the spot, ears ringing from the blast, his mind unable to comprehend what he'd just seen.

He felt a hand gently squeeze his arm. His mum, her eyes red from crying.

An implant glowed blue on her neck. Just like his. Just like everyone else's.

'Sean, sweetheart.' Her voice trembled as she tried to keep it together for him. 'Our bus is ready. Come on.'

It became clear after a few weeks inside that the robots were serious about confining everyone to their homes. Those who tried to run or sneak out got one warning and that was it. A flash of light, followed by dark ashes floating on the breeze and that smell. That hot-Tarmac smell. Some mornings it wafted through the windows, and you knew someone nearby had tried to do a runner in the night.

The internet was shut down immediately. The robots had their own network that no human could access. The phone lines were all cut, and all mobiles and pagers were now nothing more than worthless lumps of metal and plastic. But the TV and radio stayed on.

The Mediator broadcasted daily, explaining the rules between repeats of old TV shows. People with VC armbands and green-glowing implants went door-to-door and handed out transcripts of the Mediator's words. They made public information films that played on a loop on every channel for days.

Sean and his mum had taken a crowded yet silent bus back to their temporary home, the shelter at the school. Their street had been totalled on the third day of the war when a Tornado fighter jet spiralled out the sky, crashing with a plume of thick black smoke, killing dozens and destroying their house.

They'd been volunteering at the shelter at the time, helping those who'd already lost their homes. Sean's first question whenever he heard a fighter had crashed – and it happened every day – was the same: 'Was it Dad's?'

His father, Danny, had left in a hurry on the first day of the war. His orders from the RAF came through at breakfast. He headed out with big hugs and a promise to be back soon.

Since then, Sean had kept count of the days and weeks, then months and years, first in a notebook at the school, then on the wall of his room in their new home. Over a thousand tiny scratches, spread in rows of green ink, red, blue, black. Each change an old pen run dry.

After a few weeks, the Volunteer Corps had found them a house in nearby Fleetwood Street, one in a row of redbrick terrace houses. Sean's mum asked who had lived there before, but none of the VC would give her an answer. Few would even look her the eye. Clearing up, she found photos of a family: grandparents, children, grandchildren. She kept them safe. 'Just in case,' she said.

Mr Smythe, who used to work with Sean's mum at the school, had pulled a few strings and pushed them to the top of the housing list. She didn't find out till much later and was furious. 'We don't want any special treatment, Robin,' she shouted loud enough from her doorstep so that all the neighbours could hear. 'Especially not from you!'

Smythe had left in a huff that day, but he was back by the end of the week, apologising, squeezing her hands and trying to make amends.

But Sean was secretly happy about it. Having a place of their own was better than a sports hall full of crying children. Better than a playground ripe with the stench of death, and flies buzzing around rows of bodies in black bags. And the occupation wasn't too bad to start with. Smythe visited regularly and kept them informed of the latest news. He reassured them that Danny would be found soon. The RAF had surrendered and the pilots were being held nearby. 'Your dad'll be here in no time, lad,' he told Sean, scruffing his hair.

And while they waited they gorged on DVD box sets, read every book in the house, played every board game a gajillion times. The first year was like a long summer holiday. The sun shone and people still smiled. You could chat with neighbours from your doorstep, so long as you were careful not to cross the threshold and set off your implant. Everyone learned that the hard way. Sean had slipped over the line when mucking about by the front door and his implant briefly turned red. It had only been a few seconds, but the Sentry on the corner registered the infraction and it cost him a day's rations. Mum had pleaded with Smythe, but he shrugged and said, 'I thought you didn't want any special treatment, Kate,' in that calm Yorkshire accent of his, relishing the opportunity to throw her words back at her. The more sincere he tried to sound, the flatter and more inhuman his voice became. Whatever spark of humanity he'd possessed had died a long time ago. 'Besides, I report to the Mediator and he won't allow any acts of clemency. Zero tolerance is the only way to keep order.'

Mediator 452. Just thinking about the robot made Sean shudder.

The only humanoid model that Sean knew of, Mediator 452 appeared on their TVs every day. It looked like a child and creeped everyone out.

Morse Code Martin, who lived a couple of doors down, had told Sean about the Mediator. They'd been scaring each other with old ghost stories, but then Martin said he had a bit of gossip that would really put the willies up Sean. Rumours he'd heard from a loose-lipped VC ration officer about the boy robot's construction.

'The robots studied us for decades before the invasion,' the old man told Sean. 'They abducted people, did experiments on 'em and found out that humans responded positively to children. So they created these Mediator robots. Made 'em look like little kids, thinking we'd all pat them on head and smile, I s'pose. One in each zone, apparently. This one's Smythe's boss. Imagine that – saluting to a robot that looks like a little kid.'

Last January it had come down their street with Smythe on a routine inspection. It had gone door-to-door introducing itself like a politician polling for votes, probably Smythe's idea. 'Thank you for your cooperation,' it said in its odd, boyish and fragmented voice.

Small children could be cute, Sean thought, no doubt. But the thing on his doorstep was a creepy, soulless automaton. Far from putting him at ease, it made him feel sick. Its glassy eyes peered at him in a mockery of human emotion and its smooth, plasticky skin made his own flesh crawl. Just looking at the odd Fuzzy Felt black hair stuck on its head, its bizarre grey hoody and shiny PVC trousers and its unblinking stare made him recoil.

'The Robot Empire appreciates your patience in these difficult times,' it said in a voice made up of dozens of different intonations, all rising and falling in pitch like bad Auto-Tune.

Some people spat at the Mediator on its rounds. They shouted and screamed, ranting about their incarceration, but Sean said nothing. The Mediator was about to move to the next door along when it stopped and looked at Sean again. The black implant on its neck pulsed, little white lights dancing across the circular display. It appeared to be studying him. Sean felt his mum's grip on his shoulder tighten.

'You are perspiring and your heart is beating at 117 beats per minute,' it said. 'Do not be afraid of me, Sean Flynn.'

Sean felt tears running down his cheeks. He couldn't help it. How did this thing know his name? How did it know what his heart rate was? He felt invaded. They'd taken over his world, his country, his street, his doorstep and now him personally. He couldn't bring himself to reply. The Mediator tilted its head in a simulation of curiosity, fascinated by this unexpected show of emotion.

Smythe's guiding hand indicated the rest of the street. 'Come, Mediator,' he said, 'lots to do today.'

That was the day when Sean realised the robots were keeping a secret. He didn't know what it was, but the fact that they could sense heartbeats, that they knew everyone's name, that they were making such an effort to be friendly, reeked of trying too hard.

They were hiding something.

He told Morse Code Martin his theory. The old man had the idea of knocking the walls through in the lofts so they could meet and talk and swap books, games and DVDs without the robots and VC spying on them. They marked the divides between each house with silver duct tape, careful not to cross for fear of setting off their implants. Sometimes he and Sean sat and talked in the loft on rainy days.

'Of course they're hiding something,' Martin said. 'They didn't come all this way for a holiday, did they? You mark my words: they're up to something. We'll figure it out sooner or later, you'll see.' They were going to get through this, he kept telling Sean. They were going to survive. He often talked about the 'Blitz spirit'.

But after the first winter, things changed and the Blitz spirit faded. The occupation felt more real and the weekly rations were getting smaller. The power, kept running by the VC, started cutting out. The water that came in sporadic hiccups from the tap looked less clear than it used to be ... And that's when it dawned on Sean: they had another six years of this to endure.

From the start, Kate did her best to keep them both active, mentally and physically. She knocked up homework from memory and Sean worked out a daily exercise routine. He hated it to start with, but what the hell else were they supposed to do with all that time?

The first winter was hard, but the second summer was even worse; seeing the sunshine but not being able to go outside was torture. They opened every window, every door, and Kate filled the windowsills with plants bedded in old baked-bean tins from their rations. Anything to bring a bit of the outside in. She ran a length of hosepipe from the guttering so they could capture rainwater in the bath, then watered the plants with an old cracked water jug.

At night, Sean was sometimes woken by flashes of light, followed by screams, made worse when Smythe stopped by to tell them horror stories of people who thought they could sneak past the Sentries to see their family in the next street. He'd become Zone Chief within a year of the robot takeover and his visits were less frequent now, and he hardly ever mentioned Danny. Sean always had to bring his dad up. He knew it upset his mum, but he had to know.

Smythe never had any news, just more empty promises.

Well, after three years, Sean wasn't waiting on Smythe's bullshit anymore. He'd found a tube of tennis balls in the loft and had an idea.

'Mum, can I borrow that photo of Dad?'

She gave it to him with caution. Everything else had been destroyed in their old house and the one in her purse was the last remaining photo of Danny. He was smiling. They all were. It was taken at the beach during their last summer together.

Sean then tore a dozen or so blank pages from his old school notebooks, sharpened a pencil and started sketching.

He traced around his dad's face. It wasn't a good likeness, and he wished he could draw something that didn't look like a bad Manga villain, but he got better with each attempt. The final one was the best of all, capturing his dad's big grin and bright eyes.

Sean then cut a slit in each of the tennis balls and carefully folded a sketch of his dad into each one with a message and a description of his dad, headlined:

LOOKING FOR MY DAD – DANNY FLYNN – HAVE YOU SEEN HIM?

The back door creaked open. Sean stood on the threshold, not daring to go any further. He felt the sun warm his face, the gentle sea breeze wafting in from the beach. He could hear the waves lapping on the shingle even from here. The gulls, too. No cars, no planes, only the occasional distant rumble from squadrons of Drones, or a Skyship passing through the stratosphere overhead.

Sean placed a message-stuffed tennis ball into a large catapult made of bungee rope salvaged from some gym equipment he'd swapped with a neighbour. He clamped it to the sides of the back door and stretched it as far as it would go. The first ball arced over their garden into one two doors down. Not far enough. He tried again, pulling harder on the bungee. One after another they flew, over fences, roofs, and into neighbouring gardens and alleys. His note urged people to pass it on. If they couldn't help, maybe someone in the next street could. Spread the word. Sean's message included a crude hand-drawn map showing where he lived, where to return it. He knew if Smythe found out he'd be in trouble, but he was long past caring what Smythe thought.

The last ball was loosed. Sean watched it go, arching up into the sunlight as it spun over the roof opposite. He desperately wanted to go with it. To rush out and hammer on every door, screaming his dad's name at the top of his voice.

'Hey.' His mum placed a hand on his shoulder and kissed his head. Now he was sixteen, she had to stand on tiptoes to do it. 'C'mon. I've got some washing. Want to help?'

'Lemme check my diary.' He flicked through an imaginary calendar. 'Ah, you're in luck. I'm free for the next four years. Yeah, why not?'

As they stepped back inside, Sean scratched at the robot implant on his neck. Its weight tugged on his skin, which was numb where its metal edges pressed into him. They left the door open, the gentle sound of waves breaking on the shore drifting through the house.

THE LAST WORKING
GAMES CONSOLE

'If this thing is screwed, then that's it, game over. Literally. I mean, what are we going to do? Read books?' Nathan kneeled over the component parts of their old Xbox, sorting them, placing them in groups on the loft boards.

'Only if someone teaches you to read first, Nate,' Alex replied, ducking under the roof beams. She slumped next to her brother, tucking her legs in and wrapping her dressing gown around her until only her head poked out. She noticed a crusty food stain on the arm, shook her hand free from the baggy folds of the gown and started to pick at it.

'I can read,' Nathan snapped. 'I read *Lord of the Rings* in twelve hours flat,' he claimed, with his usual complete disregard for facts.

'Didn't know they published an Early Reader version.'

'It's quicker if you skip all the songs.'

Alex sighed. Her brother's ability to blurt bullshit first became apparent when he developed a lazy eye as a kid. She remembered him telling the kids who'd been picking on him that whenever the doctors operated on it, all the nurses had to be naked for reasons of hygiene. Suddenly every boy in Year Six wanted a lazy eye, too.

They weren't the only ones up here tonight. Spurred on by Morse Code Martin, the walls in the roof space along the entire terrace had been removed. Alex could see down the length of it between the water tanks and beams. Around the boxes of old clothes, Christmas decorations and abandoned gym equipment they had created an extra room up here with comfy chairs. A refuge away from the prying eyes of the VC where they could talk and trade essentials. It wasn't much, but it staved off the madness that came from being on your own for too long.

She stretched her legs, daring to let them cross the divide between their house and Sean's next door. A line of duct tape marked the border between the two homes. Crossing it would set off their implants and they'd get a bollocking from Smythe and lose another day's rations.

At the far end of the terrace, Mrs Stoker was sorting through bags of old children's clothes. Every now and then she'd call out something like, 'I've got some lovely dungarees for you here, Alexandra!'

Alex gave a cheery wave, but she secretly dreaded whatever might emerge next from Mrs Stoker's bag of nineties fashion nightmares. Alex had grown out of her regular clothes years ago, so she and the others depended on hand-me-downs from neighbours like Mrs Stoker, and the goodwill sacks that sporadically came from the VC.

Her dressing gown was warm, soft and comfy, and she could shut the world out in a second. It was all she needed.

Between them and Mrs Stoker was Morse Code Martin, standing at his loft window, flashing a torch through the lashing rain at someone across the street. A coded message carrying news and gossip. Every now and then Martin would report rumours of a band of resistance fighters in the hills. Word was they were camped out in Duncombe Wood, ambushing patrolling Sentries on the edge of town. Sean and Nathan would listen to his stories, wide-eyed, but Alex wasn't so sure.

Martin was, in Nathan's words, an old giffer, but a good laugh, too. He'd served in the Korean War and could tell stories that made your skin crawl. Alex liked Martin, though. He was the one who bonded the inhabitants of the terrace together. He settled arguments, always had a kind word and hated the robots and the VC with a passion.

Alex watched Nathan frowning over the console pieces. He clearly didn't have a bloody clue what he was doing, but that had never stopped him in the past. He was a master bullshitter, able to convince himself he could do pretty much anything. The fact that he failed most of the time didn't appear to worry him. As usual, she was the one who would have to tidy up the mess. She picked up random bits of the console, trying to figure out which components slotted together.

'You just can't help yourself, can you, Nate? You have to fiddle.'

'Back off and watch an expert at work, woman.'

'Expert at screwing up.'

'I was the one who hacked into the school's network and changed your grades so Dad wouldn't be pissed off with you.'

'That was a film, Nate.' She rubbed her eyes, tired of his nonsense. 'In real life you're my loser brother.'

'At least I'm trying,' he said. 'Go back to your bridge and wait for the three billy goats gruff.'

'Why don't you go and play with your teeny winky and leave shit like this alone?'

'Go and play with *your* teeny winky.'

'Yeah, really mature, Nate.'

'Like your armpits.' Nathan leaned forward and sniffed. 'Oh, man, they really hum. When did you last wash?'

'When did you last actually fix something?'

'April. The DVD player!'

'Turning it off and on again doesn't count.'

'Well, it was better than your suggestion that we all gas ourselves.'

'I was being ironic.'

'Yeah, I guessed, since we only have an electric oven.'

'Knob-face.'

'Titless!'

They went on like that for some time, the insults getting more and more personal. They'd been a shouty family before the war. She and Nathan drove each other mad and their parents were always arguing. But then things started getting serious. Mum and Dad began acting freaky; lots of conversations behind closed doors. Nate thought they were getting a divorce while Alex didn't want to know.

Then Alex had started losing confidence. Panicking that she was going to fail all her subjects, lose all her friends, lose her family. It was clearly the most important thing in the universe. Her world was falling apart … Then the news started going on about these weird cubes appearing in the sky.

For a short while they all finally stopped shouting at one another.

Their mum had always been a protestor. She'd taken Alex and Nathan on an anti-war march when they were kids. Dad had gone mental, but Mum said it was important that they stand up for what's right.

So that night at the hospital, it was Mum who led the shouting against the robots. Alex and Nathan wanted to drag her back, but Dad held them tight. Then someone threw a rock – that was the first time they'd ever seen anyone die – and people ran, screaming. One of them had been their mum. The Sentries got her before Alex could even shout for her to stop. She'd turned her head, looked at Alex, started to say something and in a flash she was gone.

Dad was already running for her. The Sentry warned him, but Dad could only stare at the dark shadow on the ground where Mum had last stood. Where she'd last existed. And then he was next.

Nathan and Alex had cried for about a month. They were sent to the shelter at the school, where they realised they were not alone. Fresh orphans came in every day. Soon, Mr Smythe found them a home with an old couple in some flats on the edge of town. But then the oldies both got pneumonia and Smythe put Alex and Nathan in with another old lady, this one called Polly, in Fleetwood Street. She was wonderful. Strict, but totally fearless. She used to drive Smythe mad, accusing him of betraying humanity.

But then he had her cat killed. He said all the pets were being left feral or slaughtered to save on food and energy, but he appeared to take real pleasure in seeing her weep as they carried her little friend and companion away. She wasn't the same after that and she died in the big freeze last winter. Smythe was about to move them again, but then Kate stepped in and volunteered to keep an eye on them.

So now Alex was stuck with Nathan, the two of them together and alone. The smell in their house was an unimaginable combination of farts and teen BO. Thank God the VC usually kept the TV transmissions broadcasting. Repeats of *Friends* stopped her from going completely batshit crazy.

Kate next door did what she could, and it was cool that they were neighbours with Sean. They'd lived in the same street before the war. They were in different years and hadn't been friends, as such, but it was nice to have familiar faces to talk to. But now even Kate had started cracking up, too. Alex knew it. The staring into space. The long silences. She'd seen it before with their neighbours in the flats. Alex figured there was no way they'd last the whole seven years. So why bother? What was the point? Get real. Humanity's screwed.

Next door, Sean clambered up a ladder into the loft. He moved lithely around the battered sofa, casually thumping the punchbag he'd made from sofa cushions wrapped in duct tape. It jerked as it swung from a beam. Then Sean's eyes found the console. His face fell. 'What happened?'

'Numb-nuts here broke it,' Alex said.

'Nate! You total penis!'

'It's not my fault, mate!' Nathan put up defensive hands. 'It just – *fzzzt* – went dead.'

'It's knackered, Sean, like everything else in this stupid place,' Alex said, her face peering through a curtain of long, lank hair. 'Suck it up.'

'No, no, we can fix it,' Sean said, taking some of the pieces from Nathan. 'We can definitely fix it.'

'Oh, God, Sean.' Alex's voice cracked into a shout. 'Why are you always Captain Optimistic? Maybe Nathan hasn't got the first clue what he's doing? Maybe he's full of shit? Maybe – here's a thought – it's actually broken and we can never use it again?'

Sean looked like he'd just been slapped. He turned on the wounded-puppy eyes and she groaned with guilt. He didn't do it on purpose, he was just one of those people who cared. It made her sick, mostly because it almost made her want to care again, too.

Nathan waved vaguely at Alex's face. 'Massive zit on your chin there, sis.'

She ducked under the cover of the dressing gown. 'Up yours!' came her muffled voice from within, followed by her middle finger.

'Be like that,' Nathan said, 'but you know that was Polly's dressing gown and I'm pretty sure it's the one she died in, and it hasn't been washed since. But you stay in there if you want.'

Alex realised he might be right, but she wasn't going to give him the satisfaction of coming out. She listened to Sean's and Nathan's voices as they began discussing how to fix the console and wondered why they bothered. Why anyone bothered any more. They'd lost the war, and there was nothing to do but wait. And for what? The robots weren't telling them anything, and she was inclined to expect the worst.

She couldn't go on like this for much longer. Something had to change.

'You killed her!' came a voice from outside in the street.

Alex pushed back the hood of her gown a little. 'What was that?'

'You killed her, you bastards!' The same voice again.

Morse Code Martin shone his torch down into the street below. 'Oh no,' he muttered. 'Cabin fever.'

Alex dashed to their loft window. There was a man in the middle of the street, his implant flashing red in the rain. He was raving, barefoot in a faded white vest and soggy tracksuit bottoms and armed with a length of metal piping.

'Who's the nut job?' Nathan asked.

'I think it's Connor's dad,' Alex said. 'And he's gonna get smoked if he doesn't get back inside.'

YOU HAVE TEN SECONDS TO RETURN TO YOUR HOME

Connor didn't remember much about life before the robots. He was ten and it felt like they'd been around all his life. He clung on to his favourite memories, regularly reciting them to Mum and Dad. Mum used to love listening to him, but Dad was less interested.

He was at Fairfield Bay Primary School when the war began. His best friends were George, Freddie and Hrishi, and his form teacher was Mrs McGrath, and he was loving it. The last thing he remembered telling her was that he wanted to be an archaeologist like Indiana Jones, and she said that was a great idea.

Connor's other memories, hazy now but they still made him feel good, were of going to the beach with his mum and dad. He had a funny photo of them all laughing because his dad had ice cream around his mouth.

Dad fixed cars and his hands were always mucky when he came home, but after he'd had a shower and was clean, he would lift Connor up and tickle him and blow raspberries on his tummy. He used to giggle so much he could hardly breathe.

Mum worked at the supermarket, sometimes till late, but when she did, she always brought back a treat – leftover doughnuts, or those big cookies with Smarties in them. And on Saturdays they went to the library and Connor borrowed Asterix books, Tintin and loads of Horrible Histories. Actually, he still had some. He used to be racked with guilt, wondering if he'd ever be able to take them back ... and then he wondered if the library was even still there.

Connor wanted to go out so much. Just into the garden, just for five minutes. But Mum and Dad wouldn't let him. It was so annoying. Dad would shout, Mum would cry. They never used to do that. The robots made everything different.

Stuck inside now, they watched loads of TV. Connor snuggled with his mum on the sofa. He liked her smell, it was like towels from the warm cupboard upstairs. She used to tell Connor that she loved him all the time and it got annoying, and he said so. She cried, and Dad got angry and made Connor say sorry.

Mum was always worried about Gran. She was old and lived just around the corner and Mum wanted to go and see her but Mr Smythe always said no. He said Gran was happy but Mum said she needed her pills. Gran was always on pills before the war. She used to line them up on her kitchen table and Connor wondered what the different colours meant. Mr Smythe said he would take care of it. Then he hugged Mum, which made Dad really cross.

Then a couple of months ago, Mum went out one night. Connor and his dad didn't know till the next morning. She left a note on the table. It made Dad cry and he wouldn't let Connor read it and burned it on the cooker hob. Later, Mr Smythe came round to tell them that Mum was dead. A Sentry had warned her to go inside, but she'd carried on running to Gran's house.

Connor had never believed in heaven and Dad always said it was nonsense, but Connor really wanted to believe now. He knew he would never see her again. Never hear her voice. He knew it, but he couldn't fit the idea into his head.

Since then, Dad just stared at the telly. At night Connor heard him crying. He'd never cried before the war. He hardly said a word in days. Connor hoped he was okay.

Then, that morning, Connor had an idea. He knew what would cheer Dad up. He spent all day drawing an epic battle scene with

Vikings storming a Saxon castle. There were loads of arrows sticking in people's heads, and arms and legs being hacked off. This always made Dad laugh and say things like, 'You're a sick puppy, Connor. You don't get it from me, I can tell you that, son.' Yes, that would definitely make Dad smile again.

Connor skipped down the stairs, the drawing rolled into a scroll. 'Hey, Dad. You want to see my—?'

The front door was wide open. Not unusual in the day, but Dad wouldn't do it at night, and not when it was raining. Then he heard the deep, booming voice of a robot: 'CITIZEN, RETURN TO YOUR HOME IMMEDIATELY.'

Connor ran to the door, not daring to cross the threshold and set off his implant. He'd done that twice this summer already, and Mr Smythe and his dad kept telling him off for it.

The robot, an Air Drone, descended into the street, cutting through the heavy rain and tilting forward, its bird-of-prey-style wings levelling just a few feet from the houses on either side. The wind from its engines created a mini-hurricane, stirring up droplets of water, making them dance spirals in the orange glow of the street lights. The Air Drone's blinding white beam shone through the rain, casting a thin, stretchy shadow of the man standing in front of it. He was holding a long metal pipe and shouting. And that's when Connor recognised the voice.

'Dad?' he said quietly to himself. Then he screamed, 'Dad! Come back!'

The Drone spoke again: 'YOU HAVE TEN SECONDS TO RETURN TO YOUR HOME. THIS IS YOUR FINAL WARNING.'

The Drone's hull split open and a cannon slid from its belly. It looked like a bee-sting.

Up and down the street, bedroom lights came on, doors swung open. But no one stepped outside.

The cannon crackled into life, the barrel spinning. The Drone began counting down, 'TEN, NINE …'

Across the street, Connor saw Mrs Flynn and her son standing in their doorway. They were shouting at his dad. 'Go back inside. Do as it says!'

Next door to them, two teenage kids were doing the same.

'Go home, you dingus!' the boy shouted.

'Run, now!' shouted the girl.

'FIVE, FOUR ...'

All this time, Connor had been yelling, too. 'Dad, *please*!'

Connor's dad turned to them, his arms wide. 'They're gonna kill us all anyway. Might as well take me now!'

'TWO, ONE—'

The air shimmered and there was a deafening bang. Windows rattled and with a flash of light and heat, Connor's father exploded into a million charred fragments, which were swept away in the rain.

'*Dad!*' Connor screamed, charging out into the street. With a loud beep, his implant switched from blue to red, and his pyjamas were instantly drenched in the downpour.

The Drone turned its weapons towards him. 'CITIZEN, RETURN TO YOUR HOME IMMEDIATELY.'

Mrs Flynn and the others were all shouting at him to come in. Her son even lunged forward, his implant briefly flashing red, but Mrs Flynn grabbed him and held on tight.

'THIS IS YOUR FINAL WARNING.'

Connor stumbled to a dark smudge on the street. All that remained of his father. He fell to his wet, soot-stained pyjama knees, his body shuddering with sobs. He was numb. Tingly. Dizzy. The world became a bad dream.

'FIVE, FOUR, THREE ...'

'Connor, get inside! Please!' cried Mrs Flynn.

'Run, you little knob!' shouted Sean.

The Drone's weapon hummed as it powered up again.

'TWO—'

'Stand down!' a voice snapped from the darkness. A man stepped before the Drone, his hand raised. He said some words to the Drone that Connor didn't understand.

'Authorisation code: 97-ZCRS. Request: half-hour amnesty. Reason: citizen intends to return home.'

The implant on the Drone's nose pulsed rapidly like the lights on the old Wi-Fi box in Connor's living room used to do.

'AUTHORISATION CONFIRMED.'

With a high-pitched whine and another blast of air, the Drone peeled away, screeching into the night sky.

Then the street was silent. Connor's ears were ringing. He shivered, and sniffed through his tears. The man peered out from under his black cap, rain dripping from its peak. Connor recognised the gold star on the man's cap, his red bow tie, long brown coat and tidy beard.

The man's faced hardly moved, but his eyes scared Connor more than the robot. It was like he was being inspected by a predator, a lion watching for a weak zebra to kill.

Finally, the man spoke. 'Past your bedtime, isn't it, son?'

It was Mr Smythe.

ZONE CHIEF SMYTHE

'Let me take him in,' Kate pleaded. 'We've got a spare room. He'll be well looked after.'

The lad Connor was upstairs. Kate and Sean had beckoned him in and whisked him away before Smythe could intervene. He could hear the boy's sobs drifting down the stairs. Sad, Smythe supposed, though he'd become so accustomed to seeing people cry that it had little effect on him any more.

The house he'd found for Kate was falling apart at the seams. A long crack split the living room wall. Damp in the corners. Peeling and torn wallpaper. But the biggest affront was a bloody great hole in the wall, connecting them to next door. Completely against regulations. They'd piled bricks in neat little stacks beside it, as if to indicate that this was only a temporary measure, but he'd had to get the VC to install a couple of props to stop the whole place from collapsing. The hole was so big that they'd had the cheek to plonk their sofa right in the middle of it, one half in this house, the other half next door. They'd stuck a line of duct tape down the sofa's centre. The dividing line between the two houses. Crossing it would set off their implants, and Smythe recalled the many times his people had to come out here on a false alarm, each costing Kate and the kids a day's rations. He grudgingly admired their ingenuity, but this kind of rule-bending could lead very quickly to escalating insubordination and vaporisations.

Kate's side was Buckingham Palace compared to the vile neighbouring sixth-form bedsit. The little reprobates, Alex and Nathan, had barely left an inch of it untouched, with graffiti scrawled on every surface; vulgar little stick men, sickening hippy flowers and love hearts, and the words 'ROBOT-FREE ZONE' splashed above the fireplace.

Sean sat on this side, tinkering with the innards of a broken games console. On the other was that cocky little rodent Nathan, sneering at Smythe from under his ragged fringe of hair.

'Robin?' Kate's gentle voice brought him back into the world. 'Please, he's got nowhere else to go.'

'You're an angel, Kate.' Smythe said, stroking her arm. 'But you needn't shoulder the burden. We have homes for orphaned children. Good homes. Good people.'

'I'm good people.' She said, her voice suddenly terse.

He caught himself looking into her hazel eyes and had to snap away. 'Of course, of course, I didn't mean it like that.' Smythe coughed a laugh. 'The Volunteer Corps has a screening process for foster parents. I guarantee he'll be safe and happy.'

'Yeah,' piped up Nathan, 'stick him in with one of your – whajacallem? – collaborators.'

Smythe stiffened and his blood started to boil.

'Nice one, dickhead,' muttered Sean.

Smythe threw a hurt glance at Kate, who at least had the good grace to look ashamed. ' "Collaborator" is a word with all sorts of nasty connotations, son,' said Smythe.

Didn't he know it, having had the word spat at him by so many on his rounds. He endured the ignorant abuse, knowing that what he was doing was not only important, but vital to the survival of the human race.

Like many, Smythe had been terrified when the invasion began.

He'd stood on Duncombe Hill and watched Tornado fighters swoop in tight formation over Fairfield Bay. In moments they were dashed against the rocks on the beach below. It had been instantly clear to Smythe that the invaders could not be bested.

Where others saw disaster, he saw an opportunity to become part of something bigger, part of history. He joined the Fairfield Bay Council war committee, overseeing the provision of shelters, medicine, food and welfare. The fools around him still clung to the idea that the war could be won and were slow to grasp the inevitable: the humans were going to lose.

The war was over in eleven days. Humanity's losses were devastating, the insistence on continuing to fight a futile conflict coming at a huge price. And yet those responsible for prolonging the conflict failed to see that they had done anything wrong.

The robots were gracious in victory. Their terms were clear: a seven-year incarceration for all humanity while they studied us. No one really knew why they were doing this, or what their methods were. No one was ever interrogated or interviewed, but Smythe soon learned not to ask too many questions. Those who did never got an answer, and those who became insistent had a habit of disappearing. But they needed people to step forward and help keep the remaining infrastructure up and running. This was Smythe's calling. He was one of the first to join the Volunteer Corps. That fool Dr Porter became the first Zone Chief despite his obvious failings, but Smythe knew his time would come. He would make a difference.

When the Mediator arrived, that strange little humanoid, the others in the war committee stammered and faltered. But Smythe stepped forward, hand held out. 'I, for one, welcome our robot overlords,' he said proudly. In return, the Mediator gave his hand a little squeeze. It was a cold grip, but soft. Tender, even.

It was people like Smythe who saved humanity from a quick

annihilation. And what gratitude did his fellow humans give him for it? None. Just ungrateful little scrotes calling him a collaborator.

Smythe loomed over Nathan and Sean. 'The Volunteer Corps puts food on your table, boy. We put this nice roof over your head, keep your lights on, the water running,' he said. 'Not that you look like you've had a wash in weeks, you revolting little urchin.'

Nathan started to reply, the thought no doubt unformed even as it was leaving his mouth, but Sean gave him a warning glance and the boy shut up.

'The robots would punish you for this' – Smythe gestured at the hole in the wall – 'but me – a *collaborator* – I protect you from them. I am here to keep the peace. I—'

'He didn't know what he was saying, Robin.' Smythe felt Kate gently take his elbow and his body shuddered in surprise. 'I'm sorry,' she said.

'It's not you, Kate,' he said. 'You're a wonderful mother, and Sean's a good lad, but those two ...' He waved a dismissive hand at next door. 'You can hardly care for them through a hole in the wall.' Smythe turned back to Nathan, finger wagging. 'It's high time we found you somewhere to live with proper adult supervision.'

Another voice. 'We can look after ourselves, Mr Smythe.'

Smythe winced. The girl. Alex, wasn't it? By God, she made his skin crawl sometimes. Filthy creature, long, lank hair, hooded eyes and a permanent sneer that Smythe wanted to slap off her face.

'Can you, child?' he said. 'Look at the state of you.'

She glared at him, lips twisted into a sneer. He waited for the inevitable barrage of abuse, but then Sean moved between them, a peacemaking smile on his face.

'Have you heard anything about my dad?' he asked. 'You said you'd ask around. Do you remember?'

Smythe sighed. Every time, the same question. And every time he had the same answer. 'Indeed I did. I've also checked the records, as I promised ...'

So give it a rest, boy!

Smythe shrugged. 'Nothing, I'm afraid.'

Sean looked unbowed. 'He's alive, Mr Smythe, I just know it.'

'Of course he is.' Smythe scruffed the boy's hair. He was getting tall. Nearly a man. Smythe received fresh requests every month from Kate for new clothes for all of them. If he'd had his way he'd let them all suffer in tight trousers and split shoes, but the Mediator insisted that a clothes-exchange programme was good for morale.

'Never give up hope,' Smythe said, unsure why. It was one of those things people trotted out, wasn't it? He used to think empty platitudes served no purpose, but he was finding that when used properly they could quell the weak and bring an end to awkward conversations. 'Hope will see you through,' he added.

There was a strange choking noise from behind Smythe. He spun to find Kate trying not to sob and wiping her moistened eyes. Smythe knew exactly how to react. He pulled Kate towards him, embracing her, squeezing her against him. His eyelids fluttered shut for one blissful moment as he inhaled the sweet scent of her hair.

'Oh, Kate, I'm sorry. Be strong.' Smythe kept his eyes closed. She could be as strong as she liked, but that wasn't going to suddenly produce her husband out of thin air, Smythe knew that for sure. But then much of his job was to calm, reassure, keep order. And if that meant the occasional white lie, so be it.

Smythe opened his eyes as Kate wriggled out of his grip and looked straight into Sean's accusing scowl. What was that boy's problem? His mother needed someone to dispel her fears. A man's reassurance. Where else was she going to get it?

'You can take the boy in,' Smythe announced. 'Of course you can.' He couldn't believe he just said that out loud, but if that was the price to feel Kate's body pressed against his, then it was worth paying. He'd find somewhere suitable for Connor in a month or so and everything would be back under his control.

'Thank you so much, Robin,' Kate said. 'I really appreciate it. You've been so good to us.'

'That's what I'm here for.' He addressed them all. 'It's what the Volunteer Corps are here for. These are difficult times, but if we all work together, if we all obey the rules, then we can get through this.'

Nothing. No cheers. No thank yous. Just a bunch of ungrateful ingrates with vacant faces. They'd learn. They'd all learn soon enough.

He left Kate a gift. A small tub of vitamins and a packet of tea bags. Smythe loathed any kind of favouritism, but for Kate he sometimes made an exception. She always understood. Always had a kind word. Had been the only colleague at the school who'd never mocked him. She was everything he had ever desired: intelligent, cheerful, charming, carefree, comfortable in her own skin. Everything he was not. She'd even made an effort to keep her figure, unlike many women her age. She needed a man who shared her appreciation of literature and culture, someone to match her wit. Sadly, despite evidence that this was futile, she continued to hold a candle for her thug of a husband, Danny.

He bade her farewell, clasping her hands in his. And then he took great pleasure in doing something that none of them could. He stepped outside into the pouring rain.

A DAY IN THE LIFE

There was a new sound in the house when Kate awoke the next morning. Connor's sobbing had been stop-start all afternoon, then around five he'd finally worn himself out. But now, as the morning sunlight hit her pillow, he started again.

She went to him straight away, held him, said whatever she could to calm him. She kept him busy, helping with breakfast, sharing out the rations, cleaning up afterwards, but he still spent much of his time staring into space, then suddenly bursting into tears. Every now and then Sean would zip by, hurtling up and down the stairs to keep fit, doing chin-ups in his bedroom doorway, half an hour on the makeshift punchbag. There was so much pent-up aggression in her boy now and this was the best way to get it out of his system.

'Can I join in?' Connor asked, his voice still tender and broken.

'With what, poppet?' Kate dropped down to his eye-line. He was back in his pyjamas, the only clothes that fitted him in this house, finally dry again after a night in the airing cupboard.

At that moment Sean gallumphed to the bottom of the stairs, kicked up a load of dust from the ancient paisley stair carpet as he landed and then stomped back up again.

'That.' Connor pointed.

'Let's ask, shall we?' She took Connor's hand, led him to the bottom of the stairs and called up. 'Sean?'

Her son's head popped over the bannister. 'Yeah?' he puffed.

'Connor would like to join in, if that's okay?'

She saw him hesitate. Just for a moment.

She and Danny had worried about having only one child, that he might end up selfish and spoiled. But in the end Sean always enjoyed playing with other kids, often taking the lead, deciding what to play and where. But Connor was much younger, and prone to start crying at any moment. And this was Sean's private time. When he exercised, Kate could see him thinking, trying to make sense of the world, remembering his father.

'Yeah.' Sean said, beckoning Connor up the stairs. 'C'mon, you little squirt.'

Connor bounded up the steps and Kate was surprised by how relieved she suddenly felt. The truth was, she could do with a break from the grief for a little while, too.

They played all morning, but by the end Connor was seriously winding Sean up and they were yelling at each other. You'd never have known that Connor had watched his dad killed in cold blood fewer than twelve hours ago. Kate had seen this before with kids in her class. So many of them were RAF babies who had parents working at the airbase, and too many had lost fathers and mothers, either in the robot invasion or the human wars that preceded it. They were tough little buggers at that age. They could be fine for weeks, then suddenly something would snap and they'd be howling in floods of tears and all you could do was hold them tight.

That's all Kate seemed to do these days. Play umpire, psychologist, nursemaid and emotional firefighter. Nathan appeared to exist in his own little bubble of denial, his sarcasm all that prevented it from going pop. Alex was turning into a surly little madam. She was such a sweet girl when they first arrived, but she'd completely given up hope. They were watching TV last week – repeats of old sitcoms transmitted by the VC from God knows where – when the picture flickered and turned to snow. Where a commercial break might have been, the robots now inserted their own propaganda: the same public information films they'd been playing every day for the last three years, with titles like 'What To Do When Someone Dies', 'Mental Health' and 'The Dangers of Tampering with Your Implant'. This one was 'Boundaries'.

'Ugh,' Alex said with a sigh. 'You're shitting me.'

'Alexandra! Swear box.' Kate slid a glass bottle half-full of coins along the floor towards her. Alex jolted upright, her pretty face now scrunched in anger.

'I tell you what, Kate …' Alex started rummaging in the deep pockets of her dressing gown, coins jingling as she dropped pennies into the bottle. 'I'm gonna buy four more years of swearing. Bums. Tits. Twats.'

'Give it a rest, Alex.' Sean snapped.

Alex leaned as far as she could into Sean's face without crossing the sofa's duct tape divide and snarled, 'Arseholes!'

Nathan gleefully joined in, dropping his last few pennies into the jar. 'Sheep-shagger, shaft-tickler … Can I borrow 10p? Great, hairy, fishy—'

The sudden noise made Kate's head throb, and she was just wondering who was screaming when she realised it was her. And from the freaked-out expressions on the kids' faces, she was properly hysterical. She hated losing it in front of them. Hated showing them how fragile she was. Hated seeing herself for what she had become.

Did the job, though. They were all sweet as pie for a few days afterwards.

She continued their schooling, which they weren't best pleased about. She had a few resources to hand, and Mrs Stoker found a stash of her daughter's old GCSE revision books that were perfect

35

and helped jog her own memory. There was no real curriculum, but she insisted they at least work on their maths and English. And they had to keep reading. The whole terrace swapped books and thankfully Morse Code Martin appeared to have more books than the Bodleian Library. She wasn't sure she approved of Nathan reading only comic books, but what the hell: a book is a book.

That morning she tried to gather them together for a class, but only Sean and Nathan turned up on the divided sofa and they were more interested in talking about the only major event to happen in the street during the last three years.

'I mean, did you see it?' Nathan said, head jutting forward. 'The whole guy, just zap, flash, bang, whoosh! Gone. Poor bugger. I wonder what it feels like?'

'Where's Alex?' Kate said sharply, making both boys jump.

Nathan's eyes rolled up as he tried to remember Alex's exact words. 'She said: "Education is pointless, the rations are late, I'm hungry and we're all going to die anyway, so what's the point?"'

Kate sagged. Sadly she was beginning to agree with Alex. Maybe they were better off without her. During their last maths lesson, Alex had a tantrum and threw her calculator out of the window. It took some considerable begging with Smythe to get it back. 'We'll start without her, then. Listen, boys, do me a favour: none of that zap-talk around Connor, okay? Poor kid's just lost his dad.'

'Hey – join the club.' Nathan said, matter-of-factly.

'And mine's missing in action.' Sean's grin matched Nathan's. She knew he was trying to be light-hearted, she knew that boys could joke about this stuff, but she found herself shouting again.

She missed Danny so much. Every morning she hoped she'd wake up without that pain in her heart, that hole inside her.

Sean was on his feet and holding her tight, saying reassuring words.

Nothing appeared to faze her son, though sooner or later she'd have to sit him down and make him face reality. Danny wasn't coming back. Kate had seen the planes drop out of the sky like everyone else. She got a sinking feeling in her gut every time she thought about it. All she could hope was that it had been over quickly, that he hadn't suffered.

'Okay, I'm all right, I'm sorry,' she said, rubbing her eyes. 'Let's not bother today, eh? Yeah, the rations are late, you haven't eaten properly, you won't be able to concentrate anyway, so just … read a book. Do whatever.'

Not long later, she found Sean and Connor side by side in the kitchen. Sean was making more of his tennis-ball messages and Connor was trying to help. She stood back, observing, not wanting them to notice her.

'I hope you find him, Sean,' Connor said, handing the bigger boy the knife.

Sean cut into the tennis ball and stuffed his message inside. 'Thanks, bud.'

Kate was relieved they were getting along. Though not ten minutes later, she was making the bed when she heard Sean yelling, 'Connor! You complete toss-wad!' Yeah, they really were getting along like brothers.

Just before lunch, a Volunteer Corps woman finally came with their rations and a message.

'You are the guardian of Connor Reid?' the VC asked. Her eyes were glazed and distant and her voice had a nasal call-centre quality to it. All VC became like that eventually, the grim monotony of their day-to-day job robbing them of any remnants of humanity. They all dressed the same: black with a red armband on their left arm, the hand-cut letters 'VC' clumsily stitched on the armband like a Cub Scout's badge.

'Yes,' Kate replied. 'Now he needs to—'

'By order of Zone Chief Smythe and in agreement with the

Mediator' – the VC ignored Kate and rambled on regardless – 'Connor Reid has been allotted a period of time to collect essential items from his home.'

'Good. I'll go with him,' Kate said firmly.

'No, just the boy,' the VC said. 'Three o'clock to three-oh-five precisely.'

'Five minutes? You're joking.'

'A Sentry will oversee the procedure. You must obey its commands without question. Is that understood?'

'But he's just a boy, you can't expect him to—'

But the VC woman was already making her way back to the ration cart, ticking another chore off her list.

The contents of their weekly ration box tumbled across the kitchen worktop. Gnarled carrots, a few potatoes, unleavened bread and a chunk of indeterminate brown meat. Kate guessed there must still be someone farming out there, no doubt under constant robot supervision. They'd managed to keep the lights, water and gas on for this long, so planting and ploughing fields should be pretty straightforward in comparison. The meat worried her, though. It didn't look like anything she'd seen in a butcher's window.

'Please, God, don't let it be people,' she said under her breath, only half-joking.

The food had been delivered a day later than usual and there appeared to be even less than they got last week. A black thought entered her mind, tempting her. She knew Smythe lusted after her; if she gave him what he wanted then they'd probably get more. Could she do it? Could she give in, lie back and think of England?

Kate shuddered. What was happening to her? Had she become so dulled by the grind of the occupation that something once so unthinkable was even being considered? She was grateful when Sean strolled in, turned on the tap, picked up a few carrots and

started scrubbing them, cleaning them in the grey water cou[...]
from the spout. *It never used to be that colour*, Kate thought.

'Remember before the war?' he said. 'You used to come back with bags and bags of stuff. Treats for me and Dad.'

'He always wanted the same ice cream,' Kate said. 'What was it?'

'Ben and Jerry's Chunky Monkey.'

Kate smiled. A bottomless well of choice. All gone.

'Yeah, well, I miss Fruit Corners,' she said, 'but no one's making them now. Get used to it.'

'They might do one day.'

'I'm not sure little pots of yoghurt with fruit in them will be at the top of the government's agenda when the robots are gone.'

'Would be if I was in charge,' Sean said, cleaning another carrot. 'You think they'll really go?'

'"Robots never lie",' Kate quoted. 'Why say they're going and then not?'

'Keep people hopeful. Stop us from topping ourselves, or fighting back.'

Kate tried to maintain a poker face, but she'd had exactly the same thoughts.

'You really think they'll just leave? For good?' Sean asked.

'Maybe.' Kate shrugged as if nothing else had occurred to her. She didn't want to dwell on the alternative.

'I mean, they've got no problem killing anyone who steps out of line,' Sean continued, 'so what would stop them killing us all when they're done? And done with what, exactly? If this is genocide, they're taking their bloody time about it.'

'Sean, can we stop talking about this, please?' Kate took his hand and squeezed it hard.

'We hear rumours, y'know,' Sean said. 'Morse Code Martin gets messages about whole streets being emptied, dozens of people disappearing overnight.'

'Oh, God, I wish he'd stop filling your heads with this crap.'

ands up, exasperated. 'He's not the one who has
...all, listen to your nightmares and calm you down

...nightmares!' Sean said, indignant.

...t, Kate thought, *but I bloody do.* It didn't even have
to be dark. Sometimes, during the day, she'd find herself suddenly
crying. When that happened she tried to find somewhere quiet,
somewhere Sean wouldn't see her and get upset, too. She didn't
always succeed.

At three o'clock precisely there was a knock on the door. More
VC, accompanied by a Sentry. Kate watched it from the window.
It marched along the middle of the street, towering over all of
them, as tall as the houses lining each side, its weapon-arm quietly
crackling like bacon in a pan. It moved past an overturned car,
one of many abandoned during the invasion, and came to a stop
outside Kate's house.

'Ah.' Sean nodded in recognition as he joined her by the window.
'Shit-head.'

Kate nearly choked. 'What? Be quiet.'

'Look.' He pointed to the Sentry's head, where months' worth of
bird droppings had collected in unflattering streaks. 'It's because
he stands guard by the big oak tree on the corner under the birds'
nests. All the birds shit on him. They're on our side, y'know.'

'Fine, but keep it to yourself,' she said. There was more knocking
at the door as she and Sean headed downstairs.

'All the regulars have names.' Sean said cheerfully as he followed.
'There's Shit-head, Stompy – that's the one with the dodgy left leg.
Splashback is covered in paint where someone clearly tried it on
with a paintball gun, and there's Treebeard – he's got a bird's nest
on his right shoulder.'

'And what do you call the one that killed Connor's dad?'

'Mum, you can be such a *downer* sometimes,' he said. 'I know it's sick, but if we didn't do this we'd go mental.'

Another insistent knock at the front door.

'Connor!' Kate called. 'Get ready.'

Kate and Sean stood in the doorway as Connor, still in his pyjamas, dashed across the street to his old house, a shopping list of essentials fluttering in his grip. He dodged around the cracks in the road, the weeds and the rusting cars.

'CITIZEN, YOU HAVE FIVE MINUTES,' the Sentry announced as Connor's front door clattered shut.

'Can't he stay with one of Smythe's lot?' said Sean. 'He's such a spaz-wit.'

'Be nice.' Kate gently slapped his arm. 'Anyway, I thought you liked him?'

'In teeny-weeny, microscopic doses. He's under my bloody feet the whole time: "Sean, can we do this? Can we do that? Can we play a game?" It's bloody exhausting.'

Kate surprised herself with how loud she laughed. 'You were the same when you were his age. Give him a break. Poor kid's been stuck inside with his mad dad for three years – you can't blame him for wanting a bit of a run around with someone closer to his age.'

'Then let Smythe put him in a home with other little kids,' Sean said. 'There must be someone out there better than us.'

'Would you trust Smythe with him?'

'I wouldn't trust Smythe with anyone.'

'Exactly. You kids have to stop thinking only of yourselves for once,' Kate said. 'We have to take care of one another, or the robots will.'

After a few minutes, Connor came bounding through his doorway, a black bag slung over his shoulder. He was dressed in a Viking costume: a helmet with horns, plastic chain-mail tabard and a wooden sword hanging around his waist. He had various toys, games and books piled high in his arms.

Kate slowly shook her head in despair. 'I said essentials, Connor!'

'See what I mean?' said Sean.

'THIRTY SECONDS,' the Sentry boomed.

Connor dropped half of what he was carrying. Clothes and toys tumbled across the street.

'Oh, bum,' said Connor as he stooped to pick it all up. In the process, he managed to drop everything else. 'Double bum.' He grabbed his box of Lego and gathered his Nerf guns.

'Not the toys, Connor!' yelled Kate. 'Get some clothes!'

'I need all these! Waitasec.'

'No you don't! Just bring the clothes!'

'Can't wear Lego, Connor,' said Sean, laughing. 'He's such a doof.'

'FIFTEEN SECONDS.' Shit-head remained still as its voice bounced off the walls around them. Every time Connor picked something up, he dropped something else. Kate only just resisted the urge to dash into the street to help him.

'YOU HAVE TEN SECONDS TO RETURN TO YOUR HOME.' The Sentry jolted upright and trained its laser cannon on Connor. Sean's grin disappeared. Kate tensed.

'Oh, for— Quickly, Connor!' she yelled.

The Sentry's weapon crackled into life, the barrel spinning as it stomped across the street toward the boy.

'THIS IS YOUR FINAL WARNING.'

'Connor!' Kate screamed. 'Now!'

'Connor, c'mon!' Sean shouted.

Connor dropped a bag of clothes, snatched up what he could and rushed across the street, the Sentry hot on his tail.

'FIVE. FOUR. THREE. TWO—'

Connor crashed through the door and into the house. His implant blinked from red to blue – safe!

'Genius,' Sean said, waving away the carpet dust kicked up by Connor's landing. 'You're gonna be dressed like a Viking for the next four years.'

'Did you know they used to give their swords names?' said Connor, excited to be talking about a topic he loved, the danger of just a few moments ago already forgotten. 'Like Head-Biter, or Skull-Smasher ...'

'Er ... no,' said Sean.

'Connor, sweetheart.' Kate's heart was still thumping. 'Please shush.'

With a series of heavy clangs, Shit-head marched back down to the end of the street. Kate shut the door behind them, watching the boys talk as they made their way upstairs.

'Some Vikings took drugs and went completely mental in battle. They were called berserkers and they were totally unafraid of dying.'

'Vikings were mental?' Sean said, patting the younger boy on the back. 'Another thing you've got in common.'

There was a new sound that night in the house. Two boys laughing, swearing, calling each other names, and a contest to see who could do the best armpit farts.

Kate slept better that night than she had since the invasion began.

DOINKING

Nathan narrowed his eyes, assessing the games console parts spread out across the loft boards. He squinted thoughtfully at them in the hope that he looked like he knew what he was doing. Wires trailed from the games console to the DC/AC power inverter, then over the loft's duct tape divide to a twelve-volt car battery over on Sean's side.

'Okay,' Alex said, nudging Nathan out of the way and turning the console off, 'power off on the battery, Connor.'

Connor was kneeling over the old car battery. He detached red and blue crocodile clips from the battery terminals while Alex cleaned the gold-plated connectors on the console's video card. They'd carefully taken the console to pieces and were now systematically testing each component to see if they could find the faulty part.

Then what, God only knows, thought Nathan. It's not like they could order a replacement on eBay. Sean was convinced they could find someone in the street who might have another console kicking about, and that maybe they could trade spares. It probably hadn't occurred to Sean that anyone who had a working games console probably wouldn't want to take it apart for a bunch of kids.

Nathan sometimes wondered if Sean lived on the same planet as everyone else. He talked about escape, finding Danny, the end of the occupation, like these things were inevitable. You had to admire his optimism, but Nathan wasn't sure it was worth the energy.

Nathan needed most of his energy to avoid arguments with his sister. Yesterday's fight was over washing-up powder, or lack of it, and today she accused him of wasting toilet paper. He hadn't wasted it, he'd just needed an awful lot of it that particular time. But now they were out of it till next week's delivery and might need to resort to wiping with pages from the romance novels Polly left behind. Well, it wouldn't be the first time and definitely not the last.

To avoid her, he came up here to the loft and chilled out reading Morse Code Martin's old war comics, where square-jawed British Tommies threw themselves at Nazi machine guns, yelling, 'Go to hell, you filthy traitor!' before either being blown to pieces or walking away with hardly a scratch. 'Take that, Fritz! This is for the cap'n'! The war's over for you, Jerry!'

One day, Nathan asked Martin, 'Really? Who talks like that?'

'Heroes.' Martin coughed into life, leaning closer to Nathan. 'Men who put their old lives behind them. Men willing to sacrifice everything, their very lives, so others could live in peace. Heroes, son.' Martin gave him a wink. 'Heroes.'

But Nathan wasn't sure those kinds of heroes existed outside comic books.

He had his own escape plan, of course. It was bloody genius. He'd been up late one night, staring through the window in his room, bored out of his mind, when he saw a fox move in the shadows across the street. It was creeping up on Shit-head the Sentry. To save power, the Sentries went on standby at night with only their sensors running, waiting to detect any sign of motion.

That night the fox moved like a ninja, creeping slowly, stealthily, towards the metal giant. Shit-head remained shut down ... until the fox, driven by some unknown urge, darted between its legs. Then the Sentry clunked upright, the sudden movement snapping it out of standby mode. It only took a second to register that the fox wasn't a threat and then settled back into standby.

Nathan was trying to convince the others that it was worth a go. He even practised on the burglar alarm motion detectors: nine times out of ten he could make it across the hall without setting them off. How hard could it be?

'Our implants would still be live,' Alex told him with a weary shake of her head. 'The robots could still track us.'

'We only think that 'cos they tell us so on the TV every day,' he said. 'All we'd need to do is make it far as the resistance in the hills.'

'We wouldn't make it to the end of the street, doofus,' Alex said.

This didn't faze Nathan one bit. 'Maybe we should send someone out first as an experiment? Connor?'

'Hey!' Connor yelped.

'Only joking … a bit.' Nathan gently nudged Connor's arm. 'C'mon, I have to get outside soon, I'm going mental.'

'That makes all of us,' said Alex.

'Look at that creep.' Sean's voice cut through Nathan's dreams of escape.

Nathan glanced up at Sean, who was leaning against the attic window and staring down at the street below where Smythe was chatting up Kate. They could hear her polite laughter drift through the window as Smythe finished another of his boring anecdotes.

'I wish he'd stop perving on her.' Sean slowly shook his head. Nathan could tell his mate would love nothing more than to rush down there and punch Smythe's lights out.

'Nothing's changed,' said Alex. 'He was a sleaze when he was head of Year Ten, and he's a sleaze now.'

'You can hardly blame him, though,' Nathan added. 'He needs a new wife, and Kate's well fit.'

'Um … That's my mum you're talking about!'

'Sorry, mate. But it's true. For all we know she could be the last attractive woman on the planet and Smythe needs her to repopulate the species.'

'Does your mouth ever engage with your brain, Nate?' Alex snapped.

'Don't worry, Alex – Smythe probably can't tell if you're a boy or a girl, so I think you're safe.' That earned Nathan a smack around the head from his sister.

'Why does Smythe need a new wife?' Connor piped up.

Nathan lowered his voice, itching to share the secret. 'Morse Code Martin told us. Mr Smythe caught Mrs Smythe doinking some other bloke, plus his son was flogging stuff on the black market.'

Sean joined in. 'All well dodgy for a VIP Zone Chief, so now' – he clicked his fingers – 'gone. Both of them vanished. No one knows where. Dead, probably.'

Alex sighed, trying to return to the task at hand. 'Power on, Connor.'

Connor, deep in thought, attached the clips to the battery. Alex checked her multimeter device … nothing.

'What's "doinking"?' Connor asked, all innocence.

Sean rested a hand on the smaller boy's shoulder. 'You'll get it once you've grown a few pubes, mate.'

'That's no way to talk to your little sister.' Nathan grinned mischievously.

'I'm not his sister! I'm a boy!' Connor whined.

'Power off, Connor,' said Alex, handing Nathan the console's graphics card.

'Really?' Nathan took the card, while recoiling in mock horror. ' 'Cos you sound like a girl.'

'I'm a boy and I can prove it.'

'No need, mate. Seriously, keep your trousers on,' Nathan said.

'Make sure it clicks.' Alex nudged Nathan. 'Nathan? Make sure the graphics card clicks when you—'

'Yeah, yeah.'

But Connor was getting more high-pitched. 'Tell him, Sean!'

'Leave him alone, Nathan,' Sean said.

Nathan moved to put the card back in the console. 'Aww. Your big sister's sticking up for y—'

Nathan's world suddenly shrank and went black. There were actual stars in his eyes, then purple and green glowing balls of light, and for a moment every nerve ending in his body went tight and burned in searing agony. Then he felt light as a feather, the world tumbled around him and when he regained his senses, he found himself lying in a tangled pile on the far side of his loft.

His back ached where it had hit the wooden beams and he could smell burning. He was pretty sure his hair was on fire. Everyone else was looking at him with saucer eyes. His hands trembled as he tried to put together what just happened to him. Connor. Bloody Connor hadn't turned off the car battery and Nathan had touched something live in the console. He'd been electrocuted.

'Connor! You dozy little tit!' he yelled.

'Shit, man.' Sean was smiling now, relieved his friend was still alive. 'You flew! You actually flew.'

'My gums are numb!' Nathan cried, exploring his mouth with his fingers. 'That can't be right.'

'Whoa, look … Look!' Sean reached over the beams and grabbed Nathan's head.

'Get off me, you bummer!' Nathan struggled, but Sean twisted Nathan's neck around to show something to the others.

'Holy crap,' gasped Alex.

'What, what?' Nathan yelped. They were all staring at him. Well, not straight at him, maybe a little bit to one side of him. At his neck.

'It's dead!' Sean said.

'What do you mean, dead?' Nathan was suddenly worried that

48

he'd died and was having an out-of-body experience. Certainly no one here was bloody listening to him.

'Your implant, Nate.' Alex grabbed Nathan's hand and held his palm up near his neck. Normally he'd see the blue glow of his implant reflected back, but now it was dark.

'But that means ...' The significance of this couldn't quite slot into Nathan's recently frazzled brain. Instead, they all said it together: 'We can go outside!'

'Awesome,' said Connor, the unwitting architect of their freedom, holding up the crocodile clips like six-shooters. 'Who's next?'

OPERATION HARIBO

Their celebrations were cut short by a cry of, 'What are you lot up to?' from Kate downstairs.

They froze, and it was Alex who took the initiative, calling down through the loft, 'Nothing. Just the boys arsing about.'

'Then tell them to arse about quietly,' Kate yelled back.

Sean looked back and forth along the terrace lofts. Nothing up here but dust-motes lazily drifting in the beams of sunlight. They were alone. He gathered the others around him by the duct tape divide. 'We have to keep this quiet,' he said.

'Balls to that,' said Nathan. 'Let's get everyone out while we can.'

'Yeah, Sean, let's leg it,' Alex said, in a rare moment of agreement with her brother.

'Where to?'

'Join the resistance up in the hills,' Connor said.

Alex shook her head. 'That'll take days.'

'Look, no one wants to get out more than me,' Sean said, 'but we don't know if this is permanent.' He thought for a moment. 'Let's test it. One mission, one night out.'

'Like what?' asked Alex.

'Oh my God,' Nathan smacked his forehead, suddenly in the

grip of a new idea. 'There's a newsagents at the train station – that's like half a mile from here. Piece of piss.'

'You need nudie mags that badly, Nate?' said Alex.

'Actually, no, that hadn't occurred to me, but now you mention it—'

'Sweets!' Connor said, wide-eyed and salivating. 'They have sweets.'

'Bags and bags of them, mate.' Nathan stared into empty space, imagining candy Nirvana. 'All factory-fresh, sealed in plastic. Those little rubbery chews last for ever. Sweets and porn! Yes, we have to do this.'

'Half a mile.' Sean thought about it. 'Good for a test run, at least. That's not a bad idea. Let's do it.'

'Midnight tonight?' asked Alex.

'It's a date.' Sean said, then realised what he'd said as Alex's expression changed. 'I mean ... not a *date* date. I mean a date ... You know what I mean. Anyway, this is just a fantasy unless we all get zapped. What if it doesn't work on the rest of us? Nate could just be a fluke, something to do with the way his brain's wired.'

'Or his lack of one.' Alex said.

'Hey!' Nathan jabbed her arm.

'C'mon, let's do it!' Connor still had the crocodile clips ready.

In their excitement, they zapped one another right there and then. Sean volunteered next. He bit on a cushion as Nathan applied the crocodile clips to his palm.

Sean's eyes squeezed shut and a throaty growl reverberated through the cushion. He didn't fly like Nathan; instead he shook for a few seconds like an alarm clock. But it was done. His implant was also dead.

'We should've stuck our fingers in the socket years ago.' Nathan said.

'Don't be an idiot.' Alex shook her head wearily. 'That'll kill you stone dead. This is going through a car battery, a dodgy adapter and a broken console. It's not lethal, but there must be something about this combination that works.'

'Like what?'

'I don't know, just— *mmf.* Alex struggled to speak as Nathan held the cushion in place. She shook as the shock ripped through her.

They all turned to Connor.

'Oh, look at him,' Nathan said. 'I can't shock that – it'd be like shooting a little puppy.' He glanced at Sean and Alex, who also looked reluctant to electrocute a ten-year-old boy.

'Oh, give it here.' Connor said, snatching the crocodile clips.

He screamed. He flew. His implant died. And Alex had to apologise to Kate again about the noise.

As they all nursed sore heads and hands, Sean realised something. 'We're complete idiots,' he said.

'Why?' asked Alex as she checked her dead implant in a hand mirror.

'We're gonna have to spend the rest of today hiding our dead implants from Mum.'

'Not us.' Nathan leaned against his sister. 'We'll just keep out of sight. She can't see us if we're upstairs in our rooms.'

'Connor, listen up,' Sean said as he rearranged the collar on the younger boy's shirt to conceal the implant. 'We'll tell her you're tired and need to go straight to bed. Make like you're upset.'

'I am upset,' Connor replied. 'My dad just died.'

Sean faltered. 'Sorry, I meant ...'

'No, it's okay.' Connor said as he misted up. 'It's weird ... If Mum and Dad hadn't been killed, then I wouldn't be here with you, and you guys are the best. I hate what happened and every time I think of it I feel sick, but being with you makes it better. Does that make sense?'

Sean smiled and nodded. 'More sense than anything I've heard in years, mate.'

No one spoke much after that.

Midnight took an eternity to arrive.

Sean spent the afternoon working out on the punchbag while Nathan paced in his room like a caged animal. Alex was the only one who managed to get any sleep, and Connor nearly dropped them all in it by saying, 'It feels like Christmas!' in front of Kate. Sean explained the younger boy's excitement by circling his index finger alongside his head, making 'He's mental' faces.

Kate went to sleep at about ten. Sean wanted to rush outside as soon as she closed her bedroom door, but he resisted and waited. And waited.

Two minutes after midnight, the back door to Sean's house creaked open. He stood on the threshold, his implant deactivated.

Taking a deep breath, he stepped into the garden and paused.

Nothing.

No warnings, no Drones, no Sentries. *Bloody hell, this might actually work.*

He breathed in. It had been raining earlier and the air was sweet and humid. As it filled his lungs, he felt more than alive than he had in years.

There was a squeak as Nathan and Alex's back door opened, and they were soon clambering over their garden fence into the alley.

Sean was astonished to see Alex wearing something other than her floppy old dressing gown. She looked cool in matching black jeans and jacket. Her hair was in a ponytail, and from the way it shone, it looked like she'd even washed it.

Both siblings carried heavy backpacks – the car battery in one, the games console and dodgy adapter in the other. That had been

Alex's idea. 'Let's divvy up the shock-kit and take it with us. That way, if the implants come on again we can shut them off.'

It was a good idea, but the bags were cumbersome and tugged at Nathan's and Alex's shoulders as they disappeared over their back fence.

Nathan's hand appeared over the fence. Thumbs-up. All clear.

Sean gave Connor a thumbs-up and they moved commando-style through the tall grass, brushing aside spiders' webs, feeling rain droplets trickle down the back of his neck as he climbed over the fence.

They landed next to Nathan and Alex. All four were dressed in the best camouflage they could muster: Alex's black ensemble, Nathan's green combat jacket, Sean's dark hoodie. Connor could only manage a faded blue and yellow baseball jacket, but it would have to do.

They paused for a moment, looking around them. This was it! They were actually outside – properly outside – for the first time in three years. Their eyes were wide, chests heaving with fear and excitement, big grins on all their faces. They desperately wanted to speak but knew that any human vocal noises would surely be heard by a patrolling robot.

From overhead came the familiar screeching of robot Drones. Sean looked up to see three of them pass by in a tight V-formation. All the smiles disappeared. If they were going to be caught, then this was it. They froze. Waiting.

But in seconds, the drones were gone, their engine growls echoing off the hills around the town and fading away. Sean gestured for them for move forward.

The alley was thick with tough weeds that hissed as they moved through them and tugged at their trainers. Sean warned the others, putting a finger to his lips and moving more carefully, avoiding the taller grass.

Connor dawdled behind – he'd found something in an

overgrown bush by the gate. Sean snapped his fingers twice – *Come on, Connor.* Connor's head jerked up and he nodded. He stuffed whatever he'd found into his pocket and raced to catch up.

All Sean could hear was his own panting and his sneakers crunching on the ground, occasionally splashing into a puddle. He was trying his best to be quiet, but with so little background noise to disguise his movements, he was sure he sounded like an elephant tap-dancing down the alleyway. He was first to the end. A shadow moved and he raised his fist. The others came to a halt.

They felt it before they heard it: the heartbeat boom of a Sentry's footsteps stomping down the street on patrol, search beam blazing into dark corners, inner gears whining and hissing, weapon-arm humming and crackling with energy. It was Stompy, the one with the dodgy left leg. Something inside squeaked like a rusty gate every time it moved.

Sean couldn't remember ever being this close to one of them before. He was barely breathing. They were all glued to the shadows, but Stompy only had to turn and it would see them.

But it marched on. Rounding a corner and out of sight, its squeak fading further and further away. Their heartbeats settled from mortal fear to mild panic.

They scurried across the street, coming to a crossroads where four streets met in the shadow of two housing blocks. Overturned cars littered the road, some with black scorches from robot weapons seared into the bonnets and doors. There must have been a fight here at some point. A long time ago, though. Green and black ivy had wound its way through the smashed windscreen of one car and draped itself over the driver's seat.

Sean could hear music playing from one of the flats. Judging by the crackling that accompanied it, he suspected someone was using an old record player. Martin had one and he played it at weekends. Sean even recognised the song – 'Dream a little dream'. His gran used to play it when they went to visit her before the war.

'Shut that bloody racket off!' came an angry voice from another flat.

'Shut yourself up, you miserable old fart!' a woman's voice replied.

'I'll report you, I will!' the angry voice yelled. 'I'll see that Mr Smythe hears about this, you see if I don't!'

Sean was suddenly aware that the houses around them weren't empty. They didn't just have to hide from the robots, but also from the people around them, too. Reporting someone who infringed the rules could bring rewards: extra rations, clothes and shoes.

Sean waved everyone forward, then had to go back again for Connor who was gazing up at the robot mother ship in orbit above them. A massive, doughnut-shaped space station, looking down like an all-seeing eye as it moved silently across the star-filled sky.

Sean sighed. Was Connor going to be like this all night? Was Sean going to have to run back for him every five minutes? He began to question the wisdom of bringing such a young kid along. But leaving him behind risked him blurting everything to Mum.

Sean grabbed Connor by the shoulder and dragged him away.

The Fairfield Bay train station was only a few streets away, but by the time they came to its Victorian redbrick exterior, Sean felt like he'd climbed a mountain. All this sneaking about was exhausting.

Connor and Sean hurdled a white picket fence to find Nathan kicking at the door. The wooden door-frame cracked and snapped and Sean winced at the sound, but it didn't appear to draw the robots' attention, and the station's arched windows, looking like hooded eyes, were dark. There was no one inside.

After three kicks, the door splintered and swung open, and the gang squeezed through into the storeroom. It was pitch black. Connor clicked on his clockwork torch, its weak beam revealing stone steps leading into the main shop area.

It was part newsagents, part gift shop. A place for commuters to bide their time while waiting for a train, or to buy a souvenir after enjoying the museum. Under the brick arches were shelves lined with dusty models of steam trains, next to racks of newspapers and postcards.

Now they were here, they couldn't quite believe it. They were still alive. Alex's hand suddenly snapped to her mouth. For a second, Sean thought she was going to be sick, but then she giggled. Nathan was next, followed by Connor. Sean couldn't help but join in.

'Quiet!' He was serious for about a second, but it didn't last. The adrenalin pumping through them all eased their fears a bit and broke the almost unbearable tension.

Soon they were helping themselves to fistfuls of chocolate, cans of cola, bags of chewy sweets, fresh as the day they were factory-sealed. Alex found pairs of outsized toy sunglasses, and she and Connor put them on, giggling with delight.

Connor bit into a chocolate bar that had turned white with age. He spat it out again. 'Bleaugh! That's disgusting!'

'Connor!' Sean hissed. 'Shh!'

Alex found a jar of fruit salad chews. She scooped up a handful and peeled away the wrappers stuck to the tacky, chewy sweets. She groaned with pleasure as she shoved them into her mouth.

Nathan poured a whole tub of sweets into his bag, congratulating Connor as his jaw worked overtime on a mass of gummy bears. 'Connor, you mentile electric-zapping genius.'

Connor grinned as he jemmied open a display case full of fireworks. He tried to bundle the boxes into his backpack but there wasn't enough room. He tipped the contents across the floor – a stopwatch, the SAS Survival Handbook and a book about Vikings – and started shifting stuff around to make room.

Nathan's eye was drawn to a Plexiglas cabinet of lighters. With a *snick-snick* he lit one up. A Zippo. The flame danced as the ground began to tremble like a bass drum.

Something big was coming.

'Everyone get down!'

Nathan snuffed out his lighter and they all ducked, seconds before a searchlight swept through the tiny arched windows.

Sean and Alex dared to peek over the counter as a Sentry thumped by right outside without stopping. It wasn't Stompy, Splashback or Shit-head. Sean didn't recognise this one at all. They were only a few corners away from Fleetwood Street, but he suddenly felt miles from home.

'Let's, uh, let's find a place without any windows,' Sean said.

THE REPLY

Of course it was Connor who knew all about the steam train museum next door.

'Came here on a school trip just before the war,' he said. 'Did you know that most people think the first steam train was Stephenson's *Rocket*? But they're wrong. A man called Richard Trevithick built a locomotive in 1804.'

'Oh yeah, I heard about that,' said Nathan. 'That was just before the boring kid who wouldn't shut up about trains was shoved into a bin head first, right?'

Connor lashed out, trying to kick Nathan in the shin, but the bigger boy dodged him. 'Arse biscuit!' Connor said, using the worst combination of words he could come up with. It wasn't as insulting as he would have liked, but at least it left Nathan with a puzzled expression on his face.

Still a bit cross, Connor led them through the abandoned turnstiles into the main hall. Small glass display cases contained train sets depicting scenes from the station's history. Tiny Edwardian commuters waiting for Hornby trains. Carriages full of toy soldiers going to war, waved off by their scale-model wives and children.

Pictures lined the walls, showing the town over the past hundred years. A world before the robots, where people complained if their train was five minutes late. A brass pocket watch took pride of place inside a bell jar. Connor glanced at the display card. It was made to commemorate the centenary of the railway. Just before everything changed for ever.

But the main reason Connor loved this place was because of the handful of steam engines standing huge, silent and forgotten under the corrugated roof. A few were under dust-sheets, but some still shone brightly and looked like they'd recently been polished. Connor wondered if some of the VC were trainspotters who cleaned them in their spare time. The trains' rivets and steel plates made him think of the robots. But where the robots were functional and ugly, these trains were things of beauty, designed to make the onlooker gasp in admiration, not fear.

Nathan slumped to the ground holding his stomach. 'I think I'm gonna puke,' he groaned, 'and it'll probably be a hundred per cent pure gummy bear vom.'

'Thanks for sharing, Nate.' Alex grimaced.

'Of course, you know what this means?' Nathan said.

'You're a sick puppy?'

'The robots definitely can't trace us. We're off-grid,' Nathan said. 'This is just the beginning – man, think of what we can do.'

Alex and Sean looked full up, too, and they sat with their backs against the huge wheels of a shiny green steam train. Its name was emblazoned on a shining brass plaque: *The Fairfield Thunderbolt*.

Connor dropped next to Sean, but something poked into his bottom. What was it?

'We could join the resistance,' Nathan continued, 'kick some robot arse! My uncle, he was in the SAS. Taught me guerrilla warfare techniques.'

'Is this the same uncle who showed you how to kill a man with one punch?' Sean said wearily. Nathan appeared to have a new and different uncle with every tall story he told.

'You want proof?' Nathan stuck his chin up, offended that his skills had been questioned. 'Connor, c'mere – I wanna show Sean something.'

But Connor had remembered what was in his pocket. He'd found it in the weeds outside their back garden gate just as they left.

'How come Uncle Chris never once talked to me about the SAS?' Alex asked Nathan.

'Duh,' he sneered, ''cos you're a *girl*!'

'Sean,' Connor said, suddenly excited, 'I found this.' He handed Sean a tennis ball. One of Sean's messenger tennis balls. And there was a slip of paper poking out of the slit. 'I didn't open it yet, honest.' Connor was bouncing with anticipation. 'But maybe someone found it and replied, eh, Sean?'

'Cool your jets, Connor.' Sean was calm as he squeezed the tennis ball and removed the message. 'Where did you find it?'

'In the alleyway.'

'Well, there you go.' Sean shrugged as he unfolded the message. 'It's probably one of the ones that fell short, so don't … get—' As he read the message, his eyes widened, glittering as they darted back and forth. 'Hey, listen up …'

But Alex and Nathan were still too busy arguing to hear him. 'Uncle Chris was an accountant,' Alex said. 'Dad took us to his offices in Dorking.'

'That was his cover story, dingus.' Nathan said. 'That place was an MI6 safe office.'

'Hey, listen!' The urgency in Sean's voice stopped them, and the squabbling siblings turned to look at him.

He held the note up for them to see. 'I got a reply.'

Alex took the note. Someone had written over Sean's original message in neat cursive handwriting. An older person, perhaps?

Alex read aloud: 'Danny was captured after the fighting. All the RAF prisoners were put onto ration duty. He was a nice man, who said how much he missed you.'

She glanced up from the note, amazed. Sean's insane plan had actually worked. Even Nathan looked impressed. Connor wanted to give Sean an encouraging smile, but the older boy was lost in deep thought.

Nathan snatched the note and continued in a slower, less-practised reading voice than his sister's: 'After a few weeks they were moved on, I don't know where. The Zone Chief keeps files at the school if you know anyone who works there. Good luck. A friend.'

Sean suddenly stood, grabbing his bag. 'I'm going to the school. To see if I can find Dad's files.'

'What?' Alex snapped. 'The sweet shop and back again, you said. A test run.'

'You don't have to come with me,' he said. 'This is my risk alone.'

'Nah, we're with you, man.' Nathan stood and took his place by Sean's side.

'We are?' Alex looked really worried now.

'My dad always said that being frightened of something is the best reason to do it,' Sean whispered, half to himself.

'I'm not frightened,' she said. 'I'm just not stupid.'

'I know, I know, I'm sorry.' Sean said. 'Look, you take Connor home,' he said.

That made Connor sit bolt upright. 'You're joking, yeah?' There was no way he was missing out on this adventure. 'Alex, please,' he whined.

She ignored him, instead focusing her glare on Sean and Nathan.

'We have to stick together,' Connor told them. 'That's how it works, in the stories. We're like the Three Musketeers, or the Famous Five.'

'Only there's four of us,' said Alex.

'Okay, we're like the Famous Five without the dog,' Connor snapped.

He held his clenched fist forward.

'What's that?' Alex asked.

'We bump fists, y'know, like a team.'

'This isn't a football match, Connor.' Alex folded her arms. 'There are robots out there who will kill us as soon as they see us.'

'That's not true,' he said. 'They always give a warning.' His fist still hovered in the empty air. 'So, do we stick together?'

Sean and Nathan bumped Connor's fist. They were with him.

'The fight-back starts here.' Nathan said.

Alex still held out.

Connor couldn't help himself. 'All for one and one for—'

'Shut up, Connor.' Alex clenched her jaw, took a deep breath, and her fist bumped, too. They were all in.

WATCHING THE GRASS GROW

The weeds were getting high again.

Libby Hardy sat on her back doorstep, her bottom pressed as far as it would go against the sill, and stretched her legs into the noon heat. Then she spread out her arms, inviting the sun to turn her pale skin to freckles, daring it to burn her red. Mum harped on about vitamin D deficiency constantly and Libby preferred the quiet life to nagging. But it was torture to be so near to the garden and forbidden to enter it.

Especially when the weeds were so high.

This was Libby's twelfth summer and her third stuck inside.

Every summer a man from the VC went from garden to garden with a blowtorch, burning back the wall of weeds that had grown in the past year, reducing them to scorched ashes. But he was late this year. Mum had asked the ration people about it but they only muttered about priorities, being overstretched, very busy, blah, blah, blah.

Libby had asked if she could have just one day a week to get out there to keep it tidy. The man looked at her like she'd farted.

It wouldn't take much. She and Mum would clear the weeds, rotavate the earth and get planting in no time. Grow some carrots, potatoes, beans and tomatoes and spend a little time in the sun to soak up a bit of vitamin D – and get Mum off her back. It would be paradise.

Mum had hoped they might get some kind of special treatment, having volunteered at the school during the invasion, but the VC didn't appear to care anymore.

So now all Libby could do was watch the garden be slowly strangled to death as the weeds rose higher and higher.

She leaned forward, her eyes closed, hoping to feel the heat on her face without crossing the threshold and setting off her implant again. Mum nagged her about that, too. She inhaled the warm scent of the grass and the wild flowers, listened to the toiling buzz of the bees and the gentle wind swishing through the overgrown grass.

But her reverie was short-lived as the *thud-thud* of a tennis ball snapped her out of her trance.

She opened her eyes to see it bounce a third time, disappearing beneath the canopy of weeds, landing where the rose beds used to be. She leaned over to get a better look. There it was, resting against the fence. Where had it come from? A neighbour?

'Hello?' she called. 'Is someone out there?'

Perhaps it was a VC playing a trick on them?

'Is this your ball? I … I can't reach it if you want it back.'

Then she noticed something odd about it. Someone had cut into the ball and stuffed a sheet of paper inside it. A sort-of message in a bottle.

'Oh, wow,' she said.

It was out of reach, some ten feet from the door. She could risk a day's rations by dashing out to get it, but questions would be asked: why did she go out for so long? Most infractions lasted just a few seconds, usually someone accidentally crossing the line, but if she had to rummage through the weeds it might take longer than that to retrieve the ball.

A fishing rod would be handy, but neither she nor Mum fished.

But Mum did play golf. Or she had before the war.

'Mum, where are your golf clubs?' Libby hollered as she rushed back inside. 'Didn't Dad put them in the loft?'

She checked the cupboard under the stairs, the airing cupboard, the wardrobe in the spare room, under the beds and even in the larder. The loft would be a last resort as the only way to gain access was by teetering on a stool on the landing, and that was how Mum had—

Libby shook her head, dismissing the thought. There was nothing else for it. She prodded the loft hatch open with a broom. Paint flakes and dust drifted down into her eyes, making her sneeze. She dragged the stool from the bedroom and positioned it beneath the dark hole.

It wobbled as she pulled herself up. *This used to be easier*, she thought, sighing as her legs kicked at empty air and her arms strained to take her weight. She'd been fitter when she was at school. Goal shooter for netball, usually in the top three for the sports' day sprint, and she'd been an attacker in hockey. But that felt like a very long time ago as she inched her way in, gripping the loft boards, knowing all the time that this was the easy part. Getting down would be a blimming nightmare.

It took a few minutes for her eyes to adjust to the gloom. She crawled on her hands and knees, moving boxes, looking for the familiar shape of the golf bag.

'Are you sure it's up here, Mum? I can't … No, wait! I see it.'

The bag was tucked away near the eaves and she had to crawl on her tum to reach them. She dropped the bag through the loft hatch, apologising profusely for the terrific racket it made as it clattered on the landing. Getting down was ungainly and unladylike, but at least she made it to the landing in one piece. Unlike—

'Now, now, Libs,' she told herself, 'no time for bad thoughts.'

Finding herself full of energy and enthusiasm, Libby spent the next hour stringing together a three wood, a nine iron and a putter to construct an elongated makeshift arm. She took her time. She wanted to get it right; and besides, the ball wasn't going anywhere and neither was she.

It took her a further half-hour to retrieve the ball. She kept tossing her substitute golfing-fishing rod into the bush, hoping to get close to the ball and drag it towards the house by cupping it in the putter's embrace. Even when she managed this – 'I've got it, Mum! I've got it!' – some imperfection in the ground sent the ball slowly spiralling away and she'd have to start again.

But once it was free of the forest of weeds and onto the patio the job became much easier. As soon as she'd manipulated the ball close to the back door, she eagerly snatched it up and squeezed it to open the cut and free the message.

She found a hand-drawn illustration of a man and a message from a boy called Sean.

HAVE YOU SEEN MY FATHER?

There was a map with a return address. It was from just across the way in Fleetwood Street … and then it hit her.

'Hey, Mum, Mum! I know this man!' she exclaimed. 'He was a volunteer at the school, remember? He was sorting the rations with us. Oh, God, what happened to him …?'

She racked her brains. Time had become twisted in the past three years. Time and people and faces and the order of things. An image of Mum falling from the loft hatch came to her. A still body at the bottom of the stairs. Libby stepping around it like it wasn't there.

She shuddered, trying desperately to think straight.

'He got into a terrible argument with Mr Smythe,' she said. 'Yes – oh, the poor man, he's most probably …'

She couldn't bring herself to say it, but she knew that Smythe had little time for dissent. Libby and Mum had kept their heads down and got on with the job, but Danny and the other pilots hadn't liked the idea of surrendering. Libby saw at least two of them killed by Sentries. The same thing had most likely happened to Danny.

But could she bring herself to break a boy's heart?

She carefully wrote the reply in her best handwriting. A message of hope. She knew how hard it would be for this boy Sean to get through the next four years if he had nothing to live for. She knew only too well. And it's not like Smythe would admit to the father's death, or that the boy could check any other way. No, a little white lie might get him through the storm ahead. If it even was a lie. For all she knew, Danny was alive and well and thriving. But then Smythe and his robots would have tracked him down and found him, wouldn't they?

Libby made sure the golf tee was firmly wedged in the bottom of the door-frame. She rested the tennis ball carefully on it before lining up with the sand wedge – good for chipping over the fence and into the gardens opposite. *Concentrate, Libs, concentrate. Only one shot at this, so get it right.*

She swung back, head down, then swung forward …

The ball arced over the garden fence. A slice! Damn. She couldn't be sure if it made it to the boy's garden or not. Perhaps a neighbour's? Hopefully not in the alley.

'Well, Mum,' she said leaning on the golf club, 'I did what I could … Yes, I love you, too.'

THE FILE ROOM

The gang moved with purpose now, dashing across their old school playing field, keeping low and fast. This wasn't a game, nor was it a midnight-snack run any more. This was a mission. Alex's heart hadn't pumped this hard in years. She thought back to the school cross-country runs she'd endured in this very field. She'd been good at them, even won a few, but she was out of practice, out of breath and her poor lungs were straining to keep up as she started to get a stitch. Of course, she hadn't been carrying a car battery in a backpack then, but this was no time to complain.

Insects buzzed and clicked unseen in the darkness around them, thriving in humanity's absence. A few lights from the old stone school building illuminated the row of oaks around the field's perimeter and threw long shadows across the patchy grass. Alex veered to stay out of the light, glad she'd worn something dark. Actually, she was glad just to be out of her dressing gown. The jeans were a bit of a squeeze, but that was more through lack of use than anything else. Her fake shark's teeth necklace rattled like sleigh bells and she was beginning to wish she'd left it at home, but getting ready for tonight had felt like getting ready to go out before the war. Like a night out with friends. She even had a bit of make-up on, but she began to realise that she'd maybe misjudged the tone of the evening. She glanced over at Sean. He'd clearly washed his hair and scrubbed up a bit, so at least she wasn't the only one.

Breathless, the gang skidded to a halt in the stone archway beneath the school's clock tower. The building loomed above them, old grey stone buffering the classrooms from the harsh winds that blew in from the nearby coastline. As Sean and Nathan worked to quietly open the tall wooden doors to the quad, Alex glanced up at the rows and rows of dark windows gazing across the empty field. That was where she used to have double French, she remembered. Those were the science labs, and next to that her old form room. Yeah, she used to be good at this stuff. She belonged here. It was weird seeing it after all this time, now repurposed as the VC HQ.

'Oi, dozy,' Nathan hissed at her. 'Wake up. C'mon!'

He beckoned her through the wooden doors. They were heavy and prone to squeaking. They were open just enough for her to squeeze through and join the others.

From inside the archway she could see the quad where she'd spent quiet break times reading or revising. Despite the tufts of weeds growing between the cracks in the flagstones, it was much as she remembered it: a grey stone courtyard with unlit windows staring down from all sides. She saw her bench by the water fountain, a place where she'd laughed with friends, fretted over exams, discussed TV, films, music, books, boys and all the other nonsense that felt so irrelevant now. The only light came from an amber lamp high on the wall. To their left were steps and a door into the main school. Sean positioned Connor by the wooden doors of the archway.

'Connor, mate.' Sean held the smaller boy's shoulders. 'I need you to stand guard. Use the stopwatch. If we're not back in an hour, get yourself home.' He said it seriously. 'Tell Mum what happened.'

Connor nodded, wide-eyed and terrified. He'd wanted to come

on this great adventure, but the further they got from home, the more worried he looked.

'Don't be afraid – we won't be long,' Alex said, giving him a reassuring hug, which made her backpack's straps dig further into her shoulders. Swearing quietly, she adjusted the straps and started kneading her lower back.

'Heavy?' Nathan said, shrugging off his own bag. 'Leave it with Short-arse the Viking.' He nodded at Connor who stuck his tongue out in reply.

Alex wriggled her pack off and it hit the flagstones with a clunk. As they followed Sean into the school, she glanced back to see little Connor, all alone with the backpacks, looking very small and forlorn like a boy on his first day at big school. She thought about volunteering to stay with him, but the lure of the unknown was more tempting. And as she watched Sean and Nathan dodging from shadow to shadow, she wondered who else would look after those two overexcited loons if she didn't?

The school was a nightmarish echo of its old self. The faint gluey smell of floor wax triggered memories in Alex, but there was something missing, a vital ingredient of school life: *school dinners*. She used to love the omnipresent whiff of shepherd's pie mingling with custard as she went from class to class around mid-morning, but now it was gone. And the noise, too. The place had been a racket of laughs, shouts and screams as more than fifteen hundred kids elbowed their way along narrow corridors on their way to their next lesson, but in this silence all she could hear were her ears ringing.

Classrooms and hallways were cluttered with abandoned desks and chairs. Students' artwork was still pinned to the noticeboards, along with photos of group trips to Spain and France. Alex saw a few familiar faces – old school friends she used to see every day. She realised with a sad pang that she couldn't remember all their names. And then she wondered if they were even still alive. There was one girl, red-haired and freckle-faced, beaming out at her from one group photo. Alex tried to recall who she was. She used to be mad on comic books and Doctor Who. Oh, God, who was she?

A bright beam of light from a passing Drone swept through the broken classroom windows, reflecting off pools of water where the roof was leaking. Alex ducked down. Sean and Nathan had already moved further on, gliding silently through the shadows. She hurried to catch up.

They came to the admin office next to the staff room. With a 'wait-there' wave, Sean ducked through the door, leaving Alex and Nathan loitering outside for a moment. She looked to her brother for some kind of explanation, but he just shrugged.

Alex slipped inside to find Sean opening drawers, rifling through the paper-scattered desk. He grabbed a sheet of paper, scrunched it into a ball and hurled it against the wall with a curse. He hadn't found what he was looking for.

He was angry but keeping it under control. He always did that. She rarely saw him lose his rag; instead he internalised it, digging down into his thoughts. She often caught herself looking at him, as she was now, wondering what was going on behind those deep brown eyes.

'Okay.' He puffed out his cheeks. 'If you were Smythe, where would you keep the files?'

'You mean we're just going to wander around all night?' Alex said, open-mouthed. 'That was your plan?'

'Who said anything about a plan?' Sean grinned and moved on.

So much for deep brown eyes. 'Sean!' Alex followed him into the hallway. 'We can't do this. We have to get back before Kate wakes up. Every minute longer we spend here, we run the risk of being caught.'

'Which is why I wanted to come alone, Alex.' Sean turned to face her, and he looked doubtful for a moment. 'He's my dad,' he said. 'I have to know.'

They soon found themselves in the assembly hall, a cavernous place lined with stained-glass windows and wood panels. The smell of floor wax was stronger here, more like fresh paint. The wood shone, reflecting the blue and red glow from the windows. But Alex and the others were drawn to the centre of the hall. A strange machine stood there, surrounded by a ring of tripod-mounted floodlights.

'What the hell is that?' Alex asked as she moved around it.

Circular, like a giant eye, it was tall enough for a person to stand in. Around the back there were dozens of cables, as thick as tree trunks, snaking across the floor and out of the room. It resembled a kind of metallic octopus about to pounce on its prey.

Nathan tentatively tugged at the slots for people's hands on the machine. Placed at the side of the body these clamps seemed designed to hold the victim in place like someone in a sarcophagus. Nathan then swung a brace back and forth, positioned just below head-height.

'What do you reckon this does?'

'Could be a neck brace?' Sean shrugged. 'Might hold someone's head in place? I dunno.'

'Looks like we found Smythe's perv dungeon.' Nathan said, pulling a face.

Alex dreaded to think what kind of weird shit Smythe got up to with this thing.

The echo of a cough reverberated around the room. There was someone in the corridor outside. The three of them ducked behind the machine as a shadow crawled under the hall doors along with the green pulse of an implant. That meant one of the VC.

Sean gave a signal, and they followed.

73

They caught up with the Volunteer Corps officer in a stairwell. A gaunt, elderly man with a stoop and a grey, wrinkled face. They didn't recognise him. As he descended, his green implant danced in the gloom like a firefly, throwing a dull glow on the walls around him. They dared to peek over the bannister, ducking back quickly before they were spotted.

'See what he had in his hands?' Sean whispered.

Nathan shook his head.

'Files!' Alex said. The old man was clutching them like a monk carrying a Bible.

There was a glimmer of hope back in Sean's eyes. 'This guy's going to take us straight to where we need to be.'

The gang stalked the VC Officer through dark corridors, down stairwells, further and further into the belly of the building. Twice he stopped and looked back, but they were quick to flatten themselves into the shadows. This was one game of 'What's the Time, Mr Wolf?' they couldn't afford to lose.

He finally entered a strange room-within-a-room, a space partitioned presumably to give its workers peace and quiet to concentrate. It was surrounded by dirty, smudged windows, and the gang, huddled in the shadows outside, watched him move through a door and into what had to be the file room. He edged around a small maze of metal shelving stacked with box files towards the grey filing cabinets lining the walls. The workers were gone now, but the desks inside were littered with paper, files teetered on every flat surface and the smell of stale cigarette smoke drifted out through the open door. It suddenly occurred to Alex that there wasn't a single computer to be seen and she wondered if that was the robots' orders or Smythe's. He was the kind of old-school boss who probably hated computers and preferred the secrecy that paper gave him. Or maybe he wanted his own separate paper filing system that the robots would never think to access?

An Ordnance Survey map of the town hung on one wall, riddled with crosses, Post-it notes and string. The VC man switched on a lamp that gave the room a yellow sepia glow, and he huffed and puffed as he climbed a stepladder to tidy his folders away in a tall cabinet. After what felt like an eternity of paper-shuffling and folder-sorting, he ambled from the room.

The gang waited a full minute before moving, just to be sure he was gone. Then they emerged from the shadows and dashed to the filing cabinets, their fingers soon shuffling through folders. Alex dragged open a drawer marked "DEEP SCANS: DISCIPLINARY". There was a file on everyone, apparently: mugshots of ordinary people, fearful and defeated. Some had red crosses on them.

'What do you think the red crosses mean?' Nathan asked.

Sean found a file with a photo of Connor's dad, which had a red cross, too.

'I think it means they're dead,' Alex said, brandishing two more files: a morose-looking woman and a sullen teenage boy, both with red crosses.

Nathan recoiled. 'Yikes, who's the boiler?'

'Sarah and Tobias Smythe,' she read from the files. 'Smythe's wife and kid. Morse Code Martin was right.'

'I've found him!' Sean called to them from the other side of the room. 'I've found him!'

Alex peered through the high shelves to see Sean holding his dad's file. And there was no cross on the photo!

'He's alive!' Sean's eyes blazed. 'I knew it, I bloody knew it!' He scanned the document for an address. 'Region 623-7560. Where's that?'

Sean ripped the photo out and tucked it into his back pocket, then jumped down from his stepladder and rushed to the huge map showing the entire zone. Twenty miles square, it stretched from the sea to the hills, with the town snug along the coast.

Alex allowed herself to relax a little. At least they could go home now. Sean could confront Smythe with the truth and then maybe he would be reunited with his dad. She was happy for him. Her heart ached for her own parents, but any glimmer of happiness was welcome these days.

Out of idle curiosity, she and Nathan continued to scan the files. Alex flicked through face after face. Young and old, each one looking more miserable than the last.

Alex saw a flash of orange and stopped. She flipped two files back.

'Alison Lewis,' she said to herself.

'Eh?' Nathan rolled his file drawer shut and leaned against it.

'I saw her photo in the languages corridor,' Alex said. 'She was in most of my classes, went on the French exchange. Loved comics and Doctor Who. She was on the netball team, too. Nice girl. Honking laugh and she fancied a boy in the year below. We used to tease her about that.'

Alex showed him Alison's file. It had a red cross over the photo.

'And now she's dead,' Alex said, her eyes brimming with tears. 'Thing is, I'll probably never know how she died, or why. I want to cry, I want to scream, but I'm so used to death, I'm so bloody exhausted by it that I can't be bothered. What the bloody hell have I turned into, Nate?'

She slammed the filing cabinet shut, letting it prop her up, holding her head in her hands.

Nathan wrapped his arms around her. She couldn't hear what he was saying. She knew from the tone of his voice that he was being reassuring, but she was back in her bubble and didn't want to come out. She wanted to curl up in her dressing gown again.

He was holding her at arm's length now. He had his serious face on, which often made her laugh. But there was something wrong about her brother, although she couldn't quite put her finger on it. Then she realised what it was, and a cold dread poured over her. Her skin crawled and she felt faint.

'Nate,' she said, her voice cracking, 'Nathan, your implant ...'

It was pulsing blue. Weak at first, but getting stronger.

'It's coming back on.'

'What?' Nathan spun like a dog chasing its own tail, trying desperately to see the implant just out of his range of vision. Then he looked at Alex with horror. Hers was coming back online, too. 'Where's the console? The battery?'

Yes, Alex thought, *a quick shock and we'll be back offline.* But then she remembered where they'd left the components.

'They're with Connor,' she said, not wanting to believe it herself.

'You twunt!' Nathan screeched.

She thumped Nathan hard in the chest. 'You told me to leave it!'

'Not with Squirtacus! Why'd you leave it with him? Oh, God, I'm gonna be fried 'cos you left our lives in the hands of a ten-year-old Viking nerd.'

'We can argue about who's to blame later,' Alex shoved past Nathan and dashed to Sean, who was atop a ladder, scouring the map.

'Region 623-7560,' Sean muttered to himself. 'C'mon, c'mon, where are you?'

Streets were crossed out on the map. Entire neighbourhoods now empty. Someone had scrawled the word 'Resistance?' over the hills, then scrubbed out again.

'Sean, the implants are rebooting!'

But Sean ignored Alex, his fingers flying over the map.

'Sean, let's go!'

'Here he is!' Sean jabbed the map with his finger. A small peninsula by the sea. There was a pin with a label and some words scrawled on it. 'The Poseidon Hotel,' he said.

'Sean!'

Alex jolted him back to reality. He turned to her with a 'What's up?' expression. Nathan was by her side, neck craned to one side exposing his flashing implant. And now Sean's began to flash, too.

'Oh, crap. We need to go!'

'Duh! You think?' Nathan was already halfway to the door.

Sean leapt off the ladder. 'Back to Connor! Now!'

IMPLANT FAIL

Connor's mum had always told him that sitting on damp spots would give him piles. He didn't know what they were exactly, but he was convinced he would be plagued with them after tonight. Wherever he sat it was damp and cold and the smell reminded him of his granny's cat's litter tray.

His initial fear had quickly melted into boredom and he was counting the bricks in the archway – four hundred and thirty-seven so far – when he noticed a strange blue glow pulsing on the walls around him. He briefly wondered if it was a police car light shining through a crack in the door, but then he remembered there were no police cars any more.

His implant was coming back online.

'Uh-oh … Er, Sean …? Sean?'

He gathered up the heavy rucksacks – one with the battery, one with the console and adaptor, and one with his fireworks and sweets – dragging them on the floor behind him, and rushed into the school, half-whispering, half-shouting, 'Sean? Sean?'

But no one answered. He passed an old vending machine and saw his implant reflected in the glass. It was throbbing like a heart-beat.

'Ballbags!' he whispered, the worst swear word he knew that he was allowed to say out loud.

He could run and tell the others, but he had no idea where they were. He had to zap his implant and zap it now.

He unzipped the backpacks and took out the damaged console, the dodgy power adapter and the car battery.

He lined them up precisely as they had been in the loft yesterday, making sure to connect them exactly the same way. He attached the jump leads to the car battery and a little red light glowed on the console. It was on.

Okay, now all he had to do was give himself an electric shock.

Only he didn't want to, because last time really, really, *really* hurt. It made him scream, his head ached for ages afterwards and a little bit of wee came out.

But if he didn't, the robots would find him and then … he thought about what happened to his dad. It made him sad and angry at the same time.

He decided to ask himself the same question he always did when he was afraid. What would a Viking do? They were an honourable people. Brave and noble, ready to overcome their fears and fight any enemy. The warriors were trained to endure pain and suffering, so they would definitely step up.

But they were also much bigger than him.

Size matters not, said a Yoda voice in his head. And now Connor was confusing his favourite things and his thoughts were getting jumbled up.

Nervously, he reached out to touch the exposed innards of the console. This was really going to sting.

Sean, Nathan and Alex ran hell for leather along the school's main hallway, their feet splashing through puddles, startling pigeons that flapped away through shafts of light. Alex hurdled an upturned table. They crashed through the emergency fire doors and into the quad.

We're close, Sean thought as they charged across the courtyard, *we'll get the console, jack it into the battery and zap, we'll be offline again. Then it's just a question of staying out of sight of the robots, and we've done that before, right? But then, they weren't looking for us before, were they? We weren't on their most-wanted list. And what if the implants act like a tracking device? Will that bring the robots straight to us?*

He dismissed the thought. They could do this. He knew it. They just needed to zap their implants first.

He shoved the wooden doors aside. 'Connor! Fire up the—'

But Connor wasn't there.

Nor were the backpacks.

'Connor?' Alex called his name again and again. 'Connor!'

'Where are they?' Sean looked in every corner for the bags containing the console, battery and adapter. Maybe the kid had run and hidden them? He couldn't have taken all the bags with him, could he? Had he been captured?

He glanced up to see Nathan's implant reach full brightness, glowing blue, and then with a beep it winked to red.

'Oh, tits,' Nathan said.

The ground rumbled. Something big was approaching. Behind Nathan, Sean saw a light sweep through the crack in the door. A Sentry outside.

The wooden doors shattered into splinters as the Sentry's arm punched through in one sharp motion. Nathan tried to run, but the Sentry snatched him off his feet, gripping him tightly around his torso. In a blink, he was flying through the air, his arms pinned to his body.

'Nathan, no!' Alex screamed, reaching after her brother.

'Run!' Sean yelled, shoving her towards the door. 'Go! Go! Go!'

The Sentry's voice boomed as Nathan wriggled in its grip. 'CITIZENS, YOU ARE UNAUTHORISED IN THIS ZONE. SURRENDER IMMEDIATELY.'

They ran out onto the playing field, driven more by fear than logic. More lights came on as the VC in the building were alerted to their escape and Sean suddenly realised they were exposed. Another Sentry was on them, and it hoisted Alex off her feet with one swooping motion. She cried out, arms pinned, legs kicking.

'Alex!' Sean cried. He saw that her implant was red now, so maybe his was, too?

'Go!' she shouted back. 'Get home!'

Sean ran full tilt across the moonlit grass, his mind telling him to save his friends, his body driving him away from the danger. He felt sick. Cowardly. And, at the back of his mind, there was another part of him saying that whatever he did, however fast he ran, he wasn't getting away. He was stupid. Stupid to have dared to do this. Even more stupid to drag his poor friends along. And the worst thing was, he knew he'd probably have to throw himself on Smythe's mercy. Well, if he did have to face Smythe, then Sean had a few words to say to that old bastard.

From above he could hear the terrifying Stuka-howl of an Air Drone above him. The earth shook as a Sentry thundered towards him across the grass.

The Drone dropped down directly in his path. Its central section split open, and its sting-like weapon fell into place and began to crackle with deadly energy.

Sean juddered to a halt. No way out.

'CITIZEN' – the Sentry behind him was powering up its weapon also – 'SURRENDER IMMEDIATELY. THIS IS YOUR FINAL WARNING.'

'I am!' Sean raised his hands. 'I'm surrendering. Look at me surrendering!' He closed his eyes, waiting for the worst, when a voice cut through the engine noise of the Drone.

'Stand down! Authorisation code 97-ZCRS.' Smythe emerged from the shadows under the Drone, his coat-tails whipped by the downdraught.

Sean's fear evaporated, replaced by cold hatred. 'You lying shitbag! My dad's alive!'

Smythe puffed his cheeks out, sheepish, as he strode towards Sean. 'I meant no malice, lad, no harm,' he said. 'But if you were one happy family, I wouldn't have a reason to see Kate again, would I?'

Sean felt nauseous. So it was true. His dad was alive and Smythe had kept them apart just so he could leer over Sean's mum. He clenched a fist.

'I wouldn't, son.' Smythe raised a warning finger. 'You have a choice: it can end here, in pain and ashes, and I'll tell your mother how you died raiding VC property … or you can come inside and we'll settle this like civilised people. So what's it to be?'

COLLABORATOR

Noun

kə'labəreɪtə

One who cooperates traitorously with an enemy (esp. an invader or occupying force)

Well, Nathan thought, *here we are again.*

He'd been dragged back to the school hall with Sean and Alex and handcuffed to a chair. The cold metal bit into his wrists, but at least he was still alive. He was convinced the robots would just vaporise them, but Smythe appeared to want them in one piece for some reason.

Alex struggled in her chair but Nathan knew it wouldn't make any difference and so remained still and conserved his energy. If they were going to get out of these cuffs they needed a key, which a VC Corps member had placed on a windowsill nearby. He'd done it deliberately with a 'You want this?' sneer on his face as he put it out of reach but in plain view, the man's grey handlebar moustache rustling as he smiled. Nathan wondered how you applied to join the VC. The first question on the application form had to be: Are you a sadistic bastard?

Smythe stood before the eye-like machine in the centre of the hall, the one the gang had wondered about back when this was a bit of a laugh. The spotlights circling the device were shining now, and they bathed the Zone Chief in a harsh white glare. The machine itself glowed blue and hummed like an electricity pylon. Nathan could feel the heat it generated starting to slowly warm his face.

The VC had searched them, confiscating all their gear, though they missed the Zippo lighter in one of the many pockets in Nathan's combat trousers. But what really pissed him off was when they found his bag of pick 'n' mix from the sweet shop.

'Aww,' Smythe mocked. 'Sweeties.' He tipped out the contents of Nathan's haul and empty sweet wrappers fluttered to the floor, followed by one solitary thud. Smythe picked the last item up.

'A Twix?' he said, unwrapping its golden foil wrapper and taking a bite. 'That's all that's left? A bloody Twix?'

Nathan wasn't sure if Smythe was disappointed by their poor haul, or that they had risked their lives for chocolate, or that the old man had a sweet tooth and secretly longed for a bag of Haribo Starmix. Any which way, Nathan just wished he was back at home.

'All this pain and suffering for a Twix.' Smythe shook his head slowly as he began to stride imperiously back and forth before the machine. Nathan tried not to dwell on what the old man might mean by 'pain and suffering'. 'So,' Smythe continued, 'how did you turn off your implants?'

'We're not talking,' Nathan blurted before he could stop himself. Smythe's head snapped towards him, his old teacher daring him to answer back again. *Oh well*, Nathan thought, *in for a penny, in for a pound*. 'You filthy collaborator.'

'That's a big word for you, boy.' Smythe's eyes narrowed as he finished the Twix, then handed the wrapper to the Handlebar Moustache VC officer lurking behind him. 'Co-lab-or-ra-tor – five syllables – very impressive. That's the second time you've called me that, and since I very much doubt you heard it from Kate, it made me wonder ...'

Smythe gave a nod, a door crashed open on the other side of the hall and Nathan heard a whimper come from the darkness on the other side of the machine. A forlorn figure was dragged across the polished hall floor by two more VC officers. Nathan's blood ran cold when he saw his neighbour Morse Code Martin being hauled towards the machine. The old man's eyes met Nathan's. Martin tried to call out, but could only manage a sad, soulful moan.

'But he didn't do anything!' Nathan cried.

'I beg to differ.' Smythe pursed his lips as he presented evidence for the prosecution. 'We've been monitoring the torchlight messages from his loft window for some time. This man is the very definition of a repeat offender. We arrested him earlier this evening and I'd like to show you what we do to his kind.'

The VC Officers manhandled Martin into the strange machine, lowering a bar to trap his wrists. There were bruises on his face where Smythe's men had beaten him. Nathan noticed that Martin's knuckles were red, and one of the VC had purple bruises on his cheeks where Martin had fought back and given as good as he got. Nathan wished he'd been there to see it.

The bruised one locked the neck brace into place. Then Handlebar Moustache VC passed him what looked like a rifle, a black and grey robot design. He placed the barrel over Martin's implant and pulled the trigger.

There was a crunch, followed by a high-pitched squeal like a drill bit hitting concrete. Martin flinched, clearly frightened and in pain.

The bruised VC withdrew the rifle with Martin's implant now magnetically attached to its tip. The gun had removed it like a plunger, leaving a perfectly formed metal-lined hole the size of a coin behind Martin's ear.

Nathan watched as Smythe turned away, either out of shame or squeamishness. 'Sending subversive communications on an unauthorised channel,' he said, reciting the charge against Martin as he mopped the sweat from his top lip with a handkerchief. 'A deep scan is what you get when you break the rules.'

'No,' Sean yelled. 'Let him go!'

'Save your breath, son,' Martin said through gritted teeth. 'This collaborating bastard's been looking for an excuse to do me in.'

The bruised VC officer put the gun against Martin's neck again. There was another crunch and a squeal as the device punched something into the empty hole behind his ear. The VC stood back, revealing a new implant – similar to the old one in design, but black and unlit, like a robot's.

All the kids were shouting now, but Nathan's voice was loudest. 'If you hurt him, I'll kill you, Smythe! I swear it!'

Martin grimaced in pain, barely conscious now. The new implant glittered into life. White lights flickered and pulsed.

'He is connected to the network,' Smythe said. 'Begin the deep scan.'

'Hey, Smythe ...' Martin's voice croaked, dry and weak. He struggled to form words through bruised and broken lips. 'Go to hell, you filthy traitor.'

Nathan's heart nearly broke then. His old friend, the nice guy next door who told him war stories and let him read his comics, was about to die, but he could still spit in the face of danger. Nathan thought of what Martin said a few nights ago – 'Men willing to sacrifice everything, their very lives, so that others could live in peace. Heroes, son,' – and the boy's eyes glistened with fear and pride and sorrow.

On the other side of the school, a toppled vending machine lay face down on the ground. Beside it were three backpacks and an old games console attached to a power adapter and a car battery.

The vending machine began to move, scraping noisily across the floor. Something underneath was trying to get out. Strained groans came from within. One corner lifted a few inches off the ground, then slammed back down again. There followed the sounds of muffled swearing from within, then someone counting to three.

The vending machine shifted again, lifted from underneath, higher and higher, until, with a strength he never knew he had, Connor managed to tip it over.

The electric shock had sent him flying across the hall, straight into the machine's plastic window. It had rocked back, hit the wall behind it, then come slamming down on top of him. Connor remembered banging his head, but not much after that.

He rose to his feet, battered, bruised, singed, but with a freshly dead implant. He brushed fragments of shattered plastic out of his hair and noticed the sweets and chocolate piled around his ankles. He grabbed packets of M&M's with both hands.

'Wicked ...' he panted, getting his breath back. 'Guys? Where are you?'

WE WILL KNOW EVERYTHING THERE IS TO KNOW

Martin convulsed, his eyes rolling back in their sockets. Smythe turned away, unable to watch, but Alex couldn't help herself. If she was going to die soon, she wanted to know how it would happen. She'd seen death before, but that had been instant, over in the blink of an eye. This was like watching someone's lifeblood slowly drain away.

The eye machine – the Deep Scanner, Smythe called it – had come to life on Smythe's command. Dozens of glowing filaments lit up and a semicircular arc of light whipped from the top of the scanner to the bottom and back, almost as if the eye was blinking. The light strobed over poor Martin's contorted face, creating a shimmering blue haze around him

'What are you doing to him?' she asked, her voice breaking. Only then did she realise that she was crying, too.

'The subject experiences every thought they've ever had in a very short space of time,' replied a strange boyish voice from behind the machine. Alex had heard it before on the TV during important robot announcements. It was a patchwork of words, like the announcements you used to get at train stations and airports, fragmented sentences thrown together by an artificial intelligence algorithm.

The robot known as Mediator 452 emerged from the shadows,

approaching them with a stilted walk that reminded Alex of the figures in the Lego animations she used to watch on YouTube. It might just pass for human in a crowd, but it still had that robot odour of hot metal and oil.

It continued to speak in its disjointed voice. 'The memories of a botanist from the planet you call Gliese 581d helped us develop a toxin to subdue a rebellion.'

Beside the machine, a 3-D projection of Martin's brain flickered into life. Random portions of it started to momentarily glow and fade, a rainbow hue of different colours.

'A childhood game on Kepler-22b became the basis of a battle strategy which ended a war that had lasted generations.'

The cables surrounding Martin began to glow with a soft white light, the blue haze around him began to vibrate more intensely. Martin spasmed, gritting his teeth.

'This man's mind may hold the key to defeating an as-yet-unknown enemy,' the Mediator said, the movement of its lips never quite matching the words that came out of them. 'His data will be stored, studied and disseminated throughout the Robot Empire. We will know everything there is to know.'

There was another witness to Martin's agony. Unseen, Connor peered through the bevelled glass of the hall door, jumping back every time poor Martin screamed.

Connor felt numb and helpless. His feet seemed to weigh a ton, just like when his father died. He could run into the hall and try to save his friends, but there were three VC men and Mr Smythe, plus the Mediator, and Connor didn't think he could fight them all. *Think, Connor, think.* What could he do? Again his mind went back to the Vikings. It was a great honour to die in battle. Valhalla awaited in all its glory. But then Connor remembered he was a ten-year-old boy and that Valhalla was a long-dead myth. Plus, it wasn't unknown for great warriors to retreat and rethink their strategy, was it?

Tired and frightened, Connor took a step back. Then another. And another. And soon he found himself running back down the hallway.

Smythe watched the old man in the Deep Scanner slowly fade away. This wasn't the first deep scan he'd witnessed. That had been some time ago when he reported his former Zone Chief, Doctor Porter, for sedition. But he never got over the sense of unease it gave him. He wasn't a monster, he told himself. This was a necessary part of the job. An ugly part, to be sure, but if there was to be order in his zone, then this was what needed to be done.

He reassured himself that it was not murder. The information gathered here all contributed to the robots' final mission. Merely killing or vaporising a human was seen as a horrible waste by the robots. The Mediator told him time and time again that each human brain was a precious resource, and one that could ensure the survival of the Robot Empire for millennia to come. After receiving assurances that the brains of non-seditious Zone Chiefs would not be included in the robots' harvest, Smythe felt proud to be part of something that would have such an incredible legacy, one spanning an entire galaxy, if not beyond.

He thought back to the inanity of his old self. The geography teacher going nowhere. He'd been so different then, so empty, so purposeless, it felt like another lifetime entirely.

After two decades of an unhappy marriage built on a kind of grudging tolerance, he was ready for change but dared not embrace it. His vocation had become stuck in a tedious cul-de-sac, a series of pathetic vignettes. Interviews for promotions he knew he could never have. Speaking one's mind was frowned-upon, a cancer for the ambitious. One had to stick to the politically correct script or face being thrown out of their little clique and bidding adieu to any hope of advancement.

His fate was to be stuck for ever teaching geography to ungrateful, dysfunctional misfits. An eternity as head of Year Ten. He remembered stepping out of one particularly depressing interview and having a moment of complete clarity: he could never be headmaster. Not even deputy head. They hated him and everything he represented. But if his opinions – based not on prejudice, but on years of experience – upset them, then that was their problem. It was liberating to know there was actually nothing he could do for them.

But that's not how Sarah saw it. His wife had mocked him, dismissed his determination to be true to himself. He knew she had other men. The thought disgusted him, but then so did the alternative. Their marriage bed had been cold for some time and that suited him perfectly. Her perversions had started as peculiar, and then became repulsive.

And his son Tobias, if indeed he was Smythe's son and not some bastard offspring, had devolved into an abomination to the eyes and the soul. Smythe's pleas for Tobias not to bring shame on the family fell on ears deafened by oversized iPod headphones. Every body piercing, every tattoo was a personal affront to Smythe. An attack on his position as a father. The boy's only aptitude was a prodigious grasp of the Anglo-Saxon vernacular. To be called a – what was it? – a 'poisonous, evil old dipshit' by one's own flesh and blood was a particular sorrow.

But he was merely a product of a society that was in rapid decline. A Sodom of soft facts, half-truths and wishful thinking. Children left unmanaged to become truculent, disobedient, rebellious thugs. And if one intervened to discipline them, one faced a barrage of abuse and alienation. A mental exile.

But that had all been swept away by the robots. Now he was important. His wife, like some amateur Lady Macbeth, had urged him on and fed his ambition. From a lowly Volunteer Corps administrator to Zone Chief in just three years. Doctor Porter was gone. Then Sarah and Tobias were gone. The old Robin Smythe was gone, too, and Kate would learn to love the new one. Of that, he was sure.

Two of the VC guards released the clamps holding Martin in place and the old man fell backwards onto the floor, where he lay motionless. His terrified eyes stared into space.

'What was the point of that?' Sean shouted at Smythe.

The girl, Alex, was sobbing uncontrollably, tears streaming down her face.

'You killed him,' she said. 'You actually killed him—'

'He isn't dead,' Smythe corrected her. 'Not yet.'

'The process leaves the subject's neurogenic motors permanently impaired,' the Mediator said. The robot appeared to be happy that they were taking an interest. 'He is incapable of feeding himself and will die of natural causes … eventually.'

As a pair of VC Officers dragged Martin's body from the hall, the remaining one took the key from the windowsill and unlocked Sean's cuffs. He pulled the boy across the hall towards the Scanner.

'Sean! No!' Alex cried.

'Let him go, you bastard!' Nathan strained at his cuffs, but they just cut further into his wrists.

Sean's arms were pinned tight in the Scanner by the VC.

'We're dead,' Alex whimpered, 'we are so dead.'

As before, the VC officer raised the gun to Sean's neck.

'Wait,' Smythe commanded, delighted to hear his voice resonate around the great hall. The acoustics in here were fantastic, one of the reasons he chose this hall for deep scans. It reminded him of his best assembly speeches.

The VC officer stepped back, lowering the gun.

As Smythe moved forward, he saw Sean and the other kids start to smile and he was momentarily confused. What did they have to be happy about? Then he realised they thought he was stepping in to stop the process.

He took the gun from the VC. 'I'll do this one personally,' Smythe said.

The scuffling and wailing from the children in the corner resumed, but they were red-eyed and exhausted from struggling.

Smythe placed the gun over Sean's implant. He took this opportunity to lean in close to the boy, to reassure him. 'For what it's worth,' he told Sean, 'I'll make sure your mother's taken care of. I want her to be happy.'

He pulled the trigger and, with a crunch and a squeal, Sean's old implant was removed, leaving a coin-sized hole.

'Bastard!' Sean spat. He suddenly appeared to find his strength again. 'Leave her alone.'

But as he struggled inside the machine, Smythe placed the rifle over the metal hole in Sean's neck and punched a new black implant into it.

'Alone?' Smythe frowned, shaking his head. 'No, lad. Oh no. Poor Kate's going to need a shoulder to cry on.'

Sean's new implant began to glow, white lights pulsing in time with the Deep Scanner as Sean gasped in sudden pain.

'He is connected to the network,' Smythe reported.

'Excellent,' said the Mediator. 'Begin.'

A DEEP SCAN FOR SEAN

Connor ran breathless through the empty hallways, only stopping to duck under robot searchlights or jump into the shadows if he heard VC boots coming around a corner. He had no idea where he was going. This place was so much bigger than his old primary school. How did anyone find their class in this maze? There seemed to be no way out, but the running stopped him thinking too much about what might be happening to his friends. Martin's screams had fallen silent some time ago, and all Connor could hear now was the blood pumping through his body, and a small voice in his head calling him a big chicken. He staggered to a halt by the science classrooms, panting for breath.

Science.

Connor thought back to his dad urging him to pay attention whenever there was a science programme on TV. 'Science always has the answer, Sonny-Jim,' he used to say, while scruffing Connor's hair. 'Don't worry about art or poems or any of that rubbish. If you need to fix anything, solve any problem, build anything, then science is your friend.'

'Millie Parker keeps trying to kiss me,' Connor had replied. 'How do I fix that?'

'That's hormones, son,' his dad said. 'Definitely science, but your mother's the expert on that front.'

But Connor couldn't see how science would get him out of this one.

Then he glanced up at a display cabinet labelled 'Ancient Stones'. Inside he could see a row of stones with tiny handwritten labels. He stood on tiptoes for a closer look.

Flint. The stones were flint. Flint could be used to make fire – he'd read that in his SAS Survival Handbook.

Then Connor remembered the fireworks he had in his backpack, and a plan began to form in his head.

The arc of light swung back and forth on the Deep Scanner, fizzing with energy. Sean's face was illuminated by the glowing data cables and the surrounding blue haze as he spasmed in agony. The scan was the weirdest sensation he'd ever experienced. He could feel his mind unravelling like a ball of wool, the implant tugging at it, pulling it away from where it belonged and into a bigger space outside his head. Sean could sense the greater network on the other side, another world entirely. The robots' world. The hum of their activity was overwhelming, like a billion bees in a hive rushing by, all connected, all of one purpose and working together.

A warm, comforting sensation was washing over him, like a Sunday-afternoon nap, and it was tempting him to give in and be swept away for ever. He fought it, but it was so hard to resist. It felt so right to just let himself surrender.

Through blurred vision and the blue haze he watched Smythe, flanked by his VC Officers, pacing in front of Nathan and Alex. 'People complain about life under the robots, but it was worse before. No sense of community or respect.'

Smythe's VC men nodded in agreement. One of them had just brought Smythe a cup of tea, which he sipped as he waffled on. 'In this very hall, I had children – well, animals, more like … monkeys! – swearing at me … and if I were to take them outside, teach them some manners, suddenly I'd be the villain!'

Sean's ability to think clearly was fading and he struggled to keep a sense of where he was. Which side was real? This one, or the place where his mind was going? The robot network was where the warmth was. To step through into it would be so comforting. To be part of something so vast. He wondered if it meant he would live for ever.

'Sean!' Alex's voice – distorted by the barrier of the blue haze, cracked like a bad phone signal – cut through the fog. A spark of humanity in the dark. 'Stay with us! Stay awake!'

Sean felt the cold flush of reality. He focused on his breathing, his heart beating – this was the real world. This was where he belonged. He shut his eyes tight, clenched his jaw, bit his lip. Any kind of sensation to keep him on the right side of sane.

'If you play by the rules, it's not a bad life,' Smythe continued. 'But kick up a fuss and this is where it gets you!'

'Did your wife and son play by the rules, Mr Smythe?' Sean managed to utter through the pain.

Smythe didn't turn, but Sean saw the man's shoulders shift and tighten. The VC men's eyes widened. They'd no doubt witnessed one of Smythe's shit-fits before and didn't want to be around for another.

'Is that why you betrayed them?' Sean spat. ' 'Cos you're more loyal to robots than your own family?'

Smythe, still calm but clearly rising to Sean's bait, inclined his head towards the boy. 'You know nothing about my—'

'Everyone knows!' Sean shouted, his voice echoing off the hall walls. 'Martin told us all. You killed your son 'cos he was a crook, and you killed your wife—'

'Silence!' Smythe cried.

Sean saw the VC men share a look: so they'd heard the rumours, too.

'—'cos she was shagging half the blokes in town! We've all been laughing at you behind your back!'

Smythe hurled his tea mug across the hall, stormed towards the Deep Scanner and grabbed Sean by the lapels. 'You dirty little bastard, I'll—'

'Zone Chief Smythe.' The Mediator raised a hand. 'Calm yourself.'

The Deep Scanner's arc of light swung up sharply, connecting with Smythe's jawbone like a boxer's haymaker. There was a loud crack, like an electric shock, and Smythe reeled, rocking on his heels, woozily reaching out to steady himself. He grasped a fistful of the Deep Scanner's cables, wrenching them loose as he staggered and fell to the floor.

With a descending moan, the machine powered down, its glowing cables growing dark. The blue haze vanished, and the neck brace and wrist restraints automatically snapped open and Sean pitched forwards, collapsing heavily onto the floor.

He could barely keep his eyes open, but he was still smiling. His mind felt free again, disconnected from the robot network. The lights on his new implant flickered out, fading to black.

Smythe was sitting on the floor, knees up against his chest like a naughty child in assembly, waiting for the Mediator's wrath.

The Mediator's usually vacant face managed to look disappointed. 'A Deep Scanner is a complex device, difficult to repair. This is a costly mistake.'

'I'm so sorry, sir.' Smythe clambered to his feet, staring at the broken machine, fearing for his life. 'Please forgive me.'

'You must learn to control your emotions, Zone Chief Smythe.'

There was a banging noise as the hall doors swung open. What now? Sean, still exhausted from his ordeal, craned his neck up to see what fresh hell he had to deal with.

Someone stood silhouetted by the lights. A small someone, still in shadow. Another Mediator? There was something under his arms. Poster tubes. Three under one arm, four under the other, all taped together like the barrels of a revolver. Whoever it was, they looked like a mini Apache helicopter.

Sean looked closer and saw tiny colourful cones pointing out of the poster tubes, sparks dancing behind them. There was a familiar smell, too. A gunpowdery whiff of cordite that made him think of Bonfire Night on Duncombe Hill.

And then he realised what they were. The fireworks Connor took from the train station newsagents.

Sean twisted his face away, ready for what was coming next. The Mediator stared, confused but unafraid.

With a banshee wail, the first firework spiralled through the hall, searing a bright white trail across everyone's vision. The former teacher tried to turn away, but it smacked into his ribs in a ball of flames and he howled in terror.

Connor pivoted on his heels like a ten-year-old Terminator, taking aim as multiple whizz-bangs, whistles and crackles filled the hall as more fireworks shot out of the tubes. He moved forward, trying to target the VC officers and Smythe. Flaming rockets hurtled towards them as they scrambled for the doors.

Sean woozily lunged to the windowsill, grabbed the handcuff key and then returned to Alex, clumsily unlocking her. She took the key from him and freed Nathan.

Connor tossed away the smoking poster tubes and steered Nathan and Alex towards the heavy backpacks, 'All yours guys!' he said, happy to be rid of them. They were ready to run when they found the Mediator standing between them and the door. They knew the thing before them was a robot, but Sean had never made a habit of hitting anyone smaller than himself. They hesitated.

Except Connor, who shoved the childlike robot to one side. 'Come on!' he yelled.

The gang charged along the main entrance hallway, feet pounding the floor. Sean could see the school doors, the moonlit field beyond, but he was so tired after the deep scan that he could feel

99

his brain twinge, almost like it was still trying to make sense of itself after the ordeal.

The ground began to tremble with the familiar *thud-thud* of an approaching Sentry. Even if they got out of the building, there were no guarantees they would make it home.

Sean stumbled as Nathan peeled off into one of the science classrooms.

'Nate? What ...?'

'C'mon!' Alex cried, holding the main door open.

'Waitasec—' Nathan's voice yelled from within the classroom. Sean staggered back to see his friend jumping from table to table turning on all the Bunsen burner gas taps. Nathan coughed and spluttered as he tumbled out of the room.

'Go, mate, go,' he told Sean as he flicked his Zippo lighter into life. He carefully placed it on the hallway floor, its flame dancing silently.

'Nathan,' screamed Alex. 'Now!'

'Right – go, go, *go!*'

Moments later, Nathan, Alex, Connor and Sean were racing across the grass. Every step was an almighty effort for Sean, but he knew that if he slowed or stumbled now he wouldn't stand a chance.

A clattering noise came from the school, like someone smashing plates. Sean dared to glance back just as a Sentry clambered onto the school's clock tower, dislodging tiles and bricks that crashed onto the flagstones below. From that vantage point, they were an easy target.

'CITIZENS.' Its voice carried easily across the field. 'YOU ARE UNAUTHORISED IN THIS ZONE. SURRENDER IMMEDI-ATELY.'

They kept running. It raised its weapon-arm, ready to blast them all to ashes.

A surge of adrenalin kept Sean going, but having just been so close to death, he was ready for it this time. He wondered how it would feel. A quick burning sensation, followed by nothing? Or an agonisingly slow death as each of his atoms was incinerated?

There was a noise like a sail catching in the wind and Sean saw a flame rise up the clock tower. Moments later an explosion consumed the Sentry. Sean could feel the heat from here, and the shock wave nearly knocked them all off their feet. Alex tumbled over, and Sean darted back to help her up again.

As they ran, there was a chain reaction of fiery bursts as all the gas pipes inside the school caught the flame and whisked it around the building.

Sean saw Nathan grinning like a loon as fireballs rose up into the night sky. This was his mate's crowning triumph: blowing up an entire school. Sean stumbled, and it was Alex's turn to help him up. They ran flat out, looking for the nearest shelter. The Drones would be on them soon, and they had to hide. But Sean was flagging now, his eyelids heavy, his muscles aching, his lungs on fire. They had to find cover, and he desperately needed to sleep. But he allowed himself a smile. His dad was alive, and Sean would find him.

NO GOING BACK

Sunlight crept across the empty pillow next to Kate, rousing her a little later each morning. Usually she was the first to wake, though recently Sean had been getting up early for his exercise routine. Sometimes Nathan and Alex started a shouting match next door over breakfast rations, but most mornings it was just Kate and the songbirds twittering their dawn chorus, happily oblivious to what was happening to the humans they shared the world with.

She remembered the morning chaos before the war. The rush to get into the bathroom before Danny and Sean, constantly checking her watch to make sure she didn't miss the bus. She woke with purpose then. She mentally ran through what she had to do that day, and how to catch up on anything she hadn't managed the day before.

But now she got out of bed just because she had to. Otherwise, she knew she would curl into a ball and never get up again.

'Sean,' she called, her mouth dry. 'Any chance of a cup of tea?'

Some mornings he treated her to it in bed. He still remembered her birthday and Mother's Day, and he sometimes brought her tea on a Saturday or Sunday. Funny how they clung to those old routines.

'Sean?'

No answer.

The kids had been acting really weird last night. They started by making an almighty racket in the loft, then they went suspiciously silent. Alex and Nathan did the unthinkable and went to bed early, while Sean and Connor did their best to avoid her all night. Sean also insisted on wearing an oversized grey woolly hat that covered his entire head and neck and Connor looked unusually happy for a kid whose dad had just died, and even made an odd comment about it feeling like Christmas. Maybe that's why he was wearing a scarf? She hoped this wasn't some new stage of cabin fever. The beginning of the end of their sanity. She'd grill them about it over breakfast and then try to find a solution. She had a horrible feeling that any solution would mean more contact with Mr Smythe. Whichever direction her life took, it always appeared to lead into that man's arms. She was beginning to wonder why she fought it anymore. She had become very good at putting on a smile when Smythe was around, pretending not to find him repulsive. So good, in fact, that she wondered if it was still an act. And part of this pantomime was pretending to be okay that Danny wasn't around. Was she now okay with that too?

She shook the thought away and checked Sean's room first. Empty. His bed hadn't been slept in, or he'd made it already, and how likely was that? She called his name again as she came downstairs, with a growing sensation that told her she wouldn't get a reply. She ran from room to room, calling them all, Alex, Nathan, Connor, but her words just echoed back off the walls.

She finally found herself in the kitchen, staring through an open back door at footprints leading through the long grass to the gate. Her worst fears confirmed. Somehow they'd sneaked out in the night.

The ground began to tremble. A Sentry approaching.

Her front door crashed open and a handful of black-clad VC surged into the house, shouting warnings to get down, don't run and stay where you are.

'What are you doing?' she shouted. 'Get out of my house!'

One of them, a crew-cut VC with jutting jaw and narrow eyes, shoved a sheet of paper in her face. He was carrying an assault rifle. The others were armed, too. Smythe's personal goon squad.

The paper was signed by Smythe. An arrest order with all the kids' names on it.

'Where is he?' the VC growled. Kate recognised him. Smythe's Deputy Zone Chief. McGrath, she thought his name was. She was sure his wife had been a teacher at the local primary school, and she'd seen him knocking on Martin's door last night, just as she was going to sleep. She hadn't thought anything of it at the time, but with a chill she wondered if they'd taken Martin, too.

McGrath's team moved through the house, turning over tables, beds, cupboards, cushions. Cups and plates smashed in the kitchen. One of them clambered up into the loft.

'I don't know,' Kate said quietly, realising this was not the time for shouting and screaming. 'I just got up and he was gone. So's Connor. What have you done with them? Are they okay? Please tell me.'

'He's not here!' one of the goons called from upstairs.

McGrath grabbed Kate's arm. 'Zone Chief Smythe wants a word with you.'

Shit-head the Sentry gave Kate little attention as she was dragged into the street. The VC bundled her into the back of an old transit van. In its rear window she saw her reflection. Her implant had changed from citizen blue to VC green. As the van pulled away, she wondered if she'd ever see Fleetwood Street or that house again.

'Jah! Ffff—! Jesus Christ on a frickin' tricycle!' Alex watched her brother dance in little circles, trying to shake off the pain of the electric shock. All their implants were now disabled again. 'How many times do we have to do this shit?'

'They rebooted after thirteen hours,' Alex said, glancing up at the clock on the wall. It still seemed to be working, though she couldn't be certain that it was telling the right time. She couldn't even be sure how much time had passed since they left Fleetwood Street. 'At least, they did this time. I mean, who knows next time? They could be set to a random interval, it could be a set time, I ... I just don't know.'

'Oh, brilliant.' Nathan shook his head, his ears still ringing from the shock.

'We should watch each other's implants,' she said slotting the console, adapter and car-battery combo snugly in their backpacks. 'First sign of them rebooting, shout it out. Don't be shy. If one of us is caught, we're all caught.'

They'd found shelter in the bowling alley near the bypass. They sprawled across the lanes, all their implants now freshly deactivated. Sean lay unconscious in his own lane, arms splayed out, looking like he'd just been flattened by a bowling ball. Alex anxiously touched the edges of his new implant. Now dormant and matt-black, it looked just like the robots' implants. What had it done to him? And if it came on again, would the shock work? There were far too many questions she couldn't answer.

They had run for as long as they could before Sean began to stumble. He was exhausted. They all were. Connor remembered going to a birthday party at the bowling alley and they headed straight for it. The first thing Alex did was fire-up the console-adapter-battery combo and zap them all. They were off-grid now. If the robots wanted them, they'd have to come and find them the old-fashioned way. And Alex was sure it wouldn't be long before they did.

'I was too slow. Poor Martin,' Connor said in a voice so delicate and quiet, it made Alex want to cry. 'Why do people have to die?' He was choking back sobs now. 'I miss Dad. And my mum.'

'Hey.' Alex held him tight, and he buried his face in her hair.

'We'd have died too if it wasn't for you. You're our hero. You saved our lives.'

'I couldn't save them, though, could I?' he said.

Alex didn't have an answer for that. What were they even doing here? Was it too late to go back? Beg forgiveness? The sun was probably over the horizon now. It suddenly occurred to her that Kate would be waking up soon.

'Dude, you're badass.' Nathan slapped Connor's back. 'Cool move with the fireworks. Vlad the Impaler would be proud.'

'Vlad the Impaler?' Connor scrunched his forehead in confusion.

'Yeah.' Nathan shrugged. 'He was a Viking, wasn't he?'

Connor shook his head. 'You're such an idiot.'

'Oi!' Nathan said, mock-offended. The two of them began a playful slapping match and Nate soon had the younger boy in a headlock.

Sean jolted back to consciousness, woken by the noise. Coughing, gasping for breath, he gripped Alex's arm.

'The Poseidon ... Poseidon Hotel,' he spluttered.

'Hey, hey.' Alex made soothing noises. 'Take it easy.'

'We have to find my dad,' Sean said, his voice hoarse. 'He always knows what to do.'

'What about Kate?'

'Smythe wants to pork her,' Nathan said, releasing Connor from his headlock and suddenly looking snide and angry at Sean. 'She'll be all right.'

'Ugh.' Alex scrunched her face. 'I just sicked up in my mouth.'

'Yeah, shut up, Nathan,' Sean said, eyes closed as he massaged his aching head.

'*Me* shut up? *You* shut up!' Nathan launched himself at Sean and started punching him. Not a game, but for real. Sean tried to grab his arms and it descended into an ugly playground scuffle.

'Martin's dead and it's your fault!' Nathan cried as his punches found Sean's ribs.

'Pack it in!' Alex jumped between them, breaking them apart. 'Stop it!'

They backed off, both breathing heavily, fists still clenched.

'*You* started this,' Nathan yelled at Sean. 'And who's next?' He pointed at Alex. 'Her? Connor?

'We all had our chance to go home,' Alex said. 'All of us. Don't blame Sean. There's no going back now.'

Nathan scowled, tears welling in his eyes. Connor looked more frightened than ever.

'Save it for the robots,' Alex told them. 'For Smythe.'

'I'm sorry about Martin, Nate, I really am,' Sean said. 'And God only knows what will happen to Mum. Maybe you're right. Maybe Smythe will … Ugh, I can't even bring myself to say it … Look, if we go back, we're dead. We have to find someone who can help us, and the only person I can trust to do that is my dad. But …'

Alex saw Sean's confidence slip just a bit. A moment of realisation, perhaps? That simply saying something would happen didn't make it so.

'I thought I could do this alone, but I can't.' Sean offered Nathan a hand of peace. 'I need you all with me. What do you say?'

Alex watched her brother make his decision. He could be blunt sometimes, gross much of the time, but he wasn't stupid. They all knew the only way was forward.

'C'mon, knobhead,' Nathan didn't take Sean's hand, but instead punched him in the arm. Sean took it. His mate was back on board.

They dried their tears, hefted their bags onto their backs and were on the move again.

Once outside, they followed a stream until it tumbled away into grated sewers. They climbed up the bank and kept close to hedges, slipping between buildings and along back alleys without a word.

Now and then they spotted a Sniper on a rooftop – a spider-like robot with a gun that swivelled from target to target. Alex had seen them on distant rooftops when staring out over the town from her loft. Like all robots they were patient, silent and mostly still.

She and the others hid in the shadows for ten, twenty minutes or longer, waiting for it to turn away from them so they could scurry to a new hiding place.

It was excruciating. It took them all morning to travel a few hundred yards, and the Poseidon Hotel was on the seafront, over a mile away. Alex hoped they could make it before dark. The robots wouldn't be so easy to spot once night fell.

Smoke drifted across the rubble of the school. The explosion had been catastrophic, causing the collapse of the old clock tower and sparking a fire that had ravaged the entire building. Without a fire brigade to put it out, the blaze was still raging and the school was a mess of grey stone, red bricks and twisted girders.

Smythe watched through the haze of brick dust as hapless VC members chased slips of paper blown on the breeze. All that remained of his precious filing system. Records of everyone in the town. The robots had it all in their system, of course, but Smythe had been more comfortable with the feel of paper. There was something more definite about it. You could watch grown men wilt as you physically presented the evidence against them on nothing more dangerous than a sheet of foolscap.

There was a clang as two VC dropped a charred filing cabinet rescued from the detritus. Smythe shook his head slowly. *Hardly the brightest and best*, he thought with a sigh. But he had to make do. He would never let on to the general populace, but resources were stretched thin. Despite the benefits of membership, there were few VC to police the town, and not nearly enough to manage a situation like this.

Smythe had asked for extra aid from the robots, patrols of Drones or Sentries to hunt the children down, but the Mediator had been clear: 'This is your error, Zone Chief Smythe. We do not have the resources to spare from our main objective. You will resolve this in twenty-four hours or face the consequences.'

That's gratitude for you, Smythe thought at the time. But he now realised the Mediator was right. And every crisis was an opportunity. He could now show the Mediator how he handled a difficult situation.

'Mr Smythe!' A red-faced VC came running towards him over the mounds of bricks. 'I have it – the record you wanted.' He handed Smythe a file. Sean's file. The boy's photo had a red cross over it. Smythe had taken the liberty of declaring the boy dead when he heard they'd been captured. It would save time later on, he'd reckoned.

Smythe scowled, tearing the red tape off the photo.

'And what of the boy's mother?' he asked.

'Deputy Zone Chief McGrath reports that he has her,' the red-faced VC replied.

'Good,' Smythe said. At least something had gone right. 'If we have her, then it won't be too long before we have him.'

SEARCHING FOR POSEIDON

Alice had spent most of the morning yelling at her little brother
Jake and was now exhausted. It had started during a heated game
of Monopoly and ended with her tipping over the board and
throwing all the Community Chest and Chance cards at him. Then
Mummy and Daddy started screaming at each other and she had
been sent to her room.

Now, her head resting on one hand, she was picking at the flaky
paint around her bedroom window and watching the vapour trails
of Drone patrols slowly fade away across the blue sky.

Then she saw something move in the garden.

Alice had seen plenty of foxes rummaging in the bushes, a
few cats and dogs, too, and once she'd even seen a baby deer, but
nothing could prepare her for the sight of four children sneaking
over her neighbour's fence.

'Ohmygodohmygod! Jake! Jake! Come quickly!' she squealed.

They were led by an older boy, who paused to help the other
big boy over the fence. The other big boy didn't appear to want
any help, however, and shoved him away. Alice didn't know what
a 'bummer' was, but he called the older boy it twice.

Then the girl clambered over by herself. She was a few years
older than Alice and wore a cool black leather jacket and had red
lipstick on. As she watched the girl vault the fence, Alice suddenly

wanted to be her best friend. She wanted to ask her where she'd found clothes that fitted, where she got that necklace, what books could they swap, what films did she like and how did she get out there and were the boys as annoying as her brother and was the older one as nice as he looked.

The girl was followed by the smallest boy, who did need help getting over the fence. His feet kicked at the air as he pivoted on his belly.

'Jake! Come on!'

The older boy heard her voice outside through the double glazing, and his eyes caught hers. For a moment, he looked scared. And he should be. Mummy and Daddy had been very clear about what happened to anyone who stepped outside. Alice hadn't seen it, but she'd heard about when Mr Phipps two doors down had tried to escape on the motorbike he had in his garage. Daddy said he'd got as far as the end of the street before the Sentry vaporised him. 'All they found was a bit of a carburettor and the fillings from his teeth,' Daddy had told them, though quite how he knew that Alice couldn't fathom.

The older boy smiled at her and put his finger to his lips – shhh.

Alice wanted to scream, 'Take me with you!' but knew she couldn't go. This boy's implant was strange, black like a robot's, and it looked broken. Hers was still pulsing brightly. One step outside and she would end up like Mr Phipps. Just then, Jake stomped into the room. 'What?' he grunted. She dragged him to the window, but the boy and the other children had gone.

'What?' Jake asked again, weirded-out by his sister's behaviour.

'Nothing.' Alice's heart sank, and for a moment she wondered if she'd imagined the whole thing.

'God, you're such a lame-o.' Jake slumped out of the room, slamming the door behind him and causing Mummy to shout again.

Alice propped her head in her hands again and returned to watching the skies with renewed daydreams filling her mind.

Sean thought they'd had it then, but the girl appeared to understand.

He didn't want to risk crossing people's back gardens – that was asking for trouble – but they'd ended up stuck in a wooden fort on a playground and the only way forward was across the expanse of an overgrown field.

They were exhausted and hungry. It felt like a lifetime since the sweets they'd eaten at the train museum, and coming down from the sugar rush, combined with the adrenalin from their situation, gave them all sugar-shakes and headaches. Nathan had found a half-melted Yorkie bar in his coat pocket and they shared out the misshapen rectangles, but it wasn't enough. They'd last had a drink before they left the path next to the stream. The water had been so cold it hurt their teeth and they didn't have much more than a mouthful each.

And not only did they need to avoid robot patrols, but they had to do their best to avoid being seen by any humans, too. How could they know who was friendly and who was ready to snitch to Smythe? They had to stick to whatever cover they could find, but it was only when you were outside that you realised how little there actually was.

And now this field. The grass was tall, so they could maybe crawl through it, but that would take ages and they'd be completely exposed to any passing robots.

'What's that, a hundred metres?' Sean reckoned, gazing across the field. 'Maybe more?'

'We'll be spotted by a Drone, for sure,' Alex said.

'Piece of piss.' Nathan rotated his shoulders in a mini warm-up. 'I was county sprinting champion. I'd make it in less than ten seconds, but I can't say the same for you slackers.'

'We're only as fast as our smallest legs.' Sean glanced at Connor.

'Hey, I'm fast!' Connor insisted, ready to lunge forward to prove it, but Sean held him back.

'You know where we are, don't you?' Nathan said with a wistful grin, gesturing at the fort around them.

Sean vaguely recognised it. The wooden surfaces inside the fort were riddled with carvings, a combination of declarations of love, hearts crossed with arrows and libellous insults regarding named locals and their sexual peccadilloes. Some even had mobile phone numbers inviting you to call them to partake of these rather specific abilities. But Sean couldn't pin down where they were. His mind was fuzzy and hungry. He shook his head.

'This is the rec.' Nathan beamed. 'I used to come here all the time when I was a kid.'

'Oh, yeah.' Alex said, remembering happy summers playing with her friends.

'And this very spot' – Nathan's eyes lit up as he pointed at the woodchip below his feet – 'is where Kelly Foster would let you feel her boobs for a pound.'

'Oh, for God's sake, Nate, you have to ruin everything!' Alex thumped his arm.

'If this is the old rec, we're closer than I thought,' Sean said, then something occurred to him. 'Our old street.' He snapped his fingers. 'Bingham Road.'

'That was flattened, mate,' Nathan said.

'Yeah, but it'll take us closer to the High Street,' Sean said. 'We can cut through the alley behind the old Budgens to that row of B&Bs and hotels on the seafront. The Poseidon is the one on the end, I'm sure.'

And so the gang didn't cross the field after all, but instead dared climbing over back garden fences where Alice caught them in the act.

Nathan was right. All they found in Bingham Road were ruins: a rubble-strewn crater, long abandoned, with the twisted and charred remains of a jet fighter at its heart. Nathan, Alex and Sean lay low in the rubble and tried to recognise the place where they used to play and ride their bikes, but there wasn't much left for them to latch on to. Most of the houses were just piles of bricks. The one on the corner looked like it was intact, but when they moved closer they realised that only the front of the house was still standing, propped up by a few girders.

'Mum's greenhouse survived,' Sean said, pointing to a glass-free structure in his old back garden. 'How weird is that?'

'We could get our bikes,' Nathan said, only half-joking. 'Mine's probably still in the shed. If the shed's still there ... Not sure I remember the combination on my lock, though.'

Sean liked the idea, but knew it wouldn't help them. 'Bikes wouldn't be any good over this rubble, mate. C'mon, let's keep moving. We need to find more cover and stick to it.'

'What's the point of being outside if all we do is sneak about in the shadows?' Nathan moaned.

'It's called "staying alive", doofus,' Alex said.

'Hey, look.' Connor nodded at a bush, flicking through his SAS Survival Handbook. 'Raspberries. Completely safe. Let's eat.'

They took one last, lingering look at their old street while devouring wild berries, clearing the bush of every single one of them. The flavour burst in their mouths, the colour stained their fingers purple, their bellies rumbled less and their minds cleared a little.

Sean led them through alleys and as the sea breeze grew stronger, its salty, low-tide aroma more potent, he knew they were close.

Soon they found themselves hiding in an alley overgrown with stinging nettles across from a once glorious Edwardian seaside hotel. Faded pink paint flaked from its cracked exterior around dark windows shuttered behind rusting balconies. A sign, red plastic letters – a few of them missing – on a white backlit box, read:

This is it, Sean thought, his heart racing. *Dad's inside.*

They checked up and down the High Street for robots. Empty.

'Go!' Sean whispered. They scrambled across the street, sneaked through wooden gates hanging on rusty hinges and found themselves in the hotel's delivery bay. Crates and beer barrels littered the ground.

'I know this isn't the right time,' Connor said, his legs twisting awkwardly, 'but I really need a wee!'

Sean shushed him as Nathan tried the door. 'It's locked!'

'Wait, let me,' Connor said as he ducked down and tried to squeeze through a large catflap.

'Connor, no!' Sean said as he watched the younger, thinner boy wriggle his head and one arm into the opening. Then he stopped moving, his head and arm now wedged inside the catflap.

'Ah!' came Connor's muffled shriek. 'I'm stuck!'

'You dipshit, Connor!' Nathan growled.

'Quiet!' said Alex.

'Help!' Connor yelped.

Nathan and Sean each grabbed one of Connor's legs and pulled.

'Stop kicking your legs, Connor!' Nathan said.

'Move your arm,' Sean said. 'Give it a wriggle.'

Connor did as he was told and suddenly popped free. Nathan and Sean stumbled back, losing their grip and tumbling into the metal beer barrels, sending them crashing with a deafening clang that echoed from the walls around them.

They stopped in their tracks as the noise reverberated in their ears for what felt like an eternity.

Maybe the robots didn't hear that, Sean thought. *Maybe they thought it was a fox or a dog or something? Maybe ... maybe we got away with it?*

The ground began to tremble with the *dang-dang-dang* beat of a Sentry on the move. No such luck, then. Alex dared to peek out and saw a Sentry kick a car to one side as it thumped along the street towards them. The impact set off the car's airbags and alarm, and the air was filled with its howling noise.

Alex shoved them towards the door. 'Hurry, hurry!'

Sean placed his coat against a pane of glass in the door and punched it until it smashed. He reached past jagged shards and unlocked the door, swinging it open and bundling everyone inside.

He gently closed the door just as the Sentry stepped over the gate in one big stride.

Hearts pounding, they found themselves in a dark, empty kitchen. They moved silently, hiding in cupboards and the spaces where washing machines and dishwashers used to be.

They couldn't see the Sentry peering through the window, but its searchlight swept the room, throwing shadows that grew and shrank as it glided over the worktops and surfaces.

Everyone froze, not daring to breathe.

And then Sean's new implant winked into life and its white lights started to throb. He could feel it tingle in his neck, pulsing with his heartbeat. And then it found another beat. Not his, but … that was odd. Sean felt like he could feel something just outside himself.

He shook his head to clear his mind.

And at that moment, the Sentry did the same, its searchlight dancing in time with Sean's movements, casting more weird shadows on the wall opposite.

And then the connection was lost.

The light from the Sentry's lamp faded as it backed away. Nothing to see here. Sean listened to its clanking limbs and grinding joints as it stood upright, stepped over the gate into the street and returned to its patrol.

Collectively, they all exhaled.

'Sean.' Alex looked concerned. 'You okay? You went a bit weird there.'

'Yeah, yeah,' he said, trying to shrug it off. 'Just a twinge. Nothing to worry about.'

Sean looked around him. They were all squeezed into cramped spaces.

'Where's Connor?' he whispered.

The door to a tiny cupboard opened, revealing Connor, folded up like a circus contortionist. 'You said we should take cover.' He said, untangling himself.

Sean gave a little laugh, though his mind was still trying to make sense of what just happened.

'Hey, look.' Alex moved to the window where the sunlight shone down on a cluster of a dozen or so large terracotta and plastic pots. Each one was filled with soil and sprouting green leaves.

'Yeah, so?' Nathan said with a confused look.

Alex rolled up a sleeve and plunged her arm into the soil. 'I recognise the leaves,' she said. 'Mum had these in big pots in the garden.' After a moment's rummaging, she pulled her arm back out again. She held in her hand what looked like a misshapen rock – brown, smooth and pitted in places. Connor recognised it immediately.

'A potato!' he said.

'Run it under the tap.' Alex tossed it to Connor who did just that, rubbing off the clumps of dirt. 'C'mon, there's more,' she said, handing one to Sean. 'Just don't eat any green ones.'

'Not ripe?' Nathan said, examining one closely.

'They might kill you.' She slapped one into Nathan's palm. 'Or at least give you really bad gut ache.'

He inspected it very carefully, looking for anything remotely green.

In minutes they'd plundered one of the pots and were all munching on raw spuds.

As Sean's stomach welcomed the food with a grumble, some kind of order returned to his mind. He wondered if his funny turn just now was a lingering after-effect from the deep scan. Was he slowly losing his mind, or was it just a result of hunger pangs? He started to run through what happened. He'd moved, then the Sentry moved with him. Or did it? Had he imagined that, or was it a coincidence?

His thoughts were cut short by the sound of breaking glass from deep inside the building. There were voices, some shouting, others laughing, then all of them were drowned out by a scream followed by a massive cheer.

Sean and Alex exchanged apprehensive glances.

'Smells like the old people's home where Granny died,' said Nathan, sniffing the air. 'I'm getting Deep Heat Rub, stale wee and chronic halitosis.' Alex quickly shushed him.

They had left the kitchen and found themselves moving stealthily through musty air filled with dust-motes. They trod silently on the grubby, dusty carpets, past peeling flock wallpaper, further into the labyrinth of narrow hotel corridors, ever closer to the chaotic chatter.

They came to a tall double door, its white paint stained yellow by cigarette smoke, its once gleaming brass handles now patchy and dull. The noise was coming from the other side.

Sean looked to the others: *Should we?*

They all nodded back and Sean pulled the double doors open into utter bedlam.

The hotel's once luxurious restaurant and bar now boasted broken tables, cracked mirrors and crooked chandeliers. It was filled to the brim with humanity at its wildest and worst – muscular men downing shots, mothers clutching bawling babies, elderly couples with craggy faces playing poker. The guy behind the bar had a pirate's beard covering a face smeared with lipstick and blue eyeshadow. There was a girl with conical metal horns attached to her head, and, in dark corners, men in floral dresses were playing cards. A shortage of clothes here, clearly.

In the middle of it all, two thugs were settling a dispute with a boxing match. Their bare knuckles were already bloody and raw as the raucous crowd cheered them on.

But then one reveller spotted the gang. And then another. It spread like a wave and soon everyone was staring at them. Chairs scraped the floor. Sudden silence. Everything stopped as the Poseidon residents sized up these strangers.

They looked at the gang's implants. Dead and silent. Their faces trying to fathom who these outsiders were and how they got here.

Nathan gave them a cheery nod. 'All right?'

Then one voice cried, 'Get 'em!'

They charged the kids with a roar. One of the revellers grabbed Connor as the others piled in, pushing and shoving, each trying to be first to reveal their secret.

'Hey!' Connor squealed.

'Leave him alone!' Sean yelled, and then it all *really* kicked off.

A brawling bundle of punching, thumping, chair-crashing, kids biting and shin-kicking. Sean found himself shoved against the bar by a muscular man whose nose and mouth were covered with a neckerchief and his forearms with bling. The man raised his arm for a punch. Sean scrabbled for something, anything, to defend himself with.

All he could see was a glass of water, and he instinctively flung it in the man's face.

Bling Man screamed, falling backwards as he clawed at his eyes.

'Moonshine,' said a deep voice behind the bar. Sean turned to find the bearded barkeep giving him a cheery ruby-red lipstick smile. 'Strong stuff,' he added with a wink. 'Don't get it in your eyes. Or your mouth, for that matter.'

Bling Man was back on his feet in seconds, his fists clenched for another go.

Sean tensed, ready for the worst. By the door he could see Nathan held in an armlock by one of the brawlers, Connor biting the arm of a man who was hoisting him high, and Alex trying to prise the boy free.

Then the air around them exploded. Sean's ears were ringing, and there was a hole in the ceiling that he was positive wasn't there just a few seconds ago.

The crowd parted. Through the curtain of gently drifting ceiling plaster and dust, Sean saw a man wielding a smoking shotgun. A wall of a man, towering over everyone else, muscular with a boxer's punished face. Dressed head to toe in a smart suit, he was the only person in the room not wearing second-hand clothes.

'Oi-oi,' he said, snapping the shotgun barrel open. Two empty shells popped out. He calmly loaded two more. 'What's this, a school outing?' he said, and Sean found himself looking down the twin barrels of the shotgun, his hands raised. 'The name's Wayne,' the big man said. 'Welcome to the Poseidon Hotel.'

WAYNE

'I'm Sean Flynn. I'm looking for my dad, Danny,' the older kid said. 'He was a pilot and he was moved here.'

One of Wayne's men shoved the other lad, his mate, forward. The kid's implant was dead. And the girl's, and the little'un's, too.

Wayne had seen a few people try to disable their implants, which was all well and good, but they weren't the ones who had to clean the brains off the walls afterwards. How had this lot done it?

'Look at this one!' said Magpie, his bling rattling as he twisted Sean's head around. This kid's implant was different. Strange. Black, like a robot's.

Wayne noticed that Magpie's eyes were streaming red. He'd seen Sean give him a face full of moonshine during the ruckus. Smart move. He'd have to watch that one.

'Monique'll want to see this,' Magpie said.

'I'll take 'em up now,' Wayne said as the little kid raised one hand, the other tucked between his legs.

'Er ... Can I go to the loo first, please, sir? I'm bursting.'

'Who gave you permission to speak?' he growled at the young'un, who bravely stood his ground.

'Sorry, but if I don't go there, then I'll do it here,' the kid replied.

Wayne laughed. A throaty cackle that once used to smoke a pack a day. 'I like this one,' he said, before patting the kid's cheek.

'I'm only joshing you, son. Course you can, through the door. Magpie – show him the way, eh?'

'What? I ain't no babysitter.'

'No, but y'need to wash the hooch out your eyes, so do as you're told or I'll give you a slap.'

Magpie thought about arguing back, but then cuffed the little one around the head. 'This way, Shorty.'

Wayne lowered the shotgun, deep in thought. He knew that old Swanny had managed to remove his implant, but that was with help. These kids still had theirs in, but had managed to turn them off. This was exactly what they'd been looking for. Monique would want to see them straight away.

The kids introduced themselves, as Wayne and Magpie led the way upstairs. They took them through fire doors and along hallways with threadbare carpets, the scent of damp plaster in the air and breeze-block dust drying on their lips and tongues. Rigby, one of the bare-knuckle fighters, brought up the rear in case anyone tried to do a runner.

Few of the residents ever came through these back hallways. This being a hotel, they still felt they were out of bounds, for staff only, and Monique and Wayne liked to keep it that way.

'How big is this place?' asked Nathan. Just from his tone, Wayne knew he was the gobby one of the group. There always had to be a smart-arse.

'Six floors and a basement, mate,' he replied.

'And you can, like, move around between floors and rooms and shit?'

Wayne shrugged. 'Smythe and his clankers don't care what we get up to in here. They locked us in, leave us be and we don't give 'em no cause to worry.'

'Cor. Wish we'd been locked up here,' Nathan said.

Wayne shook his head. 'Little div,' he muttered to himself.

'Let's stay!' said Connor. But somewhere in the building someone screamed. As it echoed off the walls, the boy froze in terror. Rigby nudged him forward.

'Were you working here then?' asked Nathan. 'Y'know, when it all kicked off.'

'No, son,' Wayne said. 'Power went down on my estate and they rounded us up and slung us in here. Shoved all the troublemakers under one roof.'

'Troublemakers?' the girl asked. She sounded like that posh bint in the Harry Potter films.

'Small-time thieves, mostly,' Wayne replied. 'A few bruisers, couple of mental cases. Rigby here's a certified sociopath.'

The kids all gave Rigby a bit more space.

'What's a sociopath?' Connor asked.

'He's winding you up.' Rigby said, his eyes starting to redden and swell after the fight. 'I pretended to be psycho to get off a long prison sentence. Turns out I did too good a job of it.'

'Yeah, you keep telling yourself that, Rigby.'

'I said I liked to eat human flesh and they believed me!' Rigby laughed.

'You did bite that fella's finger off,' Wayne said.

'That was purely self-defence.' Rigby looked hurt.

'Nicking your chips, wasn't he?'

'Yeah, well, I don't like people *touching my food*!' Rigby screamed. He realised he'd gone too far, laughed it off and quickly changed the subject. 'Wayne here's a champion boxer, y'know?'

Wayne bristled. He didn't like anyone knowing any more about him than was necessary. He gave Rigby a glare that made him back away.

Connor was impressed. 'Cool. Were you in the Olympics?'

Wayne laughed. 'No, mate. I just had a few fights on the London circuit when I was a lad. Old Swanny got me into it. Kept me out of trouble. Said I had a future in the sport. Trouble is, there's always some bigger bugger and after five years in the ring I ended up with a detached retina and a jaw with more cracks than a Ming vase. It's no career for a little fella like you.'

But Swanny had looked after him, found Wayne some door work at the nightclubs, a bit of regular money. And because he was a big guy, he would get some jobs off the ledgers, settling accounts with Swanny's dodgier business partners. Mostly Wayne just had to show up and people paid what they owed. Sometimes it got a bit hairy, but nothing too nasty. Broken bones heal soon enough.

Then Swanny and Monique went and retired to the coast. Sleepy little town called Fairfield Bay. Wayne felt lost without them. Swanny had been like a father to him, and Monique … a sort of sexy aunt.

'So how did you end up here?' Sean asked. Wayne liked him already. He only spoke when he needed to. His voice was quiet, thoughtful, and he had a kind of Clint Eastwood thousand-yard-stare thing going on.

'Got engaged,' Wayne said, his voice quieter now, matching the boy's. 'We started talking about settling down, starting a family, all that. But London …' Wayne shrugged. 'Too many people knew me there, y'know? Too many scores to settle. No place to raise a kid. So when I got a call from Swanny and Monique asking me if I wanted to work for 'em down here, it was a no-brainer.'

Swanny and Monique had a little nightclub down in Fairfield Bay. They'd basically retired, and their son Joe was running things, and it was all very nice. To begin with, Mandy was bored off her tits, but then she found something to do: get pregnant and start spending Wayne's money. Not that he minded. She was happy; he was happy.

'So where's your wife now?' Nathan asked. His mates all looked daggers at him, and he immediately realised it was the wrong thing to say. Even Magpie and Rigby looked nervous.

'Keep your mouth shut, kid!' Rigby stepped forward, fist clenched, but Wayne stopped him with a gesture.

'Nah, nah, it's all right,' he said. 'Clankers got my Mandy, son. That's all you need to know, okay?'

Nathan nodded. Wayne continued down the hall and the others followed.

Back then, Wayne and Mandy had a little place on an estate at the edge of town. They were some of the last ones to be rounded up and taken to the hospital. As they waited to get their implants, Mandy started getting mouthy. Only someone with her monumental sense of righteousness would try and start and argument with a bloody Sentry. She died before she even got an implant. Probably just as well, she would have hated being cooped-up like this.

There wasn't a day went by when Wayne didn't get a little heartbroken thinking about Mandy and their kid. He didn't care what they'd've had, a boy or a girl. Not fussed. He knew they'd love 'em every day. He always wanted two. A little prince and princess.

After Mandy died, Wayne stayed in. Staring at the wall. Thinking about what might've been.

Then the power went down. Whole estate. They reckon it might've been kids pissing about with the cables. Whatever it was, they threw everyone out and moved them into the Poseidon Hotel.

That's where Wayne was reunited with Swanny and Monique. They'd lost their son and they shed a few tears. They were both looking tired. Old. They'd been struggling to keep order and asked Wayne if he wanted to help. He said it would be a pleasure.

He sorted out a few troublemakers, broke the occasional bone when necessary, but they finally had control. They grew some spuds, started a couple of stills and kept enough booze flowing to make everyone happy. And now everything was just peachy.

Until these kids appeared from nowhere.

*

They came to a landing where they had to shuffle around a steaming bathtub: a moonshine still with copper pipes running in and out of it. Working in the white glow of sunlight from a tall window, two big men wearing rubber gloves were carefully pouring the concoction into aluminium barrels. Another was chopping potatoes.

'Moonshine,' Wayne told the kids. 'Don't get it in your eyes, but I reckon you know that already, dontcha?'

He saw the older kid, Sean, glance at Magpie, who growled back.

They continued up and up and up. The higher they got, the narrower the staircases. But then they found themselves in an open space again as Wayne led them onto a landing with a once spectacular fanned staircase. The entrance to the penthouse suite. The brass on the handrails was still polished, and the double doors were wide enough for a car to pass through.

Wayne paused before the doors. 'In here is Monique, the woman who runs this place. She's like a mother to me, so watch your lip,' he said, then turned to Nathan. 'Especially you.'

'Me? Don't you worry about me, I'm cool.'

'Good. Just tell her whatever she wants to know and we'll all be happy.'

'And what do we get in return?' the girl said, arms folded.

'Oh, think you're gonna give it some of that, do ya?' Wayne made a gobby mouth gesture with his hands. 'Think we haven't dealt with a bit of back-chat before, eh?' He towered over her, but she didn't budge. He was impressed. Most people backed away. He laughed. 'You remind me of my Mandy. That attitude got her killed, young lady, so I'd be a little less full of it if I were you.'

'All I want is to find my dad,' said Sean.

'Yeah, well, we all want something, don't we, mate?' Wayne jabbed him in the chest and leaned in close. 'All I want is one day. One chance to get out there and show those clankers what we're made of. One go for Mandy and my kid, and if you balls this up … Just answer the lady's questions and we'll all go home happy. Understand?'

'*Si*, Godfather,' Nathan said with a grin that evaporated as soon as he saw Wayne's glare.

'Good.' Wayne patted Nathan's cheek, and he nodded back.

Wayne swung open the doors.

DELICATE NEGOTIATIONS

Nathan's cheek still stung as the doors parted to reveal a luxurious penthouse suite. The room was cluttered with furniture, paintings, statues and rugs. Garish and ostentatious, gold leaf, clashing patterns, with two mounted impala heads flanking the marble fireplace. Nathan's mum would have used words like 'kitsch' and 'tacky', but only afterwards when talking to him in the car on the way home.

Bay windows revealed an epic panorama of the sea and the cliffs. Nathan sidled closer for a better look. In the sea was a chilling sight: the tail fin of a British Airways plane slanting out of the waves at a grim angle. He wondered about the millions of people unlucky enough to be in the air when the invasion began. He glanced up and saw Skyships – no more than tiny dots from here – heading for orbit. Patrols of Drones came swooping over the ocean, and, in the distance, the Cube was descending over the other side of the bay shore. He instinctively backed away from the window, hoping he couldn't be seen by electronic eyes.

Standing centre stage was a woman in her sixties. Tall, she dominated the room. She had flinty eyes, arched eyebrows, hoop earrings and immaculate nails. She was wearing the kind of red dress that Nathan's mum would have called 'tarty', and she definitely would have frowned over the garish diamond necklace.

There were no formal introductions, but Nathan guessed this was Monique.

She looked them over one by one, sizing them up. When she came to Nathan, he felt suddenly vulnerable, like she had some kind of built-in bullshit detector. If they made old-lady Mediators, they would look like Monique. He tensed up, getting a whiff of her perfume. It was delicate, floral, smelled expensive. She must be high up the food chain if she still had perfume.

Her eyes bored into him. His Aunt Lou used to look at him like that. Some people in his family said she was psychic, and he was getting the same vibe from this woman now. She made him think of the fortune-tellers in tents at the Fairfield Bay Summer Fair. Some of his mates dared him to try one that last summer. She'd foretold that he'd fall in love and have his heart broken. She completely failed to mention an invasion of a Robot Empire from another galaxy.

Wayne was at Monique's side, whispering in her ear.

'Show me,' she said in an East End accent.

Wayne grabbed Nathan and yanked him away from the window. 'Eh? Get off!'

Wayne dragged him before Monique. She twisted Nathan's head around to inspect the dead implant.

'How'd you do it?' she demanded.

'Oh, it's easy,' Connor blurted. 'We—'

A cacophony of voices – Sean's, Nathan's and Alex's – all tumbled over one another to shut Connor up.

'Connor, no!'

'Shh!'

'Schtum!'

Connor clammed up immediately, but Nathan could see from Monique's grin that the damage had been done.

'Nice one, div-head,' Nathan muttered as Monique released him from her grip. She smiled and scruffed Connor's hair.

'Easy, was it?' she said, holding Connor's chin in her hands. Her voice was direct. There was no disguise in it. This was a woman who said what she wanted without fear of dissent. 'How about I just take what I want? Kids aren't so tough once you break a few fingers.'

She winked at Connor, who gulped.

'Monique.' Wayne sighed with disapproval. 'Kids? Really?'

Monique tutted at his squeamishness. 'Wayne's such a softie. He'd knock seven bells out of someone for spilling his drink, but gets all gooey over little'uns.'

'We can show you,' Nathan said, 'but you have to give us what we want first.'

Her eyes darted to Nathan, daring him to say more. He suddenly wished he'd stayed silent.

He nodded at Sean, who unfolded his dad's file photo and showed it to Monique.

'I'm looking for my dad, Danny Flynn,' he said.

Monique's eyes narrowed with recognition.

'Is he here?' Sean said, a little too keen for Nathan's liking.

Monique saw it, too. Sean's desperation. Nathan ground his teeth. They just lost the upper hand. She knew they would do anything for her information.

'Let's make a deal,' she said.

And so they found themselves back in the bar surrounded by the denizens of the Poseidon. Alex had set up the car battery, console and adapter for a demonstration. The children couldn't do it on themselves, so they asked for a volunteer.

The crowd of misfits all looked eager to see it work, just not on them first.

Wayne nudged Magpie forward.

'Why me?' the masked man asked.

' 'Cos you're always moaning about how you wanna go outside

and show the clankers how it's done.' Wayne shoved Magpie into a chair. 'So put your money where your mouth is, you big girl's blouse.'

Nathan watched as Alex checked the connections again. He began to think about what would happen if it didn't work. They'd give this masked man – Magpie, was it? – a whopping electric shock, nothing would happen, and he'd proceed to beat the crap out of the person closest to him. Which, at the moment, was Nathan.

Nathan backed away carefully, imagining the riot that would follow if this went wrong. He casually looked around, trying to find the nearest exit. But there wasn't a way out that didn't involve fighting through a mob of people, most of whom had piercings or tattoos the mere application of which would have made Nathan cry like a baby. Tough crowd.

Without warning, Alex placed the live crocodile clips on Magpie's arms.

He screamed, jolted about a foot into the air and then collapsed back into the chair, his hair smouldering and his implant … dead.

The crowd roared like they'd just won the World Cup on penalties. They went bananas. The bearded barmaid grabbed Nathan and kissed his cheek, leaving a greasy red smudge. Others whooped, cheered, sang and hopped in the air, embracing each other.

Wayne grabbed Sean in a huge bear hug, spinning him around.

'You bloody geniuses!' he cried. 'There is a God!'

Monique looked on, motionless, as the celebration went on around her. Nathan could tell this was a big deal for her. This was a woman who had plans.

Alex stood by, a crocodile clip in each hand. 'I reckon it's to do with the specific voltage created by the battery and the dodgy adapter.'

'If we had something to compare it with, like a Taser—' Sean added, but Nathan was quick to cut them off.

'Whoa, whoa! Waitasec— schtum!' he hissed, stepping between them and Monique.

'We showed you ours,' he said to her. 'Now you show us yours!'

Alex grimaced, while Sean chuckled.

'You know what I mean …' Nathan said.

Monique nodded. A deal was a deal. 'There's someone you should meet,' she said.

SWANNY

The celebrations were deafening, so Monique led the kids into the hotel lobby where she could hear herself think.

'Believe it or not, we came here to get a bit of peace and quiet,' she said with a rueful smile. 'Fairfield Bay looked like a nice little seaside town, no aggravation, but trouble seemed to follow me and Swanny wherever we went.'

'Please.' Connor raised his hand. 'Who's Swanny?'

'My husband, darlin',' she said. 'He used to run things in London after his old man died, but I told him: enough is enough. You're going a bit doolally in your old age, and the nightclub-casino business is a young man's game. He wouldn't listen at first, but he always comes round. Well, he does when *I* talk to him.'

She took them around the corner to a private elevator behind the stairwell. She unlocked the shutters with a key and clattered it open. They all squeezed inside, her perfume mingling with the hot, wet scent of yesterday's laundry. She turned another key to start it moving.

'But after a couple of years of rock 'n' chips by the sea, he starts getting itchy fingers and opened a little place just off the seafront,' she continued. 'Nightclub. Classy. No table dancers. Of course, it attracted arse-ache like flies to a pile of shit. Fights, drugs, bent coppers. We didn't need none of that at our age.

'So we got our boy Joe to run the place, and we took a bit off the top,' she said. 'Swanny called it our little pension scheme. We brought Wayne down to run the door crew and keep things respectable. His Mandy loved it here and they were even talking about having kids.

'It was all right,' she said. 'Not the Caribbean, like we'd always planned, but that was never going to happen. So this would have to do.'

The lift juddered to a halt. Monique gripped the shutter handle and slid it open.

'And then then whole world decided to go tits-up.'

They stepped out into a storage room at the very top of the hotel. It was littered with forgotten paintings, broken chairs, blank-eyed mannequins and other mysteries covered in plain dust-sheets. Sunlight came through a single skylight and a billion dust particles danced in its beam.

'Do you think they have robots in the Caribbean?' Connor asked.

'Course they do,' Nathan replied. 'They're everywhere.'

'Be nicer than here though, wouldn't it?'

'Paradise on your doorstep and you're not allowed outside?' Alex said. 'I'd rather be stuck here.'

'Doesn't matter where you are,' Monique said quietly. 'Stuck is stuck.'

Monique looked up through the skylight, remembering the invasion. 'Our lot had always been rowdy, never any good at doing as they're told. Those first few days inside were a bloody massacre,' she said. 'Joe took his lads out with guns and Molotovs to do what the armies of the world couldn't. I begged him not to go, but he wouldn't bloody listen. Five minutes they lasted. One Sentry took them all out.'

Monique relived the memory in her mind. The kids all shared a look, wondering if they should say something.

'Swanny went mental,' she said finally, her voice cracking. 'I had to hold him back, or he'd be dead, too. He hasn't been the same since. No parent should lose their child. Especially not like that. Not in the blink of an eye. One second he was there …'

She felt a small hand squeeze hers. The smallest kid, Connor, looked up at her. 'I know,' he said quietly. 'Same thing happened to my dad.'

She trailed off, trying not to cry, sorting through the keys as she wandered around the maze of dust-sheets.

'So the poxy VC trashed our place and chucked us in here with the rest of the scum,' she said. 'Those first few months were hard. We had to assert our authority, know what I mean? Well, you can't have any old knobber thinking they can run the place, eh?'

She took them to a small door in the corner of the room. It had one edge sloping down at the same angle as the roof. She bent down to unlock it.

'We brought Wayne in, which helped us get established. I mean, we knew what people wanted: they'd all lost someone, they all wanted to pass the time, forget. So we ripped out a few bathtubs and set up the stills. Just enough hooch to keep everyone happy.'

She unlocked the door, opening it only so far. She turned on the kids and raised a warning finger.

'Quiet in here, okay?' she said and they nodded. 'Look … things are getting dodgy. More and more fights are kicking off. Truth is, we can't make hooch quick enough, and it won't be long before someone is killed or tries it on. Wayne's solid, I know that, but little toe-rags like Magpie can't be trusted. Smythe threw us in here to rot. He wants us to turn on each other and I don't want to give him the satisfaction. These people need hope and you've given it to them. But before you go haring off into the great unknown looking for your dad, you should listen to Swanny. After that … well, maybe you'll reckon you're better off staying here.' She opened the door fully and waved them inside.

*

It was dark on the other side of the door and it took a while for their eyes to adjust. It was a tiny storage room converted to a bedroom. Heavy curtains gently billowed in the sea breeze, allowing only the tiniest sliver of light into the room. Dust-sheets covered hidden objects, though here and there Sean could see glimpses between the folds of cobwebbed chandeliers and gold-leafed chairs stacked high. As Monique softly closed the door behind her; it creaked mournfully and a voice came from the shadows. 'Whassatnoise? Gerroudofit!'

The gang jumped back. Sean peered into the darkness to see an old man sitting in a wheelchair with a tartan blanket on his lap. He faced the window but was staring into an empty space.

'Swanny, love,' Monique said, her voice kind and soothing. 'Brought someone to see you.'

Swanny's gnarled fingers nursed a bottle of moonshine. He raised it to his trembling lips and slurped at the pungent liquid, letting some of it dribble from his lips.

'Swanny here knew your dad,' she told Sean, absently wiping away the dribble with a hankie. 'Always fiddling with his implant. Thick as thieves, they were. Never worried about all those who died trying the same.'

The gang gathered cautiously around the old man. Behind them the door creaked, and Sean turned to see Wayne standing guard. His implant was dead. The big man gave him a nod.

'And then last summer,' Monique said, 'they were gone.'

'Gone where?' Sean asked. 'How?'

Monique settled down next to Swanny. 'He's a bit deaf ...' she explained, before yelling in his ear, 'Swanny, love! Got some visitors. Can I show 'em your thing?'

Swanny said nothing, but Monique gently turned his wheelchair, revealing a cylindrical metal hole behind his ear where his implant used to be. The kids gasped.

'Sick,' Nathan whispered in awe.

'Goes in a long way, doesn't it?' Connor said, moving to poke his finger in the hole. Quick as a flash, Swanny grabbed Connor's hand.

'Gerrawayyoulittlebollix!'

Connor jumped back into Alex's arms.

'How'd he do it?' asked Sean.

'Watchmaker …' Swanny muttered to no one in particular. 'Watchmaker took it. Tiny fingers … glass eyes …'

'Watchmaker?' Alex asked.

'Tell 'em, Swanny.' Monique stroked his cheek. 'Tell 'em about the stones.'

Swanny looked at Monique as if remembering something long forgotten. His rheumy eyes glistened. 'The stones,' he said. 'They left word … the slaughter stone … shows the way.'

He repeated it over and over, muttering in a dreamlike state, as Monique told them his story.

'He did a runner back in the summer. He wanted payback for our boy. Well, so did I, but I weren't ready to die yet. He got in with this bloke called Donald who reckoned he could remove implants. Others had tried, but they had a habit of losing their heads, so I wanted nothing to do with it. Then this RAF fella arrived – your dad, I reckon – and the three of them started plotting. Crafty buggers.'

Sean thought back to the hospital. The RAF pilot who lost his head right before Sean's eyes. He shuddered at the thought of his dad ending up the same way.

'I found Swanny's note one morning. He was going to locate the resistance, he said. He promised to come back. Swore he loved me. Been a while since he'd said that sober. Three months he was gone. Came crashing through the back door at the end of the summer. His face burned red. Dehydrated. Heatstroke turned him into this.'

'Heatstroke?' Nathan curled his lip in disbelief. 'Really?'

'I'm not talking about a bit of sunburn, you ignorant little twerp,' Monique snapped. 'Proper heatstroke, the kind that boils your brain. The kind that leaves you mumbling nonsense about stones and lakes and darkness. And that's how he's been ever since.

'I hid him up here. Let him have his peace. He'll slip away, I reckon. Not much I can do for him except say sweet words, keep him fed and watered, and let him know that I love him.

'But he's started something. He's been there and back again. He's been out and survived. And now the others want a taste of it, too. They want a bit of payback.'

'... slaughter stone ...' Swanny mumbled, tired now, 'the silver lake ...'

'Come to think of it,' said Monique, 'maybe I do, too.'

Without warning, Swanny jolted forward, grabbed Sean and pulled him towards his ravaged face. 'Follow the river,' he spat, his eyes wild. The kids all jumped back, frightened as Swanny's eyes focused on something only he could see. 'Follow the river, find the silver lake!' he cried. 'Find the silver lake!'

CURFEW SUSPENDED

They left Monique and Wayne tending to Swanny. Alex could see that Sean was still a bit shaken from his close encounter with the old man. They gathered together in a tight hallway lined with shelves, surrounded by remnants of the hotel's glory days: old telephones long dead, dozens of tiny, empty plastic shampoo bottles and old posters advertising cabaret acts. Alex thought about Swanny's cryptic clues and where they might take them.

'This is bollocks, mate,' Nathan said. 'She's given us sod all. I mean, what was that?'

Alex shushed him. 'What the hell is a slaughter stone?' she asked.

'It's where druids made sacrifices,' Connor piped up.

'Vikings again?' Nathan yawned.

'Stonehenge,' Connor snapped back. 'Didn't you learn anything at school?'

'I learned that bigger boys could duff me up when I was lippy.' He punched Connor in the arm.

'Quiet!' Alex slapped Nathan's arm. She could see that Sean was trying to think, and the other two weren't helping. 'Honestly.'

'There's some standing stones on the edge of Duncombe Wood,' Sean said.

'Then that's where we head for?' she said, keen to get away from this place.

'Oh, come on,' Nathan said, flinging his arms back the way they'd just come. 'Swanny's completely mental and we're taking directions from him? He's like Rain Man, but if Rain Man was stupid. Monique stitched us right up!'

'You got a better idea?' Alex snapped.

'Yeah.' Nathan said. 'How about not wandering around lost in the woods and getting sunstroke! You want to end up like that poor bastard?'

Alex had to admit that Nathan had a point. They had no food, no water and no way of knowing how long they'd be wandering out in the woods. But she still wanted to get away from this place as soon as possible.

They all flinched as an Air Drone's voice came booming from outside.

'CITIZENS, CURFEW IS TEMPORARILY SUSPENDED. ASSEMBLE OUTSIDE FOR ZONE CHIEF ADDRESS.'

They raced back into Swanny's room and dashed to the window where Wayne and Monique were waiting.

Connor got there first. 'Look!' he said, pointing to the seafront.

Sean peered through the window to see dozens of people gathering between wooden breakwaters on the shingle beach. All their implants were green as they moved blinking in the sunlight, breathing deeply, filling their lungs with fresh air. Delighted to be outside again, but confused and fearful that this was the beginning of some nasty surprise cooked up by the robots and the VC.

A squadron of Drones hovered overhead, engines roaring as they repeated their message. 'CITIZENS, CURFEW IS TEMPORARILY SUSPENDED. ASSEMBLE OUTSIDE FOR ZONE CHIEF ADDRESS.'

Two VC heavies armed with machine guns moved to a

breakwater, flanking a familiar-looking figure. It was Smythe. There was no mistaking his long coat, bow tie and silly little hat.

'Ugh,' Monique spat, 'that bastard.'

'You're a member of his fan club, too?' Nathan said.

'He called me a barmaid once,' Monique sneered. ' "Tell that barmaid to keep the noise down," he said – bloody cheek. No one tells me what to do, and no one calls me a barmaid. Who does he think he is?'

'He used to be our geography teacher,' Alex said.

'Well, he can disappear back up his own Limpopo, as far as I'm concerned.'

'He tried to kill us all,' added Connor, a little too cheerily.

'And he killed one of our friends,' said Nathan, grimly.

'Well, any enemy of his is a friend of mine.'

They watched as Smythe clambered up onto the breakwater, extending his hand to a woman behind him. That's when Sean's heart nearly leapt out of his mouth.

'Mum,' he whispered as he watched Kate climb up to stand next to Smythe.

Without a word, Sean pulled up his hood and headed for the door.

Wayne reached out to stop him. 'Oi, son, no!' But Sean dodged out of his reach and was gone. 'Oh, you silly sod.'

Sean stepped outside, adjusting his hood, making sure no one could see his implant. He shouldered his way through the crowd, trying to get near the front. All he wanted was to catch her eye, somehow let her know that he was okay, that he was alive. And then what? He had to hope she'd keep quiet, maybe steer Smythe away from them. And then what? Oh, God, he didn't know. Their original plan to find his dad had been so simple just a moment ago.

Smythe switched on a megaphone with a whine of feedback. More than three hundred people were watching him.

'Citizens of Marine Parade,' he said in his flat, no-nonsense voice. 'I am looking for this boy …'

More VC officers moved into the crowd. They handed out printed flyers, which were passed around from person to person. The woman in front of Sean blithely handed one to him and his blood chilled. It was his ID photo; a wanted poster.

'This lad's name is Sean Flynn,' Smythe continued. 'He was involved in a terrorist incident at Fairfield Bay High.'

Sean froze to the spot. Running or making any sudden move would just draw attention. He wished he could disappear into a hole in the ground. He craned his neck to look at the hotel behind him, maybe signal to the others that he needed help, but the crowd had closed in around him, all of them looking at his picture. He couldn't move forward or back.

'Has anyone here seen this young man?' Smythe said. 'Does anyone know where he is? His mother is very concerned.'

Smythe handed Kate the megaphone. 'Sean,' she called, 'if you can hear me, Mr Smythe's given his word you won't be punished. Turn yourself in!'

Smythe took the megaphone back from Kate. 'Sean's mother will be safe with me at Lehane Castle, the new zone HQ. Spread the word.'

Sean watched as his mum was ushered away by a Volunteer Corps member. Any chance of catching her eye was gone. That was it, Sean had to get out. He tried to shrink further into his hood and began to casually edge his way back through the crush. But it was hard to make headway, people shouldered him aside, refused to move, and Sean was buffeted around.

'Anyone with information leading to the boy's safe return will receive an entire afternoon outside, for them and their family,' Smythe added. 'Yours to do with as you please!'

An excited murmur rippled through the crowd just as Sean caught the eye of a thin man, weaselly-looking with dark, sunken eyes and pale skin. The man did a classic double-take, glancing from Sean to the wanted poster and back again. Sean looked away immediately, but knew it was too late. He'd been recognised.

Sean started to push through the crowd with added urgency, head down. ' 'Scuse me ... Cheers.'

He risked a glance back and confirmed the worst: the thin man was following him, finding gaps as Smythe droned on.

'Remember, citizens ... Harbouring fugitives, withholding information – the Robot Empire see these as serious crimes.'

Sean hit a dense wall of people. There was no way through without showing his face to someone.

'Think twice before you put your lives at risk for a stranger,' Smythe said.

Sean felt a bony grip on his arm. He glanced down to see a knife pressed against his ribs.

'Back off,' the thin man hissed to those around them. 'He's mine!' Then the thin man raised his knife arm. 'Hey, Mr Smythe! The kid, he's—'

And he was suddenly silenced as someone big blurred into view. With a hollow *thunk*, the new arrival's head made contact with the thin man's and he began to topple over.

He was caught by Wayne, the headbutter, who gently lowered the thin man's unconscious body to the ground. He gave Sean a wink before standing in front of the boy, obscuring him from Smythe's view.

'Anyone says a word,' Wayne whispered through his teeth to those around him, 'I'll rip their liver out and feed it to the cat.' He glowered at a shifty-looking woman alongside him. 'Go on,' he said. 'Try me.' She glanced away.

Smythe scanned the crowd, wondering if he'd heard something. But no one came forward and he turned and marched away from the breakwater. The Air Drones began to order people back inside, but Sean already knew what he had to do next.

'I need to get to the castle,' he told Wayne.

Sean watched from his hiding place behind some yellow skips as Wayne led Nathan, Alex and Connor through the shadows.

Sean gave a short, shrill whistle and they were reunited.

'I'm gonna try and rescue my mum,' he told them. 'Then we'll head for the hills. It'll be dangerous ... Up to you if you want to come with me or not.'

'All for one and one for all, remember?' Alex said. Sean's skin tingled to see her first to volunteer.

Alex put her fist forward. Connor grinned at her as Sean and Nathan reached in to bump.

'Your mum saved me from Mr Smythe,' Connor said. 'I'm in.'

'And we can't leave her at the mercy of Smythe and his perv dungeon,' Nathan said. 'No one deserves that.'

'While you're getting all mushy,' said Wayne, 'here's a thank-you pressie.'

He produced a Taser and charging lead from his jacket. He clicked the trigger and it crackled bright blue light. 'My spare,' he said. 'Switched to the correct voltage. Save you lugging that car battery around.' He handed the bundle to Alex.

'Wicked – thanks Wayne.'

He gave a Tupperware box to Connor. 'And Aunty Moni's made you some sandwiches, little man.'

'Thanks, Wayne.' Connor smiled.

'Yeah, cheers for looking out for us, mate.' Nathan said, raising his chin in a vain effort to look taller.

'That's all right, Winkle.' Wayne patted Nathan on the cheek. 'Monique will see you safe to the edge of town,' he said, handing Sean a walkie-talkie and giving them all a salute. 'Be safe. Best of British and Godspeed!'

'Winkle?' Nathan frowned as the others tried not to giggle. 'Did he just call me Winkle?'

Monique's voice crackled over the airwaves. 'You've got about ten seconds to cross the square. Go!'

Connor hopped onto Sean's back and the gang dashed across a patch of overgrown grass surrounded by apartments, directed by Monique. 'Head for the ramps ... slip through the garages.'

The gang scuffled along the narrow space.

'Clanker!' Monique's voice squawked. 'Stop, stop, stop!'

Sean skidded to a halt, raising an arm. Connor jumped off and the others slammed into his back just as a Sniper clattered past, casting spiderlike shadows over the gang.

They held their breath, no one moving as its clanking rhythm became fainter.

'Okay,' Monique said finally. 'Go.'

As they made their way through the maze of garages and alleyways, the signal became weaker and Monique's voice grew fainter. She signed off with, 'Good luck, kids. Pleasure doing business with you.'

SMYTHE'S OFFER

Kate and Smythe spent the whole day moving around town to key spots like the big estates, the old hospital, the flats next to the bypass, the beach, Marine Parade; anywhere they thought Sean and the kids might run to. Crowds of people came squinting into the sun, rounded up and herded into place by Sentries and Drones, but no one had seen Sean. At least, no one would come forward and admit they had.

As the sun went down, they finally went door-to-door along one of the wealthier avenues on the edge of town. Big detached houses with long drives where the pools were now dry, and once immaculate lawns were dead and barren. Kate found herself talking to a face she recognised, one of her former students' mums. She only knew her as Mrs McGhie, but recalled that she was on the school's board of governors, someone who worked hard organising events, arranging meetings and charity fundraisers. Someone who fizzed with energy. Now she looked as tired and sad as Kate did. She answered all of Smythe's questions with a series of polite 'No, sorrys.' But as Kate turned back to the Jeep, Mrs McGhie took her wrist.

'Would you?' she asked in a quiet voice, one she hoped Smythe wouldn't hear.

'Would I what?'

'If my son came to you looking for shelter, would you hand him over to *him*?' She nodded towards Smythe, who was already clambering back into the Jeep.

Blood rushed to Kate's head. 'Do you have him?' she asked, gripping the other woman's hand. 'Is he here? Please—'

'No, no, I'm sorry,' Mrs McGhie said. 'I promise you, he's not here. But can you trust that man?'

She nodded back towards Smythe who honked the Jeep's horn. Kate looked long at Smythe's sharp, unforgiving face. The eyes that hardly ever blinked, the lips that rarely formed a smile.

'No,' she said. 'But he's all I have.'

Mrs McGhie gave a tiny nod and suddenly embraced Kate like a long-lost friend.

'It's funny,' Mrs McGhie said, her head buried in Kate's shoulder. 'I haven't spoken to anyone but my husband, my son and the VC ration man in three years. I'd forgotten how much I missed a woman's voice.' Her body shuddered with sobs now. 'Can you stay a while longer?' she pleaded. 'I still have some tea bags, we could—'

The horn honked again.

'I'm sorry,' Kate said, extricating herself from the other woman's hold. 'I'm so sorry.'

A funny kind of panic crossed the woman's eyes. 'I wish you'd never come,' she said, now red-faced and tearful. 'I wish you'd never bloody come! Why did you come here just to torment me? I wish you'd never come!' She was screaming as Kate ran to the Jeep.

Kate and Smythe sat in silence all the way back to the castle, avoiding eye contact as they rocked from side to side in rhythm with the Jeep's motion. He didn't ask what Mrs McGhie's outburst was about. He didn't appear to be remotely surprised or interested in it and she realised he must witness stuff like this every day. It was part of humanity's slow descent into madness.

*

Kate had brought more school parties to Lehane Castle than she cared to remember. She could reel off facts about it even now. Built in the late 12th century, the castle had endured a number of sieges. It became a hiding place for Royalists in the Civil war, was eventually converted into a prison in the 18th century and had since fallen into disrepair. And then, in the late-20th century, it had become a tourist attraction and a regular stop for schools studying local history. They loved its high walls and battlements, the green outer bailey that hosted tents full of actors in medieval costume at weekends and a French farmers' market on the first Sunday of the month.

But now, after the destruction of Fairfield Bay High School, it had become headquarters to Smythe's Volunteer Corps and a prison again. Her prison.

The Jeep swept through a stone arch at the back of the castle. As they made their way around the outer bailey they passed a trio of horses in stables, being fed by a couple of younger VC.

They were familiar faces and it occurred to her how few VC there really were.

The Jeep pulled up by the drawbridge and another face she recognised opened the passenger door for her.

'Kate, you know Deputy Zone Chief McGrath.' Smythe indicated the man who had burst into her house that morning.

'How could I forget?' she said, tight-lipped. McGrath just gave her a sleazy smile.

'He's going to show you to your quarters.' Smythe took her hand a little too firmly. 'I'm sure you're exhausted. Get some food inside you, get some rest, and we'll resume our search in the morning.'

'First thing?' she asked.

'At the very break of dawn, I promise,' he said as he turned away, hurrying off to some other appointment.

'I keep seeing the same faces,' she commented.

'I beg your pardon?' Smythe said, the gravel under his feet scrunching as he turned back to her.

'How many VC are there exactly, Robin?' she asked. 'I've seen a few dozen at most. Is that all you have for this zone?'

'No. No.' Smythe bristled. 'We have enough. We don't just take anyone, you know. Only the brightest, best and most trustworthy.'

Or most people find the idea of collaboration repulsive, she thought to herself. She began to question how much longer the VC could keep going with so few people. The notion gave her a little hope.

Rain lashed against a tiny stained-glass window in the stone keep where McGrath had left her. A fire crackled in the hearth and the air was both crisp and musty. Heavy red drapes and unravelling tapestries graced the walls of what had once been a banqueting room, and she was surrounded by wax dummies. A grinning Jester, Tudor nobles, ladies in wimples and fine dresses, serving boys in rags were all arranged around a long oak table. The orange glow of the flames played tricks, throwing shadows and light across their faces, making them look eerily alive. Medieval Mediators.

Kate had already pulled on the window latches and tried every door, but she was locked in.

From the main door came a grating *clunk-click* noise, followed by wailing squeak, and she turned to find Smythe in the doorway.

'Why are the doors locked, Robin?' she asked. 'Am I a guest or a prisoner?'

Smythe ignored her. 'Kate,' he said softly, 'may I show you something?'

He sat on a leather sofa by the fire, a small black cube in his hand. Kate approached him reluctantly. As she sat opposite him on a banqueting chair, she caught the overwhelming scent of his aftershave. It made her skin crawl and her heart race at the same. Where was this going?

'The Mediator gave this to me,' he said, turning the cube in his hand. 'All Zone Chiefs get them. It contains a promise. A pledge from the robots.'

The cube glowed and a holographic projection flickered into life: a globe turning slowly, white clouds clinging to familiar shores.

'That's amazing,' Kate gasped. She'd never seen anything like it; the projection was crystal clear and spinning in the empty air before her. She tentatively reached out to touch it. Her fingers passed straight through.

'Marvellous, isn't it?' Smythe said. 'Robot technology far surpasses ours. I know the robots look simple, cumbersome even, but that's simply a matter of practicality over design. They don't waste time on needless aesthetics. It's one of the many reasons I admire them.'

'It's Earth,' she said, entranced by the globe.

'Earth-to-be.' Smythe corrected her. 'Unsullied by overpopulation and pollution. A brave new world. Here, take it.' He held the cube out to her on his open palm.

She reached for it, but he moved it out of reach, his eyes glancing at a space on the sofa next to him. Kate hesitated, but settled down as far away from him as possible, perching on the soft chair's edge. His aftershave was even more pungent here. It stung her eyes and she had to stop herself from recoiling and pinching her nose.

Smythe handed her the cube, its hologram still live, with a reverse-pinch gesture he zoomed in, and in, and in on the image.

'Cradle Mountain,' he said, finally. 'Tasmania.'

The image of the globe had gone, replaced by a placid blue lake surrounded by lush greenery. Jungle-covered mountains rose up in the distance.

'It's beautiful,' Kate whispered. It really was. Green and lush, she wanted to be there right now. 'Is it still like that?' she asked. 'Or have the robots reduced it to rubble like everywhere else?'

Smythe shook his head and clenched his fists. 'This is what

makes me cross. This is what people don't realise. The robots aren't interested in destruction. The only places that have been destroyed are where we've resisted. Don't you see? The harder we fight back, the more destruction we create. They only want our compliance. I know it's a hoary old cliché, but resistance really is completely and utterly futile, Kate.'

He looked back at the scene on the holo.

'I can assure you this place is intact and as wonderful as it looks,' he said. 'Before the war it was regarded as one of the most beautiful places on Earth.' Smythe's eyes darted from the image to Kate's face. 'I've been allocated a hundred square miles on the shores of Lake Saint Clair. It's perfect: quiet, isolated, fecund.' Smythe looked at Kate through the hologram, his face soft and serious. 'I'd very much like you to join me there.'

Oh, God, thought Kate, her skin crawling. *He's finally coming on to me. And now, of all times? Really?* She struggled to remain calm as she imagined Smythe splashing on the aftershave, looking at himself in the mirror and thinking, *Tonight's the night.*

'And Sean?' she asked.

Smythe's eyes flickered for a brief moment. 'Sean, too, of course.' He flashed an insincere smile. 'He's a great kid. I'd be honoured to be his ...'

Kate watched as Smythe stumbled for the right word. She prayed he wouldn't say 'father', 'stepfather' or any variation thereof.

'Guardian,' he eventually managed, again finishing with that empty grin of his.

But it was too late. Kate had seen it. Sean wasn't part of Smythe's plan. All he wanted was her.

She was almost overtaken by the urge to run screaming from the room, but he had locked the door behind him with the only key she knew of. She put the cube down, stood and moved to the window. She needed some air and tugged it open, enjoying the cold breeze and the fresh scent of the rain. From here she could just make out the shape of the local Cube moving across the dark horizon, its engines blasting the ground beneath it to stay aloft. Even if the robots left today, what price had the planet already paid for their occupation? How could he think that running off to a patch of paradise in Tasmania would make it all better?

'Kate, look.' Smythe pulled himself up off the sofa. She could see him, a distorted reflection in the stained-glass window, his hands clasped together in a mockery of prayer. 'God knows I've tried to find Danny, there's no stone I've left unturned. But … when do we admit that we're beaten?'

'You're asking me to give up on Danny,' she said. 'Next you'll ask me to give up on Sean. And then you'll try to convince me that you are all I have. All I need.'

Smythe's face twisted and she knew she was right.

'Y'know, the kids make jokes about me not dating you if you were the last man on Earth,' she said. 'I never thought that choice would ever become a reality.'

'Reality?' Smythe said. 'Oh, Kate, the reality is that your husband is dead, and if your son doesn't cooperate then he will die, too. I'm the only person who can save him. I'm sorry to be blunt, but there we are …'

Her mind raced. She had to get out of here. She didn't know how, but she had to get out. Find Danny. Damn it, maybe Sean was right, maybe he was in the hills? Maybe there was a resistance? Anything had to be better than this.

But first, she needed to send Smythe a message.

She turned to face him, starting to sob. Real tears, but not for the reasons Smythe imagined. She motioned him closer.

'That's better,' he said, 'let it all out …' He took her in his arms and squeezed her tight, pressing his chest against hers. 'I'm not a monster, Kate. I only want to help you. I have qualities you can learn to like. Love, even.'

He pressed his nose into her hair, inhaling deeply. His eyes closed.

As Kate's knee jerked up into his groin with a snap.

Smythe tumbled back, breathless, his hands clutching the pain between his legs.

'I've put up with your bullshit for three years.' Kate towered over him as he backed away in agony. 'Your leering, your "updates" on Danny … and for your information, my face is here, not down here!' Kate pointed indignantly at her breasts.

Smythe staggered to his feet, trying not to retch.

Backing him into a corner, Kate continued, 'I know you're deluded enough to think you could get into my knickers, and I know that Danny's probably dead … but do you really believe I'm so desperate, so bloody depressed, that I'd want to run away with you? Go to Tasmania? I have a son. I want you to find him. That's all there is!'

Smythe moved closer to her, cheeks flushed, his eyes blazing with barely contained fury. 'You're coming with me, Kate,' he panted. 'When I tell you the truth about why the robots are here, what they want and how they'll take it … you'll beg me to.'

CONTROL

To get to the castle, they knew they had to make their way along the seafront and follow the crescent curve of the bay. Drones passed overhead every few minutes, patrolling the shoreline, so sticking to the beach wasn't an option. In the end they decided it would be better to move between the houses inland. This took them through the hospital grounds.

Everyone had bad memories of the place. Not only was it where they'd received their implants, but it was also where they had all seen someone killed by a robot for the first time. No one wanted to relive those memories, but they knew that going around it would take ages and increase the risk of them being spotted.

Connor had only ever been to Accident and Emergency – he was always falling out of trees or breaking or bumping something – so he was surprised to find that the hospital was actually a cluster of buildings. Some were like the maths huts at his old primary school – squat buildings with flaky paint and flat, leaky roofs. Connor remembered how cold those places were in the winter, having to wear gloves and seeing his own breath during lessons. Other buildings were brand new with little brass plaques declaring that some duchess or mayor had opened them on this date or that.

But every building was completely abandoned, and as they

gradually realised this, they stopped sneaking around. There was no point. It was nice to walk upright for a change.

'Where are all the patients? The doctors?' Alex asked. 'I mean, people don't stop being sick just 'cos they're stuck inside. If anything they get worse.'

'Maybe they go door-to-door now?' Nathan shrugged.

'But what if you're really ill?' Alex said. 'Like cancer or ...' Her voice trailed off. She'd seen something. Sean had, too.

'What is it?' Connor asked, moving around Nathan for a better view.

They were right behind the hospital now, underneath a huge chimney. Signs all around it warned about unauthorised entry, hazardous materials and the high temperatures of the furnace that lay within the sludge-coloured concrete block at its base. But it was something else that had stopped them in their tracks.

The first thing Connor noticed was a wheel when he tripped over it. Abandoned on the ground, it looked too big for a bicycle. There were other bits and bobs scattered across the Tarmac – hinges, handles, unidentified joints made of aluminium and steel, parts from unknown machines. Connor's gaze followed the trail of debris to a mountain of metal and plastic next to the chimney. It had filled up a skip in no time and spilled over into the car-park spaces around it. Crutches, wheelchairs, callipers, walking frames. All tossed away like unwanted toys.

'Why would they do this?' Connor asked. 'What about the people who need these?' He thought of a boy in the year above him at school who arrived in a wheelchair every day.

'Connor, mate ...' Nathan looked serious for once, and that alone made Connor feel uneasy. 'I don't think the people who need these are around any more.'

'They died?'

'I think they were killed,' Alex said, her face pale, her expression sickened.

'Why bother caring for the sick and disabled if you're just going to brain-drain them anyway?' Sean said, his voice soft but angry. He ran his hand along one of the wheelchair frames. Rust flakes came away with a crackle and drifted to the ground. 'These have been here ages,' he said. 'They must have belonged to some of the first to be deep-scanned.'

Nathan nodded up at the chimney towering over the furnace. The top was blackened with soot. 'Do you think they …?'

'Oh, God.' Alex covered her mouth and turned away.

Sean took a deep breath. 'I don't know,' he said, glancing briefly at Connor the way grown-ups did when they were discussing something he shouldn't know about.

'What?' Connor asked. 'Did they what?'

'Nothing, mate, nothing.' Sean gripped his shoulder and gave it a squeeze.

'I mean,' Nathan continued, 'maybe it's easier just to get a Sentry to, y'know … *pow*.' He made his fingers into a gun and fired.

'Nate, give it a rest, eh?' Sean said, nodding towards Connor.

'Oh yeah, right. Sorry.' Nathan scruffed Connor's hair.

But Connor wasn't an idiot. He knew what they were talking about. And it made him sad and angry at the same time.

They ran the rest of the way after that, keen to get as far away from the hospital as possible. They ran until it started to rain and get dark, and then, when they could find nowhere else to go, they settled in a graveyard.

Connor huddled under a stone angel, sheltering from the rain that pelted down on the gravestones around them. His trousers were soaked and he wondered if he would ever be dry again. He tried to tell himself that this was no worse than what the Viking explorers endured when crossing cold and stormy seas, but all he really wanted was a bit of warmth, if only for a short while.

The church was locked and its old oak doors unbreakable,

so they'd found a space in the cracked-open doorway of an ivy-covered tomb. Connor felt he should have been more creeped out by the graveyard, but after everything he'd been through it was going to take more than a few dead bodies underground to freak him out.

Connor shifted further under the shelter of the tomb. Water was dripping on his knee and he was sure the stone angel's eyes were following him as he moved.

He tried not to think about it as he bit into one of the sandwiches Wayne had given him. It was home-made bread, the kind his mum sometimes made before the war, but not as nice. It was hard where it should have been springy. The lettuce inside was gritty and he wasn't sure what the meat was. Too chewy for beef.

'Bit stringy,' Nathan said, picking something out of his teeth. 'Rabbit, I reckon.'

Connor stopped mid-bite and put the sandwich down. 'When can we go home?' he heard himself saying.

'Bit late for that, Connor,' Alex said, carefully tugging a long black hair out of her sandwich.

'We're fugitives, mate,' Nathan said, with a nudge and a wink. 'Outlaws.'

'But if they catch us, they'll—' Connor thought back to what had happened to his dad. To Morse Code Martin. His breath caught in his throat. He told himself that he wasn't scared, that he shouldn't be sad in front of the others, and he tried to bury it deep inside him. But he still let out an involuntary sob.

Nathan sighed at Connor's sniffling. 'Should've left him at the hotel,' he said, tossing his sandwich wrapper. It bounced off Connor's head.

'Hey!' Connor yelped.

'Shut it, Nathan,' Sean said, gently holding Connor's shoulders. 'Connor,' he said in the calm voice that always made the younger boy feel better. 'There's no one to ask for help now. It's just us. But if we look out for each other, we'll get through this. I promise. That sound cool?'

Connor knew Sean meant well, but he also knew that if a Sentry saw them, there was nothing they could do. One warning, a countdown, that was it. But he nodded and made the A-okay sign. It made him feel better for the moment, anyhow. Nathan was right, though – they were outlaws. Connor had thought it would be more exciting, an adventure, but all it gave him was a sick feeling in his stomach. Death wasn't exciting. Seeing his dad disappear into nothing wasn't cool. He'd been sad for days, crying without warning. But now when he thought about his mum and dad, it made him really cross. He wanted to lash out and punch the walls, smash windows and shout at the sky, to God, or whoever was to blame for all this pain and death. Now he began to understand how his dad had felt that night when he ran outside. Having friends, loving people, was easy when things were good, but when the bad times came it brought a burning pain in his heart.

After their sandwich, Sean led them through the winding streets towards the castle. It was late night by the time they got there. Connor had no idea what the time was. The clock outside the shopping mall said three in the morning, but he didn't feel like he could sleep.

The castle was a beautiful thing to see, glowing red, floodlit in the rain. Connor imagined what it would be like to lay siege to a place like this. Where were the weak points? He looked hard, but couldn't see any. Just grey stone walls far too high, wet and slippery to climb. There were some low windows, but they were barred. The only way in would be through the main entrance. They couldn't see it from here, but they all knew it would be crawling with VC and robots.

Many of the street lights were still on, giving them very few shadows to hide in. They moved between parked cars, some charred from the war, some overturned, others abandoned by their owners as they fled the invasion, but great cover for the gang. They dashed from behind an old camper van to the stone memorial column; the closest they could get to the castle.

A Sentry marched on patrol along a grass verge circling the castle, its footsteps making the ground tremble. It was so close that Connor could hear the gears whining as it moved. There seemed to be a whole bunch of them patrolling the castle's perimeter.

Alex dared to peek out as this one's footsteps faded away. 'There's too many, and they're too close together.'

'Then we'll have to be fast,' Sean said, his eyes focused on the distance between the memorial and the castle gates.

'What's the plan, Sean?' Connor asked.

'Come on, Connor.' Alex said. 'You should know better by now. Sean doesn't do plans. He just rushes in and hopes for the best.'

'That's …' Sean started to protest, jabbing a finger at Alex. '… not entirely true.'

'Well, it's worked so far.' Nathan slapped him on the shoulder. 'Why change the habit of a lifetime?'

'You got a plan?' Sean said. 'Because I'd love to hear it.'

'I do, as a matter of fact,' Nathan replied. 'But my SAS training requires grappling hooks, smoke grenades, MP5 machine guns and a Black Hawk helicopter. As I appear to have left them back at the barracks, it looks like we'll have to rely on you.'

'Well, maybe if you hadn't brought half a ton of bullshit with you, you'd have remembered them,' Sean snapped.

'Well, if *you* hadn't—'

'Clanker!' Alex hissed as another Sentry came around the corner. They all kept still until it was out of sight.

'We're kind of stuck out here, Sean,' Alex said, looking around the open square surrounding them.

'We can't go back,' he said. 'We've come this far – we can't just turn around now.'

'Yeah, but coming all this way and getting zapped here, right on the castle doorstep.' Alex shook her head. 'That would really take the biscuit. We should—'

'Cake!' Connor blurted.

'What?'

'Sorry,' he whispered. 'But biscuits made me think of cake, which made me think of my aunty's wedding.'

Three befuddled faces turned to him.

'There's a way in around the back,' Connor whispered. 'My aunty got married here and when I was sick from eating too much cake, they took me to the toilets by the kitchens. There's a big gate where the delivery vans go in and out.'

Nathan frowned at him. 'The way your brain works really scares me, Connor.'

'Nice one, Connor,' Sean said, patting him on the back. 'So we enter through there, sneak around, find mum and then get out again.'

'Oh yeah, a doddle. Another classic plan from Sean.' Nathan said to himself, his voice oozing with sarcasm.

'We ready?' Sean asked. Connor nodded, even though there was no cover between here and the rear of the castle, just the cobbled road and street lights. They'd be out in the open for a long time.

Connor caught Alex and Nathan sharing a nervous glance. If they were nervous, things must be bad. They didn't always include Connor in their conversations because they thought he was too little to understand. His mum and dad had been the same, but Connor knew when things weren't right. He could see it in their faces.

Connor trusted Sean. Well, he *had*, but now the bigger boy looked unsure. He was chewing on his lip. His eyes kept zipping from side to side as if he expected them to be caught at any moment, and that made Connor uncertain, too. If you'd asked him a day ago, Connor would have said that he'd follow Sean anywhere, but suddenly they were going right into the dragon's den.

But he didn't have a choice. The alternative was to wander around on his own, and that didn't bear thinking about.

Sean counted down with his fingers – three, two, one.

Bent low, they dashed across the road and leapt up onto the grass verge, racing towards the castle entrance. Connor could only hear the sound of his breathing, the rhythm of his feet swishing through the long grass. His chest pounded and he dared to hope that they were actually going to make it.

Then he heard an all-too-familiar sound behind him and his whole body flushed cold. 'CITIZENS, RETURN TO YOUR HOMES IMMEDIATELY.'

Connor glanced back. He saw the Sentry's lamp first, its light swooping across the grass, right into his eyes. Then all he could see were purple and green blobs.

'Shit,' he heard Sean say. '*Run!*'

They all sprinted flat out, but the Sentry took giant strides, catching up with them in moments. Of all the robots, Connor hated the Sentries the most. With their big arms and tiny heads they reminded him of school bullies who never listened, never stopped until you were crying.

'YOU HAVE TEN SECONDS TO RETURN TO YOUR HOME.'

The Sentry raised its gun-arm, its cannon whined, the barrel spinning as it powered up to fire. Connor kept running, but he closed his eyes. He wondered how much it would hurt. Maybe it wouldn't hurt at all? A quick flash and then it was over. Or maybe he would burn for ages. Maybe for ever? Caught in the agony of death for all time. His gran used to talk about hell, where bad boys would be sent for all eternity.

'THIS IS YOUR FINAL WARNING.'

To Connor's right, Sean slipped and tumbled forwards, then

rolled onto his back, hand held up defensively, the Sentry towering over him.

'FIVE. FOUR. THREE. TWO. ONE—'

Alex and Nathan were screaming. Connor didn't have the breath to make any noise. Suddenly he wanted to die, right here, right now, so he wouldn't have to see his friends go first.

'Sean, *no!*' Alex cried.

Connor watched Sean close his eyes, grit his teeth and wait for death ...

... but the robot was frozen above him.

Sean stared into the spinning muzzle of its laser cannon, just inches from his face.

'What the frack ...?' Nathan said, his jaw hanging open.

Connor saw the white lights on Sean's implant wink on and off, rapidly.

'Look at his implant.' Alex noticed it, too. 'Look!'

The lights on Sean's implant were pulsing in time with the Sentry's.

'What's that mean?' Connor managed, finally getting his breath back.

'I think ...' Sean said, his chest still heaving. 'I think I'm stopping it!'

'Awesome!' Connor said, his mind whirling.

While he was running for his life, he'd felt silly for trusting Sean and wished he'd stayed back at the Poseidon with Wayne and Monique. Wished he'd never left home, or joined this adventure. Wished that he was in his room, curled up with a book, minding his own business. But those dark thoughts had vanished in an instant, and he felt bad for even thinking them, for doubting Sean.

'Bull. Shit,' Nathan said, open-mouthed.

Sean slowly got to his feet and moved his outstretched arm.

And the Sentry did the same.

'It's like … a video game or something,' Sean said, moving again, the Sentry mimicking his every motion.

'Right, Sean, seriously … make it do shit!' Nathan whooped, suddenly excited.

Sean lifted a leg in the air.

And with a metallic grinding sound, the Sentry copied him.

'Whoa,' Alex said, hands in her hair. 'This is massive!'

'Ha!' Nathan was really into it now. 'Make it scratch its balls.'

Sean moved his hand over his nuts and the Sentry did the same. Connor was laughing so much he started to cough, and then he worried that he would be sick everywhere.

Sean did bad disco dancing – the Sentry likewise.

They were hysterical now, Sean laughing hard.

Then the Sentry jolted back into action, its cannon glowing as a pulse of deadly energy was unleashed, blasting into the ground. The earth exploded upwards in a huge plume.

Sean had lost control.

They all screamed and jumped back, and Connor's bad thoughts about Sean returned.

But then Sean instinctively reached out, the lights on his implant pulsing in time with the Sentry's. He had control again. As Connor got his breath back and his heart rate returned to normal, he realised he had to make a choice. And in that instant he chose to trust Sean completely. Even if things got really, really bad, he knew he could rely on Sean to make things right.

He hoped.

'Nearly shat my pants then.' Nathan puffed out his cheeks.

'Lost my concentration.' Sean said. 'Sorry.'

'Let it go,' Alex said, suddenly scared. 'We gotta leg it.'

Sean stared into space, thinking intently.

'Wait,' he said, and a wicked grin crept across his face. 'I've got an idea.'

STAND-OFF AT LEHANE CASTLE

There was still a dull pain running from Smythe's groin, down his leg, back up again and then along his right arm. That woman could really deliver a painful blow, but he knew it was a typical response for a distressed female. All she needed was some time to come to terms with the new world she was living in. Until then, he would leave her locked up to reconsider her actions.

He told her everything. Why the robots were here, what they wanted and how they were going to seize it. He took only a little pleasure in seeing her turn pale as she digested the scale of their operation and what it would mean for the rest of humanity.

Now she had heard the whole story, she'd soon realise there was no alternative. The robots will know everything there is to know. Robots never lie.

He'd sent someone up with food and drink. Good food and drink, quality stuff, clean. Just to make it clear to her that life was better on this side of the fence. Yes, she'd soon come round.

As he moved into the main hall, he did his best to hide his new limp. It wouldn't do to show the team any kind of weakness. McGrath was standing by the fire-damaged map of the town, one of the few things they'd managed to salvage from the school fire. They had to risk it – it's not like they could order another from Ordnance Survey.

'Report,' Smythe snapped.

'Nothing, just the usual mentals,' McGrath sneered. 'A few sightings around the beachfront-Marine Parade area, but nothing I'd call solid.'

Smythe's offer of an afternoon outside hadn't proved as successful as he'd hoped. They'd been flooded with tip-offs from cranks. Hoax sightings from people desperate to get outside. And after three years of incarceration there were plenty of them about. But his men had to follow every lead and they were already stretched thin.

'Any word on my request from the Mediator?' Smythe had asked for squads of Air Drones to scan the area using heat sensors. Even with all the rogue wildlife wandering about the town he was sure they'd find four kids soon enough. But from McGrath's doleful expression, he knew the answer.

'Nothing,' McGrath said. 'You have to wonder whose side they're on sometimes.'

Smythe was disappointed that the Mediator wouldn't offer more robot help, but stragglers weren't an uncommon problem. They knew there were people on the fringes of robot rule, on the run, living off the land, but they were fooling themselves if they thought they could escape their ultimate destiny. It was all just a matter of time. And if Smythe had learned one thing in the last three years, it was that the robots were very, very patient.

In the corner of his eye he could see the junior VC he'd sent up with Kate's food trying to get his attention with a half-raised arm. He ignored the boy's pathetic craving for attention – no doubt wanting some praise from Smythe for a job well-done – and concentrated on the situation at hand.

'Very well.' Smythe pursed his lips and examined the map. 'Start going door-to-door, turn over every home. It will take time, but we'll flush them out. We—'

A klaxon sounded, shouts came from outside and a VC officer crashed into the room. 'Sir,' he said, breathless, 'he's here!'

'I want the Snipers on the battlements,' Smythe ordered as he marched through the castle.

So the boy had seen sense and was turning himself in. No sign of his partners in crime, but that didn't matter. He had Sean, and that would make Kate happy. 'He is not to be harmed, do you understand?'

'Yes, sir.' McGrath said.

'Make sure the bloody Snipers understand, too,' Smythe added. He knew they would react to any kind of threatening gesture with deadly force. And if his past encounters were anything to go by, the boy would probably try something stupid. 'They're just a show of strength. I want him to know who's in charge. I don't want this turning into another unfortunate vaporisation.'

'Understood.' McGrath peeled off, shouting orders as he went.

Smythe stepped through what used to be the castle ticket office and onto the drawbridge. The night air was chilly, the first hint of dawn gave the sky a violet hue.

Searchlights swung into place, finding Sean. His hands were raised as a Sentry herded him at gunpoint through an archway and across the outer bailey.

Smythe heard two Snipers clatter into position above him, followed by a high-pitched whirring noise as their feet drilled into the rock, holding them firmly in place for a steady aim. Their gun-barrels glowed red as they homed in on the boy.

'You come with me,' Smythe ordered three VC. Two were armed with AK-47 assault rifles, confiscated during the first weeks of the occupation. It had astounded Smythe to learn so many people had these kinds of weapons hidden away in their own homes, but now they were in the safe hands of the VC. A third was armed with a shotgun. His own, Smythe recalled. The man had been a farmer before the war. An aggressive get-off-my-land type.

The Sentry brought Sean to a halt by a row of old iron cannons.

Smythe stepped off the drawbridge onto the manicured grass of the outer bailey, kept short and neat on his orders. He saw no reason why they should live in a pigsty.

The boy dragged his feet to a halt, his head hanging low. With the Sentry towering over him, he looked defeated. Being a fugitive had taken its toll on the lad. Smythe allowed himself a moment of indulgent satisfaction in seeing him beaten. Truth was, he didn't want the little bugger around at all. He'd much rather have Kate to himself, but if this made her happy and more compliant, then so be it.

'You should have kept running, son,' Smythe told him, half-wishing that the boy would take his advice. 'You're in the lion's den now.'

The cocky little urchin looked up and smirked at him. And that's when Smythe realised something wasn't right.

Sean brought his arm around, like a boxer delivering a round-house blow, and to Smythe's utter astonishment, the Sentry did exactly the same.

Just inches from Smythe's face, the Sentry's weapon-arm split open, revealing the red glowing mechanism inside as the twin barrels twisted and thrust out. The Sentry even mimicked the boy's posture, leaning forward on one leg like a Western gunslinger.

From above, Smythe could hear the Snipers' weapons crackle as they powered up to fire.

'No!' he cried, waving his hands. 'Stand down, stand down! Authorisation code 97-ZCRS.'

The Snipers' laser cannons spun down.

'Drop your weapons,' Sean ordered, 'or I'll fry him, then you!'

Smythe was about to give the nod, only to see his men already complying. He cursed their cowardice as their guns clattered onto the flagstones.

More noise as the other hoodlums, Alex, Nathan and Connor,

rushed over from the archway behind Sean to snatch up the weapons.

The cocky one, Nathan, swung the AK-47 around like it was a toy. 'Wassup, fools?' he whooped. He than grabbed a shotgun and slung it over his shoulder.

Smythe froze on the spot. If there was anything more terrifying than a child with a gun, he didn't want to know about it.

The girl also had an AK-47 now, and they started to bicker among themselves.

'Can I have the shotgun, Nate?' the little one asked, tugging at the bigger boy's sleeve.

'You want it? Yeah?' Nathan started to give it to him – teasing – then snatched it back. 'Ooh, no, sorry, mate.'

'Come on … Please?' Connor pleaded. 'I'm so responsible!'

'Maybe. Ask me later.'

Smythe, wide-eyed and breathless, stared into the barrels of the Sentry's laser cannons. He'd never seen them from this point of view before.

'How are you doing this, Sean?' he asked, trying to remain calm. 'It's incredible … You've become something wonderful.'

He watched as Sean flexed his shoulders and the robot did the same. Every tiny move the boy made was echoed by the Sentry as their implants pulsed in time. He'd formed some kind of intimate connection using the black robot implant. Smythe recalled an earlier anomaly report from the Mediator, something about one of the Sentries briefly going offline in the Marine Parade area, too. Close by. Had that been the boy's doing as well? Smythe had never seen anything like it. The Mediator had never mentioned that this was even possible. Whatever it was, and however he was doing it, it was clearly wasted on this child who just wanted to use the Sentry like an action figure.

Smythe felt a pang of envy. Oh, the things he could do with a direct link to the robots. How much better he could understand them and become part of their world. And would they be more accepting of him in turn? He wondered what fluke had led to the connection being made, and then remembered, with a pang, how he had interrupted Sean's deep scan just as the boy was connecting to the network.

However much Smythe wanted to get closer to the robots, the idea of enduring a deep scan to achieve it wasn't very appealing.

'Bring my mother here,' Sean said, his chest heaving. Smythe could tell the boy was getting more nervous the longer this went on. 'Now!'

'Yes, of course.' Smythe raised reassuring hands, determined to drag this out for as long as possible. How stable was the connection? How much concentration did it require? The boy looked strained. Was he sweating? 'Of course, Sean. Whatever you say.'

At that moment, one of the younger VC ran across the drawbridge. Smythe tried to remember his name. Mayhew, wasn't it? The one who was vying for his attention earlier. He snapped his fingers at him.

'Kate Flynn,' he barked. 'Fetch her, immediately!'

Mayhew, clearly on some other errand entirely, took a moment to register his new orders. He had the cheek to roll his eyes before dashing back inside. Smythe would deal with his impertinence later.

Smythe turned to face Sean again. 'I was like you at your age,' he told him. 'Always rushing into things. Hot-headed. It doesn't get you what you want … you'll learn.'

'All I want is my mother,' Sean answered.

'She'll be here in a minute, lad.' Smythe made more calming gestures. He started to feel more in control again. He'd survived years of dealing with the feral, uncivilised teenagers of Year Ten. He could certainly cope with this. 'Everyone relax, everyone—' Smythe faltered. There was a new noise. The pounding rhythm of galloping hooves. He spun, trying to fathom where it was coming from. '… stay … calm …'

A horse, the big black one from the castle stables, whinnied as it charged out of the keep at breakneck speed, its rider steering for the archway. Smythe recognised the rider immediately.

'Mum!' Sean cried, taking cover behind the Sentry as the horse careered past.

But Kate didn't see or hear him as she ducked down, guiding the horse through the tunnel and out into the night.

'Reckless, no plan, going like a bat outta hell,' Smythe heard Nathan mutter. 'I see where Sean gets it from.'

'Mum, wait!' Sean stepped away from the Sentry, his back to the Snipers.

The distraction was all the first Sniper needed. Smythe heard the buzz of its barrel moving up and down by tiny increments as it took aim.

With a flash that left a tang of ozone in the air, a single laser bolt punched through a tiny gap between the Sentry's head and breastplate.

The Sentry froze for a moment, then, with an ear-splitting boom, it exploded from inside, its breastplate buckling outwards. Sean clutched his head and fell to his knees as the second Sniper also took aim.

DEATH TO ROBOTS!

With a metallic groan, the mortally wounded Sentry fell to the ground, smoke pouring from every opening.

Nathan dared to glance out from the protection of the portcullis where he'd taken cover when the shooting started, and he saw Sean fall behind the downed Sentry, holding his head in pain. The Snipers rained down an incessant hellfire of flashing lasers. The noise was unbearable, hammering Nathan's ears until they rang. Chunks of stone and robot debris fell around Sean as he ducked behind the Sentry, head down.

Alex nudged Nate. He followed her eye-line to see Smythe scuttling away to cower in a corner by the stone keep.

'Sean!' Nathan yelled. 'Hold tight, mate, we'll cover you!'

Sean didn't risk trying to look at him through the blazing Sniper fire, but he did give a thumbs-up.

'Connor, stay out of sight,' Nathan yelled. The little boy, hands clasped over his ears, didn't need telling twice.

'Ready?' Nathan grinned at his sister, more excited than he had ever been in his life, and kind of unable to comprehend what they were about to do. 'Watch this ...'

He and Alex spun on their heels and leaned out of the portcullis, yelling wordless war cries as they strafed the castle roof with gun fire. Their faces were lit by amber muzzle flashes as the

AK-47s bucked and jolted in their sweaty palms. Empty shells spat from the sides of the guns, spinning through the air, and a few hit Nathan's neck, still red-hot and stinging, before tinkling on the cobblestones. Alex screamed like she was on a roller coaster, and Nathan couldn't help himself as he hollered, '*Death to robots!*' at the top of his voice. Their aim was erratic, but it did the trick by forcing the Snipers to retreat behind the battlements.

The guns juddered into silence after just a few seconds of fire, and they jumped back into the safety of the portcullis as Sean got to his feet.

'That's it,' said Alex, breathless. 'We're out of ammo.'

Sean was scrambling towards them.

'C'mon!' Nathan called, just as the sound of grinding metal came from above.

One of the Snipers had already jumped from the battlements and landed directly in Sean's path with a heavy clatter, its segmented legs rippling as they crawled, its gun spinning up to target him.

Instinctively, Sean raised his hand. His implant began pulsing in time with the Sniper's and it stopped dead in its tracks.

'He's doing it again,' Connor nudged Nathan and pointed. 'He's controlling another one.'

'Sean!' Alex cried. 'Sniper up above!'

High on the castle wall, the second Sniper was crabbing left and right, trying to target Sean.

Sean crouched again, eyes closed in concentration, hand extended. Next to him, his Sniper's barrel pivoted upwards. A laser bolt streaked towards the other Sniper and blew it apart into a thousand tiny spiralling fragments that rained down on the courtyard below.

There was a moment of silence and relief that they were all still alive.

Connor peered out cautiously from the shelter of the portcullis. 'How cool was *that*?'

'"Death to robots"?' Alex shook her head wearily at her brother. 'You're such a twat.'

'Come on, misery guts! This is like *Call of Duty* only it's real – we actually get to shoot robots, blow shit up.' He shook the shotgun from his shoulder and gripped it tight, snapping its slider back and forward. 'It's well sick!'

'When can I have a go, Nate?' Connor pleaded, hopping from heel to heel.

'In a minute, mate. Cool your balls.'

'God, my heart's beating like a rabbit's.' Alex puffed, patting her chest.

'That was the *best*.' Nathan said. 'We should definitely do this more often.'

'I have to admit, that was bloody awesome.' Alex said. 'But we need to get moving and catch up with Kate.'

Alex, Nathan and Connor were ready to move. Sean hesitated, his arm still outstretched towards the Sniper.

'C'mon, Sean,' Alex said. 'Move your arse.'

'Yeah,' Sean said, not moving at all. 'Trouble is, if I let go and this thing wakes up again … well, then we're all smoked.'

And suddenly all the fun was sucked out of the air. He was right. The second that thing woke up, it would fry them all. Nathan checked the magazine on his AK-47. Definitely empty. Only a few shotgun shells to defend themselves with, and he doubted they could outrun a Sniper. Six legs versus two.

'Hold on …' Sean said, with a look that Nathan had come to understand meant *I'm about to try something monumentally stupid*.

Sean closed his eyes, clenched his fist and punched down. The Sniper vibrated violently, and for a second Nathan was sure it was about to explode, but then it folded in on itself, forming a cube.

'What'd you do?' he breathed.

'Shut it down.' Sean said, sounding more surprised than any of them. 'Waitasec, one more thing … yeah …' He reached out again. There was a whirring noise followed by a clunk as a smaller cube fell from the Sniper onto the flagstones.

'Hey look,' Connor sounded delighted. 'It pood out a little cube!'

'What the hell is that?' Alex asked, inspecting it more closely.

'Its battery …' Sean shrugged. 'I think. Job done.' He puffed his cheeks and exhaled, glad it was over.

'Come on, Nathan!' Connor begged, desperate to have a go with one of the guns. 'My turn!'

But Nathan's eye was caught by a movement in the shadows.

Smythe. The old bastard had seen his chance, jumped out of the shadows and raced into the castle.

'Sorry, mate,' Nathan said, grim-faced. 'Unfinished business.'

He ran after Morse Code Martin's murderer, ignoring the cries of Alex and Sean to come back.

Smythe wasn't fast but he did know the castle better than Nathan. He ducked through hidden doors, up spiralling stairwells. But there were no VC left to help him; they all appeared to have legged it at the first sign of trouble. Smythe kept heading up and up.

'Go on, run, you knobber!' Nathan yelled after him, panting as his feet slapped on the worn stone steps of the castle. 'I'm gonna blow your bloody head off!'

Nathan kicked open a door and found himself on the roof, surrounded by a mix of ancient crenellations and modern glass skylights. He peered over the side. Nothing but a dizzying drop.

Smythe was directly opposite him, alone and charging along a narrow walkway. He looked desperate, shuffling from battlement to battlement, glancing over the edge for any sign of help.

Nathan had him cornered. And now he didn't know what to do.

Up to this point, Nathan's mind had been filled with revenge fantasies of blasting Smythe. He'd rushed after him fuelled by

174

adrenalin and anger, but now that it came to the crunch he wasn't sure he could go through with it. The biggest thing Nathan had ever killed was a spider that had leapt off the shower nozzle and into his hair. He'd shaken it off, stamped on it and washed it away. And then felt guilty about it for weeks afterwards.

Smythe was a bastard, but he was also a human. And now he was backed into a corner, unarmed, and Nathan could see the old man's hands trembling with fear.

'Don't do anything stupid, lad,' Smythe said. 'You're not a murderer, are you?'

'No, but you are.' Nathan raised the gun and took aim.

'What I do, I do for the greater good,' Smythe said, defiant. 'What you're about to do is cold-blooded slaughter. I don't think you want that on your conscience, do you?'

Nathan was closer now. He caught the scent of Smythe's sweat mixed with … was that aftershave?

'Well, we're in a bit of pickle then, aren't we?' said Nathan, inching closer. ' 'Cos if I let you go, you'll have me in a Deep Scanner before I get back downstairs. But maybe … maybe a warning shot will give you a heart attack? We can put that down to natural causes. You end up dead and I get to sleep at night. How's about that for a deal?'

'It won't be long before reinforcements arrive,' Smythe said, glancing over the edge again. Was he going to jump?

'How about a flesh wound?' Nathan said. 'In the arm or the leg.'

'Best turn yourself in, boy.' Smythe raised a hand. 'Don't be a hero. There's no such thing.'

A hero. Nathan thought back to Morse Code Martin's words. Men who put their lives behind them. Those who sacrificed everything so others could live in peace. Scaring an old man wasn't particularly heroic, and Nathan knew he wasn't a hero. But that didn't mean there were none left.

'A good friend of mine would disagree with you about that,'

Nathan said. 'This is for Morse Code Martin.' He pulled on the trigger.

The shotgun wasn't like the rattling AK-47. This was like a wrecking ball punching him in the shoulder. The gun jerked up, powder and flame billowing around him as it fired into the night sky.

Smythe, clearly terrified, tipped over the edge.

Nathan held his breath. Had he hit him? He rushed forward to see Smythe tumbling through empty air, thumping onto the tarpaulin of a makeshift car shelter. Its ropes snapped and the tarp enveloped Smythe as he sank to the ground.

Smythe clambered to his feet, clutching his side in agony, but otherwise unhit and unharmed. Then he ran like hell.

Breathing again, Nathan took aim – somehow it felt easier shooting at a human from a distance – and once more the shotgun kicked into his shoulder, sending him stumbling, thumping onto his back and knocking the air out of his lungs.

'Shitcakes!' He jumped to his feet, catching sight of Smythe as he vanished into the darkness.

Nathan cursed again, but then his eyes drifted to the shattered roof of the car shelter below, where two parked quad bikes flanked a Jeep.

KATE'S ESCAPE

Kneeing Smythe in the balls had felt like a good idea at the time, but all it did was bring out his darker side. He appeared to take great delight in telling Kate the truth about the robots' purpose, and it sickened her. She knew she had to get away and find Sean, or Danny, if he was still alive, and just hide, find a cave somewhere, anywhere, and stay out of sight until it was all over. Beyond that, she didn't have much of a plan, and none of it could come to anything while she was locked up in a castle keep.

Her first opportunity came not ten minutes after Smythe hobbled away. There was a knock, followed by the grinding of a key in the lock and the door squeaking like a cat in pain. A young VC member entered carrying a tray of sandwiches and a glass of milk, and Kate was sure he was familiar. A student from her past. The face had more spots now, and a few wisps of bum-fluff on the chin, but he was definitely one of hers. As he placed the tray down on the banqueting table, she caught a warm waft of stale body odour mixed with an overcompensation of Lynx deodorant, the latter no doubt a benefit of joining the VC.

'Steven Mayhew,' she said with a faint smile. 'Is that you?'

'I ... er ... yes, Miss.'

She knew it. He was much older now, of course, but he'd been in her class before the war. Academically quite bright, but a little peculiar. While all the other kids followed the latest trends, he'd been into cowboy movies and the Beach Boys.

'You were such a nice boy in school,' she said. 'What are you doing with the VC?'

'I got claustrophobia, Miss.'

Oh yes, he'd been a smart-arse, too. Always had an answer. As he set the tray down, her mind pieced together half a plan. She didn't have time to figure out if it would work, so she dived straight in.

'You can leave the key with the food, thank you,' she said with a confidence she didn't entirely feel.

'But …' Steve hesitated. 'You're a prisoner?'

'Don't be ridiculous,' she said, finding her teacher voice again. If there was one thing she did well, it was the teacher voice. It could silence entire classrooms and bend unruly students to her will. 'Did Robin – Mr Smythe – tell you that?'

'Well, yeah,' he said, his Adam's apple bobbing nervously.

Kate extended her hand and the boy cowered, curling the key in his palm. 'I'm not sure I can give it to you, Mrs Flynn—'

'Steven Mayhew, you will give me that key this minute!'

With an almost involuntary jerk of his arm, he handed over the key. She took it and hid it away behind her back.

'I'll tell Mr Smythe,' Steve whined.

'Yes,' Kate said, picking up a sandwich from the tray. 'Fetch him immediately – I want to speak to him. Tell him I'm very upset.'

That confused him. She could see his brain working overtime trying to figure it out: he'd threatened to report her, and now she was demanding to see Smythe. He shuffled back and forth, not sure if he was coming or going.

'Now!' she barked, and the boy dashed from the room.

'Still got it,' she complimented herself as she bit into the sandwich.

*

She gave Steve a few minutes' grace before trying the door. She tried opening it slowly to lessen the noise of its squealing, but all that did was prolong its mournful *creeeeeeeeeak* so much that she thought it would alert the entire castle. She froze, waiting for a VC to start yelling at her, but no one came.

She edged along an upper walkway, looking down into the main hall where a dozen or so VC members busied themselves with files, rebuilding what remained of the records from the old school. Smythe was talking to one of his cronies next to a charred map of the town and the hills around it. She'd need that if she actually got out of the castle, but knew she could never schoolteacher her way into nabbing it.

On the periphery of the main group was Steve Mayhew, desperately trying to catch Smythe's eye. Luckily for her, he was completely ignoring him.

Then a klaxon began to sound throughout the castle. A VC officer crashed into the room and there was some breathless conversation that she couldn't quite make out. Mostly Smythe barking orders. Something about Snipers.

Smythe marched outside and the room cleared. She had no idea what the emergency was and didn't care, but reckoned she didn't have long. She hurtled down the stairs, boots clanking on the metal steps, her hand squeaking on the cold rail. She pushed a table to the wall and clambered onto it. Taking a firm grip on the map, she tugged hard and ripped it free from its pins, and the map gently collapsed like a sail. She folded it badly, tucked it into a back pocket and ran for the nearest exit.

She headed for the arched entrance where they had driven in, but there was no sign of the Jeep and the gate was padlocked shut.

'Shit,' she huffed, catching her breath, kicking at the cobblestones.

What now? This was her only way out. Where might they have

parked it after dropping her off at the drawbridge? Could she make it on foot?

Hope came with the odour of horse manure and a gruff cough. She spun to find the horses she'd seen stabled when she arrived. The three of them were unattended, happily munching on hay. But the black one coughed and snorted again. He was already saddled and his groomed coat shone in the first purple light of dawn. He tapped his hooves impatiently as if to say, *What are you waiting for? Let's go.*

She stroked his mane and made soothing noises as she led him out, before gripping the saddle and pulling herself up onto his back.

The padlocked gate meant she couldn't leave the way she'd come in, so she'd have to shoot for the front gate instead. She could hear shouting coming from that direction. A confrontation. She didn't care what it was, she'd just have to plough straight through and hope for the best. Keep her head down and gallop for the main drawbridge. She pulled on the reins and her steed took off like a steam train. She struggled to keep control, but then realised that even trying was futile. This horse clearly wanted out as much as she did – and appeared to know the way. She was merely a passenger.

They rounded the corner into the outer bailey. Floodlights stabbed into her eyes and she instinctively turned her head, blinking away the blinding blobs in her vision. When she looked back towards the gates, she could just make out the huge silhouette of a Sentry and her heart stopped for a second as she waited for it to take aim. But, strangely, it never moved. Kate might have glimpsed Smythe as she made for the archway. There were all sorts of people milling about, but with the world bucking and jolting around her she couldn't be sure. She thought she heard someone call after her, but if they did it was drowned out by the pounding of the hooves. She ducked down as the horse clattered through the archway, and then they were free.

*

The last time Kate rode a horse was on an adventure weekend with the school. The horse, called Arthur, was close to retirement and had plodded at a gentle clop along quiet country paths in Dorset. The huge black beast she was riding now appeared to think he was in the Grand National with the Devil on his tail. The wind whipped into her face and her eyes were streaming as she clung on desperately. The drumming rhythm of hooves on sand was the only noise as they galloped over grassy dunes onto the beach.

The tide was coming in and the horse's hooves sent sea spray misting into the air. As she thundered along the seafront, she wondered how long it would be before a Sentry or a Drone came for her. She heard the distant tooting of car horns and dared to glance back to see headlights closing in. Two, maybe three, vehicles following her. She shook the reins again and squeezed with her calves – *Keep going, don't stop!* – but the horse's breathing was growing laboured, its hooves landed more heavily and the rhythm of its gallop was slowing.

'C'mon, boy!' she cried. 'Faster!'

She peered ahead to her destination: the hills. Merely dark shadows in the first light, they were oddly flat, like stage scenery. And they also looked so far away. No matter how hard she drove the horse, they got no closer. She was never going to make it.

Lights flashed as the vehicles pulled onto the beach, flanking her. Cars, not robots.

The larger one – the Jeep that Smythe had brought her in – peeled right and skidded around in front of her.

Her horse reared up in fright and Kate fell. Her stomach flipped and her mind stalled with panic; the last thing she needed was a broken collarbone – or worse.

She tucked and rolled instinctively, tumbling across the hard sand. She came to a stop a little out of breath, but mercifully all in one piece.

She looked around for her ride, but the horse was already

fleeing down the beach against the backdrop of a stunning sunrise, purples and reds glittering in the waves.

Oh well, it was a good try. Better than she might have hoped. She just wished she could see Sean and Danny again before she died. She raised her hands in surrender and wondered what Smythe would do to her now she knew the robots' secret.

She squinted through the glare of the headlights. Next to the Jeep were two quad bikes and the people on them were calling her name. Familiar voices.

And then a figure stepped out of the Jeep, silhouetted at first.

'Mum!' said Sean.

Her heart leapt and tears flooded her eyes.

She didn't know how he could be here, but she didn't care. Her whole body wilted with relief that he was still alive. She pulled him to her and gave him the hug to end all hugs.

'Thank God you're okay!' she said, half-laughing, half-crying. 'But did you have to throw me off the horse?'

She waved over Connor, Alex and Nathan, and they joined in the hugging, too – and only after that did Kate notice Sean's implant. Black and dead, like a robot's. She touched it gingerly.

'I guess we've got some catching up to do,' he said.

She had a million questions, but then the sand began to tremble.

'Sean!' Nathan pointed further up the beach.

Kate's heart sank as a Sentry powered across the sand, its lamp sweeping from side to side as it ran tirelessly towards them.

She backed away, pulling on Sean's arm, but he stood his ground.

'Sean, run!'

'CITIZENS, RETURN TO YOUR HOMES IMMEDIATELY.'

Silhouetted by the rising sun, Sean reached out, fingers splayed.

'YOU— HAVE— HAVE— HAVE—' The Sentry began to falter, its voice stammering.

Sean made a fist and the Sentry stumbled to its knees. In one swift motion, it powered up its weapon, placed the nozzle under its chin and, with a boom that made Kate's ears ring, blew its own head off.

The orange glow of the explosion illuminated Sean's face. He had a strange confidence about him that Kate had never seen before. For a moment he looked like Danny.

The Sentry's remains slumped onto the sand with a noise like a power tool grinding on stone.

'How …' Kate gasped in the silence that followed. 'How did you do that?'

But before he could answer, Nathan took Kate's arm and led her towards the Jeep.

'Can you drive, Mrs Flynn?' he asked. 'I nearly crashed us … Twice.'

Alex took Kate's other arm. 'We've got to sort out your implant, Kate. Er … is it okay if I electrocute you?'

'What?'

'It really hurts,' Connor said, with a grin, 'but it's so worth it.'

At the sound of a distant howl, they all turned back to the castle as half a dozen Air Drones screamed in, circling the castle keep like cops at a crime scene, searchlights blazing. Without a second thought, Kate jumped into the driver's seat, twisted the ignition key and stomped on the accelerator.

FIFTEEN HOURS AND
FORTY-TWO MINUTES

Robin Smythe had never been an athletic man. Oh, he understood the need for sport, particularly for teenage boys. What better outlet for their aggressive, hormonal urges than eighty minutes of rugby or a long run through the mud, followed by a cold shower? But he had never been much of a participant himself.

So he was less than prepared for his tumble from the top of the castle.

That idiot boy had pursued him with a bloody shotgun, of all things. And Smythe's Volunteer Corps had proved to be cowards of the first order, so he found himself alone and cornered on the rooftop.

Thinking back, he was amazed by how calmly he'd taken the decision to jump. He glanced at the tarpaulin below, reflecting on how small it looked from up here. But some kind of Darwinian survival instinct overtook him and, with nothing more than a step, he found himself falling through empty air. He was grateful that the tedium of his life didn't flash before his eyes, though the sensation did make him recall an incident at school when three of the bigger boys had shoved him off the top diving board at the local swimming baths. He had enough time for three short breaths and a twinge of regret before he slammed into the tarpaulin. Thankfully, it merely sagged under his weight like a baggy trampoline. The wooden struts holding it up slowly bent, then snapped and helped slow his descent even more. The tarp wrapped around him and delivered him almost gently to the ground.

Barely believing his luck, Smythe threw off the tarp, scrambled to his feet and ran. The boy took another shot and Smythe's back tensed, anticipating the agony of a gunshot wound, but it never came. Thankfully, the idiot's aim was as bad as his grasp of the English language.

He soon found himself breathless and bent by the doors to the castle kitchens. Hands trembling, he staggered in. 'McGrath! McGrath!' he called. 'Anyone?'

The first person he found was a teenage VC wandering aimlessly along the corridors. His mind scrabbled to remember the lad's name.

'You!' he panted. 'Mayhew, isn't it?'

'Ah, Zone Chief Smythe,' the boy said, with the guilty look of someone caught stealing from the biscuit jar. 'I can explain. Y'see, *shesaidthatyousaid* that she could have the key, so I was coming to you, to check, like, when you said—'

'What are you blethering on about, idiot boy?' Smythe took off his cap and swiped the teen about the head with it. 'Go and find McGrath. Now!'

Mayhew scurried away, a protective hand over his head.

It took all night for his VC team to regroup, and he assembled them in the main hall to give them a proper dressing-down. He was not normally one for shouting or screaming, but he had to concede that it felt good to vent, and the forlorn looks on their faces gave Smythe a sense of accomplishment.

'I should have you all bloody deep-scanned!' he said. 'Every one of you. Not that the robots would find much use for your empty minds. If you had half a brain between you, you'd be bloody dangerous.'

The main door creaked open and McGrath strode in, bathed

in the glow of the outer bailey's floodlights. There was something about his deputy's overconfident gait that Smythe didn't like. Everyone here knew Smythe had become Zone Chief by reporting his predecessor to the Mediator for sedition and recommending a deep scan for the elderly man. Now Smythe feared that McGrath, an ambitious and aggressive brute to say the least, had something similar in store for him.

'The Mediator wants to see you,' McGrath said, with a barely concealed smirk.

Smythe nodded grimly. If this was it, then he wanted to go out with honour. He thrust his cap at McGrath. 'Organise the search parties. She took the bloody map, so find another. They're probably heading for the woods, but don't count on it. Put out word that my reward still stands.' Smythe twisted his cap onto his head. 'I'll be back as soon as possible,' he said, more in hope than certainty.

And now he found himself standing by a scorched crater at a desolate end of the seafront. The stinging stench of rocket fuel filled the grey morning air as the Cube hovered above him, its thrusters growling as they kept it in position. The heat was incredible, slowly reddening Smythe's face. The Cube was open, split into four vertical sections. The super-hot core and the Cube's innards were exposed, revealing a latticework of metal struts, coiled cables and pulsing blue flashes that left glowing after-impressions on Smythe's retinas.

A ring of robots were gathered beneath it, some attached to the Cube by thick cables, powering up, recharging.

The Mediator stood beside him, its face motionless. 'The boy's interaction with our network is without precedent,' the Mediator said. Its vocalisation changed every time they met. Made up of the millions of small boys' voices accrued by the Robot Empire during the occupation, each word was selected from a vast database of phrases, utterances and dialects deep-scanned from children's minds. New ones were added every day. Billions more would follow. 'He will be examined,' the Mediator continued. 'We must capture him alive, Zone Chief Smythe.'

Smythe tried to bury his resentment. Oh, so now they were they interested in capturing Sean, when he presented some kind of risk to them.

'How did he make the connection?' he asked.

'The subject was connected to the network during the deep scan, but as for how he remains connected …' The Mediator paused. 'We do not know.'

Quite a confession for a civilisation determined to know everything, Smythe thought.

The Mediator continued, 'A deep scan has never been interfered with like this before.' It glanced briefly at Smythe, a hint of reproach in its voice. 'We suspect a unique, improbable and therefore unforeseen sequence of events led to this peculiarity.'

'Can't you just lock him out?' Smythe asked.

'To reconfigure the system would entail taking every robot offline. It's impossible.'

Smythe watched as a Sentry, sluggish and slow and in need of a recharge, took position under the Cube. A cable snaked down with a hiss and latched on to it.

'You can track his mother, though,' Smythe said, convinced that Kate's implant would still be active. 'Let me know where she is and I'll—'

The Mediator raised a hand, silencing Smythe. Its black implant pulsed as it received a communication.

'Citizens with disabled implants are at large in the Marine Parade area,' the Mediator said, echoing the message.

Bloody Monique and her band of misfits, Smythe thought, grinding his teeth. He should have had them all deep-scanned years ago.

He'd suggested it, but the Mediator was concerned about the extra resources that such an unscheduled scan would require.

'This civil disobedience spreads like an organic virus,' the Mediator continued. 'The boy's mother is not a priority.'

'But if we have her, we'll have him!' Smythe snapped, raising his voice. 'Can't you see that?'

Smythe instantly knew he'd overstepped the mark. The Mediator turned away from the recharging robots to face him.

'Such aggression,' it said, with a hint of preprogrammed disappointment. 'Perhaps your level of emotional intelligence is inappropriate for the role you have been assigned?'

Smythe's mind scrambled for an answer that wouldn't see him strapped into a Deep Scanner. 'I was his teacher, Mediator,' he said quickly. 'I know how he thinks. I'll find him.'

No reply. The Mediator's eyes were a silvery blank, devoid of any feeling. The white lights on its implant flickered as it consulted the robot hive mind.

'Everybody in this zone is now scheduled for a deep scan,' the Mediator said. 'A Skyship carrying four thousand and ninety-six Deep Scanners is en route. It will arrive in fifteen hours and forty-two minutes, approximately.'

And just like that, an entire town – Smythe's own town – was condemned to die.

'Good God,' Smythe muttered. It was so simple. So … efficient. He momentarily felt something like sorrow for those who were about to become part of the robot database. But then again, if they'd been more helpful during the invasion they might be standing by his side now, looking forward to a future in the Robot Empire. And then he felt a surge of excitement. His new life was about to begin, just as soon as he'd sorted Sean out. That was his top priority now.

A loud hiss came from one of the robots as its charging cable detached. The Mediator began to walk towards the beach, the refreshed and fully recharged Sentry by its side acting as body-guard.

'The operation will commence at noon tomorrow,' it told Smythe. 'If the boy is still at large ... the first deep scan will be yours, Zone Chief Smythe.'

THE STANDING STONES

The wind buffeting him, Sean could barely breathe as he twisted the quad bike's accelerator and gunned up the hill. Alex whooped as she pulled up beside him.

His mum was driving the Jeep, with Nathan and Connor standing up through the sunroof, arms raised, relishing their new freedom and shouting to the skies. The air was so clean and crisp it made his teeth ache.

'Bleaugh!'

Sean glanced over to see Connor trying to scrape something off the end of his tongue.

Nathan yelled over the roaring wind. 'What?'

'Swallowed a fly!' Connor chuckled, and everyone relaxed.

Gentle green hills rose on either side. Now and then they saw cows and sheep in distant fields and Sean wondered if there were still working farms under robot and VC supervision, or if these animals had been left to wander after the invasion. They didn't stop to investigate. There was no time to waste and they had too far to go.

Sean knew the hills would soon descend into rocky valleys, and beyond that was a wood with overgrown pathways. The ground was already uneven and his forearms ached from the constant tension of hanging on to the quad bike's handles.

Connor's bladder let them down again and they found a place to stop by a stream, parking under the cover of a row of huge willow trees. While Connor had a pee in the babbling brook, the others headed upstream a little way to fill their water bottles.

'You look tired,' Alex said as she joined him, their bottles glugging as they filled. 'You should have a proper rest. You haven't stopped since the castle.'

'Maybe.' He stifled a yawn. 'When we get to the standing stones. We're too exposed here.' She was right, though. He was tired. The showdown at the castle had taxed him both physically and mentally. To go from operating one Sentry like a remote-control toy to suddenly steering one in a firefight took its toll.

'What was it like?' Alex asked. 'Controlling those robots?'

'It takes a lot of concentration,' he said. 'Just to reach in and make it obey any kind of basic command is really hard ... and you can feel the weight of each move. Getting a Sentry to raise its arm is like lifting weights. It takes real effort. Snipers are different,' he continued, happy to finally share this with someone. 'I have a better level of control. They're smarter, faster and more sophisticated, they have this targeting system that ...' He trailed off.

'What?'

'It's difficult to explain,' he said, deciding to keep the really weird bit to himself. It happened when he first connected with the Sniper: he discovered that he could somehow see, in his mind's eye, the machine's heads-up display. He'd experienced similar set-ups on games and flight sims, but this had no recognisable numbers or words, just pulsing circles that moved faster when they found a target. And when he latched on to the Sniper, he'd seen that its cross hairs were targeted on him.

He'd been looking at himself through the Sniper's electronic eyes.

That was too weird, like an out-of-body experience.

'So do you think you could control a Drone?' Alex said, eagerly. 'Think you could fly?'

'I dunno,' he said. 'I'd need to be close enough to control it. When I'm in range of a Sentry or Sniper I get this weird twinge here.' He gestured at his implant. 'It's like I'm walking into a bubble … a control zone. I don't understand it, to be honest.'

'Well, it looked pretty cool,' she said. 'Almost worth a deep scan to—'

'No,' Sean cut her off. 'It really isn't.'

'Sean, I'm sorry,' she said, taking his hand. 'I was only joking.'

'I know, I know.' He thought back to the scan. The pain and the unravelling of his mind. 'It's like … you're becoming one of them. You lose all feeling. There's only your mind and your heartbeat. I could hear your voices … in the dark … that's what kept me going. Any kind of human contact. Any kind of warmth.'

Alex squeezed his arm. 'You won't have to go through it again,' she said. 'None of us will.'

He thought for a moment, staring into space. 'Here's hoping.'

'C'mon, everyone,' Nathan called. 'Let's keep moving. Chop-chop.'

He looked jittery to Sean, and he was constantly looking back the way they'd come.

'What's up with you?' Sean asked.

'Mate, let's not hang about,' he said. 'After what Kate told us in the car, we really don't want to get caught.'

'What?' Sean looked to his mum. 'What did you tell them?'

And so Kate, with interruptions from Nathan to get on with it, told them what Smythe had told her. The robots' plan to deep scan everyone. Their mission to know everything. It all clicked with what the Mediator had told them while Morse Code Martin was being scanned. It made Sean feel sick and he thought back to his first encounter with the Mediator on his doorstep.

'So can we go now?' Nathan already had one of the Jeep's doors open.

The others dashed to the Jeep and quads and were soon heading up towards the hills.

Sean had almost forgotten what it was like, just being able to have fun, to enjoy the freedom to move around as they pleased. He was surprised they hadn't seen any robots since the beach. Though, in a dark part of his mind, he feared they'd be waiting for them at the stones. And then, after what his mum had told them, he wondered if there really was anywhere safe to hide. He shoved that thought aside as Alex buzzed by, overtaking him on her quad.

He tried not to stare directly at her as she passed. Her smile, her long hair fluttering in the wind. He almost didn't recognise her as the girl who used to live next door and moaned about absolutely everything. Thinking back to those times made him realise just how close they'd all been to giving up for good. Alex looked alive again now, a young woman with her whole existence ahead of her, choices to make about how she would live. Would she fight in the resistance? Would she continue her education, or help others, or fall in love, or—?

And then she glanced over at him and he nearly lost control of his bike. He had to swerve to avoid a boulder, trying not to look like he was staring.

'There they are!' Connor cried.

Sean looked to where Connor was pointing. A steep hill rose up before them, an ancient stone wall leading up to tiny dots on its peak. The standing stones.

'Told you this was bullshit,' Nathan said, hands on hips, shaking his head.

Sean ignored him as he moved between the ancient stones. They formed a broken circle and had been covered in graffiti by some mysterious protestor. There was hardly a blank surface. Some of it was the kind of tagging you used to see all over town – Mr Smythe had called it 'the venal outpourings of a diseased mind' in one particularly ranty school assembly – but some of it was specific to the robots. There was a really well-drawn cartoon of a Sentry with its head exploding alongside the words 'Robots sukk!' But some just appeared to be random words thrown together – 'safe', 'riv', 'tim', 'to'.

'"Teh Deh".' Alex squinted at one nonsensical scrawl. 'What does that mean?'

'That the people who did this were mental?' Nathan offered. 'Or maybe this is how ancient man played Scrabble? Y'know, move that stone over there, and suddenly they make a word?'

'C'mon.' Kate clapped her hands, geeing them along. 'They won't be far behind us, get a move on.'

Sean felt vulnerable out here. He looked over at the stone wall, beyond which lay the wood. They'd be safer there, under the cover of the forest canopy. Every second they spent in the open air exposed them to detection by Air Drone.

'Swann told us they "left word here",' he said. 'Find it. Come on, we can do this — uh, oh, sorry!' He'd nearly stumbled straight into Alex coming around the other side of the stone.

'Not exactly making it easy, are they?' she said in a soft voice, flashing him her bright smile. He didn't reply, but instead shuffled left to right, and then – after a flurry of 'sorrys' – he stood back to let her pass. He watched her go, a smile warming his face. He felt comfortable around her now. Back at the house they were always treading on eggshells, waiting for someone to get annoyed by a comment or misunderstanding, but out here there were no games.

Nathan suddenly filled his vision. 'No!' Nathan scowled. 'No way, you're having a bird bath, mate.'

'Having a what?' Sean struggled to keep up with Nathan sometimes. He recalled a phase last Christmas when Nate took up speaking like a cockney after watching too many repeat episodes of *EastEnders*: 'bird bath' equalled 'laugh'.

'Really?' Nathan continued. 'Really? This is my sister! You're practically family!' He gripped Sean's shoulders, steering him away from Alex. 'Seriously, go for a walk, think about it.'

And then Sean realised what Nate was talking about. He wanted to tell his friend it wasn't like that, he was just happy to see Alex happy, but Nathan was already stomping away to look at the stones on the far side of the circle.

'Come see this!' Connor's voice squeaked from somewhere in the labyrinth. 'Hurry!'

At first Sean couldn't find him.

'Down here.' Connor waved.

He found the boy lying on a flat stone that was pointing towards the centre of the circle. Connor patted it proudly. 'The slaughter stone.' He pointed. 'Look ...'

Moments later, everyone was crouching next to Connor and suddenly Nathan's ancient Scrabble idea didn't sound so mad after all. From here some of the words on the stones aligned to spell out a message:

'X the river three times to safety'

Nathan frowned. 'Ecks the river—?'

'"Cross" the river,' Connor corrected him, rolling his eyes.

'This is it.' Sean gripped Connor's shoulders. 'This is the message Swanny told us about. Nice one, Connor.' Sean finally dared to think they might actually make it.

'Well done, Connor,' Kate said, in her encouraging-teacher voice. The little boy beamed like he was about to receive double house points. Then she dashed back to the Jeep and grabbed the map she'd stolen from Smythe's war room.

'Connor,' she called, 'you're lookout!'

He saluted, then stood on the slaughter stone, watching the horizon.

She spread the map across the bonnet of the Jeep and the others gathered round. There was one river snaking through a vast expanse of woodland.

'If we head straight to the river and cross here …' she said, moving her finger over the map.

'We end up in the middle of nowhere.' Nathan snorted.

Alex looked closer, reading aloud some of the place names on the map. 'Carshalton Wall … Stannum Valley … Selforton …'

'I've not heard of any of these places,' Kate said.

'The silver lake, Swanny said.' The map was upside down from Sean's point of view, and he craned his neck to read the tiny place names. 'Any silver lakes?'

'Whoa, waitasec!' Connor piped up from the slaughter stone. 'Stannum … I know that name … erm … ooh …' Connor squinted at them with one eye closed, snapping his fingers in an effort to remember.

'Something boring to do with Vikings?' Nathan suggested.

'No, no … Romans!' Connor's eyes darted as he tried to remember. 'We did a project on it. Stannum is Latin for tin. Tin's a silvery metal, and there's a tin mine in Stannum Valley with a lake, a tiny lake.' Connor turned to Nathan. 'And Vikings are very interesting, actually.'

'He's right,' Kate said, finding a little kidney-shaped body of water on the map. 'And here it is. Connor, you're on top form today!'

The little boy looked happier than they'd ever seen him.

Nathan nodded as he examined the map. 'If I was in the resistance, that's where I'd be – underground, out of sight.'

'Did your uncle in the SAS teach you that?' Sean said, raising a sceptical eyebrow.

'No,' Nathan snapped back with a sneer. 'That's my call, 'cos I'm a survival expert.' And then, in his best Arnie voice, 'Come with me if you want to live.'

'Guys, guys!' Connor again, now pointing to the horizon.

Rising over the crest of the hill they saw a long line of Sentries marching like forensic police looking for clues, their searchlight heads scanning the ground.

'Into the woods,' Sean said, guiding everyone towards the stone wall. 'Let's go, now.'

MARK IX TRAINING MODEL, FULLY RECONDITIONED

Alex's lungs burned as she ran. She'd done more exercise in the last few days than during the last three years combined. She used to watch Sean running up and down his stairs in an effort to keep fit and think he was wasting his time. Now, as she lagged some way behind him, she wished she'd made at least half the effort he had. Her boots were killing her, too, rubbing against her heels and squashing her toes. They were all wearing second-hand shoes in varying degrees of disrepair. Nathan's Converse were coming apart at the seams and the soles of Connor's trainers flapped like clown shoes.

It didn't help that the wood had grown wild. She was sure this used to be National Trust – her mum used to bring her here in the summer – but without anyone to manage it, the place had become overgrown. They were constantly hurdling fallen trees and dragging their feet through long ferns, and each step brought a new ache. What few paths were left were now cracked and riddled with tree roots just waiting to trip you up.

She glanced back, half-expecting to see a Sentry crashing through the trees or a Drone zooming overhead, but none came. But that didn't mean they weren't on their tail, and that didn't mean she was about to stop.

After an hour of almost constant running they came to a bend in the river and Kate called a breather. Alex slumped against a trunk and slid to the ground.

'Tired, Stropasaurus?' Nathan teased her, using a name he'd given her when they were much younger.

'Oh, shh— shh—' She was really having trouble catching her breath. 'Shut up, Nathan,' she finally managed. Her head fell back, exhausted, as Nathan and Sean crouched near the bright green moss-covered stones lining the trickling river. They scooped up mouthfuls of water, slurping it loudly. *Good idea*, she thought, dragging herself upright to join them. The water was freezing, sending an ice-cold jolt from her teeth through her skull and numbing her fingers.

'Wakes you up, doesn't it?' Sean said, splashing some on his face. She watched the rivulets of water cling to his skin. She suddenly wanted to reach up and wipe it away and brush his hair back and hold his face and— Oh, God, what *was* she thinking?

She noticed Nathan behind Sean, glaring at her.

What? She sneered at him, but he just shook his head slowly in disapproval. He really could be a complete dick sometimes.

'Here's the first one!' Kate called from around the bend.

They all got to their feet and followed the sound of her voice to find a rickety wooden bridge. The first one on the map. Cross the river three times, the message had said. So at least they were going in the right direction.

Once over the bridge, Alex looked ahead at the forest before them: a labyrinth of tall fern trees, long branches beckoning them to come and get completely lost in the distant haze.

At Sean's insistence they kept on the move, not running now, but marching. When the sun was directly above them, they stopped again. A lunch-break, Alex guessed, although there wasn't much to eat.

Kate and Connor used his SAS Survival Handbook to choose edible mushrooms from under an uprooted tree. They each had a couple raw. They weren't bad, actually, and at least no one was retching in agony, so they must have picked the right ones.

The wood became more dense and overgrown, and they had to shoulder their way through dense foliage. Thick thorns cut at Alex's ankles and the air was full of tiny midges, and she was careful to breathe through her nose for fear of inhaling any of them.

Now and then they heard rustling nearby and caught glimpses of deer hurrying away from them, bounding through the maze with an energy and confidence that Alex wished she had just a fraction of.

They found the second bridge almost by accident. It was old stone and overgrown with ivy. There were some stepping stones beside it, and Alex and Connor crossed those instead, hand-in-hand.

Sean suggested they stick to the riverbank after that. The wood was too overgrown ahead of them, and he was sure the river would lead them to the next bridge anyway.

That took the longest time. Clinging to the crumbling riverbank, constantly slipping into water so cold it stung any exposed skin, leaving it pink and goosebumpy. Alex grabbed at the stones lining the bank, her fingers slipping on the moss as she inched her way around another bend, swatting and spitting away more bloody midges. Connor was the first to roll up his trousers and just wade in. No one wanted to get wet, but they all had wet feet by now, so what the hell.

Alex was soaked, tired and her hair was full of midges by the time they found the third bridge. She vaguely remembered coming here on a school trip once and drawing it with charcoal. The bridge was supposed to be Roman and was decorated with a carving of a seashell at its apex. As they all climbed the bank beside the bridge, Alex hoped they'd find some sign here, something to tell them that their journey was at an end, but from the look on Sean's face up ahead, she wasn't sure she was going to like what he'd found.

She arrived by his side, short of breath again and depressed to see that the dirt track before them split off in three different directions.

'Oh, great. Now where?' she said, resting her hands on her knees.

Connor was already choosing with his fingers. 'Eeny, meeny, miny, mo—'

'Straight on,' Sean said, in a voice that brooked no argument. 'The lake on the map is in the east, so we keep heading east.'

'East?' Alex frowned. 'How do you know that's east?'

'The sun's going down directly behind us, so I reckon straight ahead is east.'

Alex looked back. The sun had indeed dipped below the tree-line. When did that happen? How long had they been out here? She didn't much fancy a night in the woods. It gave them shelter, but there was something just a little too wild about it for her liking.

But east sounded good. It was better than the middle of no-where, which is where they appeared to be now.

The dirt track was narrow but not overgrown, so Alex dared to hope that maybe someone had been using it recently. Every now and then, Kate and Sean checked the map and they took a breather, but no more than five minutes at a time. Connor, usually so full of energy, was lagging behind with Alex.

The dirt track eventually opened up, taking them onto a rocky rise. Beyond it, the wood sloped downwards at a steep angle, the trees stretching away in neat diagonal rows.

'I don't want to worry anyone,' Nathan said, 'but Connor's starting to look like lunch. I bagsy his legs when we resort to cannibalism.'

'Not helping, Nate,' Alex groaned, her legs starting to feel heavy.

'Actually, a joke probably does help,' he said. 'As self-appointed morale officer, I hereby order you to cheer the hell up.'

'You're the morale officer?' She look appalled. 'Kill me now.'

'Well, that would cheer me up,' he said.

'How about you go and take a running jump?'

'How about you shove your head up your bumhole?'

'Read a lot of Oscar Wilde, do you, Nate?'

'Enough, you two,' Kate warned. 'We're all tired, so pack it in.'

'I hate to resort to this,' Alex said, 'but he started it.'

'Yeah, and you know why?' he said. ' 'Cos if we were all like you, we'd still be stuck at home, moping around in our jim-jams.'

'Guys,' Sean said from the front. 'C'mon, not now.'

'Ah.' Nathan cocked his head to one side. 'I see your boyfriend's sticking up for you.'

'What?' said Sean and Alex simultaneously.

Alex glanced at Sean and found herself blushing. 'I don't know where you dredge these ideas up from, shit-for-brains,' she said, jabbing Nathan in the chest, 'but I'm telling you—'

'Shhh,' Connor said, pointing. 'Look!'

They all froze, following Connor's finger, to see a tiny figure deep inside the maze of trees.

A boy.

'Hey!' Alex cried, waving at him. 'Hello!'

Sean put his arm out, silencing her. It was only then that she realised she could have been waving at a Mediator. She narrowed her eyes, but the wood was getting darker and she couldn't quite make him out.

Then the silhouette turned and ran. Definitely a boy!

They suddenly found the energy to give chase. Alex's heart pounded as she and Connor hurdled fallen tree branches and dodged around tree trunks.

'There!' Connor pointed at a blur of arms and legs as the boy dashed out of sight around a bend.

'Wait!' Sean called. He and Nathan were leading the charge up ahead, but the boy knew the wood and its short cuts and slipped away from them, just a racing shadow glimpsed through the trees.

'We don't want to hurt you!' Kate cried. 'Please wait!'

They stumbled into a clearing and the boy was nowhere to be seen. They regrouped, panting for breath. He'd led them to the edge of the wood. In one direction there was an overgrown field; in the other, more trees. Alex found herself happy to be out in the open again, her breath coming more easily. The confinement of the wood had been getting a bit much.

'Lost him,' Nathan panted. 'Slippery little bugger.'

'What's that?' Connor nodded towards what looked like a crude shelter underneath the canopy of leaves. They shuffled closer. Somewhere in the distance a dog barked and they all froze. They'd heard dogs in the distance in town, but never in the wood so far. It barked again, but sounded even further away. With shared nods, they continued their investigation.

'Hello,' Kate called. 'Anyone there?'

They circled the shelter. It was made of netting and hessian rope propped up with thin branches cut to size. But it wasn't someone's home.

There was something large inside, camouflaged and hidden under a large tarpaulin. The thing's contours were oddly familiar to Alex.

'Everyone grab a corner,' Kate said, making her way to the far side of whatever it was. They did as she said and dragged the tarp to one side, revealing something that made them all gaze wide-eyed in wonder.

'Oh, man!' Nathan looked genuinely amazed. Alex hadn't seen that look on his face for several Christmases.

It was a Spitfire. Alex had never seen a real one before. She'd read about them at school and how these beautiful aircraft had saved Britain in the Second World War, but she didn't realise there were any still in existence. This one was a two-seater model, looking as new as the day it was built. Its paintwork was green and brown camouflage with blue and red roundels on the wings.

Another yellow, red, white and blue roundel was painted on the plane's body. Nathan ran a hand along its wing, tenderly touching the rivets, his eyes bright.

'Mark-nine training model,' he said, stroking its graceful curves like it was ancient treasure. 'Probably converted to a two-seater after the war. Fully reconditioned with four .303 Colt-Browning machine guns.'

Sean looked genuinely amazed at Nathan's sudden knowledge.

'I know stuff, you know!' Nathan said defensively.

From nowhere, Alex felt a sudden surge of pride in her brother. Maybe he wasn't completely useless.

The dog barked again. It sounded closer now. Alex looked around, trying to pin down its location.

'No one's covered up the air intakes,' Nathan said, crouching under the wing for a better look. 'It's been used. Maybe recently. Either way, they left in a hurry.'

'Uh … guys …' Connor said quietly.

Alex turned to see a man moving stealthily over a big smooth boulder. He had a long black, scraggy beard and was holding a modern bow and arrow. The arrow was pointed down, but could be aimed and released at them in an instant. He said nothing, waiting for them to make the first move. Then Alex caught a glimpse of the little boy they'd been chasing earlier as he ran into the arms of a man wearing a red waterproof. And on the rocks behind him were more people. Tens of them, standing silently, watching them. Some carrying sticks, hammers. One had a cricket bat, another a frying pan. One held a German shepherd dog on a rope. It barked at them, tugging on the frayed cord. The people's faces were fearful, unsure what to make of these strangers. Alex was amazed to see that, like Swanny, many had no implants at all, just empty metal cylinders where they had once been.

No one spoke. Kate broke the silence. 'We saw the message on the stones,' she said.

'Swanny told us,' Alex said. 'Remember Swanny?'

'I'm looking for my dad, Danny Flynn.' Sean reached for the photo in his back pocket. 'He was a pilot. Have you seen him? Is he here?'

He unfolded the file photo and showed it to the crowd. People glanced at each other, most with frowns.

Oh, God, he's dead, Alex thought. *Or he's been here and moved on.* She'd hoped this would be the end of their journey, the end of wandering aimlessly and following clues on the vague off-chance that Danny might still be alive. She was tired and wanted to stop, but she knew she wanted to stay with Sean, too. He couldn't go on alone. She was about to take his hand and reassure him, tell him that it would be okay, when the crowd parted silently.

They revealed a man standing at the back of the group. He was wearing an olive flight suit with RAF wings on his left breast. His beard was unkempt. And as he shielded his eyes from the sun, he looked like he'd just seen a ghost.

As did Sean and Kate.

Alex's heart skipped as hopelessness fell away from her. She was suddenly flushed with joy and happiness as she watched her friend whisper one word: 'Dad ...?'

As Sean, Kate and Danny fell into each other's arms, Alex felt Connor's cold little fingers grip hers. The boy was happy for his friend, but there were tears in his eyes and it triggered something in Alex. She suddenly missed her mum and dad like never before. She wanted a family now. A dad to keep her on the right path, a mum to hold her when she was sad, even someone just to piss her off and make up with later.

She gave Connor the very best hug she could.

DANNY

Twenty-five years in the military had taken their toll on Danny. Multiple postings and long hours made it physically and mentally tough, and death was always just round the corner. He had decided it was time for a change, and after two tours in Afghanistan, he had become a different person. No longer the young man looking for action and adventure, he was ready to move on.

He tried training for a while and it was okay, but every few weeks they started with a new batch of rookies on the same equipment, and it got old pretty quickly.

What he really wanted was control over his life again. One home, in one place, one family. So when the opportunity to apply for the Armed Forces Redundancy scheme came along, he jumped at it. His number came up and he got a phone call with a summons to see the wing commander.

He hadn't dared mentioned it to Kate. He wanted to be sure before he brought it up. But he knew it was what she wanted. And the timing would have been perfect, too: just after Christmas. Best present ever.

He didn't regret the life at all. It had been ace. Flying Tornado F3 jets, Pumas, making a difference in Afghanistan, visiting parts of the world he'd only have dreamed of otherwise and working with some of the best people you could ever wish to know. But enough was enough.

He had it all planned out. He promised to take Sean and Kate out for a meal that Sunday and was going to explain it to them. A new life for them all. He could be a proper full-time dad to Sean, and he and Kate could finally get some time together.

Then the phone rang. All leave cancelled. Report to base.

That was more than three years ago. Danny hadn't seen them since, and yet somehow his son, now looking like a grown man, was standing before him, with Kate at his side.

The world stopped moving. He felt giddy, numb, unreal.

'Oh my God,' he muttered.

Kate was speechless, open-mouthed, frozen to the spot, probably feeling exactly what he was now.

He rushed forward to embrace them both. A proper mess of tears and kisses and hugs.

'He told me you were dead,' he said, nearly choking on his own words. 'Smythe said you were dead, the bastard.'

He felt the huge sobs shuddering through Kate's body.

He grabbed Sean's face, unable to grasp how much his boy had grown. 'Look at you! Look at you both!'

He remembered waving goodbye to Sean after the call came. All Danny had known was that it was some emergency. He'd hoped it wouldn't take long, half-expecting a false alarm. 'I'll see you soon,' he'd told him. 'Look after your mother, eh?'

He gave his son just a quick squeeze, thinking he'd probably be home that same night.

Sean was so different then. In the gangly throes of his early teens, still an innocent, a big part of him still a little boy. Danny felt a sudden chill, hoping that some of that innocence remained. Hoping that the war hadn't exposed his son to too many horrors. They embraced again, overwhelmed with relief and happiness, finally reunited as the dimming sunlight filtered through the trees.

Danny, arm-in-arm with Kate, led the gang away from the Spitfire along a winding chalk path.

'I never believed Smythe,' he said. 'I snuck into town every week to look for you. But our street was just a crater.' He choked back his regret. Kate squeezed him tight.

'They rehoused us,' she said. 'Fleetwood Street, near the railway.'

Danny nodded as they stepped beyond the treeline onto a crescent cliff-edge. Below them was a small lake surrounded by the remains of an old tin mine. A rusty, dilapidated sign read:

SILVER LAKE

'This is our home now,' Danny told them, delighted by the smiles on the other kids' faces. Sean had introduced them all, the names still a bit of a blur, but they all knew they were safe here.

He led them down a zigzag walkway, and then along a rickety wooden platform leading to the mine entrance, past a second sign:

DANGER - OLD MINE WORKINGS - KEEP OUT!

The others went about their evening around them. Just ordinary folk washing clothes, skinning deer, repairing shelters, feeding chickens, much of it done under the same kind of hessian cloth camouflage that hid the Spitfire. Danny waved aside the clouds of steam coming from a couple of big steel cooking pots, the meaty scent of rabbit soup hanging heavy in the air. The cooks hallooed with smiles as the gang ducked under pheasant and rabbits hanging from lines. Goats bleated at them as they passed their pens.

'Looks like you've seen some action,' said Nathan, gesturing towards a washing line made from the struts of a Sniper's leg. There was also a basin built from a Drone's battle-scarred fuselage.

'Just bits and pieces we've scavenged,' Danny said.

'Where are the guns?' Nathan asked.

'No,' Danny replied in a firm voice. 'That's over.'

'So ... you're not the resistance?' Alex asked.

Danny shook his head with a rueful smile. 'We keep moving. Hiding. In spring we hunt in the woods, during the summer we follow the river.'

They moved through makeshift children's swings made from rope and car tyres. There were children running around, laughing and playing everywhere, some swimming and splashing in the lake.

Danny noticed a few people stopping and staring at the new arrivals as they passed.

'But that's your Spitfire, yeah?' Nathan asked.

'Sort of,' he replied. 'I was assigned it just before the surrender. I moved it here in case the war ever kicked off again.' He laughed bitterly. 'Feels like a long time ago.'

'I've logged over three hundred hours on a simulator,' Nathan told him proudly, 'and my great-granddad was in the Battle of Britain, so if you ever need a hand—'

'You were in the Air Cadets?'

'Er ... No. *Flight Sim X* on the PC.'

'Ah, okay, right.' Danny gave the kid a smile. All his career he'd met people who thought a few hours on a laptop made them an ace pilot, but maybe now wasn't the time to set him straight.

'Drone! Drone!' cried a voice from above.

Danny glanced up to a lookout positioned on the cliff-top above. Just a silhouette from down here, he pointed north before ducking under a coracle-shaped hide made of interlaced branches.

All around them, people did the same: hurrying into shelters, unhooking washing lines, slipping into the shadows.

Danny grabbed Kate and Sean and dragged them into a shelter, and the other kids followed. Danny scanned the commune and was relieved to see that everyone was hidden away, and the place looked abandoned again. It was a well-rehearsed routine they'd perfected through a combination of drills and genuine scares.

He scanned the sky, looking for the Drone. There it was, nothing more than a tiny dot in the distant blue, a vapour trail curving behind it.

In a few minutes it was gone, fading into the distant clouds. There was a cry of, 'All clear!' and everyone went back about their business.

'How often does that happen?' Sean asked, still watching the skies.

'So much you hardly notice,' Danny said, giving him a reassuring pat on the shoulder.

HIT AND FADE

Wayne's battle-training methods were unorthodox, to say the least. They mostly consisted of an intense night of showing the lads key scenes from *Saving Private Ryan*, *Band of Brothers* and *Heat* on the last working DVD player in the Poseidon Hotel.

He chose his team carefully. Only men he could trust.

Kevin was a copper before the war. That would normally be a black mark against him, but he was smart and fast and had been trained to handle a gun. The fact that he wore a floral dress didn't matter to Wayne. It was all they could find in his size when he arrived at the hotel, and Kevin often spoke of the additional comfort and confidence it gave him. They'd offered to make it into something more manly using one of the little needle-and-thread kits in the hotel's storeroom, but he was used to it now and Wayne had to admit that seeing Kevin in anything other than a dress would just be weird.

Del and Bill were a couple of old men whose minds had gone slightly fuzzy these days, but Wayne knew they'd both lost sons in the war. They were good in a scrap and keen for revenge.

Michael, shiny bald on top with an impressive beard underneath, had proven himself loyal and handy in a fight many times. He was fearless, and his large arms could lob a good home-made explosive further than any of them.

Rigby wasn't the brightest spark, but he was a strong scrapper and, despite what he might tell people, a fearless sociopath who would often jump into a fight just for the fun of it.

And Magpie, because … well, he was mental. He'd started insisting that people now refer to him as Colonel Magnum Pie, but no one had obliged him yet.

Monique wanted them to create a distraction while she emptied the hotel. After three years of incarceration, today was the day they would finally get out. There were more than two hundred people to evacuate, and by her reckoning that would take at least ten minutes. Everyone was drilled on which exit to use and where they should hide afterwards. They were to spread word of how to disable the implants. She hoped that within a few days, a week at most, the whole town would know. Maybe they could spread the word even further if they could get a radio working. Then people could start hitting back. They knew it wouldn't be over quickly, that this was the beginning of a long campaign, but protracted guerrilla warfare was their best hope to defeat the robots. Today was just the beginning.

She and Wayne went through the plan thoroughly. It was simple, but had so much room for error you could drive a bus through it.

They began with very simple hit-and-fade tactics. Nothing too dangerous, just a day of suddenly appearing at one end of town, lobbing a few home-made bombs to spook the VC and robots before disappearing back into the shadows.

They debriefed afterwards, comparing robot reaction times, how the VC worked together in combat – poorly, it turned out – and sharing the best escape routes back to the Poseidon. It was important that they not be traced to the hotel. They couldn't risk jeopardising the main escape.

They woke before first light for the big day.

'All right, lads, listen up.' Wayne stood before them, trying to summon up the spirit of Churchill, Patton or De Niro. 'In the next hour we'll move out to the crossroads at the bottom of the hill in front of the hotel. We'll start a bit of aggro and draw the robots off while Monique evacuates everyone through the back door into the alley by the old chippy. We have to keep 'em busy for a good ten minutes. That might not sound like much, but believe me, it'll feel like a bloody eternity.'

Magpie raised his hand. 'Can I use my grenade?'

'Now, don't take the piss, Magpie,' Wayne snapped. 'I won that from you fair and square. It's *my* grenade now.' Magpie sulked, arms folded like a child. Wayne had won the grenade in a card game from Magpie, who assured him that it was a souvenir from the Falklands War and still had plenty of bang left in it.

'I want you, Kevin, Rigby and Michael on the roofs with guns. Two on the pub, two on the flats. Crossfire. Understand?'

'Gotcha, boss.' Michael saluted. Wayne was happy to have a calming influence like Michael around Magpie and Rigby. The fact that he was a former biker who had opened fire on the robots yesterday while screaming, '*Kill me! Kill me! I dare you to kill me!*' said a lot about Magpie's and Rigby's relative states of instability.

'Del, Bill,' Wayne turned to the older men, 'are the fuses ready?'

'They're ready,' Bill replied. 'But you know how unreliable they are.'

They'd carefully removed the detonation fuses from all the Poseidon residents' redundant implants. Having tested them on the hit-and-fade missions, they soon learned that they didn't always work.

'One on its own, no chance,' Del said. 'Bunch a few of them together and they're more likely to go off, but then we get less of 'em, so ...'

'Gotcha.' Wayne nodded. 'We're not looking to carpet-bomb 'em, just make a distraction, so we only need a few but we need 'em to count.'

Del and Bill nodded.

'Now, I'm not going to lie to you boys,' Wayne said. 'There's every chance this'll be a one-way trip, but I want you to know that I chose you all because you're the best. We've all got plenty of reasons to show these metal bastards what we're made of, and we've waited a long time to do it. So go out there today and make me proud. Do it for your loved ones, the ones you've lost and the ones we leave behind.'

He produced a bottle of champagne from under the table. A bottle from Monique's personal stash.

'Gird your loins with this, gentlemen.' He popped the cork and handed it round. 'No more moonshine for you. This is the breakfast of warriors.'

They took up positions at a crossroads on a steep road that led down to the beach and waited. Wayne stood in the doorway of an abandoned house, absently turning Magpie's antique grenade in his hand like a rosary. After only a few minutes, they felt the ground begin to tremble with an all-too-familiar rumble: a Sentry on its routine patrol.

Wayne signalled to Del and Bill, who were waiting in an alley opposite. He saw sparks as they lit the fuses on their detonator clusters. Wayne wasn't particularly religious, but he said a little prayer that they would still work. He'd been planning this in his head for the last three years. His dreams were filled with fantasies of revenge, and now it was crunch time.

The Sentry came thumping around the corner. In this narrow street it looked bigger, somehow, but that was why they chose this spot: less room for the clanker to manoeuvre and a steep incline to mess with its stability. Wayne nodded up to where Michael and Magpie were lurking between pyramid-shaped skylights on the roof of the old pub. Then he looked up and to the left to see Kevin and Rigby move into position on the roofs of the block of flats next door.

They opened fire with their guns. Short bursts as instructed, just enough to engage the Sentry and loud enough for Monique to hear them. It was the signal to begin the evacuation. Wayne pictured the frightened people leaving the Poseidon right now. They were all depending on his team. The gunfire should hopefully draw away the Poseidon's own Sentry, leaving the street outside empty for them to do a runner.

The Sentry powered up its weapon-arm. There were no warnings if you opened fire on a robot – they met aggression with lethal force. A bright beam strafed the pub roof, turning bricks to dust, but Michael and Magpie had already backed away.

It then turned on the flats, but Kevin and Rigby were long gone.

'Del, Bill – now!' Wayne cried, and two black rectangles came spinning through the air. Covered in salvaged fridge magnets, the makeshift bombs slapped onto the Sentry's left leg, their fuses sparkling. Wayne put his hands over his ears and ducked down as an ear-splitting boom bounced off the walls.

The Sentry's leg smoked, twisted and buckled as it fell to its knees. It raised its gun towards the alley and fired, but Del and Bill were already gone.

Wayne saw a movement out of the corner of his eye. Silhouetted by the bright sea, Kevin and Rigby were running to safety at the bottom of the street. The Sentry had seen them, too, and raised its weapon as it crawled along.

Kevin had managed to scarper out of sight, his dress fluttering as he ran. But there was a flash and Rigby was ashes on the breeze.

'No!' Wayne cried, pulling the pin from the antique grenade in his hand. He ran up the spine of the crawling Sentry and shoved the bomb in where the head met the neck. He then jumped clear, landing badly. There was a crack, followed by a lightning bolt of agonising pain shooting up his leg. He'd broken his ankle.

As he rolled in pain, there was another flash, then a boom, and the Sentry's head shattered into tiny pieces.

Wayne whooped in triumph through gritted teeth, but the ground was shaking all around him. More Sentries. Then came the howl of approaching Air Drones.

His boys had got away. Only Rigby gone. He'd miss the old nutter, but compared to Wayne's worst-case scenario, this was a good result – he'd expected them all to be toast before it was over. He could try to get away himself but his ankle was in agony, and even with two good legs he knew how that would end. He preferred to go out facing his enemy, and maybe buy his mates a little more time.

A Sentry appeared at the top of the street. 'CITIZEN, RETURN TO YOUR HOME IMMEDIATELY.'

'Well,' said Wayne getting up on his one good leg, 'we got a problem, sunshine, 'cos I don't have a home any more. You clankers took it from me.'

'YOU HAVE TEN SECONDS TO RETURN TO YOUR HOME.'

'And you have ten seconds to kiss my arse.'

'Wait!' called another voice.

Wayne turned to see a handful of armed VC come running up from the beach, led by the Deputy Zone Chief. 'Authorisation code 97-DZCTM.'

'Oh, you tosspot, McGrath,' Wayne spat. 'This was my moment of glory. I've been waiting for this—'

But McGrath raised the butt of his AK-47 and smashed it into Wayne's face, and everything went dark.

DONALD THE WATCHMAKER

Donald had found himself a room in a quiet corner of the old mineshaft. It was deep down and could be unbearably hot some nights, but it was away from the hurly-burly around the main entrance. Most people tried to get a spot near the exit so they could flee in the event of an emergency, but Donald preferred the solitude and the darkness.

He adjusted the flame on his oil lamp, better to see the implant on the boy's neck. His name was Connor, and like all small children, he was a bloody fidget. Wriggling on the bench that Donald and Danny had built for removing implants, the lad would appear to settle, then suddenly jerk his legs or arms, or decide to explore his nose with a skinny finger.

'Keep still, boy,' Donald snapped. 'One false move and I end up covered in your brains, and I've just washed this shirt.'

'Sorry.' The boy blinked rapidly, twitched his nose and suddenly froze in position.

Donald was impressed. 'Very good. Perfect, in fact. Stay just like that for a few minutes.'

He pulled over a rusty trolley laden with his equipment. He donned a pair of magnifying eyeglasses, light, wiry things that looked a little like mini night-vision goggles. He squeezed a button on the side and two small white lights glowed into life. He then unrolled a cloth bag containing tiny pliers, pincers, tweezers, screwdrivers, hammers and knives.

'Are you a dentist?' Connor asked, suddenly concerned.

'No.' Donald *had* removed a couple of people's teeth while he'd been here, but he wasn't about to worry the boy with that.

'What are they, then?' the boy asked.

'My tools,' Donald replied. 'Actually, more than that, they were my livelihood. The first thing I grabbed when I was rounded up.'

'What did you do?'

'Repaired watches,' Donald said, moving the magnifying glasses closer to his eyes and adjusting the focus. 'I had a little hut facing the sea. People would ask me to fix their watches and that's what I did all day. I stopped at noon for a cup of tea and a bun and I watched the sea change colour as the sun moved across the sky.'

'Sounds nice.'

'It was bloody marvellous.' Donald sat back for a moment, relishing the memory. 'Sometimes people asked me to make a watch or a clock for a birthday or anniversary. Y'know, I was once commissioned by the mayor to make a pocket watch to commemorate the centenary of the old railway.'

The boy suddenly sat bolt upright, kicking the trolley and sending Donald's tools clattering to the ground. 'I've seen it!' he said. 'It's in a glass cabinet at the railway museum.'

'When?'

'Just a few days ago.'

Donald felt his insides warm. That was the first good news he'd heard in years. He quizzed the boy further as he gathered his tools and there was no doubt that it was indeed his pocket watch. It had somehow survived all the chaos of the invasion. Perhaps one day he would see it again.

'Okay, lie back down and keep completely still,' he told Connor as he leaned in. He took his finest tweezers and began to lift the implant's outer edge away from the skin.

'This might sting a bit, son,' he said quietly. 'I need to remove the glue they used first. But try not to move, okay? Otherwise, *kaboom*.'

'Okay.' Connor nodded.

'Yeah, er, and no nodding,' he snapped, suddenly moving back. 'Otherwise ...'

'Otherwise, *kaboom*,' Connor said, keeping perfectly still. 'Sorry.'

The others watched him as he worked his way around the edge of the implant, slowly peeling it away from the boy's skin. Danny's wife and son were there, and their friends. He was used to having an audience. People were always fascinated, but he suspected that they also wanted to be there just in case it went wrong.

Danny was telling them his story as the oil lamp flickered.

'The war lasted eleven days, but God only knows how we survived even that long,' he said, slowly shaking his head. 'As soon as the fighters were in range, they plucked entire squadrons out of the sky and dashed them against the hills below.'

Donald had seen it. His flat at the top of his building had given him a front-row seat to the conflict, if you could call such a one-sided fight that. On the news he'd seen the world's armies fall back again and again.

'We examined our strategy,' Danny continued. 'Tried to learn from their mistakes, but how do you defeat an enemy who can control your electronics? It hit us hard. We weren't used to being beaten.'

Donald had loosened the implant from the boy's skin. Now he gently elevated one edge and held the gap open with his three-inch divider while he reached in with his smallest anchor screwdriver. The robots didn't use anything like a regular screw, of course, but their technology wasn't as advanced as people assumed. In fact, it was often crude and blunt. If humans had designed the implant they would have spent time perfecting it, miniaturising it, refining the curves, reducing weight and sizing it down to ensure maximum comfort for the wearer. Donald got the impression that the robots cared not a jot for any of that, figured 'That'll do' when they had something which worked and started the production line the same morning. He noticed this attitude in the design of their craft too – simple Cubes, Skyships that were basically slabs of metal held aloft by gigantic jets, Snipers little more than guns on legs. All simple and functional.

Now his divider was in place, he could see a tab that could be slid to one side with a gentle nudge from his screwdriver.

'On the tenth day of the war, they finally figured it out,' Danny continued. 'I was ordered to commandeer a Spitfire from a collector in Duxford. It was one of the few left that could fly.'

'A Spitfire,' asked Nathan. 'Against Drones?'

'Mechanical flight system,' Danny replied. 'No electronics for the bots to control. They were able to access anything with a microchip … Like I said, wiped us out without even firing a shot.' Danny paused for a moment, no doubt reliving the memory. Donald had been witness to many of the pilot's sleepless nights, brought on by his survivor's guilt.

'But a Spitfire,' Danny said, 'well, that's just me, the stick, the pedals and some cables. More of a fair fight. Me and the team spent three days prepping it for combat, then it all went quiet. The orders stopped coming and the radio went dead.'

The tab Donald had been nudging finally gave way. Connor's implant was looser now, but still not free. There were three more similar tabs to move.

'Me and the team were racked with guilt,' Danny said. 'If it wasn't for the orders to grab the Spit, we'd most likely be dead along with everyone else. We ran through our options: we could launch a futile attack, a last gesture of defiance, or we could surrender. We took a vote.

'We hid the Spit in the woods, hoping that one day we'd be able to use it, and headed back to town, arms raised in surrender.

They split my team up. I still don't know what happened to them. I hoped they were okay, but all I wanted was to find you guys again.' He squeezed Kate's hand and nodded at his son.

'Smythe made endless promises about finding you, and I stupidly believed him,' Danny said. 'I was on ration duty, sorting the daily deliveries at the shelter in the school. Smythe asked me join the VC. I was tempted. I wanted to help, but I didn't want to become … him.' Donald remembered how the word 'collaborator' was always said with a sneer just out of Smythe's earshot. Any VC, in fact. They were even more hated than the robots.

'Then one day, Smythe …' Danny's face darkened and his chest began to heave with suppressed anger. 'He told me you were both dead. Said he'd found records that said you'd been killed when a jet crashed into our street.'

Three tabs done now. Donald worked on the final one. Commendably, Connor continued to remain completely still.

'I didn't believe him,' Danny continued. 'Maybe that was obvious, maybe I'd already asked too many questions, but then Smythe had me moved to the Poseidon Hotel. Basically a dosshouse for all the troublemakers.'

'Yeah, we followed your trail there.' Sean said. 'They gave us a … warm welcome.'

'Good. Back when I was there, Smythe basically locked the doors, shut us in and let us get on with it. It was bloody anarchy. That's where I met Donald and Swanny.'

Donald briefly looked up from his work to give them all a nod.

'The three of us wanted out. Donald still had some of his watch-repair equipment and Swanny – somehow – knew a few things about bomb disposal. He was so dodgy, a real character, but, y'know, any port in a storm. Between the three of us we were able to remove our implants. We kept it quiet. If word got out, Smythe would've been on us in a second. It was selfish, I know, but back then we were ready to take on the world. We'd heard about a resistance unit in the hills and we were ready to sign up and start the fight-back.'

The final tab was removed. Connor's implant was almost free.

'But once we were out,' Danny said with a shrug, 'we didn't have a clue where to go. We headed into the woods. Got to the stones, but it took us the better part of a day to find the clue that took us to where this supposed resistance were hiding. Of course, they were nothing of the sort. Just ordinary people who'd managed to be off-grid when the invasion happened, or, like us, had found a way to remove their implants. All they wanted was a quiet life. Not a fighter among them.'

The heat was stifling down here. Donald paused to wipe the sweat from his eyes and take a swig of water from a plastic bottle.

'We had a choice,' Danny said. 'Donald decided to stay.'

'I like the quiet life,' Donald said, tightening a squeaky clamp until the vice held Connor's implant tight over the hole in his neck.

'But Swanny missed Monique,' Danny said. 'He wanted to go back and bring her here. Did you see him? Did he make it?'

Nathan, Alex and Sean shared a doubtful look. 'Sort of,' Sean said. 'He's … not well. He got really bad sunstroke.'

'Went a bit mentaloid,' Nathan added.

'But Monique's looking after him,' Alex said, trying to sound reassuring.

Danny nodded. 'He was always a bit crazy.' He smiled. 'Good for a laugh. Be nice to see him again.'

'Right,' Donald told Connor. 'This is the really dangerous bit: I need to slide this out without touching the edges, otherwise …'

'*Kaboom?*' Connor said without even moving his jaw.

'*Kaboom*, indeed.' Donald moved closer still. 'But don't worry – no one's ever blown up on my watch.'

'I know you can do it.' Connor said with a serious and encouraging look.

'So why did you stay?' Sean asked his dad.

'I didn't plan to.' Danny's eyes were downcast as he spoke. 'I was only intending to use this place as a base. I decided to take a recce into town. I saw our old street. Completely destroyed, with a downed Tornado the centre of impact. That was when … I started to wonder if Smythe had been telling me the truth about you after all.'

Kate wrapped an arm around her husband.

'I kept going back,' he said, 'week after week, but it just got too dangerous. And then I began to think … maybe we'll outlast the robots, and then, when they're gone, I can start looking for you properly? Maybe …'

Danny lowered his head, ashamed. Both Sean and Kate were hugging him now.

Donald, breathing steadily, gently removed Connor's implant, leaving the same empty cylinder that Swanny had behind his ear.

'You're done, young man,' he said.

Connor leapt off the bench to do a victory dance for the benefit of Nathan and Alex.

'Shut up, Connor,' Nathan said, nodding towards the emotional scene next to him.

'But I didn't say anything!'

'Now, keep this clean.' Donald tapped at the empty cylinder in Connor's neck. 'It goes cone-shaped at the tip inside, so it won't fill you up with water if you go for a swim, but the skin around it might get infected. Some people prefer to leave it open, others wear a scarf, some make little plugs and decorate them.'

'Will I always have it?' Connor asked.

'Truth is, I don't know.' Donald said, rearranging his tools for the next patient. 'I daren't remove the whole thing – that's too much like surgery, and I'm no surgeon. Maybe one day, when all this insanity is over, a proper doctor will take it out. Of course, there'll be a very long queue. Right, who's next?'

Sean broke away from his father, no doubt desperate to be rid of his implant. He settled himself on the bench, and Donald adjusted the magnifying glass to look upon the strangest implant he'd ever seen.

A glassy, obsidian disc, black and mysterious. Much like a robot's.

Donald adjusted his magnifying eyeglasses. 'You sure you want this out?' He wasn't talking to Sean, but to his father. 'You know what some of the others will say.'

'I don't care,' Danny replied. 'He wants it out. Take it out.'

GOODBYE, COWBOY

To see a Skyship cruising overhead was a magnificent, awe-inspiring thing, but to see one land on the beach at Fairfield Bay pushed the limits of what the human mind could comprehend. The scale of it was both thrilling and terrifying. It simply didn't belong. It looked like a skyscraper had collapsed on the shore, just waiting for someone to hoist it upright.

Smythe felt tiny and insignificant, but at the same time part of something so much bigger. To think that this colossus had spent centuries roaming through empty space to come here, to his planet. He wondered about its construction, how many robots had toiled to create it, and how many more such ships were flying above the Earth at this very moment. His mind whirled at the scale of the occupation. The Mediator had told him they'd studied humanity for decades before their arrival, and had used that time to hollow out some of our solar system's larger asteroids, creating factories to assemble their army.

How could we ever think we might defeat them? Smythe knew he'd made the right decision and allowed himself to swell with pride. Everything was falling into place. After the Mediator's decision to deep scan the zone, Smythe had suggested a change of plan.

'Call off the search,' he told the robot. 'We know where he's going, but if we chase them they'll scatter and disappear into the woods, and you need your resources here.'

That much was true. A group of Monique's troublemakers had switched off their implants and were using guerrilla warfare tactics to attack robots and the VC. They had guns, Molotov cocktails, home-made bombs, machetes and three years' worth of pent-up aggression. They had killed and wounded a number of Smythe's people and destroyed a Sentry. They hit suddenly and then faded into the shadows. They were good. Organised and very dangerous. The robots needed to focus on this more immediate danger.

To Smythe's delight, the Mediator agreed. The Sentries had found the Jeep and quad bikes at the standing stones, proving Sean was acting as Smythe had predicted, so the Mediator called them back to deal with the crisis in town.

But Smythe couldn't risk another failure, and he had to be sure he was right about where Sean and Kate had gone.

With a hiss of air, a section of the Skyship began to detach from the hull and lower to the ground: a platform that would take Smythe and an armed VC guard up into the body of the ship. As they rose, Smythe craned his head back, hoping to see what so few humans had seen before: the interior of a Skyship.

He was lifted into a huge space. In every direction, thousands of Deep Scanners stretched the length of the ship, all prepped and ready for the citizens of this zone. All empty, but one.

As Smythe approached the Deep Scanner, he couldn't help but smirk when he recognised the face of its occupant. Someone who had given him so much grief in the past, always lurking behind that tart of a barmaid at the Poseidon. Smythe tried to recall the miscreant's name.

'Wayne, isn't it?' he said. 'What sort of name is that? You're a cowboy, is that it? Think you're a Wild West hero?'

Wayne, his face bruised after its encounter with the butt of McGrath's AK-47, said nothing.

'Incitement to riot.' Smythe began to recite the charges against the man. 'Breaking curfew, attacking volunteers—'

'Yeah, it's what I do,' Wayne said, his voice deeper and more cracked than Smythe recalled. 'It was a right laugh. Loved every minute.'

'People like you …' Smythe slowly shook his head. 'It's your kind who made this town such a misery before the robots came. What does CHAV stand for? Council-Housed And Violent – that's you, isn't it, Wayne?'

Wayne sniffed and spat on the gantry, just missing Smythe's shoes. 'I always wondered why you hate people so much, but those wonderful kids explained … Bet your missus got the shock of her life the day you decided to grow a pair.'

Smythe's fists clenched with rage. A familiar anger rose within him.

'But killing your son, too,' Wayne continued, 'your own flesh and blood? You're despicable.'

Smythe took a step forward, ready to wring this cretin's neck, but he recalled Sean's taunting and how that had ended. He checked himself. He wasn't about to make the same mistake twice.

Smythe peered around Wayne's neck. His implant had already been replaced with a black one, ready for a deep scan. Smythe smiled.

'The robots want to look inside your tiny little brain,' Smythe told him. 'Won't take long. But first I need to be sure the boy is headed for the camp in Stannum Valley …'

'Nah, mate, means nothing to me.'

'Maybe you know it better as the resistance in the hills? Some call it the Silver Lake.'

Wayne's eyes flickered with recognition. That was all Smythe needed to know. His instincts had been right – the kids had confided in this lunk in the hope he would help them.

'Oh, come on, cowboy, don't be so surprised,' he said. 'You

really think the robots haven't seen the fires at night? The washing lines? And believe me, they're no resistance. More like a bunch of deluded hippies. They think they're safe and sound, but their time will come soon enough ...'

The Deep Scanner began to hum as it warmed up.

'And your time, cowboy, is now. Goodbye, Wayne.'

With Wayne's screams echoing around him, Smythe joined his VC guard on the platform as it began its descent to the ground.

Now he knew for certain where to find Kate. He would make her one final offer before smashing the remnants of this so-called resistance. Then he would be back in the Mediator's favour, and a new life in a paradise on the other side of the world would be his.

JOSIE

Her name was Josie, she wore her blonde hair in plaits, and she was the first girl Nathan had spoken to, apart from his sister, in more than three years.

'You the ones who left the messages on the stones?' He found her and a trio of other girls painting the bigger boulders on the far side of the lake. They'd turned them into cartoon characters from old TV shows, funny faces, footballs, and one was covered in stars and moons in a night sky.

Josie wiped her paint-covered hands on her dirty overalls. Old spray cans scattered about suggested this had been designated the 'arty' corner. 'That's us,' she said.

'Word of advice.' Nathan said with a wagging index finger. 'Your tagging sucks balls.'

'Oh, charming,' she replied in a calm, even voice. 'And you could do better, you dickless gobshite?'

Her friends stopped what they were doing and gathered behind her, glaring at this stranger.

Nathan's neck itched. His implant was gone, but there was still that small metal cylinder in his neck where it used to sit, and the skin around it was starting to get irritated, particularly now he was agitated. What he thought was endearing irony had obviously been

229

misinterpreted, but he couldn't help but be honest, 'Probably,' he said, scratching his neck. 'Yes.'

'Well, maybe we should have left you wandering in the woods, then,' Josie said, hands on hips. 'Lost and crying for your mummy.'

'Yeah, not much point me doing that.' Nathan said. 'She's dead.'

'So's mine,' Josie snapped, 'so don't think you're special. We put that message out there because we knew only humans would figure it out. We hoped it would bring people together, show them the way to safety, so excuse me if my tagging isn't up to your high standards as it wasn't my top priority at the time.'

Her little rant ended, her angry words echoing off the cliff-walls.

There was a long, awkward silence.

'So,' Nathan said, clapping his hands together in a way that he hoped was both casual and authoritative. 'Me and the new guys were going to have a laugh in the lake, make some rafts, have a bit of a splash, and we wondered if you wanted to join us?'

One of the girls, about Connor's age with her paint-splattered hair in pigtails, peered around Josie. 'My dad says you lot are trouble,' she said. 'He says you'll bring death to us all.'

'I'll put you down as a "no", shall I?'

And so they went without them. Sean and Nathan made a little raft out of empty oil barrels, rope and wood, following the instructions in Connor's SAS Survival Handbook. He insisted that they call it Ragnarok, and that it was a Viking longship, and that he was the captain. It capsized twice, but soon they were upright and in the middle of the lake singing made-up Viking songs. 'We're Vikings, we kill and we maim! Yes, our boat's shit, but we're not to blame!'

Once the other kids saw them, a few more joined in, cautious at first, but soon they were laughing and splashing and squealing with delight. Especially when Connor poured a bucket of ice-cold water over Nathan's head. It was pure fun. Nathan had tried to have a laugh when they were stuck in Fleetwood Street, but they'd always been looking over one shoulder, waiting for a knock on the door, or for screams outside. Here he was free to properly enjoy himself for the first time in years.

They played football after that, and Danny and Sean joined in kicking around a mostly deflated leather ball. Danny told them he was going hunting in the morning and they were welcome to come along. He also promised to show them the Spitfire properly.

'Can we sit in it?' Nathan blurted.

'Yeah, no problem.' Danny said with the resigned air of someone who got asked that a lot.

'Can we fly it?' Nathan added.

'No,' Danny said firmly. 'Definitely not.'

After the game, Nathan took a breather on a wooden jetty, dangling his feet in the water. The lake was turning a glassy purple as the sun's light began to fade. Only last night they'd been battling robots at the castle, and they had been on the run all day. And now they'd found somewhere so calm and quiet that he had time to watch the stars come out. Distant laughter drifted over the water from the other side of the camp and children played along the shore. But something wasn't right. He couldn't put his finger on it. The world of the robot occupation was just a few miles away, but out here it didn't seem to exist. How could the robots let that happen? Unless they already knew that these people were here. The thought troubled him and he tried to push it down.

'Hey, look – it's dickless.'

He glanced up to see Josie striding along the jetty as she towelled herself dry. Her shorts and T-shirt were soaked, and she wrapped the towel around her as she sat next to him.

'I can assure you,' he said, 'I have a fully functional penis.'

'Maybe, but that doesn't mean you should let it do all your thinking.'

'What?'

'That was some of the worst flirting I've ever seen.'

'I wasn't flirting,' he snorted. 'I was critiquing your—'

'Don't worry.' She said, leaning back on her hands and kicking at the water. 'Whenever we get new arrivals, it's always the boys who try and play it cool. He's nice, though.' She nodded at Sean, who was knee-deep in the water helping Connor put his raft back together. As he pulled a rope tight, muscles flexed beneath his wet T-shirt.

'Him?' Nathan shook his head. 'Lovely bloke, but he's taken a vow of chastity.'

'Really?' Josie raised an unbelieving eyebrow.

'Yeah, he's deeply, deeply religious. Monk-like, in fact. Not into girls at all.' Nathan said sombrely. 'He doesn't like to talk about it, so best to just keep away from him.'

'Oh, I'll do that then, thanks.' She said, playing along. 'What's his name?'

'Jebediah.' Nathan somehow kept a straight face. 'Jebediah Minge.'

Josie laughed and smacked him on the arm. 'You lie!'

'Me? No, not often. A bit. All I'm saying is, if you marry him, you'll be Mrs Minge, so just think about it.'

They laughed some more, then sat in silence for a bit, feet gently paddling the water.

'Do you get new arrivals often?' he asked.

'Less so these days,' she said. 'You're the first ones this year.'

'How did you get here?'

Josie puffed out her cheeks. 'Long story,' she said.

'Well, there's nothing on the telly, so …'

'Okay,' she said eventually. 'See that guy over there?'

She pointed to the opposite shore of the lake, where a middle-aged man in a red waterproof was tending to some raised allotment beds.

'Farmer Giles, yeah?'

'That's my dad.'

'Oh, sorry.'

'S'okay,' she said. 'We used to live in Wandsworth, in London. But Dad's job was sending him mental, so he decided me, Mum and Toby were all going to camp out on the coast. Live off the land for a bit. Get back to nature. We just happened to leave the day before the invasion.'

'Whoa, nice move.'

'Yeah, from what we hear, London got it bad.' She stopped for a moment. Silent and still. Nathan wondered what she was thinking about. Old friends, maybe. Those she'd left behind. He'd seen that look too many times.

'So, anyway, we stayed out here,' she said, her voice quieter now. 'Dad had all these books on survival and shit ...'

'Oh, he should talk to Connor, they could bore each other for days.'

'I bet. Anyway, bit by bit we met other people,' Josie said. 'Other survivors. Most were like us, they were out and about when it all kicked off. Some escaped, like you. Those are the ones that freak Dad out the most.'

'Why's that?'

'He's worried you'll bring them here. The robots.' She looked at her dad as he tidied away his watering can. He was indecisive, putting it in one place, then moving it again, then putting it back where it was before. 'He's not been the same since Mum died.'

'When was that?'

'That bad winter last year.'

'Sorry,' Nathan said. 'Our landlady died then, too. Cold's a bitch.'

'True, that.'

There was a long, solemn silence. The moon was on the water now, doing a gentle dance on the lapping waves.

'So where'd you get the graffiti paint from?' he asked.

'A Portakabin along the shore. We think they used them in the mine. Thought we'd do something with them,' Josie said. 'Dad went spare. When your mate's dad and his friends showed up last summer, he thought it was the end for sure.'

'This place …' Nathan shook his head. 'It's not what I expected at all.'

'What did you expect?'

'Back in town, the neighbours – well, a friend of mine – talked about a resistance. Y'know, a band of rebels in the hills fighting the robots with guerrilla tactics. Okay, maybe that was too much to expect, but at the very least I thought I'd find people with a bit of defiance in them. People prepared to make some kind of stand. But this …' – he gestured around him – 'this is more like a long-term hippy camping holiday, but with drills for duck-and-cover whenever a Drone flies overhead.'

'You should talk to that guy.' She pointed to a long-haired, skinny man who was stalking through the shelters carrying a frying pan like a weapon. 'Calls himself Skillet. Keeps banging on about forming raiding parties and attacking the robots. That's your resistance.'

'Him?' Nathan watched as Skillet stopped to chat with a pale, equally skinny woman with frizzy hair who shared his taste in faded denim. As they spoke, Skillet absent-mindedly reached down the back of his jeans and scratched his buttocks. 'Oh, great.'

'Don't worry about it,' Josie said. 'We're as safe here as anywhere else.'

'You think?' Nathan kept his voice low. 'It's nice here and that, but there's no way you guys can keep this up for ever. I'm amazed you've stayed out here as long as you have, but they'll find you sooner or later.'

'Maybe.' She shrugged. 'The dogs warn us if any robots come close. Lookouts spot the odd patrol around the old farms, but they don't seem interested in us. And you saw what happens when the

Drones go over. Dad reckons we can sit it out. They'll be gone in four years and then we can start rebuilding.'

'I dunno,' Nathan said. 'They might be gone by then, but I don't think there'll be many of us left to rebuild anything.'

'What do you mean?'

Somewhere in the commune a bell started clanging. Voices shouted promises of dinner and a meeting.

'I think you're about to find out,' Nathan said.

CAMPFIRE STORIES

As the sun finally disappeared, the kids began to dry off and head for the big campfire where the adults were already settled in a circle on old sofas, car seats and repurposed park benches. Kate and Danny sat arm-in-arm. Alex snuggled with a yawning Connor.

Alex watched Sean sitting alone on a swing. Slowly rocking back and forth, apparently hypnotised by the flames.

'All right, Jebediah?' Nathan chucked Sean on the arm as he passed. The girl with him – Alex thought her name was Josie – giggled.

Sean gave Nathan a confused look, like someone awakening from a deep sleep. 'Eh?' He blinked.

'Nothing. Don't matter, mate.' Nathan said as he found a space on a sofa near the fire. It got dark quickly in the ravine, and Josie was lighting torches made from old food tins set atop high poles.

The boy they'd followed here was called Toby. He sat with his dad, the man in the red waterproof who was stoking the fire, sending bright orange sprites spiralling up into the dark. The wood crackled loudly and the stew in the big pot began to bubble and boil as Skillet and his girlfriend gave it a stir and added some herbs. A queue was forming with hungry people bringing their own salvaged plates and cutlery. Alex had none of her own and was worrying that she might have to eat the stew with her hands when

Josie passed her a chipped plastic plate and a mug with 'World's Greatest Lover' printed on it in faded ink.

'Thanks,' she said.

'Does your little brother want some?' Josie asked, nodding at Connor.

Alex didn't bother correcting her. After all they'd been through, Connor felt like a little brother. Annoying and whiny sometimes, but brave and funny, too, and she loved him to bits. He was happily snoozing away now, his head heavy in her lap. 'Maybe later. I'll let him sleep,' she replied.

Kate was already telling the crowd gathered around the fire the horrible truth.

'The scan puts you into a coma,' she said. 'You're dead within a couple of days. Not that they care – we're like ants to them.'

'That's what they did to our friend Martin,' Sean added. 'What they started doing to me … It's how they punish criminals.'

'Not just criminals,' Kate corrected him. 'Everyone. Everybody in the world.'

'Six, seven billion people?' Danny shook his head. 'That's crazy.'

Alex looked around at the shocked faces. It made her skin crawl when Kate first told them. It was no less horrifying to hear it again.

'One by one they're going to trawl through our brains,' Kate said, 'looking for new ideas.'

'That's why they're keeping us inside,' Alex added.

'Smythe told me it takes them a year to process a billion people,' Kate said. 'They can't do us all at once.'

'And Smythe's known this all along?' Danny asked.

Kate nodded. 'The collaborators won't get scanned. That's what the robots told them, anyway.'

'And robots never lie,' Sean said quietly as he stared into the fire.

'Smythe said Australia is pretty much empty now,' Kate continued. 'Everybody dead.'

'How can he possibly know that?' said a new voice, scornful and dismissive. It was the man in the red waterproof. It crumpled as he folded his arms and crossed his legs.

'Dad, please,' Josie said, resting a hand on her little brother Toby, who looked worried.

'All I know is what he told me,' Kate said.

'Exactly.' Josie's dad unfolded himself, gesticulating aggressively. 'Robots never lie, but humans often do. Smythe's telling you what he wants you to hear.'

'Yeah,' said a woman standing beside him. 'When has he ever told the truth?'

'Then why else are they here?' Skillet stood up, frying pan still in his hand. 'This makes total sense to me. They hoover up everyone's brains, get total knowledge. They're like the NSA or the CIA before the war, only, like, with massive robots.'

'Oh, sit down, Skillet,' muttered his girlfriend.

'We should strike back!' Skillet continued as she pulled at his arms. 'Gerrof!' he said, shaking free.

Josie's dad was on his feet now. 'How do we know Smythe hasn't sent these interlopers to track us down? They could be spies, brought here to root us out.'

'There not spies,' Danny said, his voice commanding and steady. 'They're my family, so calm yourself down'

'They could still have unwittingly drawn the robots to this place, and—'

'Laurence!' Danny barked.

Toby whimpered and Josie held him tight.

Their dad sat reluctantly, his face twisted with self-righteousness. A few people patted his shoulder and there were some quiet murmurs of agreement, but they soon faded into silence as Danny gestured for them to settle down. 'Look, we all agreed on this a long time ago,' he said. 'Fighting is pointless. We're outnumbered, outgunned. We're under their radar here and we agreed to stay that way. We sit this out. We survive.'

This was greeted with happy nods.

'Cushy here, isn't it?' Nathan said, his tone curt.

'Nate,' Alex warned, 'don't.'

'No, while we've been stuck inside for three years watching our friends and neighbours die, this lot have been on a bloody camping holiday.'

'A camping holiday?' Josie's dad boiled with rage. 'My wife died here, almost half of us were taken last winter, so don't you—'

'I'm sorry about your wife, mister, but at least she died with her mind intact.' Nathan was on his feet now. 'I've seen what they do to us, it's sick, and if you think you're gonna get off, you're wrong.'

'You heard Danny,' Laurence said. 'Fighting will only lead to more death.'

'You should see what Sean can do,' Nathan said. 'Finally we get to show 'em our balls!'

'What is it with you and balls?' Alex said, scrunching her face in disgust. 'Sit down and shut up.'

'We haven't given them a reason to bother us,' Danny said. 'And we won't start now.'

Skillet was animated again. 'But this is the kid who controls robots, right?' he said, slapping Sean's shoulder. Rumours had spread throughout the camp all day. 'Then let's do it! Let's give 'em a taste of their own medicine.'

'My son is not a weapon, Skillet,' Danny growled.

'But we can start hitting back!' Nathan said.

'I've done my fighting!' Danny's voice was suddenly raised. 'Done it and lost.'

Alex caught a glimpse of Sean looking through the flames. Disenchanted with his father, disappointed.

Danny looked away.

WHAT'S CHANGED?

Sean's heart had burned, seeing his dad back down like that. The meeting dissolved soon after and he found a quiet corner with Alex and vented.

'I dragged us all the way out here.' Sean paced back and forth along the lake's edge. 'I was all, "Dad will know what to do," "Dad will this," "Dad will that," and now it turns out he's chicken-shit.' He kicked a stone and stubbed his toe. 'Ow! Bollocks.'

'He's not a coward, Sean.' Alex's voice was soothing, calm, reasonable. 'Didn't you hear what he said? This isn't a fight we can win.'

'Look, I know he's seen terrible things, but so have we,' Sean said, his hands shaking with anger. 'And I know fighting them head-on is probably suicide, but to not even discuss it, to just shut the conversation down ...' Sean suddenly crouched low, grabbed a pebble from the shore and sent it skimming across the moonlit water. 'That's not my dad.'

Somewhere in the distance a petrol generator rattled into life and lights began to glow all over the mine. His dad had told him how they would syphon the petrol from cars abandoned on the edge of town. He reckoned they had enough to get through the next winter at least. Sean knew his dad was smart and resourceful, he just wished he could use that experience and intelligence to fight back somehow.

'Just talk to him,' Alex said. 'Get him when there's no one else around, when he doesn't have to be the big leader.' She took his hand and her touch stopped the trembling. 'Don't let something like this fester, Sean. You just got your dad back. Let that be enough.'

Sean's face burned, the way it always did when he realised he'd done something stupid. Against all the odds he'd managed to find his dad. Reunited his family. How many other people would get that chance? Alex and Nathan would do anything to have their parents back again, and here he was getting pissed off at something impossible.

'I'm sorry, Alex.' He squeezed her hand back. 'I'm such a dick, I—'

'No, you're not.' She said, her voice suddenly firm. 'You just expect everyone else to be up to your standards. Talk to him. I'm sure he'll listen.'

Sean found his mum and dad sitting on the edge of the cliff overlooking the mine. They appeared to be in the middle of a private conversation, so he held back for a moment and waited in the shadows.

'I gave up,' he heard his mum say. 'I'm not proud of it, but it kind of made things easier.'

'I know what you mean,' his dad replied.

'Sean, though ...' Kate began. Sean froze, unsure if he wanted to hear this. 'He never let it get to him. Never lost heart.'

'That's my boy,' Dad said. 'You believe this stuff about him controlling robots?'

'I've seen it,' she replied. 'I don't understand it, but I've seen him do it. Whether it was some fluke, or what, I don't know.'

A dull thud, like a distant thunderclap, came from the other side of the hills. Sean looked up to see a Skyship breaking the sound barrier, rising on a bead of light through the clouds and into orbit. The robots had become such a part of their lives that such sights were no longer remarkable.

'We have to do something,' he said out loud.

Kate and Danny pivoted around to find Sean standing behind them.

'They're here to stay, y'know,' Sean said. 'So do we just accept it? Keep hiding until we're all found and deep-scanned?'

'You can't save the whole world, Sean,' Danny said.

'What about some of it? Our friends? Our neighbours? The kids at our school, Mum?'

'If you're forcing me to choose ...' Kate shared a glance with Danny. 'I choose my son. I choose you.'

'You told me that we have to look after one another, or we're no better than them. So tell me – what's changed?'

Kate looked away and Danny lowered his head – they couldn't answer.

'I can shut them down,' he said, reaching out to his mum. 'You've seen me do it – tell him. I can control them, or use one robot to fight the others, the implant might be out but it's only dormant, if I put it back in I can—'

'Mate.' His dad raised a hand for quiet. 'I've seen a Cube nuke an entire airbase, reduce it to ashes. Squadrons of jet fighters sent crashing to Earth by a single Drone. Even if it's true ... Just you against the entire robot army? That's suicide.'

'I really thought you'd have the answers, Dad ...' Sean's voice faltered. 'But you're as scared as everyone else.'

'Damn right, I'm scared,' Danny said, matter-of-factly. 'And you should be, too. I'm sorry I've let you down, but this is the right thing to do. I don't want anyone else to die. It's as simple as that.'

Sean turned away and headed back down the zigzag cliff-path. Whatever he said wasn't about to change their minds, that was clear. He heard his dad call after him, 'I'm going hunting first thing. Nathan's coming. Let me show you what it's like out here. It's a good life. You'll love it.'

But he ignored him, went straight back to the mine, found a nook near where they stored the tinned food and tried to sleep. But sleep wouldn't come. He knew now that he couldn't rely on his dad. What happened next would be up to him alone.

The mine was hot at night, crowded and stuffy with people sleeping on camp beds, some on the floor wrapped in old duvets or curled up on beds of straw. In the dim glow of electric lights strung along the ceiling, Sean could see Connor twitching in his sleep, cocooned in a moth-eaten sleeping bag. Nathan and Alex were sprawled out on the dusty floor. His mum and dad were swaddled in an old blanket.

Sean was wide awake, turning his inert implant over in his hand.

He got up as quietly as possible and slowly filled his sleeping bag with stuff to make it look like he was still in it. He turned to leave.

And found Connor's wide eyes staring straight at him.

'Where are you going, Sean?' the little boy asked.

Sean raised his fingers to his lips, whispering, 'Nowhere. I just need some air.'

'You're not leaving, are you?'

'What makes you say that?'

'You look like you're leaving,' Connor said. 'It's how my mum looked when she went. Sort of sad and angry and a bit mad.'

'I just want a bit of space to think.'

'You want to put your implant back in, don't you?'

Sean grinned. Connor was only little, but he wasn't an idiot. 'And why would I want to do that?'

'So you can control the robots, fight them.' Connor yawned. 'That's awesome. I would.'

'I can't fight them all,' Sean said.

'No.' Connor's eyes were closing and he yawned again. 'But maybe you can mush the smaller ones with the bigger ones.'

Sean smiled at Connor's idea, so simple and straightforward. He looked long and hard at the implant. Such a basic, ugly bit of machinery. But it could change everything.

'I know what to do,' he whispered. 'When they wake up, Connor, tell them I know how to save them. How to save the town.'

Connor nodded, and Sean moved silently to the mine's exit. A few people were still awake, all cosy in their chosen nooks as the moonlight glowed through the mine entrance. He smiled, tried not to look in a hurry and fanned his face to suggest that he needed some air. He got sympathetic looks back in return. They knew how difficult it could be for newcomers to adjust. Once out of sight, he ran unseen up the zigzag path, up onto the cliff, back into the woods, and before long he found himself standing in the long grass of a rolling meadow with the sun peeking over the horizon.

Sean held the implant in his palm. Black and silent now, it looked like a component from the console they'd taken apart in their loft just a few days ago. It was so quiet and still here. He liked to think he could feel the planet moving beneath him, hurtling through the universe at a million miles an hour. He had come here to think. To make a decision.

Then the birds began their morning song, a cheerful cacophony of chirps and whistles. Around him insects buzzed and flower petals opened to welcome the rising sun. Time to face the day ahead.

He tilted his head to one side. He carefully slid the implant back in. With a click, he felt it re-engage with his brain. It was still off, but it was rebooting. Soon the robots would know exactly where he was. And they would come for him.

A RUDE AWAKENING

Even in the cool light of dawn, the mine was a hot and sticky place. The sleeping bag had a musty whiff and was probably flea-ridden. And however Kate moved to get comfortable, there was always some rock or pebble poking into her. But it was still the best night's sleep she'd enjoyed in a very long time.

She gripped Danny all night, not wanting to let him go. They'd talked for hours after Sean stormed off. About their son, his friends, the war, the occupation and finally themselves.

'I don't know how you did it,' he said. 'Four kids and Smythe on your back. I'd've gone mad.'

'I doubt Smythe would have fancied you as much,' she said.

'What are you saying?' he said, mock-shocked. 'The war hasn't been kind, but surely I haven't lost my rugged good looks?'

'I'm just glad I don't have to do this on my own any more.' She took his hands. 'I may never let you out of my sight again.' They kissed and held each other without saying anything. There were some tears before they fell into sleep.

She panicked briefly when he rose at dawn to go hunting with Nathan, but a reassuring kiss soon calmed her. As Danny got ready, Kate glanced over to where Sean was lying buried in his sleeping bag, hoping he would change his mind. But he didn't reply to

Danny's whispers. 'Last chance, Sean,' he said, nudging the sleeping bag with his foot. 'No? Suit yourself.'

Danny gave Kate a shrug – *I tried* – then waved goodbye, leaving with Nathan and two sets of bows and arrows.

She understood Sean wanting to do something, but there was no way she was taking any of them back into danger. If staying together and alive meant sheltering in a stuffy cave for a few years, then so be it. And Sean's connection to the robots, the way that thing in his neck worked, just made him a target for them. She was glad it was gone. She was glad it was over.

As sunlight crept further into the mine, Kate heard people rousing around her. She was determined to make herself useful. She'd spoken to some of the other parents last night, about educating the commune kids. Most of them were out of practice with their reading and arithmetic, and the younger ones knew very little at all. Her brain was buzzing with ideas, already compiling a curriculum for them, and she was excited at the prospect of working again, of having a purpose in life beyond mere survival.

Alex and Connor were already up and dressed. Kate felt a little glow of pride at their self-sufficiency. They'd done so much in the last few days. They weren't her children, but at the same time they felt like family, and she began to think about their future together. Would they want to stick around with her, Sean and Danny? Or would they create their own little family unit? At least they had options now, which had been unimaginable when they were stuck in Fleetwood Street.

Kate kicked her sleeping bag away and stretched her legs.

'Morning, all,' she said with a stretch and a yawn. 'What have you got planned for today? I was thinking we could—'

A noise so loud, sudden and close that it made Kate's head flinch, blasted through the entire commune.

Everyone around her clapped their hands to their ears, but that didn't stop it shaking the mine walls, creating cracks in the ceiling and sending people panicking in every direction.

There was a moment of silence, just long enough for everyone to remove their hands from their ears, and then it came again, closer and louder, like a thousand foghorns blasting at once.

Kate ran to the mine entrance, dodging falling dust and debris, as the noise repeated again and again.

Alex was already there, peering up at the cliffs. 'Uh … this is not good,' she said.

Kate squinted into the bright morning light. About a hundred feet above them, all along the cliff-top, were more Sentries than she'd ever seen in one place before. Dozens of them, all their weapons powered up and ready to fire. One had a loudspeaker attachment on its arm, which was sending the blaring klaxon bouncing off the cliff-walls and into the mine.

A tiny figure strode to the edge of the cliff. Someone Kate hoped she'd never see again. Next to Smythe was even smaller figure. One Kate recognised from his regular transmissions on TV, Mediator 452.

Smythe raised a megaphone to his mouth. 'Good morning, everyone. I've come to give you a chance to save yourselves.'

Kate felt someone squeeze her hand. It was Connor. 'Oh, crap,' he said when he saw the Sentries' weapons bearing down on them. She squeezed back.

'Hand over the boy, Sean Flynn,' Smythe said flatly, 'or every last one of you will die.'

Murmurs sprang up all around Kate. She knew there was no question in their minds; one child's life against that of the entire commune. It was an easy decision.

Laurence, still in his red waterproof, whom she'd spoken to about schooling only last night, suddenly blurted, 'I know where he is!' and rushed back inside to find Sean.

'Dad, no!' Josie tried to stop him, but he shook her away and others ran with him.

'No!' Kate cried, instinctively running after them. She found men and women tossing aside sleeping bags, looking in dark corners for any hiding place.

'That's Smythe,' she told them. 'He can't be trusted! Do you think for a second he'll let us go if we—?'

But Laurence shoved her aside, desperate to find Sean.

'Back off!' Alex cried. An ugly brawl followed as Kate and Alex fought to hold the group off. The fighting was clumsy and Kate was knocked to the ground, a boot connected sharply with her head and she briefly saw stars.

One woman finally spotted Sean, still sleeping. 'There!' she cried, lunging past Kate, who briefly wondered how Sean had managed to sleep through all the noise. But then the woman pulled open his sleeping bag.

All she found inside were some rocks and old clothes piled up to look like someone asleep.

Sean was gone.

'Where is he?' the woman asked, trembling with fear and anger.

Kate looked to Alex for an answer, but she was clearly as shocked as she was.

'He said he was going to save the town ...' said a young voice from the back.

Kate turned as the crowd parted to reveal Connor. 'He said he knew what to do.'

Kate took a white baby's nappy from a washing line near the mine entrance. *It will have to do*, she thought as she waved it as a flag of truce.

She dared to peer out. She looked up to see Smythe beckoning her into the open, but she kept one foot firmly inside the mine, shielding her body behind its rusty iron door. Alex and Connor peered through the bars.

'He's not here!' she called up to him.

'What?' Smythe barked back.

'He's gone,' she shouted. 'We don't know where.'

There was some kind of discussion between the Mediator and Smythe. Kate's ears were still ringing from the robot klaxons so she couldn't make out the words, but she tried not to smirk as it became clear that Smythe was getting a ticking-off from the small robot.

Smythe raised the megaphone again. 'Kate, I promise you – if you and Sean join me, you won't be harmed.'

Kate thought back to her waking moments. The hopes she had for teaching again, for the children of this commune, for their future. Her future. Her family's future. She stepped out from the protection of the mine.

'Robin Smythe,' she yelled defiantly, 'I'd rather die than spend another second in your company. You're not getting me or my son!'

Smythe appeared to freeze, his cold stare fixed on her as he made a choice. He said something to the Mediator and the very air around them began to rumble.

A shadow crept along the ravine, blotting out the sun. It was suddenly very cold.

It was a robot Cube. A gigantic obsidian block, its rockets roaring as it moved into position over the mine. It was a good half-mile away, but Kate could feel the heat and smell the oily tang of its engines from here.

Even with the megaphone, Smythe had to shout over the noise. 'The Cube will drill into the ground beneath your feet. Its thermal bore slices through rock like a hot knife through butter.'

The Cube rattled and the air cracked like thunder. Something was happening to it. Kate hoped beyond hope that it was some kind of malfunction.

'The ground you stand on will turn to molten lava,' Smythe continued. 'You're going to die, Kate, along with your husband, your son and everyone else here, because of your selfishness. This is your last chance. Hand Sean over – now!'

The Cube began to slowly split open into four equal parts, exposing its bullet-shaped bore. It was powering up to unleash fire on them all.

The man in the red waterproof, Laurence, was standing next to Kate again. He was armed with a cricket bat, though how effective that would be against the robot hordes, Kate wasn't sure. He had been a teacher like her. PE, she recalled. But she saw the fear in his eyes, the pure panic of fight-or-flight. Was he going to run? She caught his eyes and silently begged, *Please don't.*

Then someone shoved past them both and rushed out of the mine. A long-haired man carrying a frying pan. With a blood-curdling scream, he ran from the mine entrance towards the wooden walkway, desperate to get away.

'Skillet!' a woman behind Kate cried.

Skillet took about half a dozen steps, waving the frying pan while howling a war cry. There was a blinding flash of light and the man was vaporised in an instant. His slightly melted frying pan clattered to the ground.

There was a moment of breathless silence. No one knew whether to run or cry.

Then the bombardment began. The Sentries pounded the mine and the cliff around it with their weapons, their heat-beams scorching the air and temporarily blinding anyone unlucky enough to stare at them. Any thought of making a run for it vanished, and Kate and the others retreated into the darkness of the mine.

300 HOURS ON A SIMULATOR

Nathan had never given rabbits much thought. At least not beyond the yummy chocolate ones they used to scoff at Easter. They were cute, he supposed, with their little twitchy noses and fluffy bottoms. And even though he'd wound Connor up about rabbit sandwiches in the graveyard, and sometimes seen them on the menu in the posh restaurant his dad took him to as a kid, he didn't really think of them as food.

Not until this morning, that is. When Danny had suggested they go hunting, Nathan thought they might be tracking deer, but Sean's dad had other ideas. 'We'll start with something a bit more doable today and work our way up,' Danny said. 'How does that sound?'

They set off before the sun came up. Danny wanted to check the traps first. They had a number of them scattered around the forest, small wooden traps with tiny bowls of seeds and fruits to tempt the unwitting animals inside. The first two were empty, but the third held an incredible bird with golden-brown feathers, a black head and vivid red colouring around its eyes. It pecked at the few remaining raisins in the bowl.

'What's that? A pheasant?' Nathan asked as he watched Danny open the trap and reach inside for the bird.

'Yup,' Danny said, covering the bird's eyes. 'They don't run if you cover their eyes,' he explained as he took it out.

Nathan reached over and stroked the pheasant's feathers. 'Hello, mate,' he cooed. It shook its body aggressively, as if irritated by the attention. 'All right, suit yourself, grumpy sod,' Nathan said.

Danny took a step back before suddenly pulling and twisting its neck. The bird went limp in his hands.

'Ah!' Nathan jumped back, shocked. 'It's dead!'

'It's dinner.' Danny said, gently stringing the bird onto a long branch he'd brought with them. 'One more to check and then we can start hunting.' He balanced the branch over his shoulder like a knapsack and they moved on. 'Still think this is like a holiday camp?'

Nathan tried to find a quick comeback, but couldn't think of anything that didn't make him sound like a dick.

He was quietly relieved to find the next trap empty, so they had more time for archery practice. They came to a sloping field, and Danny had them hiding behind an overgrown hedgerow.

Standing in the centre of the field was a solitary rabbit.

'We'll only get a couple before they all scarper,' Danny said, prepping his bow. 'So choose one and stick with it.'

As the morning sun crept across the field, more and more rabbits appeared, happily bouncing around, unaware that they were about to be used for target practice.

'I'm not sure I can kill an ickle bunny,' Nathan said, his throat dry.

'It helps not to use words like "ickle",' Danny said. 'And they might be a bit stringy, but they're very tasty. You should know – there were quite a few of them in last night's stew.'

'Oh, *now* you tell me!'

'Shh,' Danny said, raising his bow, flexing it in his hands in readiness. It was a simple thing, made back at the commune. It had the same rustic, home-made feel as everything else there, including the toilet paper. Nathan was getting sick of this rough-and-ready lifestyle. Even though it only showed repeats, he really missed their old TV.

Danny nocked an arrow in place, pulled back on the bowstring and exhaled gently.

Nathan did the same, choosing his target. He picked a rabbit with a black patch over its eye, imagining that it was like the pirate of the warren. Maybe even a bully, one who would duff-up the other rabbits for the rabbit equivalent of lunch-money. *Yeah*, Nathan thought, *this little bugger's got it coming.*

Danny released his bowstring, Nathan a moment later. Danny's arrow pounded into the body of a large grey rabbit. Nathan's spir-alled about ten feet in the air before tumbling into the long grass. The surviving rabbits, including the one with the black patch, all pelted for cover.

Danny slapped Nathan on the shoulder. 'You'll get the hang of it.' He said.

As promised, Danny took Nathan to see the Spitfire. They stood before it, admiring its curves and sleek design.

'Well, Nathan, you're squeamish when it comes to hunting and you're next to useless with a bow,' Danny said. 'But if you can tell me three facts about the Spitfire, I'll let you sit in the cockpit.'

Nathan's mind raced. He adored the Spitfire. It was the one plane he flew again and again on his old simulator, but his brain froze and he struggled to come up with anything.

'It's a … plane?' he ventured.

'Good.' Danny said encouragingly, nodding at him like a toddler struggling with its first words. 'Anything else?'

'I swear, Danny, I can fly this in my sleep,' Nathan blurted as his mind began to trip over itself. 'This is a two-seater training model, probably modified after the Second World War. Take-off speed is about a hundred and forty, it can fly up to forty-two thousand feet, depending on the type and load it can go at between three and four hundred miles an hour, it can—'

'All right, all right.' Danny raised a shushing finger. 'In you get.' He jerked a thumb towards the cockpit.

Nathan scrambled up into the front bubble. *This is more like it*, he thought, scanning the instruments before him. Danny started running through them one by one.

'Okay, on the right,' he said, 'you've got oil pressure, oil temperature—'

'Can I pull the trigger, Danny?' Nathan asked, excited and bouncing in his seat. 'Please?'

'Definitely not!' Danny batted Nathan's hands away from the controls. 'This thing is still prepped and armed. I don't want you—'

An incredible noise shattered the quiet around them. A blaring klaxon sound, honking again and again. Danny stepped away from the Spitfire, trying to pinpoint where it was coming from.

'What the hell was that …?'

They ran to high ground – from the rise overlooking the valley they might be able to see what was making the noise. But they only got as far as the treeline at the edge of the wood before Nathan spotted it. He grabbed Danny's arm and pointed to a robot Cube moving into position.

'Oh, God,' Danny's voice became a whisper. 'That's over the mine, that's— Oh, God.'

There was a crack like thunder as the Cube began to split open.

'What's it doing?' Nathan had never seen a Cube do this before.

'That bore in the centre of the Cube, you see it?' Danny pointed. Nathan saw the dull silver bullet lowering from the body of the Cube and nodded. 'That unleashes all the energy inside the Cube. They used them on our airbases. It's like a bloody nuclear bomb going off.'

Distant echoes of screams drifted across the hills, soon silenced by the screech of Sentry weapons.

'Oh, Christ.' Danny grabbed Nathan's arm and started to pull him back the way they'd come. 'Three hundred hours on a simulator, right?' he asked the boy.

'You're not thinking what I think you're thinking?' Nathan said, trying to dig his feet into the ground, but Danny was already frog-marching him into the woods.

Before he knew it, Nathan found himself seated in the front bubble of the two-seater Spitfire with an antique flight helmet on his head. It bulged around his ears, where the radio speakers crackled and hissed.

The Spitfire taxied as Danny ran through the pre-flight checks. The clattering noise the plane made as it bumped over the uneven, overgrown field reminded Nathan of their old washing machine struggling with a heavy load, and it suddenly occurred to him that this was actually happening.

'No way, no, sorry, I can't do this, mate,' he said, shouting over the rattle of the spinning rotor. It ebbed and flowed now, rising in pitch then dropping again like an old lawnmower. He was pretty sure it wouldn't even get them into the air, let alone fly into combat, but better safe than sorry. 'I can't. It's a total suicide mission! I'm sorry.' He started unbuckling his restraints.

'What are you doing?' Danny's voice came over the intercom. 'You said you could fly this in your sleep.'

'I'm full of shit!' Nathan cried, feeling liberated all of a sudden. Being himself was kind of a relief, especially if it meant he wasn't about to die in horribly in a ball of flames.

'What about your great-granddad in the Battle of Britain?' Danny said. 'What would he say?'

'I made that up. My lot were Irish – they didn't even fight in the war!'

'You were the one who wanted to fight back!' Danny yelled.

'Yeah, but that was with Sean,' Nathan said. 'I was thinking of taking them on one Sentry at a time, not the whole army in a flying antique with a bloody Cube about to go supernova.'

'I can't do this without you,' Danny pleaded.

Now where had Nathan heard that before? Like father, like son. He looked back at Danny in the bubble behind him. This was a two-man Spit. In theory, Danny could fly it on his own, but he'd need Nathan to fire the weapons and two pairs of eyes were better than one when taking on multiple targets. Multiple targets, oh, God! This was definitely a one-way mission and he didn't want to be on it. He reached to open his bubble.

'Sorry, kid …' Danny said, and before Nathan could open the canopy, the Spitfire lurched forward and the boy fell back into his seat. They were accelerating. Something happened to the engine noise. It went from a rattling, knackered clattering to a glorious swarm-like hum.

'I haven't got time for this,' Danny said as the engine growled and black smoke belched from the exhausts and they began to gather speed. The engine noise rose in pitch even further. The racket was deafening and the whole plane began to shake. Unseen components beneath Nathan's feet started to clunk and rattle.

'What are you doing? Stop!' Nathan yelped. 'Please! I don't wanna die a virgin!'

But Danny ignored him, pushing the throttle harder, the ground beneath them becoming a rushing blur. There was no way Nathan could jump out now. He strapped himself back in as they hurtled towards a stone wall. They were either going to take off, or crash and burn.

'Oh, sssshhhhhh—'

But then the nose lifted and Nathan could see nothing but blue sky. And just like that they were airborne. The rattling ceased and the engine calmed down to a steady growl. The Spitfire banked left and the world tilted the other way, revealing overgrown green fields below them, the river they'd followed to the commune and the glistening sea beyond the hills. It was so different from any flight Nathan could remember being on as a child. In the big Boeings and Airbuses they took on holiday, any movement was slow and gradual, but this was the closest to being Superman that he could imagine. Danny just had to nudge the stick and suddenly they were veering to the right.

Danny, clearly delighted to be in the air again, gave a cry of, '*Yeeeeeeee-hah!*' before slowly rolling the Spitfire over in the empty air.

Nathan pressed his hands up against the canopy bubble, desperate not to fall out, 'You're mental!' he yelled over the intercom. 'Total shitzoid!'

But Danny ignored him, diving down and heading for the coast. 'We'll come in low,' he said, 'avoid detection and surprise them from the rear.'

'Oo-er.' Nathan couldn't help himself. 'And then what?'

'Distract them long enough for everyone to get away,' Danny said. 'Then get the hell out ourselves,' he added.

Nathan nodded. That sounded like a plan, but then he remembered what they were up against. It all sounded so simple, apart from the last bit.

NAPOLEON CALENDARS

When Robin Smythe was a little boy, his father's study was often locked and forbidden territory. It overlooked the rose garden where his mother spent much of her day tending to the flowers, but his father's chair was turned away from the window and faced a methodically arranged bookshelf. The neat tessellations of burgundy, blue, brown and black leather spines were broken up by one object. Without fail, every year, his father purchased a calendar featuring great battles from history and hung it in the centre of the bookshelves, directly in his line of vision.

On the rare occasions when Robin was allowed into his father's study, usually to discuss disappointing school reports and the like, the boy always found himself drawn to the epic scale of the oil paintings featured on the calendars. Thousands of men in uniform, often in square formations, marching across windswept fields towards the enemy, destiny and a place in history.

One summer morning when his father was away at a conference, the young Robin Smythe dared to venture into the study. He took the key from the box in the hall, waited until Mother was busy in the greenhouse at the bottom of the garden and crept into his father's domain. His mission was simple: to steal the calendar page for January 1963. It was August now and he was sure his father would not miss it; and it had made such a huge impression on him that he knew he had to have it and keep it for ever. It depicted Napoleon on horseback at the Battle of Wagram, looking through a telescope at the troops in combat below while handing orders to one of his generals. What impressed the young Robin was that even though chaos reigned around him, the great leader remained calm and focused on the battle, leading his men to a momentous victory.

His father had been livid when he discovered Robin's crime and the boy received a slippering, which left welts he imagined he could still feel today. But there was no denying the beauty of that painting. He bought a print of it as soon as he could afford to do so, spending much of his first wage packet having it expensively framed. It graced his office at the school during his tenure as head of Year Ten, though he was sure it was wasted on the stream of ingrates who were sent to him for discipline.

But not in his wildest dreams could he have imagined that he would one day stand at the head of his own army before a decisive victory. Standing atop the cliff, with the robots barraging the mine below, he felt more alive than he ever had before.

He had explained his strategy to the Mediator the night before. 'We'll come with smiles and the olive branch of peace, Mediator. A simple exchange: the boy for their continuing survival. They'll deny he's there, of course, but the threat of the Cube will turn them against one another, like rats in a cage.'

The Mediator wanted to send the Sentries in with their weapons blasting. But they could not fit inside the mine entrance and Smythe argued that the commune people would no doubt have enough food and water stockpiled to make this a long, drawn-out siege. Not something he had the time or patience for. Rather, the mere presence of the Cube would make them see sense, and if that didn't work, turning the entire area to lava would solve the problem Sean presented.

'People do the right thing when motivated by fear,' he told the Mediator. 'You'll see.'

Indeed, it had all gone as he predicted. He knew these people all too well. Kate's defence of her son was to be expected, though he was disappointed when she declared her hatred for him so publicly.

'The mother is not the priority,' the Mediator told him. 'We must have the boy.'

As Smythe stared down at Kate, wincing at her vulgarities and the two-fingered gesticulations she and the children were now making, he realised he had been wrong about her. He'd thought she would be his perfect mate in the new world, his Eve in the post-robot paradise, but she had proved as self-centred and crude as all the others.

'Very well.' He sighed heavily. 'Mediator – please remove Kate Flynn from the immunity list. She is now a viable target.'

Kate had rushed inside as the bombardment began. He had no way of knowing if she was dead or alive, and he found that he no longer cared. He glanced up the Cube. Its four sections were nearly fully open, revealing the glowing inner core, raging with pent-up energy. The bore began to lower from the main body of the Cube. It would be over soon. He wondered how the Mediator might reward him. Perhaps an early retirement to Cradle Mountain? He'd certainly earned it, though he was starting to fancy himself a key tactician for the robots. A Napoleon for their army. Scourge of resistance units the world over as they called on him for tactical advice and his insight into the human condition.

He watched as two poor fools tried to climb the cliff-face in a desperate attempt to escape. He pointed them out to the Mediator, who silently gave an order over the network.

One Sentry's implant pulsed in response and it angled away from the others, taking aim. A laser bolt flashed from its weapon and one of the climbers was vaporised. The second climber continued his upward scramble in a blind panic and lost his handhold, tumbling through the air. Any expectations he had of a messy death on the rocks below were cut short as a second laser bolt killed him mid-fall.

Smythe allowed himself a little smile of satisfaction.

Then a second deep rumble, one separate from the Cube, began to vibrate the air around him.

Both Smythe and the Mediator turned to look along the valley, where a Skyship roared into view. Most likely the same Skyship Smythe had used to interrogate Wayne the night before. Its engines were on full, blasting dirty black fumes downwards into the valley below. It turned, banking over the green fields and farms, and headed towards the mine.

This hadn't been part of Smythe's plan and he wondered what the Mediator was playing at. 'This is quite unnecessary, Mediator,' he told the robot. 'Everything appears to be under control here. I'm not sure we need reinforcements.'

But the Mediator ignored him, having lapsed into a kind of trance. 'His control is sublime. Exquisite.'

Smythe followed the robot's glassy gaze. He shielded his eyes, straining to see. There, at the end of one of the Skyship's many pinnacles, stood a person. A boy, perhaps. And Smythe didn't need the Mediator's enhanced vision to figure out who it was.

The Mediator gave another silent order, its implant glowing. An Air Drone unexpectedly swooped down from above, diving into the ravine before slowly rising at the cliff's edge, the downdraught from its engines enveloping Smythe and the Mediator like a hurricane.

The Mediator ran directly towards it, arms outstretched, and leapt off the cliff. With a clang, the child-robot magnetically attached itself to the Drone, which then banked away, accelerating towards the approaching Skyship.

Smythe could only look on, open-mouthed. 'Mediator!' he eventually cried. 'Come back!'

But the robot was already hurtling towards the Skyship, and towards Sean, who was standing on the bow, his arm outstretched, steering the ship towards the Cube.

THE MEDIATOR'S DEAL

Sean didn't have to wait long for the robots to find him. Within minutes of replacing his implant, he spotted an Air Drone high above him, a tiny silver cross against the bright blue sky.

Sean ran through the tall grass, waving his hands and shouting at the top of his voice. 'Hey! Down here! Come and get me!'

The Drone continued on its trajectory for a few heartbeats then lurched into a dive, its inhuman howl growing louder and louder as it approached.

It barked the usual warnings but Sean ignored it, reaching out, his eyes closed, waiting for that odd sensation, that weird feeling of stepping out of this world and into the bubble of the robots' control.

As the turbulence of the Air Drone buffeted him, he felt it once more. His implant ceased to pulse in time with his heartbeat and found a new rhythm. He had linked with the Drone. He could see himself though its electronic eyes, and on its radar he could sense the other robots in the area.

The Skyship on the beach.

The Cube heading towards the commune.

He was so shocked, he nearly lost the link. He forced himself to focus. Concentrate. He had come here with a half-arsed plan to hijack a Drone and start fighting back, to show his dad it could be done. But now it looked like everyone in the town, and everyone at the commune, were all going to die.

How do you take on a Skyship and a Cube?

Then it came to him. A plan so insanely simple that it arrived fully formed. What had Connor said? Mush one robot with another? Crash a Skyship into a Cube. How hard could that be?

The Drone was harder to fly than he expected. It wasn't just a question of point and steer. And it was cold up here. His fingers froze into position gripping the Drone's hull. He could hardly breathe and his eyes were streaming as the wind roared around him.

It took just a few minutes to find the coastline. He brought the Drone down to about thirty feet, skimming over the waves as they dashed against the rocks below him. The tide was out and he saw the familiar twisted wreckage of the British Airways airliner pointing like a finger towards the bay.

The wind still buffeted him, but at this low altitude the feeling started to return to his hands. As he rounded the bay, he saw the Skyship and was instantly confounded by its size. It was so much bigger than he'd expected and his mind struggled to make sense of the scale of what he was seeing. Watching these things drift past high overhead was one thing, but on the ground it dwarfed everything around it. Even at low tide, with the waves hundreds of yards from the bay walls, the Skyship had two landing claws on the beach and two in the sea. Four Sentries were positioned around its perimeter, looking tiny from here, standing guard, waiting.

Then he saw the buses.

A line of double-deckers along Marine Parade, probably the same ones that had taken the townspeople to the hospital to receive their implants three years ago, once again chock full of people. Standing-room only. The first bus came to a stop by the Skyship and a group of armed VC began waving people out and shoving them towards the Skyship's open ramp.

Sean knew what lay inside the Skyships. Smythe had told his mum and she had told them. Thousands upon thousands of Deep Scanners. The mass uploading of the town's inhabitants was about to begin.

Some of the first people out of the buses ran, hoping to escape, but they didn't get far before the Sentries unleashed their fire. Bright flashes winked silently in the distance as those who tried to flee were killed. Sean knew he had to make his move now.

He steered the Drone towards the nearest Sentry and closed his eyes. The Drone's targeting display materialised in his mind and he lined up the Sentry in his sights.

Laser bolts pounded up the beach, sending plumes of sand spiralling into the air. They reached the first Sentry, pummelling into its chest and it exploded, one of its arms clanking to the ground.

He immediately came upon the second Sentry, already raising its weapon. No time to aim, he fired instinctively, taking off its head. He swung up and around for another pass, the pungent tang of ozone in the air as the two remaining Sentries fired back, missing him by inches. He had to come in faster than before. He could feel the Drone struggling to remain stable, its wings shimmying. The last two Sentries were lined up before him. He destroyed the first in a ball of flames, but the second had longer to target Sean's Drone and scored a direct hit. The ear-shattering noise of the impact sent debris tumbling into the air. The dead Drone jerked to one side and started falling. Sean lost the connection immediately as black smoke billowed around him. The heat was intense and he jumped into empty air, hoping for a soft landing on the sand.

Instead he hit the upper hull of the Skyship, tumbling over and over and falling off its edge. Stomach turning as he fell, he reached out for one of the many long pinnacles protruding from its bow. He was lucky not to break his arms as he slammed into one of them, his feet dangling.

As his Drone smashed into the sea, Sean heard the clang of the remaining Sentry as it rounded the Skyship, looking for its prey.

He pulled himself up onto the pinnacle and closed his eyes, trying to make a connection with the Sentry to shut it down before it could kill him.

Instead, he found the Skyship.

He made the connection, trying not to think about the size of the craft. It was heavier, bulkier, slower to respond, but it had the most powerful engines Sean had ever encountered. He fired them up, lifting the Skyship just a few feet into the air.

He could hear people cheering from the buses, followed by a few cracks of bullets from the VC's weapons, but they were soon swarmed by townspeople and beaten to the ground.

The remaining Sentry had found Sean. Moving into position in front of the Skyship, it aimed its weapon-arm.

Sean raised the Skyship's bow, tilting it upwards, and put the thrusters on full. The afterburners roared, melting the Sentry's outer armour. It fell to its knees as parts of it began to form a slag pool on the blackening sand.

The Skyship was rising quickly. Too quickly. Sean struggled to stabilise it. Without wings or any concession to aerodynamics, this was like flying a breeze block kept aloft only by the incredible power of its engines. He switched to the aft thrusters and hoped their kick would keep him airborne. If they did, then all he needed to do was fly in a straight line and ram it into a Cube.

He headed back along the coast and almost immediately became aware of another presence out there on the radar. The Mediator was at the ravine. Sean wondered if it knew he was coming. He put the engines on full power, sinking lower and lower, finding the path of the ravine.

In just a few minutes he could see the Cube. It had nearly split into four sections and a white-hot glow emanated from within.

Sean leaned forward, buffeted by the relentless headwind.

An Air Drone screamed through the sky. Sean prepared to take evasive manoeuvres, but then he saw the Mediator hanging from its cannon-arm, its face blank, impassive. The Drone arced in behind Sean and set the Mediator gently onto the pinnacle.

Sean now found himself stuck at the end of the pinnacle with the Mediator standing between him and the rest of the ship. The small robot stepped forward.

'Sean Flynn, you are a fascinating phenomenon,' it said over the roaring wind, reaching out to him. 'We wish to study the connection you have made with us – our simulations cannot replicate it. We offer you and your family immunity, the home of your choice, freedom to roam wherever you want.'

Sean turned back to face the Cube, the wind whipping his hair. It was getting closer. He could see more Sentries lined along the cliff-top. Too many for him to take alone.

'Defy us,' the Mediator continued, 'and we will order an immediate air strike.'

Sean looked around. In the distance he saw black dots flying in a V, low on the horizon. Drones in formation.

The Mediator came even closer. 'There is a ninety-four-point-six per cent probability that the collision will kill you,' it said.

'You reckon?' Sean replied, hoping to sound confident and cocky.

'You are perspiring and your heart is beating one hundred and twenty-four times per minute,' the Mediator said. 'We know you are frightened.'

Sean thought back to his first encounter with the Mediator on his doorstep. How terrified he had been that it almost knew what he was thinking, knew his heart rate, knew he was afraid. It was right. Sean was scared. But the difference was that now he didn't care. For all its technology, the Mediator couldn't see into Sean's mind or work out what he planned to do next.

'Being frightened of something is the best reason to do it.' Sean said with a confidence he didn't entirely feel.

The Mediator, normally so impassive, now looked confused. 'Your decision is … foolish. Goodbye, Sean Flynn.'

The Mediator's implant pulsed as he began to send the order to attack.

Instinctively, Sean broke off his link with the Skyship and reached out to stop the Mediator. Their implants pulsed in unison and then boy and robot were connected.

And Sean could see everything.

A huge network of three-dimensional cubes stretched out before Sean's mind's eye, each representing a robot's sensory perceptions: the robot network. Millions of them, all tethered together in their own cyberspace. The noise of their electronic chatter began to crescendo.

And something else happened. A twinge at the back of Sean's mind. A horribly familiar unravelling. One he hadn't felt since he was strapped into the Deep Scanner.

The Mediator was trying to deep scan him!

Sean pulled away with a gasp, suddenly disconnected and back in the real world. He collapsed onto the pinnacle, dazed, disorientated and out of breath.

His gaze fell on the Skyship's implant, tiny in comparison to the ship, like a whale's eye. He ignored the Mediator and focused on the Skyship instead.

He had control once more, but he needed to get rid of the Mediator before it tried to connect with him again. Already the robot was moving towards him, reaching out. Sean made the engines on the left side of the ship blast downwards, tipping the colossal craft on its axis.

Sean gripped the pinnacle hard as the sky and the ground spun around him.

The Mediator slipped and fell, clinging to the pinnacle with one hand. But its tiny fingers soon gave away.

Sean watched the Mediator tumble through the empty air, getting smaller and smaller, eventually smashing onto the rocks below, its shattered body spiralling in several directions at once.

Sean heard Smythe call the Mediator's name. He looked up to see the old man bellowing into his megaphone.

And then Sean saw every single one of the Sentries turn their cannons directly towards him. A tiny figure at the end of a long pinnacle. An easy target.

As one, they opened fire.

THE FAMILY THAT SLAYS TOGETHER, STAYS TOGETHER

In the sweltering heat of the mine, Alex huddled closer to Kate and Connor, holding them tight. She watched the people around them doing the same. Some were weeping, others praying. Every time the walls shuddered, Alex's heart leapt. Dust fell in a constant rain from the rock ceiling.

Connor whimpered, clutching Kate.

'It's okay, Connor,' she said, but the little boy began to cry. 'Hey, listen to me.' Kate pulled them both closer to her. 'Whatever happens today, I'm not scared. I'm not sad. Do you know why?'

Connor shook his head numbly, eyes glistening and wide.

'Because you're with me. Alex is with me. Nathan's safe with Danny, and Sean got to see his dad,' she said. 'For a little while, we – you, me, all of us – we were a family. Not many people get that these days. But we did.'

Even though hot tears were stinging Alex's eyes and streaming down her face, she found herself smiling. Kate was right. They *were* a family. A weird, messed-up family, to be sure, stuck in the strangest situation; one that Alex could never have imagined in a million years back when she was revising for exams and bitching about homework. When she lost her mum and dad, she felt she had nothing to live for. But now she had this new family, and just when she was learning to love them she was going to lose them, too.

There came a sound like someone snapping dry wood. Alex looked up to see a huge jagged fissure had appeared in the mine ceiling. People around them began to wail. They couldn't run. Setting foot outside was certain death, and if the Cube didn't kill them they'd be buried alive. The roar of the Cube was louder now. It had started to rise in pitch, reminding Alex of when aircraft suddenly powered up their engines for take-off. She realised that something new was about to happen. Maybe the Cube was only seconds away from incinerating them all. She just hoped it would be so quick she didn't feel it.

Kate pulled Connor tighter against her and reached out to Alex. She took Kate's hand and looked into her eyes. Kate might try to calm little Connor, but she knew she couldn't fool Alex. Kate gave her hand a tiny squeeze.

'I don't want to die,' Alex said quietly. 'A week ago … maybe I didn't care. But now—'

'We're not going to die, are we, Kate?' Connor asked.

'No, sweetheart,' Kate said. 'We'll find a way, I promise.'

'Why won't Mr Smythe believe us?' he said. 'Sean isn't here!'

Kate was about to reply when Alex saw her pause mid-breath.

'Kate?'

Slowly, Kate got to her feet.

'Kate, what are you doing?' Alex was worried now.

Kate turned towards the mine entrance. 'It's me he's after,' she said in a tiny whisper. 'Not Sean.'

Kate marched forward, suddenly determined.

'No,' Alex cried. 'They'll kill you!' She tugged at Kate's arm.

'If I give him what he wants,' Kate said, breaking free of Alex's grip and starting to run, 'I can stop this.'

'Kate! Come back!' Connor cried.

But Kate ran straight into the clearing, her arms raised in surrender.

Alex waited for the inevitable flash of a Sentry's laser bolt.

But none came.

Connor rushed forward, but Alex grabbed him, holding him tight.

'Robin!' Kate called. 'Robin …?'

No reply.

'They're not shooting at us?' Kate said, puzzled and delighted at once.

'Up there.' Alex nudged Kate and pointed, tracing the robot laser fire to a Skyship hurtling along the ravine towards the Cube.

Kate shielded her eyes as she followed it. 'Why are the Sentries shooting at their own ship?'

'Who cares?' Alex didn't waste a second. She spun on her heels, yelling into the mine, 'Coast is clear! Everybody out now!'

People were hesitant at first, but once they saw Kate standing safely outside, they soon got the idea. Connor waved them on, shouting, 'Go, go, go!' and the exodus began, people dashing out into the fresh air one after another and heading for the safety and freedom of the next valley.

Sean's fingers became increasingly cold and numb the longer he clung to the pinnacle. He tilted the Skyship at a forty-five-degree angle as soon as the Sentries opened fire. Then he gripped the pinnacle with his hands, knees and ankles, shielding himself behind it. But he could only hang on for so long.

The Sentry firepower was relentless. Each impact on the pinnacle jolted Sean's grip and soon the Skyship began to weaken. He could feel it juddering, hear the bulkheads inside creaking and groaning.

His feet suddenly came loose. His legs swinging out, he was dangling over the ravine hundreds of feet below. He shifted himself to hang from his elbows, flexing some life back into his fingers, but he was an easy target. Just a matter of seconds now. He could only hope that the Skyship had enough momentum to hit the Cube.

Two Drones swooped in, keeping pace with the Skyship, swivelling into position as they took aim at Sean. They were so close Sean could feel the heat of their engines. Their main bodies split open, their sting-like weapons powering up as they emerged from the fuselage.

Sean glared at them defiantly, ready for the worst—

—when they exploded into fireballs, their twisted wreckage spinning to the ground.

Sean looked around for his saviour.

But he heard it first. The legendary growl of a Merlin engine. He looked up as a familiar shape spiralled out of the morning sun, its .303 Colt-Browning machine guns pounding.

Danny leaned on the controls in the rear bubble of the two-seater Spitfire. In the front, Nathan thumbed the fire button, yelling as he did so. Danny grinned as he watched the two Drones crash and burn.

'Nate,' he called through the intercom, 'hold off for a second. We're going to come round again and strafe the Sentries on the cliff-top.'

'Roger that!' Nathan replied excitedly.

The Spitfire swooped underneath the Skyship, curving in towards the row of Sentries and Snipers on the cliff-top.

'Now!' he yelled.

He saw Nathan hunch forward and moments later Spitfire bullets ripped and pounded and clanged through the robots. Some exploded instantly, others fell, tipping over the cliff-edge and crashing on the rocks below.

'Nice work!' he told Nathan.

'I wish my careers teacher could see this,' Nathan replied.

'"Suited to accountancy", my arse!' Maybe it was the pure adrenaline coursing through his veins, or maybe it was the fumes from the Spit's exhausts filling the cockpit, but he was delirious with excitement. All Nathan's fears were gone and he couldn't imagine being anywhere else.

Danny glanced down to see Sean standing on the pinnacle of the Skyship again, both the boy's and the ship's implants pulsing in time.

'He's doing it,' he said in utter disbelief as he watched his son control the massive ship, steering it back towards the Cube. 'He's actually controlling it!'

'Told you,' Nathan replied. 'He's as mental as you!'

A flash of light momentarily blinded Danny and he looked to the cliff-top. Now all the remaining Sentries were firing at him.

He pulled back on the stick, skimming the cliff-walls and evading the laser blasts with a barrel roll.

'Danny, no,' Nathan yelled over the radio. 'I'm gonna puke!'

Danny pulled on the stick, coming up and around for another run.

The Skyship was still on its side. This way up, the pinnacle was only a few centimetres wide. Sean bent his knees to keep his balance as he steered the Skyship, concentrating intently. The Cube filled his vision, the white light from its core making dazzling patterns on his retinas.

Time to get off. He turned and ran full pelt away from the imminent collision. It broke his connection with the Skyship, but there was nothing the giant machine could do to stop itself from crashing now.

Sean reached out, looking for an Air Drone to connect with.

The hull jerked and buckled violently underneath him and he hit the deck. The Skyship had impacted with the Cube. He didn't dare look back, but knew he only had seconds.

He took a deep breath, got to his feet and jumped blindly into the air.

His legs kicked and his arms waved as a pair of shadows flickered over him. Two Air Drones!

He reached out, briefly making a connection with one of them. But it was moving too fast and the link broke.

Sean was falling again, the ground coming up beneath him faster than he liked.

Another Drone spiralled past. One last chance. He reached out.

The lights on the Drone's implant pulsed and the link was made. It pitched towards Sean and he grabbed its wing, clinging to it with white knuckles.

He glanced back to see the Skyship spear all the way into the Cube's core, knocking it away from the mine and over the top of the cliff in the direction of the wood. The light was blinding, the sound a wall of pure white noise as the rippling waves of energy blasting out of the Cube vaporised the other two Drones.

Sean closed his eyes and commanded his Drone to hurtle skywards.

'C'mon!' he cried as the rushing air tried to rob him of his breath. He felt the Drone shimmy as the shock wave threatened to overtake them, but he clung on tight and put everything into the thrusters.

With a cheer of pure joy he cleared the wave, riding high into the clouds.

Kate, Alex, Connor and the survivors of the commune watched as successive explosions consumed the Skyship and Cube, the debris from the fallen machines cascading down, some splashing into the lake.

The cheers around them were deafening, but for now all that mattered to Alex was the little part of her family that was here. She clung to Kate and Connor in a hug she hoped would never end.

'Look! Look!' Connor was pointing at the sky. Alex looked up to see a Spitfire, glinting in the sun, pitching into a celebratory barrel roll. She knew that her brother, who even threw up on the kiddie rides at theme parks, would be happy and crapping himself at the same time, and that made her laugh harder than she had in years.

THE ROBOTS' PROMISE

Smythe's mind scrambled to process what he'd just seen as he ran through the woods. Everything had been so clear a few minutes ago. Sean would be dead, along with all those reprobates in the mine, the town's deep-scanning underway and Smythe given the choice of early retirement to Tasmania or taking an important position in the Robot Empire elsewhere in the world. It had been so straightforward. He was always a believer in having a clear vision, a plan of action mapped out before him. And if something like an invasion came along, then he would merely rethink the plan to bend the new world to his advantage.

But so much had unravelled in the last hour, he wasn't sure he could salvage anything. He just needed to get away and think.

It had been so quick. Sean's arrival on the Skyship, the Mediator, the Spitfire. Where on Earth had that come from? Perhaps the boy was right – maybe his father was still alive?

But Smythe was not to blame for this, that much was clear. The Mediator had abandoned his post to indulge his fascination with Sean, and Smythe had screamed at the Sentries to keep their fire on the boy, but being nothing more than idiotic cyphers they reacted instinctively to the new danger and blasted the Spitfire instead. It would all go in his report, though quite who he would report to was unclear. He'd seen the Mediator break into two halves on the rocks below him. It had been odd enough to answer to the peculiar boy-robot; saluting half of one would be stranger still.

Smythe clambered over a rock wall, hitting the dirt hard and spraining his ankle. He cursed as he got to his feet and limped towards a set of ancient standing stones covered in graffiti. He was momentarily so disgusted by this act of wanton vandalism that he didn't see the two Sentries march out from behind the treeline until they were almost into the next field.

'Wait,' he called after them. 'Where are you going? Take me with you!'

With much grinding and clanking, the Sentries turned to inspect him. He noticed that their implants were flashing red. 'CITIZEN,' the first one boomed, 'RETURN TO YOUR HOME IMMEDIATELY.'

'Authorisation code 97-ZCRS,' Smythe recited, breathless with exhaustion. 'Help me, please.'

The Sentries' implants pulsed as they communed with the robot network.

'THE LOCAL CUBE HAS MALFUNCTIONED,' it said. 'UNABLE TO AUTHORISE.'

The air crackled as the first Sentry's laser cannon powered into life.

'CITIZEN,' it said, stepping towards him. 'RETURN TO YOUR HOME IMMEDIATELY.'

Smythe backed away, hands raised in surrender. 'Now, just wait a moment, let me explain – I am Zone Chief Smythe.'

The second Sentry chipped in now. 'YOU HAVE TEN SECONDS TO RETURN TO YOUR HOME.'

'Oh, for … Can you see any houses around here?' Smythe said, exasperated. 'How the hell am I supposed to—?'

Now the second Sentry raised its weapon-arm.

Smythe found himself standing in the centre of the stones, flanked by the Sentries.

'Stand down!' he cried, angry now, red-faced with flecks of spit on his lips. 'Stand down! I order you to stand down! You must obey me! Don't you know who I am?'

'THIS IS YOUR FINAL WARNING.'

'I am Robin Smythe, Zone Chief and loyal subject of the—'

The air around Mr Smythe shimmered and he suddenly felt warm. No, not warm, hot. Hotter than hot. He'd seen this happen enough times to know that he would be dead in less than a second. He tried to run, but his legs simply wouldn't move. And as his blood boiled, as his eyes evaporated and his body exploded into a million tiny carbon flakes, Smythe died happy in the knowledge that there was still an entire world of robots, an occupying force of millions, that would eventually do the same to that interfering little brat Sean Flynn.

Days later, people came looking for Smythe. All they found was a tiny black cube in the circle of ancient stones. They couldn't get it to work, but Kate identified it as Smythe's. His future. His promise from the robots.

Nearby was a dark smear on the slaughter stone that might once have been Robin Smythe, Volunteer Corps Zone Chief, and loyal subject of the robot empire. But no one could tell for sure.

ROBOTS NEVER LIE

It was Connor who found it first. Sean heard the boy shout from the lake shore. 'Sean! Sean! It's here!'

It was a pathetic sight. The once creepy and intimidating Mediator was dragging its severed torso along the rocky shore with its remaining working arm.

'Hold it down,' Sean said, and Alex, Nathan and Connor grabbed the broken robot, pinning it to the ground.

Its head ticked like someone winding a grandfather clock as it rotated a hundred and eighty degrees to look up at Sean. 'You must desist from interfacing with our network, Sean Flynn.' Its eyes were dark, sunken into black sockets.

'Keep it still.' Sean kneeled by the Mediator, closed his eyes and reached out.

'Uh … you're sure you want to mess with a Mediator, mate?' Nathan asked. 'You're gonna get us nuked.'

He wasn't wrong. There were still plenty of robots out to kill them. An entire world of them, some still in orbit with weapons of mass destruction. But Sean had an idea how to stop them.

'This one's different,' he said. 'When I connected with it, I could see their network.'

'Their what?'

'Controlling a Sentry is pretty straightforward – like controlling a remote-control car.'

'That's easy for you to say, matey,' Nathan said.

'A Sniper, a Drone, they have different levels of sophistication,' Sean said, his eyes still closed. 'But the Mediator's a step up. It's like when I was in the Deep Scanner. They're both hubs for the robot network's data. I just hope it goes both ways.'

Sean's implant went into overdrive again, flashing and pulsing wildly. The Mediator's, too.

'It's resisting,' Sean's eyes briefly flickered open. 'I knew it.'

'You … must … desist—' the Mediator said, its voice strained.

Sean felt their implants pulse in unison. The connection was made.

Eyes closed, he was back in the network. Billions of cubes floated around him in this new dimension, each one a robot, each one connected to the network. He found one nearby and reached out with his mind. A Sentry. One of many looking for a new Cube. Sean knew what to do. He could feel the retreating Sentries obeying his command as they froze in their tracks. With a thought, he made them all eject their power cells. They winked out of existence before him, disappearing from the network.

He sought out more, and more, shutting down millions of robots all over the world. Distance meant nothing here. His commands and thoughts passed through other Mediators at light-speed, all blissfully unaware that they were under attack.

Sean saw through the robots. Glimpses of every corner of the world as robot after robot shuddered and died when their power cells left their bodies.

He could sense the bigger robots, the Cubes and Skyships, beginning to realise what was happening. Urgent transmissions pulsed through the network. One simple order: *Retreat*.

'Sean.' He could hear Alex's voice from the other side. It sounded muffled, like he was under water and she was on dry land. 'They're leaving!'

'I know,' he said, feeling the sweat pour down his face. 'I can see ... everything.' He sensed the Cubes rising all over the planet. But he couldn't let them get away. He sent his own simple command.

Self-destruct.

When the first Cube exploded, somewhere over the Indian Ocean, he was so surprised that he nearly lost the link. His eyes opened briefly and he was back in the real world. No, not yet. He had to go back in.

But now the Mediator was fighting him. Sean felt the robot tugging at his mind. The Mediator was still trying to complete Sean's deep scan.

Sean did everything he could to ignore it. More and more Cubes and Skyships were imploding all over the world, Drones tumbling out of the sky.

But his mind grew darker, and the colours faded. He was losing his thread of thought. It was like warm water rising around him. Comfortable, quiet, painless. If this was death, then it came with a welcoming embrace.

He heard the Mediator say something, then Nathan and Alex, but the noise was faint, distant.

Something happened. The Mediator winked out of existence. Gone, as if he were never there.

But Sean remained in the network. He felt himself falling. Nothing he could do would get him up again. He began to feel cold. But the robots were offline. Those that had not been destroyed, the ones beyond his reach, were now running, leaving the planet. The network was corrupted and broken, and without its reassuring hum they were nothing more than machines acting on survival impulses.

All light around Sean faded. All sound was gone. He floated in empty space, lost in the network. He wondered if he would die, or stay in limbo like this for ever. He couldn't feel his arms or legs, only the pounding of his heart. He told it to keep beating. To stay alive.

As Alex gazed up at the Cubes and Skyships exploding in the distant skies, the Mediator began speaking in a broken voice. 'This … is not … the end … robots never … never—'

'Robots never lie,' Nathan said. 'Whatever!'

'It's just you don't always tell the truth, do you?' Alex reached into its torso and ripped out its cube-shaped power cell. Its eyes went dark. *Good*, she thought, *it's dead*. But then Sean's body started to convulse.

'Give him mouth-to-mouth,' Connor cried as he flicked through his SAS Survival Handbook.

'I ain't doing it,' Nathan said.

He said it was like the Deep Scanner, Alex thought, shoving Nathan aside and leaning over Sean's body. *Any kind of human contact*, Sean had told her. *Any kind of warmth.*

She took his hand in hers and gently kissed his lips.

'That,' said Connor, 'is not mouth-to-mouth.'

A glimmer of warmth. A touch on his hand bringing his nerve endings back to life. Pressure against his lips. Light and sounds rushed around him and his lungs burned as Sean took a breath. It felt like his first for a long time.

He found himself sitting upright, gasping for air. He saw Alex's smiling face, welcoming him back to the world.

Had she just kissed him? He saw the Mediator's power cell nearby. His friends had yanked it out. They'd saved him.

'Thanks, guys,' Sean croaked, his throat dry.

Their eyes lit up when he spoke. There were hugs and cheers and they helped him to his feet.

They stood on the lake shore by the defunct Mediator's motionless body and looked up into the bright blue sky. Sean hadn't imagined it. He couldn't help but smile as he watched black smoke trailing from Cubes and Skyships as they fell back to Earth.

The robots were defeated.

There was a celebration at the castle that night. Sean watched from the parapets as the aimless exodus of newly freed townspeople were drawn to its stone walls, billowing flags and flaming torches. Nathan and Connor had returned to the Fairfield Station gift shop and liberated what fireworks Connor hadn't already pinched and set them off over the castle as the sun went down. A crowd of grateful survivors danced and sang around the blazing bonfire glowing in the outer bailey.

Sean wandered aimlessly, enjoying the happiness, the new optimism. A band played acoustic instruments, a deer roasted on a spit, a woman was acting out a story for a group of enthralled toddlers, Toby and some of the older children played tag, racing through the crowd, laughing. Sean saw familiar faces. Michael, Del and Bill from the Poseidon were singing a rude song while Kevin danced the cancan on a table in his dress. Magpie grabbed Sean in a headlock and kissed his hair before letting him go.

A woman called Mrs McGhie tearfully hugged his mum, whispering, 'Sorry,' again and again and again. The little girl who had spotted Sean climbing over her fence came to say hello, introduced her brother and asked Sean to confirm that she really had seen him and wasn't a lying spod-head. He was happy to oblige.

He wondered if his anonymous friend was here. The one who sent the note saying that his dad was still alive. Danny couldn't imagine who it might be. They asked about, but no one appeared to know.

They raised a glass to whoever it was and Sean's mum and dad started to cry and they all hugged and he got embarrassed.

'Sorry I doubted you,' his dad said, shaking his hand. Something he'd never done before. A grown-up gesture. Sean felt weird about it. He didn't want to grow up quite yet. He wanted to enjoy what little of his childhood he had left. But then his mum attacked him with a salvo of wet kisses and he felt five years old again.

A memorial shrine began to grow as the night passed. On a table teeming with candles, people placed photos of loved ones lost, missing or dead. Wild flowers were heaped around them. Sean took a closer look. He found Morse Code Martin, younger and in his army uniform, and one of Wayne with his wife Mandy, both smiling, in happier times. Connor placed a photo of him with his parents at the beach, laughing at the ice cream on his dad's face. Some, like Nathan and Alex, no longer had photos, but instead lit a candle each.

Nathan was talking to Josie and her friends. He was regaling them with tales of his adventures, miming Spitfire strafing runs. Later he saw Nate slow-dancing with Josie while everyone else was jigging along to the band's frenetic songs of freedom.

The party went on all night. As the sun began to rise, Sean saw his mum and dad huddling near the dying embers of the fire, chatting with a young mother about school and the future. Connor nestled against Kate, wearing his Viking helmet and tabard. His eyelids drooped and she hugged him tight.

Monique filled Alex's glass with champagne. They toasted the new world. Alex took a big sip and got a case of the giggles as she nearly spilled it down her dress. As she patted herself dry, she caught Sean's eye. She made her excuses and they found a quiet spot away from the noise of the celebrations.

'Thank you,' he said.

'For what?'

'For saving me.' Sean took her hand. 'I know it was you.'

'No one seems to know what really happened,' she said. 'Some people think the army finally fought back, others that the robots got some kind of virus. I've been putting them right, but none of them believes me. You should tell them what really—'

'Y'know what?' He said, looking around. 'Don't. I'm not sure I want that kind of attention.'

'So what do we do now?' she asked.

'I have no idea.' He linked his arm with hers and they strolled back towards the bonfire. 'I never thought that far ahead. How about we start with tomorrow and see how we go from there?'

'Sounds good to me,' she said.

Arm-in-arm, they stood by the bonfire. Sean's gaze followed the embers carried upwards on the breeze. Then his eyes found the stars.

The robots' orbital ship inched slowly towards the full moon, every bit as bright and reflective in the dawn sky. Together they resembled a pair of glowering eyes.

Sean knew it wasn't over yet.

He stared back. Brave. Unbowed. Waiting.

An afterword on living life dangerously ...

My editor, publisher and some very nervous lawyers have asked me to make it clear to you, dear reader, that some of our heroes' activities are extremely dangerous and should in no way be attempted by your good self.

Now, I know you're smart and not a monkey-see, monkey-do kind of person, but just in case any of your slightly dimmer acquaintances get hold of this book and try something stupid, here's a rundown of all the particular no-nos in the story ...

Electrocution

When Jon and I were writing the screenplay we wanted the gang to be able to disable their implants in a believable way. We didn't want a technobabble solution – *'How about we re-route the power source through the main bypass coupling felange maguffin wotsit?'* – nor to make one of them some unbelievable genius at unraveling robot technology (though there was a character in the early drafts called Ajay, who was exactly that!). Nor did we want it to be something that any Tom, Dick or Harry could figure out for themselves.

Many of the great discoveries in science happened by accident:

Alexander Fleming discovered penicillin on a discarded, mouldy petri dish, Charles Goodyear spent years tampering with rubber, nearly asphyxiating himself in the process, before accidentally discovering the vulcanised rubber that we use on our tyres today. So, like these great discoveries, we wanted an accident that no ordinary person could replicate, and we wanted it to be tinged with danger and pain. After all, you don't want to make life too easy for your heroes, do you?

We liked the idea of somehow short-circuiting the implants, but a full-on electric shock from the mains was out of the question: the amps are so powerful you'd be dead before you hit the floor (volts hurt, amps kill). So we consulted with electricians, investigated the difference between AC and DC currents and hit upon the idea of a shock from a set-up so convoluted that it would be impossible to replicate (even the robots couldn't figure it out!): a damaged games console, via a faulty DC adapter, via an old, half-charged car battery. There's simply no way of really knowing how strong or dangerous the shock in our story is. But it's enough to be so painful that no one wants to do it twice.

My father-in-law is a retired builder and would always work cautiously with electricity. It always baffled him that people would be nervous about tinkering with their plumbing, but would gleefully fiddle with their home electrics and often nearly kill themselves in the process. Maybe it's because we're all taught to wire plugs at school? A little knowledge is a dangerous thing. I speak as someone who recently blew a fuse installing our porch light. The money I paid the expert electrician to come and fix my mess was worth every penny.

Fireworks

I'm genuinely astonished that we're still allowed to buy fireworks over the counter in shops. I suspect that if it wasn't for our annual celebration of the attempted assassination of James I this wouldn't be the case. Anyway, should you find yourself in the possession of these little packets of gunpowder, do not be tempted to ignite them. Rockets can hit a top speed of a hundred and fifty miles an hour, some travel 200 meters, and the majority of fireworks-related injuries recorded in the UK are for children under 17. Worse, the pain from firework burns is intense and long lasting and will scar you for life. Don't believe me? Look up 'firework burns' images on the internet and enjoy your subsequent nightmares.

Eating raw potatoes

You'll find plenty of folk who will tell that eating raw spuds is fine, and others who will tell you stories of deathly poisoning. I suspect that anyone who eats a raw potato might be a little odd, and could have a constitution peculiar and tough enough to cope with solanine: a poison found in raw potatoes, aubergines, tomatoes and nightshade. Give me well-cooked chips, wedges and roast spuds with garlic instead!

So for the record: never, ever eat potatoes that are green under the skin.

I once got mild green potato poisoning at a publishers' conference. It was like being stabbed in the gut. The pain lasted about forty-eight hours, and I was lucky. It's been known to kill.

Mushrooms

The internet is littered with stories of entire families being accidentally poisoned by mushrooms picked in the wild; some dying, others surviving after long and agonising pain. The SAS Survival Handbook that Connor uses to find edible mushrooms in the wood is a real book and really does have colour illustrations of fungi, both edible and poisonous. When our gang tried it they had no choice: they had to survive in the woods and had no idea if they would reach their destination. All mushrooms start to look alike to me after a while, so on the whole I prefer to choose mine in the safe confines of a grocery. You should too.

Punching glass

As the gang run from a Sentry and hide behind the Poseidon Hotel, Sean places his coat against a pane of glass and smashes it through. He was lucky that the glass was weak and smashed easily. When I was ten I was asked to open a sticky window for a decorator who was working on our house. That glass was weak too, and I put my hand straight through it. The decorator nearly passed out – he hated the sight of blood – and I was rushed to the hospital where I got nine stitches for my trouble. The doctor said I was extremely lucky not to have severed any arteries in my arm. If I had, I would have bled to death in minutes. I recall waiting in the A&E and showing a woman my cut, which was in a V-shape just below my right hand ring finger. I could lift it up like a little flap! She nearly passed out, too.

Should you ever meet me, ask about the scar and I'll show it to you for a small fee.

And that's it. Curiously the nervous publishers and lawyers seemed okay with the assault rifles, blowing up your school with bunsen burner gas, and riding Skyships into giant robot Cubes. However, personally I would steer you away from these too. Try paintballing and skateboarding and always wear the correct safety gear.

And if you want to live dangerously? What should you do? Join the Scouts or a similar organization. You get to do some awesome stuff and it's supervised and safe. I would also recommend the SAS Survival Handbook and The Dangerous Book for Boys (Girls: don't be put off by the title, it's an awesome book for all).

Well, I hope you enjoyed this rundown of the more deadly parts of this book and I hope you'll survive long enough for when the robots return …

Mark Stay

ROBOT OVERLORDS: THE MEDIATOR PROTOTYPE

A SHORT STORY BY MARK STAY

Based on characters and situations created
by Jon Wright and Mark Stay

INTRODUCTION

This story predates the events told in Robot Overlords, *and we won't be meeting Sean, Nathan, Alex or Connor. However, in the test screenings for* Robot Overlords *people always wanted to know more about the creepy Mediator. Why is it so different from the other robots? Why is it a boy? Why does he talk like that? And can he please stop giving me nightmares now, please? Well, just for you curious types who have to know everything, here's how he came to be…*

The first time Alfie Winters was abducted he assumed, naturally, that it was by aliens. Well you would, wouldn't you?

That day had been perfectly normal. Like most days, it had ended with a massive argument at home.

'Who started it?' his mum yelled. As if that was important. As if the cause of a fight was what really mattered. Truth was, Alfie paid so little attention to what people said and did these days that he simply fell back on stock phrases, 'It wasn't me! You never listen to me. You never believe me. You always take their side!'

What *had* happened was that some kid had said something, Alfie gave back as good as he got, and then the fists started flying. This was how most days panned out, so why did everyone get so wound up about it? People sucked. That was the truth, and the less he had to do with them the better.

Having his form tutor call his mum was such a regular event that it didn't worry him anymore; the police joked that they'd brought Alfie home so many times that he should have some sort of loyalty card.

'Mrs Winters, your son lacks … motivation,' Mrs Keynes, Head of Year 7, had said at the most recent parents' evening. 'If staring into space was an Olympic sport, Alfie would be a gold medallist. Any attempt to include him in the lesson results in aggression and abuse. I'd like to discuss how we can …' After that the words faded into background noise. Alfie found an empty spot of sky outside and stared at it. His mum was fiddling with her e-cigarette thing at the time, so he knew she wasn't paying attention either. He had tried so often to make people hear his side of the story, but they all refused to listen, so he'd given up on it.

He didn't bother with school much after that.

Instead, he would run off to his secret place – a ramshackle tree house in the woods near the bypass. He and his mate Riz had built it last summer. They'd nicked some wooden pallets from round the back of the supermarket, hauled them up the tree and nailed them together in a rough box shape. There was no roof, and the whole thing creaked like a ship at sea, but it was solid enough for him.

Riz had moved away after Christmas, so now it was all Alfie's. This was where he came to get away, where no one would find him. After the argument about the fight, and some door slamming and shouting, Alfie left the house. He made his way through the maze of alleys around the estate, slipped through the gap in the concrete wall by the kids' play area, followed the stream into the wood until he could hear the distant, never-ending white noise of the cars on the bypass. He pulled himself up into the tree house using the blue tow rope his dad had been trying to find last weekend.

This is where Alfie would try to sort his thoughts into some kind of order. But in between concocting revenge fantasies and dreaming of living on a desert island somewhere, troubling thoughts about the future would leak into his mind. School was boring as hell, but a job might be even worse. What was the point of life if he couldn't do what he wanted? What was the point of life anyway? And what the hell was that bright light up there?

The last question brought a new distraction. A police chopper, maybe? Alfie glanced up to see a black cube floating above the treeline. It was about the size of a house, with four blinding white searchlights swirling underneath it. The only noise it made was a low buzz. The sound reminded Alfie of when the TV broke just before Christmas – an electronic distortion that set his teeth on edge. So, no. Not the police.

Then all four searchlights converged on him. Alfie closed his eyes, jerked back, began to fall, and then …

He woke in darkness. The floor beneath him was cold, metallic. Alfie wondered why his right cheek ached, then he realised he was lying face-down, probably had been for some time. It was pitch black. He couldn't even see his hand in front of his face.

'Hello?' he croaked. His mouth was dry. How long had he been there?

He stayed lying down, not sure if moving about was a good idea. Was this a cell? Had he been arrested? No, cells usually smelled of piss, puke or detergent. This smelled of … nothing. Sterile air.

'Alfie Winters,' a voice said. It didn't seem to come from a speaker, but instead filled the blackness around him, soaking into his ears like bathwater. 'Do not be afraid. We wish you no harm.' The voice was strange. Machine-like. A patchwork of words from different voices, male, female, old and young. 'The first test will begin in moments.'

'Lemme out!' Alfie said, afraid, but doing his best to hide it.

Then the floor beneath him began to glow, first a dim grey, then a bright white.

He looked around, getting to his feet. The room was square, about the size of his bedroom at home. There were no windows or doors, or even joins in the floor, or wall. It seemed to be one continuous smooth surface. He'd never seen anything like it.

'Let me out!' he said, louder this time.

All the walls were glowing bright white now, and Alfie's eyes twisted into a squint.

Images began to flash on every surface. No noise, just a blur of photos: faces, places, animals, vehicles.

Every few seconds the slideshow would slow down, as if particular images might have greater impact on him. Certain pictures seemed to appear more regularly than others: spiders, insects, snakes, dogs. Big, aggressive men, fists clenched. It was as if someone was sorting through them, finding the ones which would scare the crap out of him the most.

Then came the noises: women screaming, men wailing, animals howling, babies so distressed that they could scarcely catch their breath between sobs. A surround-sound cacophony of nightmare noises.

Alfie wanted to pound the walls and beg to be freed, but he'd learned from a lifetime of detentions that begging achieved nothing. Alfie knew the secret to driving his teachers mad was to just look through them, as if they weren't there. And so that's what he chose to do. He stared into space. Lids halfway down his eyes. His face slack, the epitome of *whatevs*.

The room suddenly fell dark again. Alfie couldn't be sure how much time had passed, but he was beginning to feel drowsy. He fell to his knees.

The smell of wet soil filled his nostrils. Alfie woke by the pond in the wood. It was raining and it was night, but a bright moon shone through the wood's canopy. He could hear the cars on the bypass and there were no strange, silent cubes floating above him.

He ran the whole way home.

'You lying toe-rag, Alfie!'

'But, mum—!'

He got the bollocking of his life when he got home. He'd been gone five hours. 'I was worried sick,' his mum screeched as she gathered her handbag and coat and headed for the door. 'You know if I'm late for work that old git docks my pay. Next time, I'll lock you out, see how you like that.'

'It was, like, a space ship or something.' Even as he said it out loud, Alfie knew it sounded lame. 'I was abducted!'

'I bloody wish,' Alfie's mum said as she took a drag on her e-cigarette, which glowed green in the dark hallway. 'Dinner's on the side in the kitchen, your dad said he'll be home by ten. Any more lies, Alfie Winters, and I swear to God I'll smack your arse so hard you won't be able to sit down for a month.'

And with the bang of the door and the clattering of the letter-box, she was gone.

Alfie found dinner, a cold and greasy burger from the van by the bus garage – mum got them at the end of the day for free from a mate who worked there – and tried to chill out with a bit of FIFA. But his mind was racing as he tried to make sense of what had happened today.

Mum had updated dad via text, so when he got home after midnight he smacked Alfie around the head, called him a 'lying scrote' and sent him to his room.

A week went by and, since no one believed Alfie, he stopped talking about it.

The kids in his class said he was mental. Tyla and Gid, the bigger kids he hung out with on the estate, thought he was on drugs, and he knew the local police and hobby-bobbies would just laugh.

Night after night he would go back to the treehouse, shouting at the moon and the stars, 'Come on! Come and get me!' but the only reply was the occasional coo from some solitary wood pigeon.

He wondered why he had been taken. Maybe it's because they knew no one would believe him? Who would listen to a lying scrote like Alfie Winters?

Alfie, fed-up with cold, greasy burgers, was passing the local allotments one night when he thought about all that free food just waiting to be plucked out of the ground. He hopped over the fence, ignored the chickens that clucked at him from a nearby enclosure, and looked for whatever was ready for picking. His granddad, the only person who had ever listened to Alfie, used to bring him here when he was little. 'Can't beat fresh fruit and veg, Alfie,' he had told him. 'Better than the crap your mum slops out of those tins.'

Alfie hadn't been convinced, but suddenly anything seemed better than going home and listening to his parents shout at each other.

Carrots. Alfie recognised the leaves. He reached down, gave one a yank, and up it came – bright orange and twisted. He brushed off the soil, then bit down with a satisfying crunch. He took a few more, carefully replacing the leaves, making it look like the carrots were still underground, so no one would notice they'd been taken until they came to harvest them.

He was taking his second bite when he got the nagging feeling that something was wrong. He couldn't quite put his finger on it. Then he realised that the chickens had gone quiet. He looked round to see the last of them go scurrying into its coop.

A bright light beamed down from above. Alfie winced and he fell into unconsciousness.

He found himself in the same cell again. Or was it? Did it seem bigger this time? He couldn't be sure. Every surface glowed a dull white, so at least he could see.

Silently, one of the walls slid back, revealing a corridor stretching away into the darkness beyond. Then another wall did the same, and another.

The room went dark. The corridors began to glow white.

'No point hanging round here, then, eh?' Alfie said to himself in the gloom, choosing the nearest exit and stepping into a brightening corridor.

The wall closed behind him, but more gaps slid open, more ways to get lost. Alfie had never been one for staying still for long, so he just kept moving, turning randomly left or right through the maze, as more doors slid open.

'Alfie?' a familiar voice called.

'Mum?' he stopped in his tracks.

'Alfie?' the voice repeated. But the tone was exactly the same. Some kind of recording. They were messing with him, and he ignored it.

'Alfie, boy, get back here!' His dad this time. Alfie thought about running, but he wouldn't give them the satisfaction. He stood still, trying to shut it all out.

Images began to appear on the floor, ceiling and wall. Some were like those before, others were ... just strange. Alfie was distracted by the looping image of a man's arm folding back unnaturally, revealing glowing fibre optics inside. 'What the what?' he muttered to himself, both repulsed and fascinated.

There were fewer creepy images this time. Some were kind of cute: happy babies and yapping puppies accompanied him down one corridor.

One bark sounded a little closer than the others. Alfie spun on his heels to find an actual puppy, an adorable Golden Labrador, skittering towards him. Its eyes darted from side to side. It looked afraid, unsure of what was real.

Alfie slapped his thighs and got down on his haunches, 'All right, mate? C'mere.' The puppy ran into his arms, tail wagging, its nose sniffing him all over as if to make sure Alfie was genuine. His uncle had three dogs at home that Alfie would play with all the time. Big ones. So this soppy little thing was no problem.

Without warning, the corridor went dark and quiet. The pup whimpered and Alfie held him close, 'It's okay, mate, don't worry.'

The puppy suddenly wriggled in Alfie's grip, its ears alert.

Alfie strained to listen. A *slap-slap-slap* sound getting rapidly closer. Someone with flat feet running blindly down the corridor. The puppy broke free of Alfie's arms and hurtled in the other direction. 'Yeah, I think you're right, mate,' Alfie muttered, running after him.

The pup was fast, but Alfie was used to legging it on demand and was quick to catch up. He followed the puppy round corner after corner, not caring where he ended up, so long as he was away from those heavy footsteps. But as he turned on sharp bend, he found it waiting for him, turning in little circles. A dead end!

'Shite,' Alfie cursed. He looked back the way they'd come, where a long shadow was looming larger. The footsteps were getting louder. After a moment a man came gallumphing around the bend. A big man, huge biceps, fists clenched, teeth bared like he wanted a fight. Another abductee? He looked angry, lost, even a little frightened. Not a great combination in a situation like this.

'Oi, son!' he rushed towards Alfie, and for a second the boy wondered if he was actually going to stop or just run into him. 'What's goin' on? Where the bloody hell are we?'

'I dunno.' Alfie went immediately on the defensive. 'Don't blame me.'

'You got summink to do with this?' the man demanded, grabbing Alfie by his shirt.

There was a chirpy 'Yip!' from the pup. Alfie craned his neck and saw that another door had slid open. The pup was already halfway down the next corridor. The man had seen it too, and Alfie took advantage of the distraction to shove the restraining hand away. In the blink of an eye, Alfie was chasing the pup.

'Oi! Get back here!' The big guy was after him in seconds.

Alfie was fast, but this fella had a long stride. Alfie could hear the man's rasping breath closing in, making the hairs on the back of his neck stand on end.

The puppy took a sharp left, catching Alfie unawares. He turned too late, twisting his ankle and tumbling into one of the glowing walls. The man was on him in a moment, hoisting him off the ground and slamming him against the wall, knocking all the breath out of him.

'No more pissing about, son.' The man clenched a meaty fist. 'What the bloody hell is this place?'

Peering round the corner, the pup watched them, whimpering. And that gave Alfie his idea.

He turned on his secret weapon. The puppy-dog eyes.

It was a technique that had once worked on his mum and dad, though they didn't fall for it anymore. Even the police were starting to suss it out, but this guy ...

'I don't know, mister,' Alfie said, in his best *I-didn't-do-it-nothing-to-do-with-me* voice. 'They took me too. This is my second time. I was just minding my own business when this bright light comes out of the sky, and I was really scared, and I miss my mum and dad and—' He was lying like a pro now, so adept at the puppy eyes that he could feel a layer of glistening tears gathering on his eyeballs.

The man relaxed his grip on Alfie's shirt. Then his hands actually began to tremble. He fell to his knees, sobbing and shaking. 'What's happening? Please! Somebody help me!'

The walls flickered to bright white again. As the man pounded on one wall it swung around like a revolving door. 'No! Wait!' the big guy yelled, as he was swept away like dust off a shelf.

Alfie was left alone with the puppy. It felt like the end of a test.

'A question.' That voice again. It came from everywhere at once. 'How was that achieved?'

'I ain't talking till I get some answers,' Alfie said with all the defiance he could muster. 'Who are you lot? And where am I?'

As if in reply, the walls changed to show the planet Earth from orbit. For a second, Alfie thought he was suspended in space, but when he stumbled back he could feel the hard floor of the cell under his feet. An illusion? Some kind of webcam from space? The puppy barked, leaped out of Alfie's arms and started sniffing around the South Pacific.

I'm in a space ship, Alfie thought. I've been abducted by aliens and they've got me in space.

Cool. Freaky, but cool. His heart began to race as the idea settled in his head. He began to realise there was no way he could get home without his abductors' permission.

Okay, not so cool.

The image of the Earth disappeared, and once more the room fell dark.

'Again: how was that achieved?' the voice asked.

'How was what achieved?'

Something like a face appeared on one of the walls. A blank, featureless face. White as a ghost and just as formless.

'Our apologies, Alfie Winters. This must be very disorienting for you.'

As it spoke, the face began to shift and move. The skin became hollow where the eye sockets should be. Cheekbones formed, a mouth, ears. It reminded Alfie of the time his mum left one of his Star Wars figures on the radiator and its face melted.

'How did you prevent the aggressive man from hurting you?' it asked. 'We calculated that his level of testosterone, combined with an excessive alcohol intake and low IQ, would lead to a violent encounter. Yet you avoided that outcome. We are curious to learn how this was achieved.'

As the face continued to take shape, Alfie realised that it was trying to look like him.

'Puppy dog eyes, innit,' he shrugged.

There was a pause. Alfie could almost feel the room thinking.

'Meaning you adopt the characteristics of a young canine in order to gain sympathy, and thus defuse the situation?' Another pause for thought. 'An interesting strategy,' the voice said eventually. 'We must confer further with the network.'

The walls around Alfie began to glow brighter and brighter. The puppy leapt back into his arms with a yelp. Alfie held him close and shut his eyes tight, and then …

*

304

Alfie awoke back on the allotment. It was morning and the first gardeners to arrive were running towards him, shaking their fists and shouting something about stolen carrots. Alfie and the puppy legged it.

'Dad … where's the Xbox?'

About a week had passed since that last encounter and Alfie was having a miserable time. Mum was yelling at him even more, the school was threatening to permanently exclude him for non-attendance, and now his Xbox had gone.

'Down the dosh shop,' his dad said, referring to the pawn shop in town. Every now and then something in the house would disappear in return for some ready cash from the pawnbrokers. It was usually some of mum's jewellery. Sometimes it came back, but more often than not it stayed there for good, when dad was unable to pay back the loan. 'Just till the end of the month,' he continued. 'Caught short, ain't I? Bills and such. All be sorted payday,' he scruffed Alfie's hair in a way that he thought would be reassuring. It wasn't. Alfie knew where his dad's money went, and it wasn't on bills. He watched as his dad activated a gambling app on his phone.

Worried that his dad might even sell the puppy, Alfie had kept him a secret. He named him Minotaur and kept him at the treehouse. At the weekend Alfie had nicked a box of dog food from the delivery bay around the back of the Tesco Express. He also borrowed one of mum's plastic fruit bowls and left it outside the treehouse to collect rainwater.

Alfie was taking Minotaur for a walk one evening when he stumbled across Tyla and Gid and a group of about a dozen other kids roaming the concrete walkways of the estate.

'Alfie, blud, you recovered from having Uranus probed, yeah?' Tyla cackled and the others joined in.

History does not record what Alfie said in response, but it

involved a slander concerning Tyla's mother, UFOs, and a sexual act illegal in most States of the US.

Seconds later, Alfie was running for his life across the old rec.

So when the bright lights appeared above him this time, they were rather more welcome.

He awoke in the cell, as before. But this time he was no longer afraid. In fact, he was beginning to enjoy these encounters.

'Greetings, Alfie Winters,' the voice said, its face appearing on the wall. This face had a bit more detail. It was like looking at his own reflection in a milky white pond.

'We have reviewed your tests, analysed your strategy with the aggressive man, and found that it might suit our needs. We should like your opinion on our experimental models.'

'Look, mate, I, like, understand the individual words you're saying,' Alfie said, 'but you gotta learn to speak proper English.'

A panel slid open, revealing what looked like a toy baby doll. It was life-size and uncannily realistic. Apart from the eyes. They weren't quite right. Dull. Empty.

Alfie, fascinated, leaned closer for a better look. 'That's not real, is it? Tell me that's not a dead baby, or something, I don't—'

The baby jerked into life with a high-pitched whine and a smell of hot oil that made Alfie think of his uncle's garage, littered with greasy car parts. The baby's head rotated with a *click-click-click*, till it stared directly at Alfie with glassy, lifeless eyes.

'Holy crap!' Alfie jumped back in fright.

'Yes, that was a common reaction,' said the voice. 'Our analysis – and your solution to the violence simulator – has shown that humans share collective responses to other humans of a particular types: you fear large arms, shoulders and tiny brains, like the man we pitted you against.'

The baby got to its feet and started to walk around the cell with eerie, jerky movements.

'And humans react positively to creatures with oversized heads and big eyes,' the voice continued. 'Thus, this smaller model should work, but all of our subjects have reacted with the same mixture of terror and revulsion that you have displayed. We have pursued the theory with other models ...'

More doors slid open and other mechanical children appeared: robot toddlers, robot six-year-olds, all with the same jerky movement and dead eyes, accompanied by that smell of hot oil.

'But we cannot recreate the reaction you elicited, Alfie Winters.'

The small machines all limped towards Alfie like child zombies, their arms reaching out for him. He soon found himself backed into a corner.

'You want people to find *these* cute?' Alfie shook his head. 'You're doing it all wrong, mate. These are freaks, man. You made the eyes way too evil. They need to be bigger. And look less ... dead.'

One of the toddlers took Alfie's hand. He shook it off, 'Get that weird-arse crap away from me!'

'We have further concerns,' the voice said. 'The smaller models—'

'Babies,' Alfie corrected it. 'We call them babies.'

'These babies are fragile and their mobility is limited. Their use in the field will be significantly constrained by these shortcomings.'

'Just make 'em bigger.'

An image flashed up on one of the walls. A baby robot. It suddenly warped in size.

'No, no,' Alfie waved his hands at the image. 'Not some giant baby. That's even worse. Nah, make it like me. My size.'

'And the puppy eye phenomenon will still be effective?'

'You saw it work, didn't you?'

Another pause as the voice considered this.

'We thank you, Alfie Winters,' it said. 'We will contact you shortly.'

*

'Where is it? Good boy! Good boy!' Alfie was training Minotaur to sniff out food hidden under fallen spring blossom when the pup suddenly bolted upright, its nose twitching, ears pricked up on high alert. Alfie followed Minotaur's sharp stare to see someone moving through the wood, approaching the tree house through the daffodils.

He looked like a boy, about Alfie's age. But he walked strangely. Stilted, stiff. As it got closer Alfie saw that its face was much like his own. There were the same freckles, little human imperfections – but it wasn't quite right. The head was too big, the arms a little short, and the smell of hot oil was a dead giveaway.

'Alfie Winters.' It spoke with the same voice as the face in the cell. 'Greetings.'

As it moved, Alfie could hear machinery and gears whirring.

'You're using my face?' he complained. 'You can't use my face. I've got copyright on that.'

'We thought you would find the familiarity pleasing,' the boy robot said.

Alfie's face scrunched in disgust. 'You've got lots to learn, mate. And what's that?' He pointed to a round device attached to the thing's neck. It was black, like a tiny ice hockey puck.

'My implant is used for communication and tracking,' it said.

'Uh, right,' Alfie said, not bothering to follow that one up. 'What are you supposed to be, anyway?'

'I am a field-test prototype of a Mediator-Class robot,' it replied. 'We wish to conduct an experiment in the wild and we should like to request your assistance one last time, Alfie Winters. We require an adult male capable of grievous bodily harm, with a low intelligence quota.'

'Huh?'

'Who is the most aggressive, stupid man in this zone?'

'Oh, easy,' Alfie said, without hesitation. 'Nine-inch Neil.'

'Take me to him.'

Tyson's was a nightclub off the high street, squatting in the shadows under the old iron railway bridge. Alfie's mum had worked the bar there a few times, and she would come home with stories of booze-fuelled punch-ups that would start with two people bickering over something trivial and end with the entire dance floor becoming a flurry of fists, smashed glasses and bloody noses. The hero of these stories was the club's doorman and bouncer, Nine-Inch Neil. With a torso shaped like an inverted mountain, and a head capped with hair shaved into a Saint George cross, Nine-Inch Neil would calmly stride into the centre of the melee and start peeling combatants off each other like foil off a ready meal.

For a big man he had a surprisingly high-pitched voice, but no one ever, *ever* pointed this out to him twice. His hands were like outsized goalkeeper's gloves, and could do a lot of damage.

As Alfie and his robot companion approached the flickering neon lights of the main entrance, Neil was in the process of hurling one of the nightclub's more intoxicated patrons into the street.

'And if I see you come here again,' Neil's voice hooted like an owl's as the unfortunate evacuee tumbled across the pavement, 'I'll rip 'em off and give 'em to me sister for earrings!'

'You sure about this?' Alfie said, hesitant, with a slight tremor in his voice.

The Mediator Prototype looked on, totally fascinated, as Nine-Inch Neil started to boot the man in the ribs, 'He is perfect,' it said.

Neil had returned to chatting with a pair of his fellow doormen as Alfie and his companion came closer. The Mediator took up a position before the group of doormen, hands folded before itself like Alfie's Head Teacher at assemblies.

One of the other doormen glanced at the Mediator Prototype, did a classic double-take, then nudged Neil.

'What the bloody hell is that?' he said.

Neil frowned and tilted his head to one side, 'Help you, boys?'

'Nah,' Alfie grinned. 'Just hanging out.'

'Then sod off and do it somewhere else.' Neil jabbed a thumb down the street. 'This ain't a crèche.'

'The subject's use of language suggests bilingual capabilities,' the Mediator Prototype said. 'He may not be as imbecilic as is required for the experiment.'

'What you call me, shortarse?' Neil bristled, his voice rising even higher in pitch. 'I ain't bi-nuffin'!'

'Perhaps, he is perfect after all,' the Mediator Prototype decided. 'I shall begin the experiment with a series of statements designed to provoke an aggressive response.'

'I know your mum, don't I?' Neil turned his attention to Alfie. 'You're Alfie, innit? Right, listen up, Alfie: you, and your mate, piss off!'

'Free country,' Alfie sneered.

'Is it now?' Nine-Inch Neil moved forward, ready to show him just how un-free this bit of it was.

The Mediator Prototype stepped between them, 'I question your virility, and the efficacy of your genitalia.'

Neil stopped in his tracks and turned to his two bouncer companions, 'What was that?'

'Something about your knob, Neil,' said the first with a chuckle.

'What?'

'He's saying your willy don't work,' said the other.

The Mediator Prototype continued, 'Your body odour suggests your level of personal hygiene is insufficient at best.' It leaned forward. 'And an analysis of your breath reveals trimethylaminuria: chronic halitosis caused by your body's inability to breakdown trimethylamine, which is then released in breath, sweat and urine. This is also known as "Fishy breath". You should arrange for immediate urine and blood tests.'

'Fishy breath?' Nine-Inch Neil's nostrils flared, his lips puckered angrily, revealing jagged teeth.

Alfie took the Mediator Prototype's arm, 'How about we give it a rest now, eh?'

But the robot would not budge, 'You have just released faecal matter into the air,' it told Neil. 'Malodorous flatulence. Analysis suggests you see a physician about your anal fissure.'

Nine-Inch Neil – so named, because he claimed to have survived having a nine-inch nail thrust into his skull by an ex-girlfriend – had clearly had enough. He stepped forward, rolling up his sleeves and clenching his huge fists into mallets of meat.

'You, sunshine,' he said, his voice higher than ever, 'have had it!'

'No, wait!' Alfie tried to intervene, but Neil shoved him aside and grabbed the Mediator Prototype by the scruff of its neck, hoisting it off the ground. Neil's companions made disapproving noises.

'Lay off him, Niners,' the first said. 'Poor kid's mental, in't he?'

'Looks like he's had some kinda plastic surgery or something,' said the second, taking a good look at the Mediator Prototype's face. 'I seen skin like that on a show on the telly. Were you in a fire, mate? Burned, was ya?'

Alfie picked himself off the ground. Part of him thought about stepping in, but he really wanted to see how this played out.

'What's that smell?' One bouncer sniffed the air, then asked the robot, 'You been drinking motor oil?'

'He'll be drinking his own snot and blood in a second,' Nine-Inch Neil drew back his right arm, ready to land his first blow.

Which is when the Mediator Prototype turned on the puppy eyes.

Even Alfie, who was expecting this, recoiled in horror.

The robot's eyes suddenly bulged, looking like they were about to pop out of their sockets. The skin around them stretched, deforming the face, pulling up its top lip, revealing bright red plastic gums, and unnaturally white teeth.

'Jesus!' Neil dropped the Mediator and backed into his companions. 'What the bloody hell is that thing? Get lost, both of you, now! I'm calling the police.'

'Come on!' Alfie pulled the Mediator Prototype away. It didn't resist this time.

'You still haven't got the eyes right,' Alfie told the robot. 'And your face ain't supposed to go all stretchy.'

They were back under the tree house. It was night, but a bright moon shone beams of white light through the trees.

'The subject did not assault me, despite provocation,' the machine replied, pacing back and forth, scrunching through the dry grass. 'That suggests the experiment was a success.'

'Yeah, he didn't thump you,' Alfie nodded. 'But not cos you were cute, but cos you're a freak …' Alfie suddenly remembered that he was speaking to something that could throw him back into that empty, windowless cell. 'No offence.'

'He did not attack me because he feared me?'

'Yeah.'

The robot thought for a moment. The implant on its neck came to life, flashing white lights, like it was sending a signal.

'Fear may be sufficient, for the time being,' it said, finally. 'In the meantime, we shall continue to develop this model and experiment further. We thank you for your contribution, Alfie Winters. Your mind has already made a significant contribution to the knowledge base of the robot network. Would you like to be deep scanned now, or later?'

Alfie had no clue what the machine was going on about. 'Er … how about later, eh?'

'Very well, Alfie Winters. This will be our last communication with you until the occupation. We will meet again. Robots never lie.'

*

Well, it must have been lying, because Alfie never heard from *that* robot again.

Life got back to something resembling normal. Alfie really missed the regular abductions. Looking back, they were easily the most exciting that had ever happened to him. What was once simply boring, now felt like an endless black hole of tedium. It made him want to scream, 'You're wasting your lives! There's a whole universe out there of robots and spaceships and shit!'

And he finally did, during one particularly awful English lesson.

He was sent to the Head, whom he called a name so unrepeatable that the man swore in shock. 'Detention for you,' Alfie smirked.

Alfie was permanently excluded after that and he spent almost all of his time with Minotaur in the woods.

And then, one afternoon, giant cubes began appearing in the sky.

Long, howling air raid sirens sounded and fighter jets took the air. Alfie thought about running home, but the screams of fear and panic from the town suggested he should stay right where he was. He clambered to the top of the highest tree in the wood, and watched the robot invasion unfold. He saw RAF fighters fall out of the air without firing a shot. In the middle of the night, a red and orange glow filled the sky, followed by a noise that sounded like the Earth cracking in two. He later learned that had been an airbase being incinerated by a Cube.

Alfie saw his first Sentries marching in rows, unchallenged, along the bypass and into the town. Then Drones flew overhead. Snipers scuttled about on the roofs of the blocks of flats on the estate.

He didn't want to stay at the tree house. That robot knew where to find him, and Alfie wasn't about to hang about and wait for it to show up.

He and Minotaur kept on the move in the woods and around the town.

Alfie became a horrified observer of a changed world. The streets were silent now. Everyone was stuck inside. The background hiss of the bypass traffic was gone, and the only noise in the sky came from squadrons of Drones rumbling high overhead. In the first summer, Alfie watched unseen in the shadows as people would chat on their doorsteps. But the winter that followed was a cold one, and those people who opened their doors again in the spring looked much older, worn, tired. The reality of the occupation was taking its toll. They all had implants in their neck, like the one in Alfie's robot, but theirs glowed blue, not white. Alfie once saw a toddler run into the street, pursued by its screaming mother as both their implants turned red. The Sentry at the end of the street jolted into life, its weapon powering up, ordering them to go back inside. They did, the mother scooping up the child, both wailing in terror.

Sometimes, Alfie would hear someone being killed by the robots. It always played out the same way: shouting and screaming mixed with warnings from a Sentry, followed by a flash, a bang and a strange smell in the air. Like a burnt Sunday roast.

Minotaur would alert Alfie to any robots whenever they snuck into town on a food raid. The allotment was good for veg and chickens. Sometimes Alfie thought he saw others like him, free and flitting between trees in the wood. Or maybe it was an illusion brought on by hunger? Either way, he chose not to reveal himself. Alfie didn't see how making friends would make things any easier. Just other mouths to feed. No. Minotaur's companionship was all he needed.

Alfie sometimes wondered about his mum, and how she must hate being kept indoors. Did she miss him? She never seemed to give him much thought before the war, so he didn't think it likely. He was surprised to see his dad out and about one day. Unlike those people stuck inside, his dad's implant was green. He wore a long black coat with a red armband and the letters VC sewn onto it. Alfie later learned that this stood for 'Volunteer Corps', the people who chose to work with the robots. It shamed Alfie that his dad would side with the bad guys, but he wasn't surprised. Dad was like a cat. You could throw him out the fiftieth floor of a skyscraper and he'd still land on his feet.

Then Alfie saw his first Mediator. It was going door to door with a man from the VC.

Alfie felt sick. The thing no longer looked like a child, but it was child height and now spoke with a child's voice. They still hadn't got the eyes right, but it was an improvement on the one that had wound up Nine-Inch Neil.

The worst of it was – Alfie knew where they'd got the idea from. It was one thing for his dad to side with the invaders, but Alfie had helped them develop one of the tools of the occupation.

The thought chilled him to the bone. It's funny how much growing up you can do in one moment. Alfie recalled the days when he wanted everyone to listen to him, to believe him … and now he never wanted to speak to anyone ever again. Just in case they ever asked about life before the robots.

ROBOT OVERLORDS
SHOOT DIARIES

INTRODUCTION

The following diary extracts were written at a very exciting time for me. The final money for the film's budget had just come in, and suddenly all the 'Will we? Won't we?' doubt was gone and the unstoppable production machine was up and running: we were going to make the film.

There was only enough budget to keep me on location for a few days of the eight week shoot, so I looked at the schedule and chose those days very carefully. They would be for my favourite scenes, or ones that I thought might be tricky and need rewrites.

This was also a hectic time for me. I still had a full-time job; my employers were kindly letting me take six months off work to concentrate on the production and the writing of this book. So there was lots of flitting back and forth from London to Belfast and the Isle of Man, with phone call updates from the director, Jon Wright, in between.

It was an incredible experience and I'm delighted to share it with you here.

Mark Stay

Sunday 26th May 2013

Belfast

Got a few days off work to attend rehearsals before the shoot begins on Friday. Staying at the Crescent Townhouse Hotel, ready for the start of rehearsals tomorrow. Met with Jon tonight to run through the schedule and work on ideas.

The extra money we need for VFX is now in place, so the movie won't look like a bad episode of 'Blake's 7'.

Monday 27th May

Belfast – rehearsals

Read throughs. We're in a room in the production offices on an industrial estate at the edge of town. It's bare, but we can work in relative peace and everyone's raring to go. I had already met Ella* and Milo† at the audition stage and was probably more excited than they were to start rehearsals.

* Ella Hunt, who plays Alex in *Robot Overlords*.
† Milo Parker, who plays Connor in *Robot Overlords*.

Met Callan* for the first time – nice guy. Our new Nathan†, James Tarpey, fits right in. For him, today was as much an audition as it was a rehearsal. Happily, Jon offered him the part at the end of the day. We needed a couple of adult actors to read-in the other parts, and we got the fabulous Jo Donnelly and Lalor Roddy (who will play Swanny). Jon loved working with Lalor on his previous film, *Grabbers*. He's huge fun. Jo was terrific, such a good actor and a delight to be with through the long days.

I was taking notes throughout the day and we have some minor tweaks to make to the script, which I started tonight.

One fly in the ointment. Jon's not happy with the prototype prop for the implants. They're bulky, with poor illumination. Jon wants to investigate a CG solution, if we have the budget.

Tuesday 28th May

Belfast – Rehearsals

Read throughs. We got to the end of the script today. James is really making the part of Nathan his own.

There's still no easy solution to the implants issue. We might resort to single colour devices that we can tweak in post. Not ideal.

* Callan McAuliffe, who plays Sean Flynn in *Robot Overlords*.
† We had another actor lined up for the role, but the schedule clashed with a TV series he was working on, so James was found at the last minute.

Wednesday 29th May

Belfast – Rehearsals

Jon had a frantic day sorting out the implant situation, so he asked me to run today's rehearsals, while he popped in and out.

We kept off the script and improvised scenes not featured in the film – little moments before or after key scenes on the film, so the actors could get an idea of their characters' lives outside of the script. I was worried I might become the kind of hippy-dippy workshop-happy drama teacher I hated at school, but actually it all went really well.

Had a good one-on-one session with James going through his lines. In the middle of our meeting he got a call from M&M World, his current employers, whom he had to inform that he was quitting his job to make the film.

The kids got to try out the quad bikes today. Great fun if their excited squeals were anything to go by.

Our new Executive Producer, Chris Clark, arrived today with an armful of script notes compiled by him and the BFI. Chris is an experienced producer who's worked with Gillian Anderson* and Sir Ben Kingsley (SBK)† before on films such as *Johnny English* and *Thunderbirds*. I was worried by the number of notes he had, but none of them were drastic, mostly to do with clarity, and Chris' objectivity has helped focus on a few weak spots.

I like Chris a lot. He's very calm and methodical. When I first heard we were getting an Exec Producer to look at the script from a creative perspective, my writer's paranoia kicked in, and I was concerned that he would sweep in and demand huge changes or

* Gillian Anderson, who plays Kate Flynn in *Robot Overlords*.
† Sir Ben Kingsley, who plays Robin Smythe in *Robot Overlords*.

declare: 'You're fired.' I needn't have worried. All of his suggestions have so far improved the script.

The only trouble we've had is pinning Jon down to go through the changes. He's so busy with the implant issues and other shoot prep that if we're going to do this properly I might have to extend my stay until Saturday.

Thursday 30th May

Belfast – Rehearsals

A frantic day for Jon, an odd one for me. I wrote some additional dialogue for a scene at around 9.30am this morning, but couldn't get Jon to approve it till around 6pm (it's for tomorrow's shoot). He was around for some rehearsal this morning, but also had to visit the set for tomorrow, look at the finished implants (much improved), and then go clothes shopping with Callan because they couldn't find him a suitable outfit (and Jon hates clothes shopping).

Rehearsals were okay, but they just want to get on with it and I don't blame them. But it was nice to hang out with Jo Donnelly again; she's a lovely person and a fine actor.

Paddy* turned up in the afternoon and I was happy to see a familiar face. He showed us a few pre-viz VFX clips which were just terrific. Some of the images and framing seemed to have been plucked directly from my brain.

Tonight we finally finished our script notes with Chris. Jon and I will use Saturday to do the final rewrite.

* Paddy Eason, the VFX supervisor.

This has been a great week. Tiring, sometimes worrying (the implants), but a great learning experience. The team at the production office have been friendly and helpful and it's been humbling to watch all these people work so hard to bring this story to life ... and the shoot starts tomorrow.

Friday 31st May

Belfast – First day of the shoot

The first day of filming couldn't have gone better. We were at the Belfast Metropolitan College, an abandoned edifice, now mostly used for filming. Gillian Anderson's TV series *The Fall* was shot there and we even re-used one of their sets for the file room.

The day started with shots of the VC guy coming down a stairwell followed by the gang, then lots of sneaking around and running down corridors. Then, in the afternoon, the file room scene.

The rehearsal paid off: the kids work well together and they look so good on camera.

I snuck off to a nearby hotel lobby (the Fitzwilliam) where they had a nice open fire (it was quite chilly for June) and worked on the rewrites. Both Chris and Piers* have asked me to pay attention to SBK's line changes.

It was good to see Jon in action again. Very calm, very sure of what he wants and very good at getting it out of his young cast.

As I watched all this unfold, I wanted to go back and tell my 10-year-old self that one day I would get to make a cool movie ... and that the next 30 years would just fly by.

And so we're off! They have a night shoot on Monday – rather them than me – and this is when SBK and Gillian will join the cast.

* Piers Tempest, Producer of *Robot Overlords*.

I have rewrites with Jon today – hopefully the last major pass – before I fly home later tonight.

Sunday 2nd June

Home

Jon and I did a solid five hours of rewrites at the hotel yesterday. Mostly small chunks here and there. We pored over the BFI notes and Chris's marked-up script.

Then not one, but four cabs arrived to take me to the airport! Slight mix-up at the taxi company.

Today saw intermittent bursts of rewriting as Jon sent stuff over for me to check or change. In particular, we worked on Roy Hudd's 'Heroes' speech.

We sent the production draft to Piers and Chris for approval tonight. Any changes after this will be issued as 'pinks' (additional side pages).

Sunday 9th June

Home

Jon called today with an update on the week's filming. Gillian threw herself into the fight scenes with gusto, nearly flooring one of the stuntmen and banging her head on the ground! But she dusted herself off and carried on without a word of complaint*.

Jon, completely in awe of SBK, says he's chosen to do the role in a Huddersfield accent! Not what we wrote or expected, but it fits

* I heard later that she'd been accidentally kicked in the head during this scene!

perfectly and he's completely in the zone and often nails it on the first take. Jon said he was giggling watching the edit – it's *that* good.

The overall message was it's going very well. The crew are outstanding and they're on schedule. Jon sounded relaxed too. Can't wait to get out there again.

Tuesday 11th June

Home

My phone suddenly went mad at about five to eight this morning with people texting and tweeting me. *Robots* was featured on BBC Breakfast News! I managed to catch a couple of minutes, then saw the rest online. It was part of a piece asking if Northern Ireland is the new Hollywood, after the success of *Game of Thrones*, *The Fall* and now *Robots*. They interviewed the stunt team, together with Piers and SBK. It was a great plug for the film.

Mum called, very excited. She was in the canteen at work when it came on. She was proudly telling all her friends.

Wednesday 12th June

Home

Had a call from Jon this morning for an emergency rewrite: needed a few lines between Danny and Sean talking about his powers. Jo C (my boss) kindly let me duck out of the office for an hour while I zipped to the relative peace of the Curzon to have a go.

Emailed the new lines to Jon and Chris, but haven't heard back yet (night shoot tonight).

Thursday 13th June

Home

Got a very brief call from Jon tonight. He had to cut it short when he realised the restaurant he was in was about to close, and he had to eat!

Got some additional notes from the BFI today. After Jon and I speak first thing, Chris is going to run through them with me tomorrow.

More BBC coverage tonight. BBC Northern Ireland interviewed Gillian Anderson at the ravine location. Top marks to our publicist.

Friday 14th June

Home

Sent Chris my comments on the BFI notes. He seemed happy. I'm going to tweak sc200 – when Sean links with the Mediator.

Tuesday 18th June

Belfast and back again

Left work early, hopped on the Gatwick Express and was in Belfast City Airport by nine o'clock.

No sign of my taxi driver, but I was greeted by hordes of teenage girls, weeping, with mascara running down their faces … turns out I'd just missed JLS passing through Arrivals.

*

When it eventually arrived, I shared the taxi with Martin Chamney* from (our VFX company) Nvizible. It pulled up in Newcastle, a few miles south of Belfast, outside a magnificent hotel facing the sea. The hotel had around 200 rooms, and a golf course, spa and luxurious marble lobby. 'This,' I thought, 'is more like it.' Of course, it was the wrong bloody hotel! We were directed to our more modest, but still very welcoming, accommodation in town.

We arrived at Tollymore Park bright and early. I jumped in a minibus with the VFX guys and we made the bumpy journey up twisting, narrow roads. The location was terrific. Sweeping views of hills and mountains and a lake and, in a clearing, our standing stones. Made of polystyrene coated in concrete, they looked so real that some of the crew thought that we'd desecrated an ancient monument (the story requires that they're covered in graffiti).

SBK was up first. He had to converse with two robots who weren't there, but he really delivered and put everything into it, take after take. We had a Panavision crane on rails, which swooped above him for the robots' POV, and the shots were very cool.

Between set ups it was great to catch up with the crew, and I got chatting to SBK's stand-in, Brian. A very affable chap, not only a veteran of *Game of Thrones*, but also an architect. This is something I came across again and again today: many of the NI crew and extras already know one another from shows like GoT. They work so well and efficiently together that they save us time and money, essential for an indie movie like ours.

I was interviewed by a couple of guys from Radio 4, and *Total Film*. I hope I didn't say anything slanderous ...

* The CG Supervisor for *Robot Overlords*.

After lunch, Gillian and the kids arrived and the energy levels went back up a notch. They've clearly bonded brilliantly during the shoot.

Unfortunately, I had to leave earlier than I wanted as I was sharing a cab with Piers and producer Steve Milne. Uneventful flight home, though I did see Air Force One land at Belfast International (it's the end of the G8 summit).

Saturday 22nd June

Belfast and Carrickfergus

Crikey, where do I start with the last couple of days? I had a meeting with my accountant, which doesn't sound terribly exciting, but he did explain and reassure me about a few things. I came out with the confidence that I can get through the next six months of unpaid leave from work in one piece.

Then, first thing on Friday, Claire* dropped me off at Gatwick and I was Belfast-bound again. First stop was at the production offices to see our editor Matt Platt-Mills, his assistant Vicki Webbley, and the rushes and first assemblies of the film. It's looking very good. You're going to hear this a lot, but SBK is fricking awesome. His interpretation of Smythe is nothing short of bloody genius and his improv lines really work†.

But also Milo in the scene where his dad dies … bloody hell, he really nails it.

* My wife.
† The whole cowboy Wayne bit is his. So good I pinched it for the book.

Scene after scene I was cackling with glee as each beat either surpassed my expectations or came very close to it. I left Matt and Vicki in good spirits and headed to the set on an industrial estate on the other side of Carrickfergus.

Within a cavernous warehouse stood a huge bluescreen cyclorama, and next to it a set of the interiors of the houses in Fleetwood Street. I loved the details inside the houses: the multi-coloured piano keys, the plants in old baked bean tins, the graffiti on the walls: 'Robot-Free Zone!'

When I arrived they were in the middle of the scene where Kate asks Smythe if she can look after Connor. Everyone was on form, and I was sorry to be pulled away to do my EPK (electronic press kit – the kind of interviews you get as extras on DVDs).

These took place in the warehouse next door, with the standing stones behind us as a backdrop. Trouble is, we were in a warehouse and not a proper soundstage, so we had to keep stopping for the noise of trucks reversing, generators thrumming into life and jet aircraft zooming overhead*.

The noise did create problems throughout this section of the shoot: feet scuffling in the adjacent hall could ruin a take and our First Assistant Director, Barry Keil, had to lay down the law a few times.

The EPK was fun. My interviewer, Ian Thompson, asked interesting questions and, thanks to everyone at Orion showing an interest over the past few months, I already had some well-rehearsed answers.

But when I returned to the set the scene they were shooting was not going well.

It was the swear box scene. Designed to show that the kids were sick of being cooped-up, and that Kate might be losing her marbles.

* On Saturday we had about forty minutes of the Red Arrows flying overhead.

There were two problems: tonally it was just too broadly comic, and these beats and ideas were covered in other scenes. It's the kind of thing you desperately try to iron-out during rewrites, but this one had somehow slipped through.

We finished shooting the scene, but concentrated on coverage for the montage that followed it.

I was then asked to rewrite a couple of bits for Milo's scene with his home-made rocket launcher, and I got to write it in an empty trailer at the unit base.

Yes, I finally had my own trailer.

For a bit.

They finished the day with an exterior bluescreen shot of Kate driving the boys in the Jeep. When the huge fan they had wasn't strong enough to suggest driving at full pelt through the hills, the SFX guys managed to find two canisters of compressed air. Very resourceful!

Gillian had to dash to catch a flight right after, and so I missed my opportunity to say hello. Big shame, but hey ho …

This morning was all about the bluescreen stage and Tamer Hassan* and SBK facing off in the belly of the Skyship. It looked fricking amazing, like something from *Star Wars*. All of us, including Jon, were geeking out. Tamer's best known for playing hard men in movies like *The Business* and *Kick Ass*. He's certainly a hard man in our movie, but he seems to be having huge fun, holding his own against SBK in today's scene.

There was some discussion about yesterday's failed scene, and we decided to shoot some *ennui* boredom ideas for the montage. I was despatched to write them, but rather than go to the trailer (at the unit base about half a mile away) I sat on a sofa in the currently-unused house set.

* Who plays the part of Wayne in *Robot Overlords*.

Which was where I found myself chatting to Sir Ben Kingsley and his PA, Todd Hofacker. Sir Ben said some very nice things about the script and asked what I was working on next. I told him it was a World War II movie and he seemed intrigued and definitely knew plenty about the period. We parted company, but ten minutes later he was back and asked if I knew the film *A Matter of Life and Death*. I told him it was a big influence on my new script and he approved. Since then I feel like I've been levitating about a foot in the air.

Callan and James came in on their day off to work on the scene I had written and they were about to start when my taxi arrived. A shame I couldn't see them play with it, but I know I'll enjoy the finished result.

And now I'm home. A tired, but very happy, writer.

Monday 24th June

Home

Got an email from Jon today with some great character ideas from Geraldine James*. Wonderful stuff. She's even outlined a scene where Monique confronts Smythe. I'm going to see if I can weave it into the book.†

Speaking of which, the official offer for the novelisation came from Gollancz. I'm going to be a bloody Gollancz author! I'm in some very esteemed company. Guess I'd better get on with it, then.

---

* Who plays the part of Monique in *Robot Overlords*.
† I couldn't in the end, but the line about Smythe calling her a barmaid and the phrase 'He can stick that up his Limpopo,' are remnants of this idea.

Friday 28th June

Home

Lou* had a good time on set last night. All the extras on Twitter were buzzing about it. Sounds like the celebrations were properly raucous.

Matt called this morning. All the castle battle stuff is looking very heroic.

Monday 1st July

Home

First day as a freelancer, and a good start. Some 3,000+ words on the novel.

Sunday 7th July

Douglas, Isle of Man

I managed to convince Jon to cast me, my wife Claire, our kids George (11 and suffering from growing pains) and Emily (13), my dad and his friend Kevin as extras in the Poseidon Hotel crowd scenes. By this point the shoot had moved to the Isle of Man.

A rather noisy and thrumming flight on a prop engine plane to the Isle of Man this morning. Movies have taught me two things

* My friend Lou McGhie works for the Army out in NI and arranged for some of her troops to appear as extras in the final celebration scenes at Carrickfergus Castle.

about prop engines: 1) they conk out, usually mid-flight; and 2) they're good for slicing-up Nazis. Disappointingly, the engines on our plane did neither.

Our taxi driver did his best to sell the island to us: there are no foxes, moles or badgers on the Isle of Man, there are some stretches of road with unlimited speeding and we had to say hello to the fairies as we crossed over the fairy bridge. Very peculiar.

Met with dad and Kevin for lunch and, later, dinner. Dad got all proud and soppy over dinner. It was very sweet.

We'd had a stroll along the front earlier to find the location for tomorrow, on the way bumping into Ella, then Callan, then Aidan Elliot*. Claire had to take George back to the hotel early. Still tired from his growing pains. We relaxed in the hotel room all afternoon, watching Andy Murray make history winning Wimbledon. The room is nice, but stuffy. I did nod off, but was awake to see him win the final set.

Monday 8th July

Douglas – Isle of Man

A fun, but exhausting, day as an extra at the Castlemona Hotel. We all arrived at 8.15am for costume. Our clothing was deemed 'not outrageous enough' and the costume dept. got to work kitting us out. Dad looked like a 60s acid casualty, and Kevin ended up in a dress with a mohair cardigan (the costume lady took one look at Kevin – a former police officer, over 6ft tall with a beard – and said, 'I'm putting you in a frock!').

I got off lightly with a cotton paisley gown.

We soon realised just what the costume department meant

* Our Co-Producer.

when I met some of our fellow extras. They looked amazing. Many came in their own clothes, with terrific hair and beards and one girl had these incredible metal cones on her forehead. We, in comparison, were quite the squares. Paddy got roped-in too, and his paisley gown complemented mine*.

We started with an energetic scene – a punch-up between two brawlers, and the crowd went wild cheering these guys on. Claire had to pretend to be drunk/unconscious while all this was going on as Emily tried to wake her up, and George joined in the yelling with gusto. I couldn't see, but apparently dad was cheering while standing on a chair at the back.

We worked our way through shot after shot, and the room got hotter and hotter, but spirits remained high. I got chatting to Jon's dad Bill – also, with Jon's sister, roped in as an extra – who looked like Willie Nelson in his get-up. He was always quick with a joke to gee people on.

George began to flag and he had his head on the table between scenes. He was tired and in pain, not a great combination. But Emily was having a great time. She and I ended up in the scene where our heroes are grabbed by the mob. Em was pulling at James Tarpey's coat, while I was wrestling with Ella Hunt. She was fighting me by jamming her hand under my chin. Her refrain between takes would be, 'Right, let's have the chin ...'

Tamer Hassan, though suffering from a broken foot and burdened with a cast, soldiered on through a key scene with a shotgun. We all somehow kept the energy levels up ... except George who spent some of the afternoon with the nurse. His growing pains are so bad that if you listen carefully you can hear him creaking like bamboo.

*And in any subsequent script revisions we were referred to as the 'Camp Gentlemen in the gowns'.

Jon seemed to think we'd all be in it, though so much would depend on the final cut. But he was happy, and with two and a half weeks to go there's a feeling that we're in the final straight.

While Claire and the kids rested, I went for a drink with dad and Kevin. Ella was playing the piano and singing in the hotel bar – and very good she was too. Had a quick chat with Ella and her mum before turning in. Early start tomorrow.

Thursday 9th July

Douglas to Epsom

We did our longest school run ever today. Up at 4.45am to get to Douglas airport (where George and I saw the actor John Rhys Davies queuing in security. We somehow held back from sidling up to him and whispering, 'Asps … very dangerous …'). We were on a plane a couple of hours later, then dashed from Gatwick to a local supermarket for packed lunches and quick change into school uniform and they were both in school by 10am.

Damn, we're good. And knackered.

I did a little writing in the afternoon, but kept nodding off. Back on track tomorrow, hopefully.

Oh, and I bought a new office chair. Exciting!

Also got a very nice text from Jon. I'd thanked him for letting us join in all the fun, and he replied saying that he hoped I'd like the finished film, and that he was putting everything into it. I don't doubt him for a second and am massively impressed with his efforts.

Sunday 14th July

Home

Jon called. Swanny's scene is very powerful and Lalor is terrific in it, but now the scene that follows feels weak in comparison. He asked me for a quick rewrite and I duly obliged. To help, he sent me assemblies of these scenes. It was great to see the film coming together already.

The main shoot finished just a few days later. Oddly, I don't seem to have recorded this in the diary, so we'll jump to when I saw the first assembly of the film. A first assembly is by no means a finished edit, more a compilation of takes assembled by the editor. It's often very rough and overlong…

Tuesday 6th August

Home

Jon called to soften me up before I see the first assembly tomorrow. He still thinks it's a good film, but he's got a mountain to climb during the edit. We agreed that there's no way we can go toe-to-toe with the mega-blockbusters, but we have made one of the most ambitious British films out there. Can't wait.

Wednesday 7th August

Home

Saw the rough assembly of *Robots* today. No VFX, no sound design, a temporary score from other movies etc, just a very rough cut, but

I'm delighted. It's going to be a belter. It starts lo-fi and indie and then just gets bigger and bigger and bigger. It's quite extraordinary, the performances are great, and I can't think of another film to compare it to.

What's clear is that Jon, Matt and Vicki* have a huge task ahead of them. At least 10-12 weeks of editing. Also at the screening today were Christian Henson†, Jeremy Price‡ and Dan Johnson§. By the end they looked googly-eyed at the prospect of all the work ahead of them. Again, it's an ambitious film and people have been befuddled by it (in meetings when we were trying to raise the money, people were sometimes sceptical that we could pull it off) but once they get their heads around it, they're cool. Nvizible now step up. They've designed shots of the Sentry powering up that are so cool we might use it for the opening titles‖.

Thursday 26th September

Molinare, London – Financiers' screening

Today saw the financiers' screening of *Our Robot Overlords*. Jon warned me that these can be brutal affairs, where the money people wonder why they bothered to invest in the first place, and who the hell hired these clowns and: 'I don't understand the ending, so let's go straight to DVD and cut our losses'.

I didn't need to be there, but it was being shown on the big screen in Molinare's in Soho and I wanted to take notes for the novelisation.

* Vicki Webbley, our Assistant Editor.
† Our composer.
‡ Our Sound Designer.
§ Our Dialogue and ADR Supervisor.
‖ We didn't!

Jon and Matt were both outwardly calm, but nervous. Piers arrived with an infectious energy about him, which definitely helped the mood. The financiers started arriving soon after. People from NI Film, Pinewood, Steve Milne from Molinare, Natascha Wharton and Jamie Wolpert from the BFI, and our sales team and producers Tim Haslam and Hugo Grumbar.

What I saw was a much slicker cut of the film with a few VFX and pre-viz sequences. It's far from finished or perfect, but it's really feeling like a movie. There were cheers at SBK's death scene and effusive applause at the end, and I blubbed a bit.

The lights came up and Tim gave Jon a bearhug and congratulated him on a job well done.

There were one or two notes, but nothing unfixable and that we hadn't considered ourselves already. It could not have gone better and we were all buzzing afterwards. Already people were talking about sequels, TV shows, games and even theme park rides! If all goes to plan I could end up writing about nothing but robots for the next ten years, but I don't think I have a problem with that … yet.

As an added bonus the new issue of *Total Film* arrived. SBK was interviewed and mentioned *Robots* as one of a number of 'wonderful scripts' he's worked on. I am currently floating on air.

Oh, and I spotted dad and Lou McGhie in the film. Claire, Emily and I are still in it. No sign of George*.

Monday 25th November

First test screening

This evening saw a screening of *Robots* for children. There were about 30+ of then and alarm bells began ringing when we saw how

---

* He's in it, behind Tamer Hassan when he's just fired the shotgun. We just weren't looking hard enough.

young some of them were. Jon asked who was youngest during his introduction: eight years old. A bit too young, maybe.

So it wasn't a complete surprise when one poor traumatised girl asked to leave during the Morse Code Martin deep scan scene (referred to by many afterwards as 'the torture scene').

But, that aside, it was a hit. Considering how few completed VFX we have, and the temp score, dialogue and sound effects, it scored very highly, with boys between 9-14 really liking it. Not a massive surprise, as that's exactly who we designed it for (though Jon said he was impressed by a couple of 8-year-old girls who loved it and asked some very intelligent questions in his Q&A).

We split them into age groups for the Q&A. Chris Clarke and I got 12s and up. The 12 year-old boys loved it. The older girls thought their younger brothers would love it too. The older boys – 16, 17 – liked it with reservations. A bit too young for them, clearly.

Reading the cards afterwards was great fun. Lots of effusive praise, apart from the girl who walked out who WOULD NOT RECOMMEND THE FILM TO ANYONE! But then she listed her favourite film as *Babe*, so she's not our target market. From the comments made by the adults it was clear that dads like it but some mums don't. Some of the younger boys noted that they liked it, but their parents probably wouldn't take them to see it. Poor kids.

This kind of testing is always a blunt instrument, and I'm uncomfortable with lumping genders and age groups together – as if we're all alike and the same – but it does give you some kind of steer, and so far it's working in our favour. I'll surely complain when we get negative feedback!

Wednesday 22nd January 2014

Pinewood

Another test screening, but this time in screen 7 at Pinewood studios. More kids this time, maybe 60+.

Matt and I were sat behind an 11-year-old boy called Abdi ... Well, I wish we could clone him. He was hooked from minute one. I know because he talked all the way through the film, which was a handy barometer of when he was engaged and when not. My favourite moment was when Nathan points the shotgun at Mr Smythe and this kid shouts, 'SHOOT HIM!' Matt and I punched the air at that point. At the end Abdi turned to his teacher sitting behind him, 'That was awesome!' He told Jon that he was the best director ever and we signed autographs for him and his friends. Great to see that more girls seemed to like it this time, too.

Afterwards there was a focus group of about twenty kids. By and large the 11-14 year olds loved it, but the title got a thumbs-down. Hugo perked up like a meerkat when he heard this ... I fear a title change is on the cards. The word that gave them a problem was 'robot'. The older kids felt it was too childish and off-putting. One 16-year-old said he thought the film was much better than he thought it would be because he was down on the title. We'll wait to see what the other cards say, but there's a feeling of inevitability about this.

Jon and I felt the younger kids' answers were being influenced by the attitude of the older ones, who were very down on it overall. There was fun moment when they realised that Jon was sitting behind them, hearing all their comments. They were mortified, apologetic, and bugging him for advice on how to make it in the movies.

But, overall, a very positive screening. The new edit is good

– rattles along – and everyone feels good about the progress Jon and Matt have made since the last screening. Onwards and upwards!

Monday 27th January

Home

After a long weekend of panicky emails between producers about a new title for *Our Robot Overlords* (including *Cyber-Lords*, *Robo Warrior*, *iDrone*, and, my favourite, *Alien Scrapers**) we finally went for …

… drum roll …

… can you bear the tension …?

… *Robot Overlords*.

This is a result. I hope this is finally put to rest.

So after many test screenings, we identified the points in the film that needed pick-ups. Not re-shoots, but little scenes that help glue the film together. Some were very small – a finger tracing a line on a map – others were a little more involved, such as blue screen shots for the finale, and new scenes to help clarify the story. We had always expected to shoot these and there was enough in the budget for one day at Pinewood.

I also saw this as an opportunity to ask the actors to read an extract from the book on film. The plan was to record them saying

*What the what?

individual lines as they moved around the studio. I had originally envisioned maybe doing this with my cheap old camcorder, or even my phone, but an old schoolfriend – Jeremy Mason – who now makes documentaries and has done more reality TV than any one person should endure, came to the rescue and offered to film everything!

Sunday 2nd March

Pinewood

Really tired, but if I don't write this now …

Friday night was a rehearsal and reunion with Callan, James and Ella (Milo had only one line and it seemed unfair to drag him across town to rehearse that). Jon and I had written two scenes for the following day's pick-ups and we had a couple of hours booked in the Millennium Hotel in Sloane Street.

Any fears we had that we couldn't recapture the gang's camaraderie instantly evaporated. They clicked back together like they'd never been away.

On Saturday morning I picked up Gillian Redfearn*, and Jennifer McMenemy† from Slough Station and we made our way to Pinewood Studios, up Goldfinger Avenue and into stages N&P. Shooting was already underway: the finger on the map.

Not long after, Jeremy and his sound guy Matt Johns turned up with some serious-looking kit … and to think I was going to do this with my poxy little camera.

I had explained the book reading idea to the kids last night, and that I didn't want to get under their feet, and that I knew it was a long day etc. Well, once again, I needn't have worried. We had

* The book's editor.
† Gollancz marketing manager.

everything we needed by 2pm. They threw themselves into it and we shot all over Pinewood. Just fantastic. I couldn't have asked for more. A particular highlight was Milo learning a gory bit for the dinner table and all the others walking away in disgust.

In the afternoon, Jenn interrogated me for author interviews, and thank God she was there to coach me, otherwise the messages from me would have been 'All teachers are weirdos like Smythe,' and 'This book will give you nightmares'.

Jeremy and Matt were just brilliant. Quick to react to an actor's sudden availability, they were professional, discreet, fleet of foot, and the few clips I saw at the end of the day looked extraordinary.

And then Louise Mason turned up and did the impossible: took some photos of me where I don't look like a gurning idiot!

Jon and his crew worked tirelessly through the schedule. The scene we wrote at the wall overlooking the school (shot against blue screen) worked really well.

Then we all decamped to the container park on the edge of the studio. It was dark now. Clear skies and bitterly cold. We arrived just after 8pm and we had to release Ella and Milo at 9.15 (there are strict rules about how long child actors can work for). The crew sprang into action. A crane rose in the distance with a powerful light beaming down on us, a smoke machine added atmosphere and fresh sandwiches, cookies and tea helped keep us warm(ish).

The kids must have been chilled to the bone in their costumes, but there wasn't a word of complaint, just singing and fart jokes (we could hear all this via our headphones picking up their radio mics).

We got what we needed in time and everyone hurried back to the relative warmth of their cars. I gave Jon a lift to Gerrard's Cross train station. He was tired but happy with the day's work. Mission accomplished.

Wednesday 17th April

An incredible day, watching and listening to the recording of the score for *Robots* at AIR Studios in Hampstead. Situated in Lyndhurst Hall, an old mission house designed by Alfred Waterhouse (who also designed the Natural History Museum), the studios aren't as big or as famous as Abbey Road perhaps, but the sound in that hall is incredible.

When I arrived at 9.30 most of the musicians were assembling and getting ready. I found Paddy in the studio cafe and we made our way to the sound-proofed control room room. Christian Henson and his team were raring to go. He gave a short introduction, explaining that we only had the budget for one day of recording, and there was lots to do, and then they were off.

That was when my jaw dropped.

The score is amazing.

I'd had a taste of it last night at the Pinewood screening, but it was Christian's demo, recorded with synths and samples. It was great and it gave the film a whole new feel. But nothing beats the English Session Orchestra going at full pelt.

As they rattled through cue after cue, we watched the scenes on the monitors, each one of them elevated to another level by the soaring music.

Jon arrived about 10.30ish, then he, together with me, Paddy and Piers sat looking on with silly grins on our faces.

We learned that the musicians hadn't had any rehearsals. They were all sight-reading the music and often nailing it on the first take, all playing in time to a click track synchronised with a timecode on the screen. It certainly put my amateur fumblings on the guitar into perspective.

The main orchestra played from ten till one, then after lunch it was reduced to a smaller group of strings who played overdubs that made the orchestra sound even bigger than it was. The afternoon ended with a quartet playing a Haydn piece that will be heard on Monique's gramophone player during a scene set in her room.

Just as we thought it couldn't get any better, the choir arrived. Just eighteen voices (including, we were told, the deepest bass in Britain), but in that hall they sounded legion. One of my favourite parts of the score is a 'Day in the life' style crescendo of strings and horns (Christian's tribute to AIR studios' founder and Beatles producer George Martin). But then they added eerie, Kubrickian *2001* voices to it and it was transformed into something spine-tingling. By now Tim Haslam, Chris Clark and Steve Milne had joined us and we were all agog.

The day ended just before 10pm. A crammed session, but the score is not yet complete: guitars and flutes will be recorded at Christian's studio tomorrow. Sadly I can't make it, but I can't wait to hear the results.

Tuesday 13th May

Home

The press release for the book went out today. Lots of nice comments on Twitter and Facebook. Paddy and Simon (Jessey – friend and the guy who 's been updating the *Robots*' Wikipedia page) questioned the use of the word 'Mankind' in the shoutline. Annoyed that I didn't spot that. Was never a fan of the 'Mankind will fall, heroes will rise' thing anyway. Will probably go with 'Robots never lie' or whatever our eventual distributor comes up with.

So … it's out there. It's real. No stopping it now, I don't think.

Wednesday 28th May

Home

Tonight I was invited to Molinare, where I sat with the guys who've been working like mad these past few weeks to put the final polish on *Robot Overlords*. The ADR, the sound effects, the sound mixing, the score, the VFX and the grading. All of the dark arts of post-production have finally come together to present the finished film.

I can't see into the future, so I don't know if the film will be a massive hit, a red-stinging bellyflop, or the kind of film that sneaks into cinemas for a fortnight then disappears forever. But I can tell you that we've made the film we set out to create. A fun adventure for the young at heart. So many people have worked above and beyond the call of duty to make it happen. It deserves to be seen and enjoyed, and I throw myself prostrate before the mighty gods of cinema praying that it will.

Tim and Hugo will now start screening it for distributors. They think they'll get dates for the end of June. Hugo says they'll fill a big cinema with excited kids, stick the distributors in the thick of it all, pump them all full of sugar and away we go.

Sounds like a plan.

Wednesday 25th June

BFI Southbank, London

Had my *Chubby Rain* moment tonight.

At the end of the movie *Bowfinger*, Steve Martin's character – a deluded and naive filmmaker (can't imagine why I relate to him?) – gets to see his finished film *Chubby Rain* with an audience. And it's a magical moment as he hears the laughter and applause. Yeah, we've had test screenings, but never with a completed film, and always with an audience primed to give us notes. These guys were here just to enjoy themselves.

The preparation for this night has made me a nervous wreck. The plan was to invite as many distributors as possible, then surround them with children and hope that the good buzz heightens the film and gets us a distribution deal. But it's NFT1 at the BFI on the South Bank ... 450 seats to fill!

So we invited everyone we knew. I had about sixty people coming, including family and folk from Orion. But Harry had been inviting coachloads of kids and suddenly we were massively oversubscribed. So most of my guys were dropped ... then they weren't (after some cancellations) ... then they were again (more kids!).

I've been told that there will be more screenings for those who were dropped, soon.

I bumped into Jon as I came down the steps from Waterloo Bridge. I chatted with him, his dad (who's in the film!), and to Piers, and Jon's agent Marc.

Inside, Tim and Hugo were handing out bags of sweets to the kids as they came into the foyer. I stepped inside to find the place pretty crammed already. I managed to find a few familiar faces (or they found me), and then Emily arrived with her Film Media Academy (FMA) class from school. After a brief introduction from Jon, Ella and Milo the lights went down, there were some excited whoops and then the only noise in the darkness was the hissing rustle of about three hundred bags of sweets being rummaged in.

90 minutes later ...

They dug it. Lots of laughs and gasps, a big cheer when Smythe gets vaporised, a very big 'Eww!' as Alex moved in to kiss Sean, and a massive round of applause at the end.

Chubby Rain.

There was a mum with her two kids behind me who both declared it to be 'Well sick!' and said they would definitely recommend it to their friends.

Ella was mobbed by the FMA girls in the foyer (Milo, who had come with his class from school, managed to get away from the scrum), and everyone was effusive in their praise. Piers reported that all the distributors that he managed to nab on the way out made positive comments, so it's looking good.

Now it's a waiting game. Will any of them bite?

Hung around afterwards with Jon talking sequel ideas.

Friday 27th June

Been getting some lovely comments from friends and colleagues and everyone genuinely seems to have enjoyed the film. Then Jon sent me a paragraph from Damon Wise of *Empire Magazine*. He'd had a private screening a few weeks backs for the article he's writing on the film. He said …

'Rooted in Hollywood's joyously anarchic young-adult adventure films of the '80s, *Robot Overlords* combines intense cutting-edge VFX spectacle with warm, fuzzy British humour to create a unique futuristic throwback that fuses the digital fantasy of *Transformers*-era mayhem with the heartfelt analogue pleasures of *The Railway Children*. It is the stuff of daydreams and nightmares, tears and laughter, hopes and fears – an intimate blockbuster with a keen sense of home.'

Well, you can stick a fork in me. I'm done.

And of all the films I thought we'd be compared to, *The Railway Children* would never have even made the top hundred, but a quote like this makes my heart soar. Now let's see what the rest of the world thinks.

Acknowledgements

Well toppermost of the poppermost has to be Jon Wright, who started this whole thing with an email about a bad dream he had where there were huge robots outside his house, waiting to blast him if he stepped outside. Without his constant faith in me as a writing partner, I just wouldn't be where I am today.

Our producer Piers Tempest not only has the best name in British film, but has been champion flag waver and drum beater since the very beginning, and it was he who suggested that I start thinking about a novelisation very early on. Were it not for his encouragement, this book might never have happened, or at least been a hurried afterthought.

The film's sales team at Embankment, led by the mighty Tim Haslam and Hugo Grumbar, have also been supportive in making this not just a film, but a whole universe, and their enthusiasm for the book has been infectious.

Without the input of our story development brain trust, the Tiny Tank Think Tank, this would have been a very different kind of tale, so a massive thanks to Mark Huckerby, Nick Ostler, Matt Platts-Mills, Rick Warden and Paddy Eason. Paddy gets bonus points for reading an early version of the novel, tipping me off as to how the finished VFX would look, and allowing me to see the top secret stuff at Nvizible during post-production. And on top of

349

that, he kindly shared his own Spitfire flight experience, giving our heroes' flight an added authenticity.

Thanks also to the film's assistant editor Vicki Webbley for sending me reference clips whenever I needed them.

Our cast were incredible, and being able to draw on their performances to flesh out these characters on the page was a gift that few writers get. I also hereby acknowledge that I've gleefully pinched their wonderful moments of improvisation to make me look good. I especially want to thank Callan McAuliffe, James Tarpey, Ella Hunt, Milo Parker and Craig Garner for taking time out of a busy day's pick-ups at Pinewood to be filmed reading an extract of the book for a promo video that turned out so much better than I could have possibly imagined.

Speaking of which, a huge thanks to Jeremy and Louise Mason for filming, editing and producing the promo and many other of the book's flash online stuff, and for doing the impossible and making me look good on camera.

I should also mention our beloved extras on the film, especially Laurence Doherty and Michael Stuart, whose online excitement and encouragement can keep a writer going when it's not quite coming together. They also have this uncanny knack for finding news about the film before I do, so follow them closely on Twitter (they're good for *Game of Thrones* news too!).

At Orion I've been blessed with the support of Jo Carpenter, Dallas Manderson, Jennie McCann and Jo Jacobs, all of whom have covered for me when I've not been around. And I'd like to thank everyone else at Orion for not being weird about this!

Thanks to Jon Wood and Lisa Milton for pushing the big, red 'Go!' button, and to Paul Bulos and his team for untangling the most complex contract ever with my wonderful agents Katie Williams and Hilary Delamere.

Thanks also to Jennifer McMenemy and Sophie Calder for not just their sterling marketing and publicity work, but for also steering me away from saying things in print and on camera that might otherwise completely alienate our potential readership.

Late of Orion, but my secret weapon, is Lisa Shakespeare who has guided me, Obi-Wan-like, through the dark arts of media training.

And I mustn't forget Charlie Panayiotou at Gollancz who, like Chaplin in *Modern Times*, pulls levers and pushes buttons, and knows how the scary software that sends this stuff out into the real world actually works. Without his knowhow, coupled with the production team at Orion, we'd all have to huddle around my laptop to read it.

Nick May of the Orion art department took Nvizible's robots and created a cover that made me go 'Whoa!'

My copy editor, the amazing Lisa Rogers, has my eternal gratitude for spotting several plot holes, stopping the characters from constantly sighing, grinning, smiling and nodding, and ensuring that I don't look like a complete numpty.

And last, but by no means least, my editor Gillian Redfearn for taking a gamble and, with her sage wisdom and advice, proving once again why she's the best in the business.

ROBOT OVERLORDS

Directed by Jon Wright

Screenplay by Mark Stay and Jon Wright

Produced by Piers Tempest

Producers Justin Garak, Ian Flooks, Steve Milne

CO-PRODUCERS ROBERT NORRIS, AIDAN ELLIOTT

EXECUTIVE PRODUCERS STEVE CHRISTIAN,
CHRIS CLARK, IVAN DUNLEAVY

EXECUTIVE PRODUCERS CHRISTIAN EISENBEISS,
HUGO GRUMBAR, TIM HASLAM

EXECUTIVE PRODUCERS NIC HATCH, MARK HUFFAM,
STEVE NORRIS, AQEEL ZAMAN

DIRECTOR OF PHOTOGRAPHY FRASER TAGGART

CASTING DIRECTOR AMY HUBBARD

COMPOSER CHRISTIAN HENSON

PRODUCTION DESIGNER TOM McCULLAGH

EDITOR MATT PLATTS MILLS

VFX SUPERVISOR PADDY EASON

COSTUME DESIGNER HAZEL WEBB-CROZIER

SUPERVISING SOUND EDITOR JEREMY PRICE

Cast

Smythe	BEN KINGSLEY
Kate	GILLIAN ANDERSON
Sean	CALLAN McAULIFFE
Alex	ELLA HUNT
Nathan	JAMES TARPEY
Connor	MILO PARKER
Mediator 452	CRAIG GARNER
Danny	STEVEN MACKINTOSH
Wayne	TAMER HASSAN
Monique	GERALDINE JAMES OBE
Morse Code Martin	ROY HUDD OBE
Watchmaker	DAVID McSAVAGE
Swann	LALOR RODDY
Connor's Dad	JUSTIN SALINGER
VC Teenager	JONATHAN McANDREW
Rough Teenager	SONNY GREEN
Thin Man	ANDY LINDEN
VC Member	MARK ASANTE
VC Officer	JAMES SWAIN
Commune Member 1	MARIA CONNOLLY
Commune Member 2	CIARAN FLYNN
Tomboy	ABIGAIL CASTLETON
Voice of Mediator 452	JUDE WRIGHT
Voice of Robot Sentry	NICOLAS FARRELL

Stunt Coordinator	NICK CHOPPING
Utility Stunt	TOLGA KENAN
Stunts	RACHELLE BEINART
	MICHAEL BYRCH
	JAMES COX
	KELLY DENT
	LYNDON HELLEWELL
	MARK HIGGINS
	PAUL LOWE
	MARC MAILLEY
	KIM McGARRITY
	ANDREW MERCHANT
	CASEY MICHAELS
	MATTHEW STIRLING
	ROCKY TAYLOR
	TONY VAN SILVA
	REG WAYMENT
	ANNABEL WOOD
	MATT DA SILVA
Stunt Wire Technician	BEN MAHONEY
Stunt Wire Rigger	RICHARD MEAD
	PAUL HARFORD

Crew

Production Manager	JAMES SMITH
1st Assistant Director	BARRY KEIL
Visual Effects Producers	GIL JAMES
	SIMON KENNY
Robot Concept Designs	PAUL CATLING

Casting Associate	SIMON COX
2nd Assistant Directors	JO TEW
	JONNY BENSON
Art Directors	FIONA GAVIN
	CAIREEN TODD
Set Decorator (Isle of Man)	SALLY BLACK
Script Supervisors	LAURA MILES
	RIK BOEYKENS
Sound Mixer	DEREK HEHIR
Sound Maintenance	TERRY McDONALD
2nd Assistant Sound	ROBERT JOHNSTON
'A' Camera Operator	PETER FIELD
'B' Camera Operator / Steadicam Operator	DEREK WALKER
1st Assistant 'A' Camera	STEVE BURGESS
1st Assistant 'B' Camera	ANDY GARDNER
2nd Assistant 'A' Camera	ANDREW JONES
2nd Assistant 'B' Camera	DARREN CHESNEY
Digital Imaging Technician	STEVE EVANS
Lab Technician/Data Manager	ADAM McHATTIE
Daily DIT	PAUL CLEMENTS
Video Playback Operators	CHRIS CAVANAGH
	JONATHAN AMES
Camera Trainees	GEORGIA QUILLIAM
	ANTHONY BREEN
Stills Photographer	AIDAN MONAGHAN
Gaffer	BRIAN LIVINGSTONE
Best Boy	SEAMUS LYNCH

Electricians	DAVID MURRAY
	STEVEN LIVINGSTONE
	GINO LYNCH
	CONNOR DUNN
Daily Electricians	GERR O'HAGAN
	NIALL CRAWFORD
	GARETH HETHERINGTON
	GWILYM HOOSON-OWEN
Dimmer Operator	KEITH SHANKS
Genny Operators	STUART FARMER
	ADAM WING
Rigging Gaffer	HUGO WILKINSON
Lighting Riggers	PAUL TOMAN
	ANTOL TURLEY
	GARETT MATTHEWS
Standby Rigger	MICHAEL LYNCH
Key Grip	GARY POCOCK
'B' Camera Grip	GARY ROMAINE
Daily Grips	IAN McGURRELL
	IAN BUCKLEY
	RON NICCOL
Grip Trainees	RILEY GARRETT
	SAM CROWHURST WATERS
Crane Technicians	PAUL LEGALL
	GEORGE POCOCK
	STACEY HANCOX
Property Masters	RICHARD STEVENS
	PAUL STEWART
Props Buyers	CARLY PARRIS
	SARAH SPEERS

Set Buyer	CHRIS MOORE
Props Modeller	GAVIN JONES
Dressing Props	CHRISTOPHER STRAIN
	NICHOLAS KEOGH
	KRISTIAN EDWARDS
Daily Dressing Props	CONNOR McCULLAGH
	CHRIS SMITH
	PATRICK McCULLAGH
	BARRY CADDELL
	THOMAS ARTHERTON
	NEIL MURRAY
	DECLAN DOHERTY
	GARETH MARTIN
	STEFAN PAUSE
Chargehand Standby Props	MARK VENN-McNEIL
Standby Props	PETER MARLEY
	TOM ALEXANDER
Costume Supervisor	HARRIET WEBB-CROZIER
Standby Costume	CIARA WINNINGTON
Costume Trainee	GERI DOHERTY
Daily Costume Standbys	EVE McCOLGAN
	SOPHIE WALLACE
	LUCIE CORCORAN
	BETHANY WILLIAMS
Makeup & Hair Designer	ROSIE BLACKMORE
Hair Designer	CAROLE DUNNE
Makeup Artist	NINA AYOUB
Mediator 452 Makeup Effects Designer	PAUL HYETT

Daily Makeup & Hair Artists	MICHELLE MAXWELL
	JENN BOWMAN
	EMMA SHERRY
	CATRIONA COOGAN
	BELINDA CONNOR YOUNG
	ORLAITH WELSH
	JENNA SMITH
	KATE SMITH
	CHARLOTTE EASTON
Hair & Makeup Artist Trainees	ELAYNE SHORTELL
	DONNA McCORMICK SMITH
Storyboard Artist	GABRIEL SCHUCAN
Assistant Art Director	SARA-JO BAUGH
Standby Art Director	NENAZOMA McNAMEE
Art Department Trainee	SCARLETT CLARK
	MILLIE ALLEGRO
	CARA LYNCH
Production Coordinators	STACEY QUIGLEY
	KEVIN BAULCOMB
Assistant Production Coordinator	LAUREN SHEERIN
Production Trainee	RACHEL HULL
Assistant to Sir Ben Kingsley	TODD HOFACKER
Chaperone	LISA CURRY
Tutors	POLLY ROWN HAMILTON
	HELEN LAMMING
Financial Controller	JENNINE BAKER
Assistant Accountant	LISA LLOYD
Location Managers	PETER CONWAY
	SIAN SUTHERLAND

Assistant Location Manager	PETE MURPHY
Unit Managers	DAMIAN McDONALD
	JIM EDGE
Location Assistants	HAYLEY WILSON
	VINCENT HUTCHINSON
	ROBBIE HUFFAM
	JOHN PAUL LAGAN
	PAUL MAXWELL
Unit Publicist	IAN THOMPSON
3rd Assistant Director	PAUL GEORGE
Daily 3rd Assistant Directors	HUSSEIN YASIN
	SAM ROSS
Trainee Assistant Directors	CHRIS McCORMICK
	JO JAMES McCULLOUGH
	JESS CORLETT
	RACHEL MILES
Daily Set PAs	TANYA ROSEN
	AARON BUTLER
	EMILY CORLETT
	CHARLOTTE GREEN
Stand-Ins / Runners	DANIELLA SOPHIA ADAMS
	HOLLY HANNAWAY
Special Effects Supervisor	STEFANO PEPIN
Workshop Supervisor	JASON McCAMERON
SFX Floor Supervisor	MATT HORTON
Senior SFX Technician	NICHOLAS PHILLIPS
Senior Workshop Technician	TIM MITCHELL
SFX Technician	NICK MORTON
SFX Assistant Technician	RONNIE RACKLEY

Construction Managers	DEREK FRASER
	GRAHAM THOMAS
Supervising Carpenter	JAMES McCALLAN
Chargehand Carpenter	MARK WHITE
Standby Rigger	TUCKER McDONALD
Standby Carpenters	PATRICK PATTERSON
	LESTER ROWBOTTOM
Carpenters	ARTHUR McCULLAGH
	REUBEN SHANLEY
	LIAM McNALLY
	DAVE SMYTH
	RYAN MURDOCK
	FINLO HUGHES
	TOMMY DALZELL
	RICHARD TURK
	STEVE DAWSON
	CHRIS RUSHBY SMITH
HOD Painters	PERRY BELL
	BRUCE GALLUP
	KEVIN FRASER
Painters	JERRY OLIVER
	ROY MOORE
	KIT NELSON
Plasterers	DESSIE O'NEILL
	DOMINIC O'NEILL
Poly Sculptor	ANDY McINTYRE
Standby Rigger	TUCKER McDONALD
Stage Hand	SIMON CONIE
Master Armourer	ROBERT GYLE
Armourer	GARY CAMPBELL

Action Vehicles Co-ordinator	DAVID KINGHAM
Animal Wrangler	KENNY GRACE
Aerial Photography	FLYING PICTURES
Spitfire Supplied by	AIRCRAFT RESTORATION CO.
Transport Captain	GEOFF BROWN
Drivers	JOHN QUIGLEY
	DEREK SYMINGTON
	PAUL McCAUSLAND
	MARK STANFIELD
	PADDY O'REILLY
	MARTY DYER
	SCOTT McCULLOUGH
	STEVEN FERRIS
	GARY DAVIDSON
	TERRY McCORMICK
	CHRIS HALL
	MARTIN ISAAC
	JAMES EVES
	TOM McCREA
	JAMES NELSON
	RITSON GIRVAN
	RICKY COLE
	ADE HOLLAND
	MIKE DUCHARS
	PHIL BARRY
	FIONA SINGER
	MALCOLM QUIGGIN
Facilities Provided By	G&H FILM AND TV SERVICES
Facilities Managers	ROBERT NELSON
	LEE McFADDEN

Facilities	DAVY GARVAN
	TOM McCORMACK
	MARK READ
	GAVIN McCORMICK
	ADAM COLCLOUGH
Catering Provided by	PINK POMELO
	CHANTERELLE CATERING
	CAFÉ LATTE
	CULINARY LIBERATION
	RC CREASY CATERING
Health & Safety	SEAN BAILEY
Medics	TERRY McGERRY
	GWINETH HARRISON

Second Unit

Director	TERRY LOANE
1st Assistant Director	LEON COOLE
3rd Assistant Director	GRAHAM KINNIBURGH
Sound Recordist	SIMON KERR
Unit Video Op	EMMET COLTON

VFX Element Unit

Production Manager	SUZIE FRIZE-WILLIAMS
Artem SFX Supervisor	MIKE KELT
Artem Explosions Supervisor	PAUL GORRIE
DoP	PETER FIELD

Phantom Flex Op	JOHN HATFIELD
1st Assistant Camera	SEAN CONNOR
Grip	EMMETT CAHILL
Gaffer	PETER WING
Electricians	DANIEL O'DONNELL
	JAMIE BRUCE
	DELROY BURTLEY
	RYAN WING

Additional Photography, London

Line Producer	GUY ALLON
Production Assistant	HARRY RYLOTT
1st Assistant Director	DAVID CRABTREE
2nd Assistant Director	MARIA ANA DIAS
3rd Assistant Director	GABRIELLA WHEELER
DOP	FRASER TAGGART
Camera Operator/Steady Cam	DEREK WALKER
1st Assistant Camera	PAUL WHEELDON
2nd Assistant Camera	LUKE SELWAY
Camera Trainee	JAMES WOODMASS
DIT	STEVE EVANS
Key Grip	GARY ROMAINE
Gaffer	MARTIN SMITH
Electricians	LEE ELDRED
	CHRIS POLDEN
	MARK RAFFERTY
Trainee Electrician	ALEX SIMMONDS

Generator Operator	MITCH WISKER
Rigger	BRENDAN FITZGERALD
Sound Mixer	JAKE WHITELEE
Boom Operator	ROB NEWMAN
Supervising Art Director	NINA TOPP
Assistant Art Director	NICK AKASS
Art Department Assistant	KATIE MACGREGOR
Costume Supervisor	HEIDI McQUEEN PRENTICE
Costume Assistant	KATHRYN AVERY
Hair & Make Up Artist	ROSIE BLACKMORE
Hair Stylist	CAROLE DUNNE
Hair & Make Up Assistant	JANE OGIN
Hair & Make Up Trainee	MONIQUE GIAMATTEI
Unit Medic	CHRIS MOSS
SFX	MATTHEW STRANGE
SFX Assistant	DANNY PARKES
Catering	HONEY & THYME LONDON
Script Editor Working Group	MATT PLATTS-MILLS
	PADDY EASON
	RICK WARDEN
	NICK OSTLER
	MARK HUCKERBY
Post Production Supervisor	EMMA ZEE
Consulting Editors	MICK AUDSLEY
	JON HARRIS
First Assistant Editor and VFX Editor	VICTORIA WEBBLEY
On Set Digital Lab	ADAM McHATTIE

Editorial Assistant	JOEL DONNAN
	EDWARD CROMPTON
Post Production Assistant	HARRY RYLOTT
Sound Designer	JEREMY PRICE
Effects Editor	MARC LAWES
Dialogue & ADR Supervisor	DAN JOHNSON
ADR Recordist	RICHARD PRYKE
Assistant ADR Recordist	ROLF MARTENS
Foley Supervisor	GLEN GATHARD
Assistant Foley Mixer	JEMMA RILEY-TOLCH
Foley Editor	PETER HANSON
Foley Artist	JACK STEW
	JASON SWANSCOTT

Re-recorded at Pinewood Studios

Re-recording Mixer	RICHARD PRYKE
Re-recording Mixer	ANDREW CALLER
Sound Mix Technician	ROLF MARTENS

Pinewood Post Production

Director Post Production	NIGEL BENNETT
Director of Technology	DARREN WOOLFSON
DPS Workflow Manager	JAMES CORLESS
DPS Workflow Supervisor	THOM BERRYMAN
Post Production Booking	REBECCA BUDDS

Post Production Co-ordinator	ALISON VINER
ADR Voice Casting	VANESSA BAKER

Molinare

Chairman	STEVE MILNE
Colourist	GARETH SPENSLEY
DI Producer	KATIE SHAHROKH
DI Coordinator	STEVE KNIGHT
DI Online Editor	GARETH PARRY
DI Manager	MATT JAMES
DI Film Consultant	JUSTIN LANCHBURY
DI Conform Editors	JAMIE WELSH
	TIM DREWETT
	MICHELLE CORT
	TOM SUGDEN
	STEVE OWEN
	KIRSTY DUA
Digital Film Technician	MIKE ANDREWS
Data Transfer	JONATHAN DICKINSON
	LIZZIE NEWSHAM
Film Consultant	LEN BROWN
Consultant VFX Producer	TIM FIELD

Visual Effects By Nvizible

Managing Director Nvizible	NIC HATCH
Executive VFX Producer	KRIS WRIGHT

VFX Producers	SIMON KENNY
	GIL JAMES
VFX Co-ordinator	CIARAN KEENAN
Data Wrangler	ERRAN LAKE
Compositing Supervisor	JAMIE WOOD
CG Supervisor	MARTIN CHAMNEY
VFX Editor	TOM BALOGH
Animation Supervisor	ROB HEMMINGS
Animators	BERANGER MAURICE
	JAMES FARRINGTON
	JOHN KAY
	SAWAN THAK
CG Look Development	STEFAN GERSTHEIMER
CG Artists	BILLY PERRY
	JELLE VAN DE WEGHE
	STEPHEN THORNHILL
Lighters	MINH NGUYEN-BA
	OLIVER SULLIVAN
	PHIL BORG
Lead TD	WAYDE DUNCAN SMITH
TD	SAM CHURCHILL
Lead Compositors	ANTOINE JANNIC
	RICCARDO GAMBI
	JIM PARSONS
Compositors	ADAM ROWLAND
	CHARLOTTE LARIVE
	CHRIS SCOTT
	DARREN R NASH
	GAVIN DIGBY
	JACK HUGHES

JASON EVANS
JEREMY HEY
KEN GRAHAM
LIAM LAVERY
MICHAEL SHAW
PATRICK McCULLAGH
SANDRA CHOCHOLSKA
SIMON-PIERRE PUECH
VICTORIA FARLEY
WILLIAM G WRIGHT

Motion Graphics Designer	CHRIS LUNNEY
Technical Support	CHINTAN PARMAR
	ANDREW KINGSTON
	STEVE MADSEN
	BEN GRIMES

Nvizage

Lead Previs Artist	JASON McDONALD
Previs Artist	JASON IVIMEY
Previs Artist	AMARDEEP RATTAN
Previs Artist	ZACH DU TOIT
Previs Editor	TINA RICHARDSON

N-CAM

Technicians	DAVID STROUD
	JOANA POWELL
	BRUNO XIBERRAS

PEANUT

Matchmove	AMELIE GUYOT
	PEREGRINE McCAFFERTY
	DAMIEN BOUVIER
	FABRICE DI CICCO

SOLID STATE IMAGES

Matte Painter	LINO KHAY
Production Assistant	KRISTINA OTREMBSKAYA
Composer	CHRISTIAN HENSON
Music Consultant	NICK STEVENSON
Music Supervisor	MAGGIE RODFORD

Music Recorded at Air Studios London
by JAKE JACKSON

Assistant Engineer	CHRIS BARRETT

Additional Music Recorded at North Seven Studios, London by STANLEY GABRIEL and JOE RUBEL

Assistant Engineer	CICELY BALSTON

Music Mixed by Jake Jackson & Goetz Botzenhardt
at Soho Sound Kitchen

Assistant Engineer   LEON JEAN-MARIE

Music Orchestrated by Ben Foskett
& Christian Henson
English Session Orchestra contracted by Dom Kelly

Assistant Contractor	JAMES MARRANGONE
Conducted by	NATALIE MURRAY-BEALE
Leader	ROLF WILSON
Choir	SYNERGY VOCALS
Choir Director	MICAELA HASLAM
Featured Vocals	CHARLOTTE RITCHIE & DOT ALLISON
Guitars	LEO ABRAHAMS
Solo Cello	CHRIS WORSEY
Solo Violin	JEFF MOORE
Drum Kit	JONNY BRISTER
Euphone, Drum Programming & Pianos	CHRISTIAN HENSON
Additional Drum Programming	THE FLIGHT
Copyist	COLIN RAE
Score Reader	ANDREW COTTEE
Assistant to the Composer and Additional Engineering	SEBASTIAN TRUMAN
Additional Orchestral Elements	SPITFIRE AUDIO LLP

Mat Zo - 'Robots Never Lie'
Written and produced by Matan Zohar
Published by Xenon Music Ltd

Post Production Script Services	FATTS
Test Screening Audience Research	FIRST MOVIES
Brand Advice	ED SHARP AT FILM TREE
Merchandising Support	NIKKI GRASS
Package Artwork	OWEN BLACK
Trailer and Promo Editing	JOHN PIEDOT and ANDREW SNOOK at EDIT POOL
Cameras	PANAVISION
Lighting	PANALUX
Production Insurance	PAUL HILLIER ROBERTSON TAYLOR
Production Legal Services	LAURENCE BROWN
Financing Consultancy	THE SALT COMPANY
Accountancy Services	BROWN McLEOD
International Sale Agent	EMBANKMENT FILMS
Production Auditors and tax credit advice	STEVE JOBERNS at SHIPLEYS LLP
Completion Guarantor	FILM FINANCES, INC DAVID KORDA JAMES SHIRRAS ALI MOSHREF RUTH HODGSON TATIANA WAIT

Tempo Productions Limited

Directors	JO BAMFORD
	PIERS TEMPEST
Finance Director	IAN SEDDON
Legal Representation	GUY SHEPPARD
Production	HARRY RYLOTT

For Isle of Man Film
MIKE REANEY

For Pinewood

Head of Production	NICKY EARNSHAW
Head of Distribution	GEMMA SPECTOR
Distribution Executive	JAMES WARREN
Production Executive	JULIA HILLSDON
Legal Counsel	MAGDALENA DUKE
Pinewood Pictures	PAMELA SLATER
	GRAHAM SYLVESTER
Legal Advisors	MICHAEL MAXTONE-SMITH

AND MARNIE WILKES OF REED SMITH LLP

For Umbra Telegraph

Legal Representatives	NATALIE USHER AND
	ANTONY SWIATEK of
	LEE AND THOMPSON LLP

Financing Structured by 4knowledgeStreams Inc.

For British Film Company

Chairman	CHRISTIAN EISENBEISS
Principal	STEVE MILNE
Assistant to Mr Eisenbeiss	SILVIA SCHULTEISZ
Assistant to Mr Milne	CATHERINE MILNE
Production Runner	MARINA MICHELSON
Legal Representative	SAM TATTON-BROWN
	of LEE & THOMPSON

Worldwide Sales And Distribution –
Embankment Films

HUGO GRUMBAR	TIM HASLAM
CAMILLA HASLAM	SHARON LEE
SARA MAY	MAX PIRKIS
MAITE VILLARINO	SARA CURRAN

For BFI

Director of Lottery Film Fund	BEN ROBERTS
Senior Production and Development Executive	NATASCHA WHARTON
Development Executive	JAMIE WOLPERT
Head of Production	FIONA MORHAM
Head of Production Finance	IAN KIRK
Business Affairs Manager	VIRGINIA BURGESS

For Northern Ireland Screen

Chief Executive	RICHARD WILLIAMS
Head of Production	ANDREW REID
Head of Marketing	MOYRA LOCK
Head of Finance	LINDA MARTIN
Production Executive	NICOLA LYONS
Senior Funding Executive	SUZANNE HARRISON
Funding Executive	JENNIFER JOHNSTON
Legal Counsel	DAMIAN McPARLAND, PARTNER AT MILLAR McCALL WYLIE LLP

For Gasworks
EMMA LIGHTBODY

SPECIAL THANKS TO

The Salt Company (International) Limited, Sun House Entertainment, Robert Bevan, Cyril Megret, Marc Helwig, Katie Haines, Jonathan Kinnersley, Anna McDowell, Aircraft Restorations Duxford, Michael Kuhn, Alan Maloney, Norman Merry, Clive McGreal, Richard Walton, Peter LaTerriere, Hugo Heppell, Department of the Environment Northern Ireland, Carrickfergus Castle, Carrickfergus, North Down & Ards Borough Councils, Anna McDowell, Sgt. Ian Spence, PSNI, Hugh Whittaker, Mick Walsh, Panavision, Panalux, Dermalogica, 4knowledgestreams Film Group, Billy Levy, Virgin Gaming, Microsoft, WemoLabs, Anthony Batt, Denis 'Slim' Johnston, Laurence Doherty, Damon Wise, Amanda Davis, Claire Stay, Emily Stay, George Stay, Jo Carpenter,

Dallas Manderson, Jennie McCann, Jo Jacobs, Steve Mayhew, Jo Donnelly, Lou Mcghie, Oliver Denny, Peter & Ben Hardyment, Trevor Forrest, Robert Walak, Ann Runeckles, Masashi Kawamura, Alan Halsall, Into Film, Susan Wrubel, Slated.com, Edinburgh International Film Festival Young Talents 2012, Ian Smith, The Television Worshop, Nottingham, Doug Liman, Jenni Page, Sam, Bill, Hida & Kerry Wright, Kate, Rose, Evie, Bay & Robin Tempest

Filmed on location on the Isle of Man and Northern Ireland
www.robotoverlords.net

Made with the support of the BFI's Film Fund
© Mediator 452 Limited / British Film Institute 2014